ON A
FLIGHT TO
Sydney

J.A. FORDE

For my Grandma Dee (who probably would have told me to add more spice), you gave me the means to make this book a reality. I wish you were here to read it, and if I could send you a signed copy in heaven, I would.

Author's Note

My writing contains mature themes and some explicit language and is therefore intended for audiences 18+. On a Flight to Sydney is a fade-to-black romance with implied intimacy but no explicit scenes are depicted on the page. This story deals with several issues that could be potentially triggering, such as PTSD and panic attacks (on page) due to military trauma (described in detail), death of a friend, narcissistic parents and parental neglect, and a brief mention of an attempted sexual assault (not detailed). Your mental health is paramount, so please protect your peace and well-being if these are themes you are sensitive to.

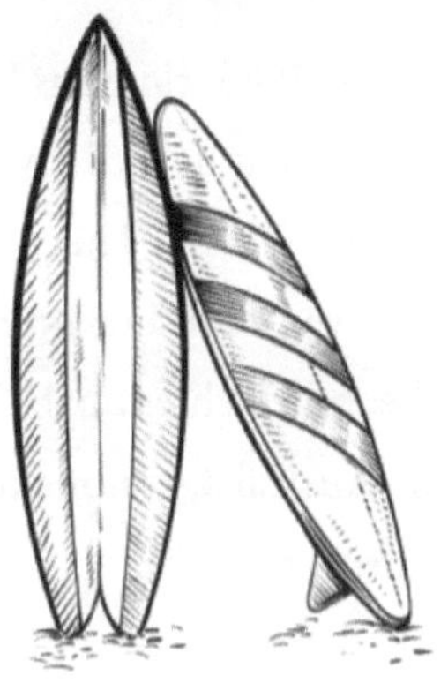

CHAPTER ONE

WES

My head snaps forward off the headrest, jolting me from the memory of *that* flight—*that* plane—to the one I'm in now. Sleep tugs at the edges of my mind as I feel the pull of the wheels on the tarmac. I've never landed a Boeing 787, but I have landed enough planes in my life to know the wind is giving the pilot hell right now.

My heart beats a frantic rhythm in my chest, my surroundings sharpening into focus. The quiet voices of the flight attendants, the frayed pages of an inflight magazine in the seatback pocket, the cold metal of the armrest pressing against my skin. Just a dream... It was just a dream. Deep down, I know it's a nightmare, but naming it as such would give it more power than it already holds. My hands shake as my lungs feverishly seek more air, the impact of this landing reminding me far too much of another. One that'll haunt me as long as I live.

I tilt my head back, eyes falling closed as I force my breathing to slow. I press the heels of my hands into my eye sockets in a futile attempt to push the memories away. This isn't my first flight since the events of *that* day, not even close, but after sitting here for fifteen and a half hours, it's been hellish enough. Flying nonstop from Los Angeles to Sydney, Australia, is no joke. Especially after the eight-hour drive to the airport.

I've been in travel mode for well over a day with minimal sleep, and even my bones ache with the weariness. Add in my anxious feelings about this move, my new job, and whether I'm making the right decision... Yeah, it's no wonder I'm experiencing flashbacks.

I scrub a hand across my face, the stubble that scratches against my palm a physical reminder of the disconnect between who I was then and who I am now. Reaching for my phone, I switch it off airplane mode. Thankful I had the forethought to set up an international plan, it picks up on Australia's Telstra network and immediately begins to ping with notifications. I fumble with the buttons, trying to silence the sounds, but by the time I do there's more than a few heads turned my way.

I sink into my seat, avoiding their eyes, and see that the first message is from my baby sister. The tension releases from my shoulders at the sight, and I feel a smile start to spread across my face. I know it drives her crazy that I think of her as my *baby* sister considering she's twenty-six years old, but with eight years separating us, I'm afraid that's how I'll always see her. Even with the age difference, Rory's one of my favorite people on the planet. She was the one who drove me eight hours from our hometown of Lake Tahoe to LA so I could fly halfway around the world. She's tried to hide how much she hates the idea of this move, but I can read her well enough.

She's worried about me.

Hell, *I'm* worried about me if I'm being honest.

Rory has always been the stable constant in my life. Meanwhile, I've been the fly by the seat of my pants guy. And I mean that literally—I spent the last twelve years as a fighter pilot for the United States Navy. I may have gone everywhere on their orders, their timeline, but when I was in that jet it was just me—my instincts, my gut, my grit and determination. I would've kept doing it too, if I could have. There's never been anything I wanted more.

My throat bobs around a stiff swallow as panic threatens to rise again. That's all gone now. That last deployment took it all from me, and no matter how hard I try, I can't get it back.

Despite the concern my move seems to have garnered, this time away is exactly what I need. Space to breathe. Space to get my head on straight. Space to not be surrounded by the worst memories of my life.

I inhale deeply and return my attention to my phone.

Rory

How's the future?

Her question makes me laugh out loud, snapping me out of my morose thoughts and earning me more covert looks from my fellow passengers. With the time change and the length of this flight, I skipped over a whole day of my life. It's not the first time I've lost or gained a day during travel, but it's always a weird realization. Rory is still living in that day, the one I'll never get back.

The *ding* of the fasten seatbelt light turning off is followed by the inevitable rustling of over two hundred people attempting to move at once. I, on the other hand, stay seated. Sitting toward the back of the plane, I'm not going anywhere anytime soon, so I may as well take my time.

Me

> Wouldn't you like to know. Just landed in Sydney. Did you make it home ok?

I made her promise she would get a hotel for the night, literally forcing the money to cover it into her hand while we stood on the drop-off curb at the airport. I didn't want her turning around and driving through the night back to Tahoe. No need for her to be in the car for sixteen hours straight, especially when she'd be solo on the way back. I do the mental calculations and work out that she should've made it home by now.

Rory

> Almost, I let myself sleep in a little and then grabbed the most amazing breakfast burrito. I bet they don't have those in Australia. You probably should have stayed here.

She's teasing me of course, but this cuts deep. She knows how much I love breakfast burritos. Plus, with nothing but airplane food and snacks to keep me going, I'm positively ravenous. As if trying to prove that fact, my stomach growls audibly, as if a yawning pit has opened inside me, ready to swallow a cow.

Me

You're the worst, you know that? I'd kill for one right now.

I'll give you a call once I get settled in, ok?

I know she's going to want reassurances that I'm all set and don't need rescuing. I swear, for a little sister, she's more like a mom these days.

Rory

You know you love me. Yes, please call me. Anytime.

Her message lifts the corners of my mouth into a small smile, and I feel a pang in my chest. It'll be a while before I see her again, which is especially hard since this time it's my choice, not school or the military keeping us apart.

Another message from her pops up just as my thumb moves to lock the screen.

Rory

And Wes, I love you.

There's a weird sting behind my eyes at her words. I must be more tired than I thought because I don't cry. Not that I'm crying now, it must just be the stale air kicking up dust in here or something. I blink a couple of times to clear the *dust* and start gathering my belongings.

My forceful tug on the straps of my backpack is followed by the sound of ripping fabric. A groan slips out of me, shoulders slumping forward, and I rest my head against the plastic tray table. I take a gentler approach to finish pulling it free but can see there's a decent tear down the side. Huffing out a breath, I move the bag with care, like it's a bomb that could detonate at any moment.

The aisle ahead empties out so I stand to grab my larger carry-on from the overhead compartment. The wheels get stuck somewhere between a Hello Kitty suitcase and a diaper bag, and my patience wanes.

"Shit." I mumble the curse under my breath, but a mother in the row behind me still gives me side-eye.

Seriously, I need off this damn plane. Is that really so much to ask? Stretching up higher, I give it a yank, only to lose my balance and go careening backward. My back collides with the person behind me, and when I turn to apologize the loosed bag slides down and hits my shoulder, pushing me further off-balance. My right knee, already pulsating with pain from sixteen hours of sitting, twists and buckles.

The moment stands still but also moves in high-definition, and I can do nothing but let it happen.

The thud of my bag hitting the ground is nothing compared to the loud *oof* that comes from the flight attendant I land directly on top of. Our faces are only inches apart, bodies pressed close, my throbbing knee bracketed between her thighs.

Shit. This is not just any flight attendant. This is *the* flight attendant. The one I've struggled to keep my eyes off the entire flight. The one who's been resolutely avoiding said eyes for the *entire* flight. I have her full attention now and I am not prepared for what I see in her gaze. There's fire in the stunning grey depths, like molten graphite, and she looks like she could burn through me with just a thought. I can't exactly blame her. With my body pressed against hers, the difference in our stature is accentuated. At six-two, I'm pretty sure I'm crushing the woman beneath me, who must be at least a foot shorter.

Oh god, I'm crushing her.

I pull an arm free, but all I manage to do is grab her chest in my attempt to push myself up. She makes the most adorable squealing sound that in other circumstances would have me laughing, but the look that follows it replaces any humor with mortification.

"I'm so sorry, I was just... I wasn't... I mean, I didn't..." I'm a bumbling fool who can't form words.

I manage to press the offending hand to the floor next to her and push up until I can leverage myself into a standing position. I suck in a breath through my teeth as I put weight on my knee. A sharp pain radiates out from where my scars pull the skin tight. I should have wrapped it like Rory told me to. Freaking know-it-all little sisters. The shooting pain in my knee, though, is no distraction from the sight in front of me.

Now that I've put space between us, I can really see her. I can also feel the stares of everyone still on the plane pressing in on me. They can relax—it might feel like a full hour since I collided with this woman, but I know it's only been a minute or two at most. I avoid their gazes as I let mine roam over her, telling myself I'm just making sure she's alright, but knowing it's really because she's stunning.

Her skirt has ridden up a couple inches and her blouse is askew, not tucked in neatly like it was the whole flight. Her chestnut brown hair is splayed out behind her and, in my own disheveled state, I'm having an even harder time not staring. How is she more appealing now than when she was all prim and proper? I catch her eye when I reach her face, and the blush across her cheeks at my perusal matches her perfect pink lips. She glances away again, clearly embarrassed. Is it bad that I really like that blush and the fact that I put it there?

Her eyes flick back to my face as I reach down, offering her my hand, but they drop again when she slips her smaller one into mine. It's soft and warm against my calloused palm, and I can't stop my thumb from grazing across the top just once. I decide to flex my muscles a little when I pull her up, and she has to stop herself with her free hand so she doesn't slam into my chest. I suck in another breath at her touch and her grey eyes lock onto mine.

Well, this is new. I can't remember the last time I felt such an immediate attraction to a woman. The connection between us breaks just as quick when she pushes away, releasing my hand to busy herself with straightening her uniform.

"Sorry, I—" I'm stopped from continuing when a throat clears and I come to the startling realization that we are still blocking the aisle. The passengers in the rows ahead are long gone, and I can sense the impatience from those remaining behind us. I sidestep into the nearest row of empty seats, grabbing my bags as I go, and she steps into the row opposite me. Now there's nothing to do but watch each other.

My watching is blatant and bold, because that's who I am. Hers is more covert, stealing glances from under her long, beautiful lashes that bring out the smoky color of her eyes. I should say something, but every time I'm about to, another person walks between us and breaks our eye contact. I was nearly at the back of the plane, yet now it feels like there's an infinite number of passengers streaming up the aisle. With every passing moment, the tension builds and tightens like the string of a bow pulled taut.

When the last passengers have exited the plane and it's only me and her remaining, we stand locked in a stare down across the aisle. She doesn't seem to have any trouble making eye contact now, although I'm not sure the blazing look of irritation is what I was going for with my glances earlier.

"Are you planning to deplane?" Her Australian accent would make me weak in the knees if I wasn't already. I imagine the way she's crossing her arms over her chest is to close herself off from me, but its effect is outright sinful. Her shirt pulls tight across her chest, and I'm doing everything in my power to be a gentleman and keep my eyes on her face right now.

The other flight attendants are already moving about the cabin and getting their turnover checklists complete, yet here we stand.

"Oh, yeah. I just wanted to apologize again. Are you okay?" The words tumble out as I give her another once-over.

"I'm fine, thanks." She bites out the words, but then her voice softens a little when she asks, "Are you?"

I'm pretty sure she's only asking because it's her job, but I delude myself into thinking it's because she cares.

"I'm fine." My brain tells me to stop there, but my mouth just keeps going. "I'm also sorry that I grabbed you... your... I didn't mean to. It was an accident."

Have I never held a conversation before? I rarely stumble over my words, but the fresh blush staining her cheeks makes me lose the ability to form sentences altogether. Damn, she is beautiful.

She holds up a hand to stop me. Clearly, talking about how I grabbed her breast is not what she wants to do right now.

"It's fine. Really." Her reply is curt, a dismissal. It says she's done talking. *We're* done talking. She steps into the aisle and walks to the back of the plane without another word. Throwing my backpack over my shoulder, I grab my rolling bag and head for the exit. I allow myself one backward glance, but she's determinedly looking the other way.

I feel the sting of pain in my knee with each step as I make my way off the plane and into the terminal, heading for baggage claim. My thoughts never stray from the beautiful brunette whose name I never even learned.

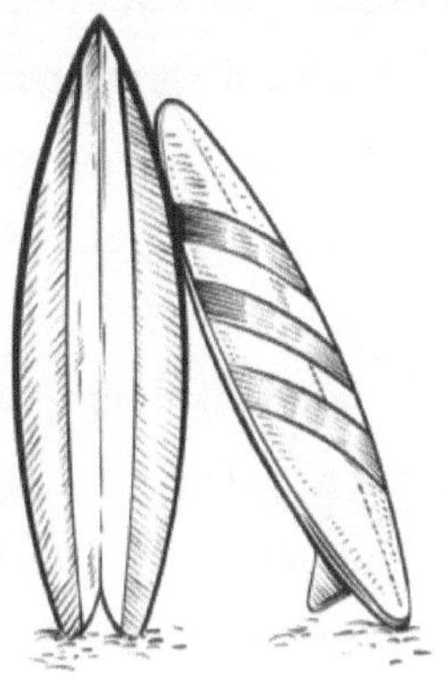

CHAPTER TWO

Joss

My heart is still beating a mile a minute, the heat still lingering in my cheeks from my interaction with Mr. 32C—better known inside my head as Weston J. Anderson. The fact that I looked him up hours ago on the manifest is a tidbit of information I'll happily take to the grave. No one needs to know that my desire to find out his name came well before we accidentally made it to second base in front of forty-odd passengers.

Good grief, did that really happen? *Why me?*

In the back of my mind, however, there's a miniscule yet irritatingly loud thought rolling around saying *lucky me*. I swat that idea away like a gnat—inconsequential, unimportant, and wholly unhelpful.

I rarely take note of anyone in particular on my flights, but when *he* boarded the plane in LA, I couldn't help myself. His tall, lean frame in a pair of jeans and a T-shirt stretched across his broad chest was like a beacon. I'll admit to checking out his muscles for a few seconds too long and I thought he might have seen me looking because every time I walked by after that, his eyes were on me as well. So, being the mature adult that I am, I started averting my gaze, avoiding him entirely. It was working so well too, right until I ended up with those startling blue eyes staring directly into mine with less than six inches of space between us.

With his body pressed on top of mine, it was difficult not to get lost in their depths, their color rivaling the brilliant blue of the ocean outside. I also couldn't help but wonder if his unkempt brown hair was as soft as it looked. I'd nearly lost all control of my faculties, wanting nothing more than to run my fingers through it, when I was brought back to the moment by his hand on my chest. That shook me right out of my delusional fantasies about his hair.

I couldn't seem to keep my emotions locked down like I usually do, causing my embarrassment to manifest into anger. For me, it's that or tears, and I've trained myself well over the years that I do not cry. So, anger it is whenever something mortifying happens. Like, you know, having a beautiful man fall on top of me, grope me, and then pull me into his chest. If not for his abrupt intake of breath, like he could feel the same zing of awareness that I did, I'd swear he'd done that on purpose.

A shiver courses through me as the memories replay in my mind. *Oh my god, I cannot believe any of that actually happened.* I refused to look at him as he left, not wanting him to see the way I was completely flushed from my cheeks all the way to my toes. He could thank his stuttered attempt at an apology for that.

I distract myself as best I can, going row by row to tidy up anything left behind. I try to let all thoughts of Weston go as I fall into the familiar routine—pick up rubbish, straighten magazines, check for belongings. On and on it goes. It's redundant but it's easy and it keeps me moving, busy, my brain focused on the task at hand. As I reach row thirty-two, I notice something on the floor. My stomach sinks as I reach for it, knowing what it is and who it must belong to. Because, really, why wouldn't it?

I flip open the navy-blue US passport, and yup, there he is in all his glory. Weston James Anderson staring back at me. How is this gorgeous man still taunting me long after leaving the plane? He's probably being held up at customs as we speak.

Crap, crap, crap.

"Hey, Amala. 32C dropped his passport. I'm going to see if I can catch him," I call out to our lead flight attendant before I can think better of this idea. She nods, a little smirk playing around her lips. I don't even want to know what she's thinking as I rush past her without a second glance.

Let me just say, though practical, my work shoes are not meant for running. Neither is my skirt, which is a bit tighter than I'd prefer. Alas, there's nothing I can do about either of those things right now as I charge up the gangway. If I don't catch him, he'll eventually panic when he realizes his passport is missing. At least I assume that would be a typical response for just about anyone entering a foreign country without their passport.

I scan the crowds of people, looking for any sign of his messy brown hair. I know this was his final destination—because I'm a stalker apparently—so he won't be at any of the other gates. But he could have stopped at Duty Free, or gone to the bathroom, or he could have rushed straight for the exit.

The point of no return looms before me as I turn on the spot, hoping I won't have to track him down in the long line at customs. My heart sinks when he doesn't magically appear. Shoulders slumped, I let my feet carry me back toward the gate. I get about ten meters before I stop short. *One last look*. I'll take one last look around just to be sure. I scan the seats, the gates, the streams of people walking past, and that's when I see him.

It's his broad shoulders and messy hair that draw my eye as he turns away from the water bottle filling station. He's heading straight for the security exit. *No, no, no.* There's too many people and I'll never reach him in time. Before I can give it a second thought, I accept my fate and take a deep breath.

"Weston Anderson!" I shout, my voice carrying across the sterile corridor, and his head snaps around so fast he likely cricked his neck. His eyes catch mine and widen in surprise, and I wonder what he's thinking. *"Why is that rude flight attendant chasing me down?"* sounds about right.

I wave his passport over my head and his eyes go even wider, his mouth popping open in a comical little O. The sight makes me smile. He jogs back toward me, something else falling from his backpack along the way. Does he not have it zipped? He stops and mumbles something under his breath, irritation written all over his face as he bends down to pick it up. Five more strides and he's in front of me.

I should say something. *Come on, Joss, any words will do.* I'm almost coherent enough to speak when he beats me to it.

"Hey." His one-word greeting comes out breathless.

"Hey."

The way his shoulders and chest rise and fall has me dropping my gaze and giving him a very unprofessional once-over. He either doesn't notice or chooses to ignore me ogling him as he plants his hands on his knees, bending forward to catch his breath. His backpack falls to the floor with a thud—that didn't sound good—and he rubs at his right knee, eliciting a small grimace. He gingerly stands up straight and we finally meet eye to eye once again.

Well, not exactly eye to eye. I have to tilt my chin up, up, up to look into his. He runs a hand across his jaw, his stubble long enough that I can hear the scrape of it against his skin. I may have been speechless before, but now I'm just as breathless as he is. Because this man is... well, truly breathtaking. His skin is flushed from the jog over, accentuating his high cheekbones. He's objectively good-looking, but he doesn't wear it like a badge, which makes it all the more irresistible.

I hold out the passport, finally finding my words. "You dropped this on the plane."

He reaches for it, and when his fingers brush mine, I feel a shock of electricity. I pull my hand away and take a step back, needing space. Nope, nope, nope. That whole "shock of attraction" thing only happens in romance novels. That was clearly just static from us running.

"Thank you. Wow, that would have been a disaster." His voice is rough, and his American accent does things to me that it probably shouldn't.

"I can't believe you chased me down to give me this." He stops for a second, and his mouth quirks up into a small smile. "Or maybe you just really wanted to see me again."

That's what he's thinking? What, I chased him down because I just couldn't resist him? The audacity of this guy. I mean, yeah, I could have just dropped it at a ticket counter and had them call him, but—

Wait, why hadn't I done that? I wipe the emotion from my face and refuse to let him see me blush. Again.

"How did you manage to get off the plane with that big head of yours?" The words are out before I can stop them, and there's no going back.

His eyes narrow on me, like I've challenged him and he *likes* it. Oh brother, he's one of those guys. The best thing I can do now is hold my ground. That's probably why he was paying so much attention to me on the plane, because I wouldn't give him any. He figured I was playing hard to get, which I decidedly was not. I quirk a brow and cross my arms, but his smile only widens, as if that was actually his plan from the beginning.

Dammit, I think he won this time.

"Would you like to get a cup of coffee?" His voice caresses the word coffee in a way that should be illegal. I blink and shake my head. I can't have heard him right. I just called this guy big-headed, and his response is to ask me out?

"Wh-what?"

"Coffee. Brown liquid. Sometimes with milk or sugar in it. Tastes good. Gives you energy." His smile grows with every word, making his perfect dimples stand out beneath his beard.

Why, oh why, does he have to have dimples?

Stay strong, Joss.

"I know what coffee is. Why would I want to get it with you?"

"Well, because you're obsessed with me obviously. Why else would you chase after me in an airport?"

"Ob-ob*sessed* with you?" I continue to stutter out my words. This is going really well.

"Yup, completely obsessed. The way you yelled my name before, I could tell."

Lord help me, the pair on him. His eyes gleam with mirth as he runs a hand through his hair, whereas my brows have drawn so close that I'm about to go cross-eyed.

"You're kidding me, right?" I'm indignant now, and I have zero chill where he's concerned. He's delusional. Yet, when he leans into my space, I can't help my sharp inhale or the way my pulse quickens. I can't help but breathe in his scent that, despite having spent sixteen hours on an airplane, is somehow crisp and clean and entirely masculine.

His voice is soft and teasing as he speaks low into my ear. "Yes, I'm kidding." He laughs then, a full, boisterous laugh, and his hand finds his hair again. It's either a tic of his, or he's really trying to drive me insane. "I'm just messing with you. Although, I am a hundred percent serious about getting you a cup of coffee, I owe you that much."

"Oh, okay, yeah. I mean, no. I'm working, sorry. I have to go actually. Just wanted you to have that. Good luck, Weston."

I'm backing away now, looking anywhere but at him. I can't get away fast enough. Not wanting him to see how he affects me, I turn and walk away. Again.

"It's Wes!" he shouts after me. "And what about you? Aren't you going to tell me your name, or should I just call you Grey?"

This man has no shame, yelling across the terminal, drawing all sorts of attention to us.

"Grey?" I call back, turning to face him even though I know I shouldn't encourage him.

He has a devilish grin in place that is even more delectable and wicked than the one he had on before. What on earth? How does he get under my skin like this?

"Like your eyes." And though he's talking about *my* eyes, it's his that are burning bright.

I scoff but feel the corners of my mouth lift. Goodness, he's smooth, but I am not falling for his charms. He lifts his hand in a little wave and it's so cute and endearing that I lose my mind for a second and find myself shouting back to him.

"It's Joss!"

Why did I do that?

He seems to inflate, like he just won a game I didn't realize we were playing. We each turn and head our own way. He's off to take on the Emerald City while I'm headed back to my airplane to finish cleaning up before I get to go home. I have almost a week off before my next trip, and I'm beyond ready for some R&R.

My feet carry me across worn carpet, down the metal gangway, and back into the stale air of the plane. All the while, my feelings are a riotous contradiction. Weston— *Wes*—has me completely off-kilter. He's undeniably hot, thus the reason I felt flustered around him during the flight. But he's also over-confident and cocky, which are not qualities I typically find attractive. He nearly flattened me, which was irritating to say the least. Sadly, it was also the most action I've seen in a while. So, there's that.

I roll my neck to clear the confusing thoughts. It's a good thing I won't be seeing him again. Even if he is staying in Sydney for a while, this is a huge city—it's not likely I'll run into him on the street. Not that I'd want to. After everything that happened with Eric last month, I need to keep my emotions in check and steer clear of trouble.

And Wes Anderson screams trouble.

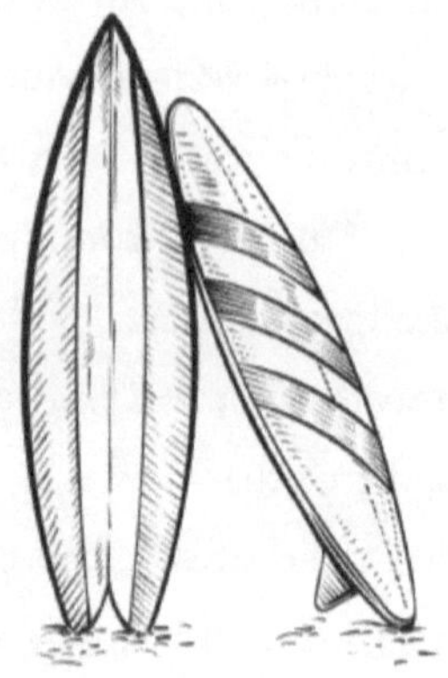

CHAPTER THREE

Wes

*I*t's *Joss.*

Two little words.

Two words that keep ringing through my head in her perfect accent. *It's Joss.* Just her name, but a win is a win, and dammit, I didn't realize how much I needed one after a string of so many losses. I can't believe I dropped my passport, or that she took it upon herself to get it back to me. What a clusterfuck it would have been if she hadn't.

No, officer, I swear I had a passport when I boarded the plane.

I scrub my hand across my face before sliding it through my hair. I can only imagine the state it's in right now—I'm counting down the minutes until I can take a shower. Bringing myself to care is difficult though. God, what a way to end an already excruciating travel day.

It's not lost on me though that if I hadn't dropped my passport, I wouldn't have seen her again. *Joss*. Her name rolls around in my brain like the best kind of distraction. I was serious about getting her coffee, anything to repay her for the effort of chasing me down. Yet, if I'm being completely honest, it wasn't her kindness that put this stupid grin on my face. The one I can't seem to get rid of. No, it was getting her riled up. Who knew a girl giving me sass about my ego would be such a turn-on?

That's the most like myself I've felt in months. It was easy to banter with her. Fun. My smile stays in place even as I walk away.

I clear the security exit, baggage claim, and customs with no additional issues. My passport is safely stored in my sadly ruined backpack—now slung across the front of my body. I take a seat on an outdoor bench to wait for my ride, taking the weight off my knee and stretching my legs in front of me.

My suitcase, surfboard bag, and carry-on sit beside me. I got used to traveling light in the military, taking only what was necessary. Now, my behemoth of a bag seems almost comical. On the other hand, considering I'm here with a work visa and no return flight, I guess this could be considered light. Most of my belongings I either sold or donated before I left, with the remainder going into storage to be dealt with at a later date. I wish locking up my emotional baggage were as easy. If only I could put it in a box and throw away the key.

I tip my head back and slide my eyes closed, letting the crisp June breeze coast across my skin. I left an eighty-degree summer day behind me in Los Angeles only to be greeted by a sixty-degree winter day in Sydney. The reverse of the seasons has always thrown me off. Even when I was in college here it messed with me when we'd be on summer break for Christmas. Of course, winter in Sydney isn't like winter in Tahoe. When you're used to feet upon feet of snow, days with highs in the sixties and lows in the forties aren't exactly what I'd classify as "winter" weather. But I won't complain, not when it means I can surf year-round while I'm here.

I let my thoughts wander and, unsurprisingly, am taken right back to today's flight, when I was right on top of Joss. I've been attracted to many women over the years and enjoyed the fruits of that attraction even more, but there was something different with her. Like a moth to a flame, I feel like Joss could burn me and I wouldn't resist.

Anyway, none of that matters. Sydney's massive, and chances are she doesn't even live here. She could be based anywhere in Australia for all I know. The likelihood of seeing her again is slim to none, which is for the best. Given my current mental state, I'm not in a position to start anything with anyone. If I'm being honest, I have no plans to ever seriously date again.

My phone buzzes and I pull it out of my pocket. My ride's almost here. Breck, my closest friend from my years at the University of Sydney, offered to come get me, but I'm glad I told him I'd see him tomorrow. With how tired I am right now I wouldn't be the best company. Fortunately, it's only a couple minutes before I'm sitting in the back of a sleek black SUV and headed toward what will be my new home for the next twelve months. I'm so glad that this driver isn't the chatty type.

The next thing I know the car is pulling to a stop in front of a very tall, very swanky building near the city center. I can't believe Breck was able to swing getting me an apartment here. It's nice to have friends in high places, and he's well-connected in Sydney. There's no way I would've been able to afford this place at their normal rates, but he called in a favor and scored me a deal.

I gather my luggage and board bag from the back and make my way inside toward the security desk. Apparently I live in a building with a security desk; that's a first. Of course, most of the places I've lived have been in the middle of nowhere and had no need for luxurious anything.

The guard at the desk looks me over as I walk in. He's older, maybe in his mid-fifties, and looks stern. For a security guard, I'll take it.

"Hi, I'm Wes Anderson. I'm moving into apartment 16A and was told I could pick up my keys here?"

All I get in return is a gruff nod. Maybe he's tired today too. He types something into his computer and then pulls a set of keys from the drawer to his right.

"You've got two keys here. If you lose one, you're responsible for replacing it." He slides my lease across the desk with the keys. It's straightforward, and after thirty-four years on this planet—twelve spent on the move with the military—I've signed my fair share of them. "You've also got this key card to access the gym, pool, and other amenities on the property. Here is a welcome packet with all the information you need to get settled. If you have questions, you can reach out to management."

He trades out the paper I just signed for a heavy folder that I'll likely never open. I wonder what part of Australia he's from to have such a thick accent. I remind myself to ask him the next time I catch him wearing a smile.

"Thanks so much. Are you usually the guard here"—I look at the badge on his chest—"Frank?"

I'm one of those people who is great with names. Frank seems unsure of me though, as if he's sniffing out ulterior motives.

"Yup." Okay, a man of few words. Got it.

"Thanks again. Have a good one, Frank." I offer him my friendliest smile and barely get a nod in return. I'll break down those walls eventually; it's what I'm best at.

I pocket the keys, grab my bags, and trudge across the marble floors toward the elevators. I haven't lived in a big city since the last time I was here, and I wasn't living this high life then. It was more like college dorms or trashy apartments and lots of cheap beer and ramen. This is going to be a whole different world compared to the Sydney I experienced in my early twenties.

I open the door to the apartment and let out a low whistle. Breck has really outdone himself here. The open floorplan stretches from the entryway all the way to the windows, where a stunning view of the city greets me. The glistening water of the harbour shines in the low afternoon light, and I give myself a full minute to appreciate the sight.

The apartment came fully furnished, and the decor is all modern and chic. The galley kitchen on my left is separated from a small dining room by a granite bar, and I spot a rack of copper pots and pans hanging above it. I'll need to learn to cook more than pasta with a kitchen like this. A grey sectional sits in front of a flatscreen TV, flanked on both sides by tall black bookcases. I didn't bring many books from home, but I'm sure that those shelves will fill up over time. I'm kind of dumbfounded that this place is going to be mine.

I kick off my shoes and pull my bags down the hallway, passing the laundry room and a half bath as I go. The bedroom is light and airy, with big windows facing the same gorgeous view. A sprawling king-sized bed with white linens and way too many pillows contrasting against a black bed frame commands most of the space. It looks like a cloud that I'd like to sink into and never get up from. There's a leather armchair in the corner next to a small table, and a dresser opposite the bed.

I catch a glimpse of myself in the mirror above it and flinch. I really need a shower—this bedhead situation I have going on is out of control. I drop my bags at the foot of the bed and sit down, leaning back against the mountain of pillows. I know I should stay awake, maybe go out and find something to do so I don't mess up my transition to this time zone, but my eyes are heavy. The weight of everything I'm carrying falls away and I'm pulled under in seconds.

A chiming sound from the nightstand pulls me from sleep. I blink my eyes open, trying to register where I am. It's a slow dawning. Right, I'm in Sydney. This is my new apartment.

I rub the sleep from my eyes and pick up my phone.

Breck

Hey mate, you make it ok?

Me

Hey, yeah, sorry. I meant to text you when I got to the apartment, but I totally passed out. Dude, this place is incredible!

Breck

No worries, and yeah I'd kind of kill to live in that building, aside from the fact that I love my house. Getting settled?

Me

If getting settled means falling asleep for three hours. Thanks again for setting this place up. Still good for tomorrow?

Breck

Definitely. Talia and I can pick you up and we'll go grab lunch.

Me

Sounds good. Will my favorite girl be joining us?

Breck

Willow has school, but she's excited to see you too.

Me

Tell her I brought her a present. It will be great to see you guys.

Pulling a change of clothes out of my bag, I head for the bathroom. The groan that escapes me when I see the spacious walk-in shower is indecent. There's also a separate garden tub large enough for even my long legs, which I look forward to using sometime soon. I can almost hear the shower calling my name as I strip down, wincing slightly at the pull of denim over my swollen, red knee. I make a mental note to ice it tonight even though I know I probably won't.

The hot water hits my shoulders and some of the stress and exhaustion is immediately rinsed away. I go through the motions on autopilot before gliding the most luxurious towel across my skin. This is something I could get used to. I fasten it around my hips and run my fingers through my damp hair. It's longer than I've had it in twelve years, and part of me wants to just let it keep growing. My small rebellion against the military's rigid grooming standards.

I venture out to the empty kitchen, aimlessly opening cabinets. Why didn't I think to order in groceries or something? Now I'm starving and have nothing to eat and no energy to go out. The stainless-steel fridge taunts me, and despite knowing it will be empty, I pull it open.

"No way!"

I'm talking to myself, but there's beer in the fridge, so it feels warranted. Another pull of a handle reveals a pizza in the freezer with a note.

> Welcome Home —
> Love, Breck, Talia,
> and Willow.

I imagine this was Talia's doing. Regardless, dinner is served. Or I guess it's lunch? This time change is really messing with me. I pull the pizza out and start prepping it to go in the oven, popping open a beer as I go. It's cold and slides down my throat smoothly, taking a little bit of the weariness with it. The sound that escapes my lips is embarrassing. I'm sure I'm quite the sight, standing here half-naked, moaning over my beer.

With the pizza cooking, I walk over to the windows. Two of them are actually doors leading out onto a small patio, and I waste no time opening them wide. I let the sunlight and chilly wind reinvigorate my tired body, unconcerned that I'm in nothing but a towel slung low on my hips. There are a couple of patio chairs and a small table out here, and I already know I'll be using them a lot over the next year. I lean on the railing, taking a large swig of my beer, and soak in the fact that I'm actually here.

A few quiet minutes pass, my body releasing built-up tension with each breath of fresh air. I should go check on the pizza, and I need another beer. Turning, my eyes snag on the balcony of the neighboring apartment. The vibrant coral surfboard propped against the wall is what first catches my eye. There's also a very skimpy bikini hanging off the back of a chair. Could it be that I have a surfer chick living next door? Be still my heart.

You're not looking to date, remember? I chide myself. Settling down here, or anywhere really, isn't something I'm interested in. But does that mean I can't enjoy the fun of being single in a city far away from my past and all the mess that comes with it? Would it be so bad befriending the adventurous woman next door? Maybe she's someone who would jump at the chance to do something fun and go along with all my hairbrained schemes. This living situation is looking better and better every minute.

My stomach's incessant growling tugs me away from the balcony, and thoughts of my neighbor are interrupted by the buzzer on the oven. Grabbing a second beer from the fridge, I search through all the drawers until I finally find an oven mitt. It's black, what a surprise. Everything in this apartment is monochrome. I can't decide if I like it or not.

I'm so hungry I eat the entire pizza and finish off a third beer before I'm done. With a full stomach, my exhaustion weighs on me again. Keeping my eyes open is becoming a challenge, but I want to get unpacked before I crash for the night.

I walk to my room and flip open my suitcase. I take my time hanging clothes in the closet, filling the dresser, and even unloading all my toiletries. But it only takes me about an hour before I'm all moved in and there's nothing left to distract me from the tiredness.

Bed. Now. Need sleep. My brain is functioning in single syllable words at this point. I have the wherewithal to at least double-check that the oven is off and plug in my phone before I fall face-first into the cloud that is my new bed.

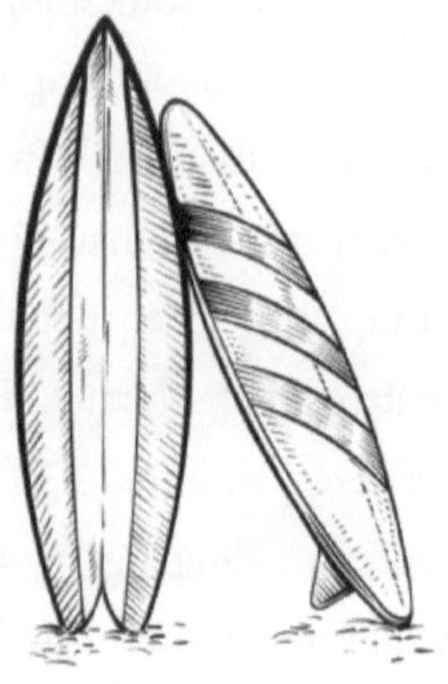

CHAPTER FOUR

Joss

I feel the strain of the day rolling off my shoulders as I unlock the door to my apartment. I haven't been home in a few days, and I've been craving the refresh button that comes with it. No matter how stressful work is, I can always let it go here. It's one of my favorite things about being a flight attendant. I get to leave it all at the airport.

Of course, I haven't completely left this most recent trip behind me. Despite my best efforts, my thoughts linger on Wes. Never have I met a man on a flight—or anywhere—that caught my attention like he did. It's kind of infuriating because why couldn't Eric, or anyone I've dated, have that pull? Maybe I wouldn't be single right now if they had. I mean, come on, it had to be a random man on an airplane? An American, no less? Likely here and gone just as quick?

It's not like I'm all that upset over mine and Eric's breakup last month. He didn't understand me, and I'm glad I never fully gave him my heart—even if his words still play on a loop, poking holes in my unaffected facade.

You never open up.

How can you see a future for us when you can't even share your past with me?

Sorry, bud, some things just don't need rehashing. Like, ever.

I pull myself out of my head—those thoughts aren't going to take me anywhere good. What I *need* to do is unpack, do laundry, get groceries, and eventually fall into bed. These intercontinental flights are brutal, but the pay is good, and I would never give up the industry perks.

I throw in a load of laundry, the comforting whir filling the apartment with a buzz of white noise. I slip on a pair of joggers and a baggy band T-shirt, ready for a day of doing absolutely nothing. I unpack the rest of my bag, sliding it up onto a shelf in the closet.

Bye, Felicia, see you in a week.

My feet sink into the soft white carpet on the way to the fridge. There's very little in there, but the cheese and deli meats I bought right before I left still look good. All thoughts of getting groceries are pushed to tomorrow. I throw together a makeshift charcuterie board—so bougie of me—and pour a glass of rosé before heading out to the balcony.

This is my favorite spot in my apartment. It may not be huge, but the view is beautiful, and the sun over the harbour is perfect despite the chill in the air. My surfboard taunts me from its place in the corner. I'm itching to hit the beach but know full well I'll wake up too late tomorrow and miss the best waves. Maybe an afternoon session then.

I set my plate on the table and walk to the railing where I lean my forearms against the cool metal. Closing my eyes, I breathe in the smell of home, then lift my glass to my lips, the crisp wine bursting with flavor against my tongue. When my stomach rumbles, bringing my attention back to my makeshift lunch, I spot a light on in the apartment next door. Has it finally been rented out? I don't see any movement, but my curiosity is piqued as I wonder who my new neighbors might be.

When I finish scarfing down my meal, I take the dishes to the sink and don't bother washing them. I'm a rebel, okay? Still feeling hungry, I pull out the package of Tim Tams. Talk about "home." The only other place I've been able to find my guilty pleasure is in Hawaii, oddly enough. I keep my gluttony contained and settle on two for tonight, dropping crumbs on my way to the bathroom.

I rush through what you could barely call a shower, pull my comfy clothes back on, then wrap my hair in the softest towel on earth. I spend so much time in hotels that I've learned the importance of good linens.

I wipe away the steam fogging the mirror and momentarily take myself in. This long day has left me with dark circles beneath my lower lashes. My distinctive grey eyes stand out in contrast to my brown hair and sun-warmed skin. They've always been my favorite feature, and they'd be completely unique to me if I didn't know exactly where—who—I got them from. I release the dark tendrils of my hair, shaking off that thought, and let it fall in wet waves past my shoulders. I'm due for a trim, but I tend to forget mundane things like appointments for haircuts.

I palm my cheeks with a huff and get to work applying my skincare. I swear with every birthday comes yet another product I "need" and with my thirtieth creeping up I feel that pressure even more. How men get away with washing their hair, face, and bodies with the same soap—and *maybe* applying a moisturizer—is beyond me. No one ever tells them they need seventeen steps in order to look good.

My bed beckons to me with its cushy pillows and soft throw blankets. *Laundry. I should rotate the laundry.* I swipe that thought away like a bad Tinder match, instead going in search of my phone and Kindle. When I'm back in my room, I fall into bed with a contented sigh. I plan to stay right here the rest of the afternoon.

Unfortunately, it's not long before the exhaustion takes its toll, and I can't spare a thought for the romance in my book. I'm asleep in no time, completely oblivious to the world.

I wake up in the morning feeling well rested but frustrated. Frustrated because a certain beautiful man featured heavily in my dreams last night. I can still feel a light blush on my cheeks thanks to said dreams.

Goodness, Joss, get a grip.

I roll myself out of bed, knowing the groceries aren't going to buy themselves. The laundry probably didn't move itself to the dryer while I slept either, which is unfortunate.

I pad to the bathroom, splashing water on my heated skin. My favorite running shorts and hoodie call my name from the vanity where I always leave them before a trip. I do so with high hopes that pulling them on first thing in the morning will lead to me actually going for a run. It never does, but a girl can dream. I slip my runners onto my feet, but with no bra I've eliminated any chance I'll be jogging anywhere.

First things first—I need coffee.

I'm out the door and halfway to the elevator when I notice the door to the apartment next door is cracked. Soft music drifting from inside. I'm tempted to knock and introduce myself, but braless with a messy bun might not be my best first impression. I get on the elevator, and as the doors slide shut, I spot a man coming out from apartment 16A. Before I can take note of much more than the logo on the tattered baseball cap sitting backward on his head, the doors shut completely, leaving me more curious about my new neighbor than I was before.

The sun is shining this morning and a sense of calm washes over me. I've never wanted to live anywhere but the city. I love the hustle and bustle, the noise, the pace... it's where I thrive. There's nothing that could ever tear me away from my life here.

I pop my AirPods into my ears as I walk down the street, headed for Harbour Grounds. I slip through the door and let the heady scent of coffee surround me. I could float away on the aroma like a cloud. Jaz, the barista behind the bar, is also my best friend. She squeals with delight when I catch her eye from my place in line. The people waiting for their coffee look around as if Sting just walked in, but it's just me. They make sure to display their disappointment before turning back around.

Jaz and I moved to Sydney around the same time, right out of high school, and became fast friends over a mutual love of coffee, books, and a desire to see the world someday. I pull my AirPods out and return them to their case as she leaves the line waiting, scurrying out from behind the counter. She's in my arms for a big hug before I can even fully register that she's coming for me.

"Hi! You're here, I couldn't remember when you were getting back."

"I'm here, and I couldn't be happier about it. Except maybe if the crap service at this place was better." This last part I say with a giggle, and she smacks me on the shoulder, heading back to the counter.

She points her finger at me and shouts over her shoulder. "You get decaf for that."

I feign a look of hurt and fling my hand across my chest dramatically. "You wouldn't dare."

She ignores me and turns her attention back to her customers. Luckily, most of the locals who frequent this place know that Jaz is crazy and flighty—it's part of her charm—and she takes the next few orders with quick precision.

Before I even reach the counter, she slides me my Sleepy Sydney, a nitro cold brew with brown sugar syrup, salted caramel cold foam, and a caramel drizzle. It's basically caffeine and sugar incarnate.

She points me to the open seat at the bar so she can come catch up with me when the line clears. I watch her work, admiring my best friend. She started here as a barista and is now part owner of the place. There's more than one man in here that watches her with rapt attention. Her soft brown skin glows in the café's amber light, and her dark curls are pulled away from her face, emphasizing her shining green eyes. My friend is stunning. But her looks don't even hold a candle to the woman she is on the inside.

Beyond my parents, who I do not count, Jaz is the person who's been in my life the longest. She's seen me through the hardest moments of my adult life. She's my person. I'd bury a body with her if she asked me to, and I know she'd do the same for me. Let's just hope that particular need never arises—dead people aren't really my thing.

It only takes her a few minutes to get through the mid-morning rush before she takes up her spot opposite me behind the bar.

"Have you gotten better at making these? Or did I just miss your coffee so much that it somehow tastes better?"

"You know it's just because you missed me. How was your trip?"

My trip... Do I tell her about Wes? I chew my lip, debating it. She'll probably have more questions than I have answers. So, maybe not.

"It was good, uneventful. You know I don't love the LA route, but I always find something fun to do."

That I get to travel for my job is about the only area of my life that makes Jaz jealous. I bank my buddy passes and frequent flyer miles so we can take a vacation together every couple of years. We've done Africa and the Maldives so far, but we're still working out the details for where we'll go next.

"Don't tell me... You went to Disneyland?" She says this as if she knows me or something.

"Yes, I did. Before you say anything, I know I go there every time I'm in LA, but I can't help it. I do believe it's the happiest place on earth, outside our little slice of heaven here, of course."

"I know that, but what makes me crazy is that you could do so many things—hit up Hollywood, shop Rodeo Drive, go to Santa Monica—but instead, you always go back to Disneyland. I think you're nuts."

"I'm aware of how nuts you think I am." I add an aggressive eye roll just to drive my point home. "Maybe I'm saving those things for when I drag you to LA with me someday."

"Have you talked to Eric lately?" she asks nonchalantly, avoiding my eyes by wiping the perfectly clean counter with a rag.

Where did that question come from?

"Definitely not, why?"

"I'm just asking." She holds her hands up like I have her at gunpoint, the rag hanging limply. I guess my response came out a little defensive. It's been over a month though, so I can't figure out why she'd suddenly be interested.

"You remember he dumped *me*, right?" I try to lighten my tone, but it's still more clipped than I'd like.

"I just thought that maybe..." At the look on my face, she stops and seems to think better of where she was going with that sentence. Or maybe not. She sets her shoulders and continues. "I just thought you might have decided it was finally time to let someone in."

I clearly haven't had enough caffeine yet because I have no idea what she's getting at. I let people in. Eric and I dated for six months. It just turned out he wasn't the right guy for me.

"Look," she continues, "I love you. You know I love you. I've also known you a long time, nearly twelve years come to think of it, and there hasn't been a single guy you've dated that's scratched the surface of knowing the real you. Eric told you as much, right? Wasn't that the problem?"

I'm stunned. Where is this coming from? Maybe I should have led with the Wes story so we wouldn't be talking about this right now.

"Why would I want to put all that baggage on someone? I wish I didn't have it myself. And it's not like every guy I date dumps me for not being an emotional oversharer. I'd say most guys appreciate that about me. Some things just don't work out."

She scoffs at this. "Love, there's a difference between not working out and you ending things before you can get hurt."

"That's not what I do."

Again, she raises her hands. "Okay, okay. I wasn't trying to get your hackles up. I just don't want you to be alone forever. You deserve to be happy."

I'm about to push her on her sudden interest when I notice that Jaz is no longer looking at me. She's looking past me, which is strange. Jaz is one of those people who gives you a hundred percent of her attention. It's part of what makes her a great barista and why I keep suggesting they convert Harbour Grounds to a bar at night—she'd make a great bartender.

She lets out a low whistle, just loud enough for me to hear, and I giggle as understanding dawns on me.

"Damn... Don't look now, but you can forget everything I just said because I think your future husband just walked in." Her eyes have gone all soft and gooey, like the center of a cinnamon roll. "Yum-my!"

Typical Jaz to casually transition from debating my love life to finding my future husband. She's probably trying to keep me from being mad at her. Not that I could ever stay mad at her for long, no matter what she drops on me at nine a.m. while I'm jet-lagged and caffeine-deprived. It's working though, because I'm intrigued. Her face says enough about how hot the guy behind me must be.

I turn slowly on my stool, taking a sip of my drink as I go. You know, so it doesn't seem as obvious that the only reason I'm turning around is to ogle an innocent customer. But when I make it all the way around, I inhale sharply, cold foam and coffee clogging my lungs. The coughing and spluttering cover some of my reaction, but nothing can drown out the recognition.

Oh god. That sharp jawline. The stubbled face and dimples. The messy hair. Messy hair I wanted to run my hands through less than twenty-four hours ago.

I spin back to the counter and try to pull coffee-free air through my lips. He's just a mirage. He's not real. I wipe at my hoodie with a napkin, glad the navy blue will mask the stains of my embarrassment. All the while, Jaz is looking at me like I've grown a second head. Her evergreen eyes are round. She's also speechless, which is not something I've ever witnessed in my best friend.

"Bloody hell, what was that, Joss?"

Now she finds her words. She's also using them way too loudly and including *my name*. I act on instinct, leaning across the bar and slapping my hand across her mouth to stop her talking. If it's possible, her eyes grow even wider.

"Shhhh. Don't draw his attention. Don't look at him. Look at me," I whisper-shout, as if it will somehow undo this nightmare. But it doesn't, and as I lower my hand, she glances back to me with a *What the fuck* look. This is not going well.

"I might already know him." The words are clipped and kind of garbled. I'm honestly amazed Jaz can even understand me at this point. She makes a *keep going* gesture with her hand, a wide and far too interested smile spreading across her face. "He was on my flight in from LA yesterday. It's a long story."

"Oh my god!" Now she's the one whisper-shouting, and she follows up her quiet proclamation with a flick to my nose, making my eyes jump to hers in shock.

"Ow! That hurt."

"Did you do the nasty with him in the bathroom?" She waggles her dark eyebrows at me. "Can we call him Mr. Mile High Club?"

She's taking way too much pleasure in this, making me wish a crack would open in the ground and swallow me whole.

"First of all..." I flick her nose in return, earning me a little yelp. "Second of all, no I did not *do the nasty* with him, do you think I want to get fired? No! I just—we just... ugh, it's hard to explain when he's—"

I don't get to complete my sentence as I hear a deep voice rumble from behind me. "Right here."

Oh my god. I let my head fall to the counter, all hope of avoiding exactly this flying out the window. Did he hear all of that? No. No. *No*.

"Kill me now," I mutter, but the deep chuckle behind me tells me he definitely heard me. I lift my head and catch sight of Jaz's face. She's gone mute *again*. That's twice in 5 minutes, an all-time record. Turning, I hold my breath and take him in.

Wes Anderson.

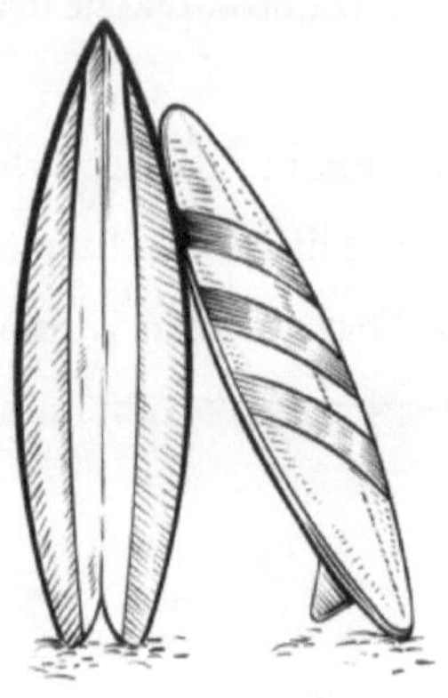

CHAPTER FIVE

WES

I can't keep the gleeful smile off my face as the beautiful—and incredibly flustered—Joss rotates in her seat to meet my gaze. The bright pink in her cheeks is even more appealing than it was yesterday, and I love that I put it there. Again.

I woke up thinking about this girl, probably because my dreams all ended with us in the same spot we were at on the plane yesterday. I rarely dream of anything these days besides the crash, so I'll take visions of her over that every night. I can't believe my luck that of all the coffee shops in all of Sydney, this is the one she chose today. Or maybe it's her regular spot, seeing as she was comfortable enough to flick the barista's nose a second ago.

"Good morning, *Joss*." I use her name so she'll know, without a doubt, that I remember exactly who she is. I feel like a kid in a candy store.

It's almost like my inability to stop thinking about her since we parted ways made her materialize here, less than a block away from my apartment. I take note of those enchanting grey eyes as they check me out from head to toe, and my smile only widens. I have to drag my eyes away from her to reach across the counter and extend my hand to her friend.

"Hi, I'm Wes."

"Jaz." Her hand flies out to meet mine, but her eyes ping-pong between me and the ice sculpture standing next to me. "I'm Joss's best friend. How do you two know each other?"

She motions between us while still holding my hand in her grip, making it more of an awkward hand-holding wave before she finally releases me. It's cute how she's pretending Joss wasn't just in the middle of telling her exactly how we met when I interrupted them.

My confident side kicks in and I sling my arm around Joss's shoulder, giving her a little squeeze. I feel her tense slightly, but she quickly relaxes and looks up to catch my eye. She's glaring at me. Fortunately, it's more of an *I'm a kitten that doesn't know how to use its claws* glare than an *I'm going to tear your heart out* glare. I grin and look right into her eyes as I address Jaz.

"I, personally, was enjoying Joss's retelling of this story. I would love to hear her tell us the rest."

Her eyebrows pull together while mine lift in challenge. Staring at her face, I can see she's still rosy with embarrassment and maybe something else. I really hope it's attraction. Her eyes flick down to my mouth while I talk. Yeah, that's definitely attraction.

I feel it too, Joss, don't you worry.

"Somebody better start talking before I'm forced to use my overactive imagination to fill in the blanks for myself," Jaz says, impatience dripping from her tone. Her eyes continue to jump between us before finally landing on Joss, urging her to explain.

At that, Joss rolls her shoulders back to shake my arm away and hops off her stool, putting it between us as she turns to face me.

"It really wasn't a big deal." She shrugs off the words. *Wasn't it?* I'm so curious to see how she spins this for her friend.

"Wes here," she begins, waving her hand at me in a nonchalant way before turning back to Jaz, "clumsily fell on top of me while we were deplaning, felt me up, and then left his passport behind. Which I kindly returned to him before he could be arrested by customs for trying to enter the country without it." Turning back to me, there's a smug grin on her face and a gleam in her eyes. "I think that about sums it up, right, Wes?"

She says my name with an edge to it, and I think I love that too. I smile wider even though I can feel the heat in my cheeks. I'm not completely immune to embarrassment, I just tend not to care what people think of me. But with Joss, I care more than I should, and I have no clue why. I don't even know her. She's gorgeous, yes, but still, there has to be more to it.

Joss has now turned back to her friend, giving me a chance to let my gaze roam. She's wearing worn-in running shoes, and her tanned, toned legs are on full display in a pair of shorts that cut high up on her thighs. She's got on an old ratty sweatshirt and her hair is pulled into a mess of curls atop her head. Honestly, I'm loving this version of her. Not that flight attendant Joss wasn't a smoke show, but this girl is so obviously comfortable in her own skin that I'm flooded with a sense of awe.

Jaz lets out a low whistle, drawing my attention away from the gorgeous woman beside me. She's still looking between us like we're the most bizarre pair of animals in the zoo. "Well, that is not what I was expecting. You're sure you didn't just hook up in the bathroom?"

A bark of a laugh escapes me and I decide, on the spot, that I like her. I also decide it's my turn to drag Joss into the hot seat.

"No, no. Joss spent so much time avoiding my attempts to catch her eye the whole flight that I couldn't even strike up a conversation, let alone convince her to help me become"—I look directly at Joss now—"Mr. Mile High Club, was it?"

Joss snorts into her coffee and Jaz lets out another laugh that screams *busted*.

"It took my bag intervening on my behalf and creating the scene Joss described for me to finally get her undivided attention." It's her turn to full-on blush as she looks at me, and I do a mental fist pump. "Oh, and as I said on the plane, the whole groping thing was accidental."

I place my hand over my heart like I'm pledging the truth to her. I mean, it is true. I'm not that guy, no matter how confident I come across.

"But I do owe you for chasing me down through the terminal to return my passport. Getting strip-searched by a customs agent would not have improved what was already a long day."

This garners me another laugh from Jaz—at least she thinks I'm funny. I think Joss is trying to hold one in as well. Good, I'm not losing my touch. I'm about to ask Joss to sit and have coffee with me, but she abruptly turns away before I can.

"Well, I'm off. I've got to get groceries." She plants her hands on the bar and hops up, leaning over to peck her friend on the cheek. "See you later." The look Jaz gives her says she's far from finished with this conversation. She turns to me as she grabs her coffee and slings her bag over her shoulder. "Wes, enjoy your vacation. Try not to flatten the flight attendant on your way home, yeah?"

She taps my shoulder once as she moves to leave, and the small touch makes my blood sing as a shock of awareness runs through me. She's good, thinking she can brush past me and that will be the end of it.

But I don't give up that easily.

"Actually..." I catch her open hand before she can sprint out of the coffee shop. "I'm not here on vacation, and my apartment is pretty bare on the grocery front. I wouldn't even know where the nearest store is. Mind if I tag along with you?"

Her fathomless grey eyes are wide as she looks down at her hand, then back up to me, and then to Jaz as if asking to be saved. Jaz, however, does nothing but regard us with an amused smile on her face.

"You two have fun," she says, giving us a wave before moving to greet a customer at the register.

As I start for the door, Joss's hand still in mine, I catch the glare she sends her friend. I'm pretty sure she mouths something too, because Jaz's laughter is the last thing I hear as we step out onto the pavement.

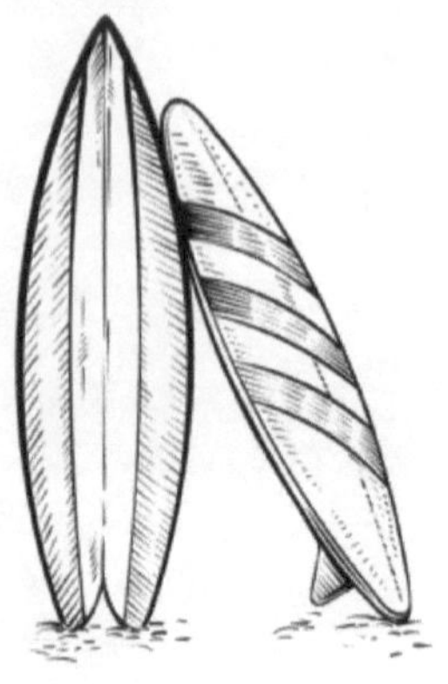

CHAPTER SIX

Joss

What is happening? What. Is. Happening? Have I entered the twilight zone or something? I swear I can hear that creepy "nehneh-nehneh nehneh-nehneh" coming from somewhere. How did my hand find itself in Wes's, being tugged from the coffee shop, while my now *ex*-best friend stands idly by. She is *so* going to pay for this.

"Where to? I really appreciate you letting me tag along." Wes says this like I had a choice in the matter. He's good—too good—and what did he mean he's not here on vacation? I need to regain control of this situation. He seems perfectly content to insert himself into my life, and that can't happen. I may have been mooning over how I wished I could find a man like him just last night, but I didn't mean *him* him. The universe is playing with me, I swear.

"I'm not *letting* you—you invited yourself. And seeing as this is a public street, I can't exactly stop you." I pull my hand from his, trying to keep my emotions in check. I should *not* instantly miss the contact of his warm skin. I turn and quickly stalk off down the street, thoughts zeroed in on all things laundry detergent and eggs and not the way this infuriating man is making me feel.

"Wait." He jogs to catch up to me, which doesn't take him long. How tall is this guy anyway? "Come on, is my company really that bad? I'm sorry I inserted myself into your plans, but seriously, my apartment is bare. I also haven't lived in Sydney in twelve years, and it definitely wasn't in this part of town. I'm all turned around."

So he just moved here, that makes sense, but still... How is this real? I let myself glance up at him, taking in his profile. Damn, he is gorgeous. My eyes slide down his body, to the white T-shirt that hugs his muscled arms and the jeans that hang just right on his hips.

Ugh, stop, Joss. It doesn't matter how appealing he is, you don't have space in your life for this.

Not that *this* is anything.

"The only reason for this little excursion is to fill your fridge? No ulterior motives?" I stop and turn to face him fully, raising a skeptical brow. I won't be his *Welcome to Sydney* conquest, if that's what he's after. Casual doesn't gel with my trust issues. Although, according to Jaz, neither do relationships, so I'm not sure where that leaves me.

"I mean, I do need groceries. But do you want me to lie and say I'm not glad we bumped into each other again? I won't. Of all the coffee shops and all the women in Sydney, what are the chances?" He gives a little shrug with his hands still deep in his pockets. He looks almost boyish like this.

Okay, fine, maybe his intentions are more innocent than I gave him credit for. He *is* new here, maybe he could use a friend. He looks down at his shoes, avoiding my eyes. Then, like he's said too much and needs to do something with his hands, he runs one through his hair. That perfect hair. I'm distracted by it until he grabs a baseball cap from his back pocket and slips it onto his head.

I immediately stiffen. No. It can't be. It's not. I shake my head, clearing the rogue thought. I'm still staring, trying to get a better look at it, when Wes looks up and tilts his head.

"What's that?" I say at the same time he says, "What?"

He reaches up to touch his hat, feeling around for something amiss.

"Nothing, it's just... I thought I recognized your hat from somewhere. Never mind. Let's go." All my words come out jumbled as I start walking again. I'm still trying to convince myself that it's a funny coincidence—*another* funny coincidence, that is.

"Are you sure? Have you ever been to Lake Tahoe? It's from a ski resort there." He motions to the weathered patch on the front. "Do you ski?"

His voice carries over the breeze, but I'm barely listening as I contemplate the possibility of Wes living right next door to me. Those aren't short-term apartments. How would I manage to avoid him if he's right there ALL. THE. TIME?

"Hey, Grey? You listening?"

He's waving a hand in front of my face now and I finally snap out of my spiraling thoughts, particularly when I hear him use the ridiculous nickname he gave me at the airport yesterday. "Sorry, got lost in thought there. What did you say?"

"I asked if you ski? Or snowboard?" He points to his hat again, and I note the word Heavenly and the large letter H logo.

"Oh, no, I don't. Always wanted to though." I can almost hear my brain making whirring sounds as it tries to process the confirmation. Yep, the universe has really done it. He's my neighbor. "Did you say you just moved here? Like, to *live*?"

"Yeah. I'm here for a year on a work visa. I spent two years here in college and have always wanted to come back."

Before I have time to unpack this, we've arrived at Woolworths and agree to branch off to different parts of the store. I contemplate making a run for it when I see him turn down the men's hygiene aisle, but what kind of *neighbor* would that make me? Instead, I veer my cart toward the chocolate section—I'm going to need lots of it as I come to terms with my new reality.

Once I've gathered what I need to get through the next couple of days, I meet Wes at the front with our baskets and check out. I smile when I see I'm not the only one with upward of three packs of Tim Tams in my haul.

"So, where are you living?" I have to hear him say it.

Not a single flicker of recognition passes across his blue eyes.

"Oh, um, I'm in those newer tower apartments. Kings Cross Rise?" It comes out like a question. "They're just a block from that coffee shop." A smile tugs at his lips, clearly pleased that we ran into each other.

Just you wait, Wes. You have no idea how much we're about to see of one another.

I let out a little groan, stopping in my tracks to face him, and look up at the sky like I'm pleading with God.

"I knew it..." I drop my gaze to look directly into Wes's eyes. "You're my new neighbor."

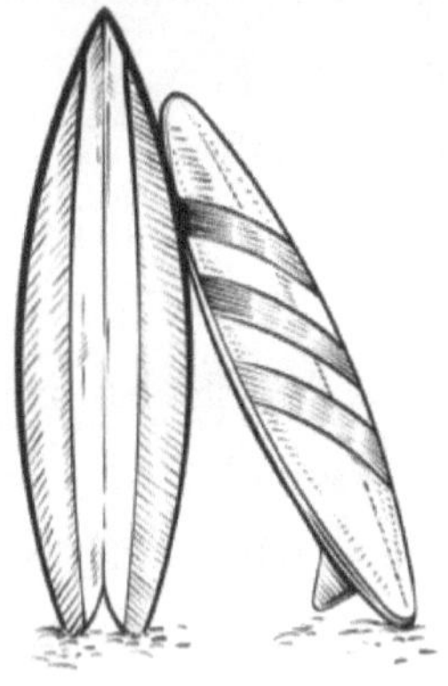

CHAPTER SEVEN

WES

You're my new neighbor.

Those four words leave me utterly stunned. I'm *never* stunned.

Did she just say neighbor? How can she possibly know this? I think my jaw might be on the sidewalk, because the first thing I register is Joss's soft finger under my chin, closing my mouth. She chuckles, likely at my imitation of a largemouth bass.

"I'm sorry. You're what now? How—I mean, are you sure?"

This is twice in two days that I've been reduced to a bumbling idiot around her, but of course this time she seems to take pleasure in it.

She gives a little self-deprecating laugh, and then reaches up to pull my baseball hat off my head. She holds it gingerly in her hands, like it might bite her.

"I saw my new neighbor walk out of his apartment in *this* hat this morning. Maybe it's just a coincidence? Maybe there are two new men in my building with this hat?"

Her building, she says, like she has ownership of the whole complex. But her logic is sound, the likelihood that anyone else in this city has this exact hat is low—I got it fifteen years ago from half a world away.

"I'm not going to lie, I'm impressed with your deductive skills, Columbo. Especially after the long day you had yesterday. I'm pretty sure I didn't even notice there was another person in the entire building this morning when I was leaving to get my coffee."

"Which you never got, by the way." Her words remind me that I'm still very much running on fumes.

"Again with the excellent deductive skills. Maybe that's why I'm so slow on the uptake this morning."

She laughs, seeming lighter somehow than she did when we first ran into each other. I don't know what's put her more at ease around me, but I like it, especially if we're going to be neighbors.

"So if you live at Kings Cross Rise and really are *my* neighbor"—I emphasize the word in direct correlation to her possessiveness of the building—"that's your coral surfboard on the balcony?"

She raises her eyebrows up toward her hairline. "It is indeed. Was too tired to get out today though. Do you surf?" she asks, sounding genuinely interested.

It's a relief to finally be leaving the awkwardness of our first encounters behind us. I feel compelled to tell her the story about how I first learned to surf as a teenager, hoping to keep the momentum going. It's an embarrassing story, but it has her laughing in earnest as we walk.

"You really rode the wave all the way in," she says through her laughter, "sitting backward on the board?"

I swear I hear a little snort as she continues to laugh.

Before I know it, we're back at our building. *Our building.* I still can't quite believe that out of all the apartments in all of Sydney, we would end up next door to each other in this one.

Joss stops short outside and looks up toward the sky, taking it in as if she's wondering the same thing. She turns to face me after a beat, and instead of feeling awkward, we just smile and walk inside.

"Hiya, Frank." Joss gives him a little wave and Frank, the monosyllabic security guard from yesterday, instantly brightens and offers her a returning wave.

"G'day, Ms. Morgan."

"Frank, please, for the millionth time, just call me Joss."

Joss Morgan. The name suits her, and I feel myself inflate learning this small detail of who she is.

Frank chuckles—actually chuckles—and waves her off before asking how her trip was. I'm once again stunned. I can charm the pants off just about anybody, and yet I got nothing from Frank yesterday.

"Frank, have you met our newest tenant, Wes?" she asks, angling toward me and motioning between us with her hand.

"Good morning, Frank, good to see you again." I offer up my brightest smile, and I'm rewarded with a grunt of acknowledgement.

I think Frank is broken. I look over at Joss to catch her stifling a giggle behind her hand. What she doesn't know is how determined I am. I will get through to this man if it's the last thing I do.

"Bye, Frank," she hollers over her shoulder, grabbing my free hand and pulling me toward the elevator bank.

I can feel her touch radiating all the way up my arm, and like a zap to my heart I'm shaken by how good it feels. She's still trying not to laugh as we get on the elevator, but I'm stuck staring at where our hands are linked. When she looks down, noticing them too, she quickly lets go. Why does our touching seem to turn us both into teenagers, incapable of adult interaction?

"You seem to be on pretty good terms with Frank?" I let some incredulity slip into my tone and she visibly relaxes at the change of subject.

"He's a hard nut to crack; it's not personal. It'll take him a while to warm up to you. Especially because you're American. He'll assume you're just passing through and won't want to get attached."

Huh, interesting.

"And what about you? Have you warmed up to me yet?" I give her my most charming smile, and unlike Frank, she reacts. Her eyes trail over my face, her cheeks heating as she bites on her bottom lip. What does that blush mean?

She's saved by the bell, or in this case, the ding of the elevator. Part of me is surprised to find myself standing outside my own door. I wasn't paying close enough attention to where we were going. The fact that I am indeed standing at my front door as Joss continues down the hall is the final proof that we *are* neighbors.

I pull my keys from my pocket as Joss does the same, and I laugh quietly at the ridiculousness of the situation. Joss narrows her attention on me, looking adorable as her face bunches up in confusion.

"What?" A hint of apprehension lines her tone, like she's concerned I'm laughing at her.

"It's just that I followed you here like a lost puppy. You could have led me literally anywhere and I would have followed. Yet here we are." I gesture at the space between our doors. "It just feels like fate or something."

I laugh again, lower this time. Fate? Do I even believe in fate? I must be more tired than I thought.

"Well, it's a good thing I'm not a serial killer," she says with a straight face, but there's a lilting, teasing quality to her voice. "Luring you to my secret lair for you to rub lotion on yourself."

I nearly choke as I bark out a laugh.

"Did you just reference *Silence of the Lambs*? Wow, you and I are going to be great friends. That was dark, Grey." She laughs too, the sound bright and enticing, and I find that I mean the words. I think I may have just found my first new friend in my new city. It makes the distance from home feel a little less overwhelming.

She unlocks her door first and steps in, then hesitates and pops her head back out.

"Wes?"

"Yeah?"

"Since you never got that cup of coffee this morning, when you're done putting your groceries away, I can make you one."

It's an olive branch. Maybe she needs a friend too.

"Yeah. That would be great actually."

"Okay, see you in a minute."

Closing the door behind me, I set my bags of groceries on the counter and begin unloading them. I can imagine Joss going through the same motions. I wonder if her floorplan is like mine or if it's flipped. Maybe her kitchen shares a wall with mine. I'm about to go tap a little "ratta tat tat" on the wall when I feel my phone vibrate in my pocket. Pulling it out, I see Breck's name on the screen.

Breck

> How'd you sleep? Jet lag kicking your ass? Let me know if you're still up for lunch in a bit.

Me

> Better than expected honestly. Just got some groceries. About to have coffee with my new neighbor. Let me know what time for lunch.

Breck

> How about 1? Neighbor, huh? Replacing me already? He better not be prettier than me.

Me

> She is definitely prettier than you

I set the phone on the counter, not bothering to read his reply before walking out my door and down the hall.

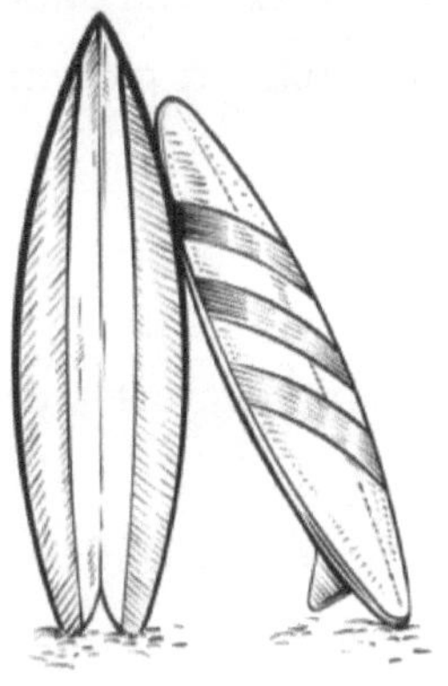

CHAPTER EIGHT

Joss

In the five minutes it's taken me to put away my groceries and put on a damn bra, I've come to a few conclusions. First, I am just as wildly attracted to Wes today as I was yesterday. Those freaking dimples may be the death of me. Second, I'd like it if we could be friends, in spite of said pesky attraction and our less than conventional first interactions. Third, I will not allow the first to keep me from making the second happen.

Was I shocked this morning when he appeared out of nowhere? Yes. Was I more than a little embarrassed at how easily he was able to throw me off-balance? Yes. However, now that we're neighbors and I've had the opportunity to be around him under less awkward circumstances, I can admit I actually like him.

A knock at the door makes me jump, nearly spilling my coffee. I get a little flutter in my stomach and consciously press a hand to my abdomen. These butterflies are going to have to scram if this friendship is ever going to work. Pasting on a smile, I pull the door open.

I can do this.

"Hey, neighbor." I surprise myself when my voice comes out cool... casual... smooth. I've totally got this. He smiles, more boyish now than when he was intentionally ribbing me earlier. He's still wearing that same baseball cap—now turned backward—dimples peeking through his stubble. I step back and sweep my hand out in invitation.

Don't look at his ass when he passes. Don't look at his ass when he passes.

My traitorous eyes absolutely check him out anyway. But I blame his jeans and the way they fit like a glove over muscular thighs. Is it possible to be an ass woman? Like, you hear men classify themselves as a "boob guy" or an "ass man", but I've never thought about it for myself. For Wes, I am definitely an ass woman.

"That coffee smells amazing. I'm not sure how I'm still upright at this point." Wes's voice snaps me out of my unneighborly thoughts and I scrub a hand over my face. This is going well.

"I definitely wouldn't be. Let's get you a cup. Do you take milk?"

I move past him into the kitchen and watch as his eyes rove over my space. At least it's still tidy, what with being gone most of the week. I look around my apartment—taking in the bookshelves, organized by color, the frames nestled amongst them with photos from my many adventures, the large floral arrangement on the teak table I bought secondhand last year—and try to see it through his eyes.

I decorated when I moved in, even though most places in the building come with the option of furnishings—like Wes's. I like a neutral color palette as much as the next guy, but the monochrome never meshed well with my beachy style. I've spent the last three years adding tans and whites paired with pops of mint green and coral to the space, and it's finally coming together.

The steam rises off the top of the freshly brewed coffee, and I top up my mug before pouring another for Wes. I meet his gaze across the counter, and he smiles.

"No milk." He reaches for it, and I meet him halfway. "Cheers." His hand brushes mine and he lifts his mug in a half salute before bringing it to his perfect lips.

No, Joss, just lips.

I lift my cup at the same time, enjoying the sweet and creamy flavor on my tongue. "Even with all my travel and overnight flights, I still can't get myself to drink black coffee." I wrinkle my nose. *Black coffee, bleh!*

A smile plays around his eyes as they dip to the butterscotch coloring of the liquid in my cup.

"You know, I didn't drink coffee at all until I went on my first deployment. When I first tried it, I'd use the creamer they had on the boat, but it was so sweet it made my teeth hurt." He grimaces and slides his tongue over his top teeth, like he's remembering it all too well. "Twelve-hour missions and days when I never saw the sun were impossible without the stuff though, so I switched to drinking it black and never went back."

He finally looks up and our gazes lock over the rims of our cups as we each take another long sip. I let my eyes drift closed, savoring the flavor as I focus on the information that was packed into those few sentences. Where do I start?

"You're in the military?" I ask, nodding at the hair curling out from under his ballcap, just brushing his ears. There's also the stubble lining his jaw, sharpening his features. "That wouldn't have been my first guess." From everything I know about military men—which isn't much, to be fair—they tend to be strait-laced and clean-cut all the time.

There's a flash of something in his eyes, but it's gone before I can pinpoint what.

"I was. I got out a couple months back." His tone has an edge to it, the lightness that was there just moments ago now gone. His entire posture has changed, it's more rigid. There's a story here, one he's probably not ready to share with a near stranger. But my curiosity is bubbling.

"Right. You said you're here on a work visa, which wouldn't make sense if you were still in the military. What did you do?"

"I was a pilot." His tone is clipped now as his eyes break away from mine, looking around the apartment again. He's clearly uncomfortable.

Time to back off, Joss.

"What are you going to be doing here?" I ask, and at the more neutral question, I catch how his shoulders settle. When he lowers his cup after another long sip, the smile is back on his face.

"My best friend from college, Breck, owns an adventure touring company here and they expanded into skydiving last year. He needed a pilot, so here I am." He gives a "no biggie" shrug.

"That easy, huh? Just pick up and move to Australia to help out a friend?" I'm finding it hard to imagine leaving everything and everyone I know for a job halfway around the world. Though, I guess in a way, I did just that when I moved to Sydney at eighteen. But I didn't have much choice. Maybe he didn't either.

I don't know where his mind goes with my question, but I must have a knack for striking a nerve because there's that look in his eyes again. And since he doesn't look away this time, I can better identify it. *Pain.* Not physical pain, but something deeper, something broken that you can't quite manage to repair, but you feel it all the way to the center of your being. I recognize it because I've had those same pains. I still do. My fingers twitch around my mug, wanting to reach out to him, but I hold back.

"I wouldn't say it was easy, no, but it was necessary," he says, all but forcing the words out. "I couldn't stay, and this became the perfect excuse to leave."

His blue eyes hold mine, an ocean storm churning behind them. I know all too well the need to leave, even when it hurts, because staying will only hurt more.

"Wanna sit on the balcony?" I change the subject and start moving that way, giving him a minute and hoping he'll follow me.

Maybe if we do become friends, Wes will feel comfortable sharing the mess behind what seems like a very put-together exterior. I wonder if I could share my mess with him too? I pull the door open and turn to watch him move through my space. He looks comfortable, at ease again.

I quickly grab my favorite teal bikini off the second chair, grateful it didn't blow away while I was gone. I'm usually better about taking things inside when I'm away for work.

I toss it into my beach bag and catch Wes's eyes following it as it goes. This particular suit is hardly more than a few scraps of material, and it's definitely not the most practical for surfing, but I love how it makes me feel—confident and sexy. Wes must like it too if the heated look in his eyes is any indication.

Instead of a small flutter of butterflies, I feel a tightening low in my belly. When the burning heat returns to my face, I have to remind myself of conclusion number two. *Friends*, nothing more.

Sitting down in the white wicker chair, I prop my feet up on the railing. My hands curl around my mug, resting it on my knees as I stare out over the city toward the harbour. I give my cheeks a minute to cool before I look over my shoulder at where Wes is lingering.

"You going to sit? Or just stand there all day?" I force playfulness into my tone.

The corners of his mouth twitch up and he moves gracefully around me to sit. His long legs stretching out in front of him and his whole body relaxing into the chair with a sigh, he tilts his head back, completely at ease. He rolls his head to the side so he can look at me, pinning me with his sapphire gaze.

"So, Joss, what are we going to do about this?"

"This... meaning what?" I know what he means, but I sure as hell won't be the one to say it.

"Oh come on now, don't play coy. I am obviously attracted to you. You're clearly attracted to me. *This*."

He motions between us, as if encompassing the chemistry stretching tight. I swallow. I guess putting it all out there might make this easier. Even still, I'd have added something a little stronger to this coffee if I knew we were going to have this conversation.

Well, here goes nothing. "Actually, I'm glad you brought that up. Better for us to just get this out of the way up front. I may think you're hot, but we're neighbors, and I'm not looking for a random hookup or any drama in my life. It's best we stick to being friends. Friendly."

There, I did it. It's out there. Wes's smile grows, but his brows pull together at the same time. Interesting. I wonder what that face means. Is it weird that I hope I get the chance to learn what all his faces mean?

"Sounds like we're on the same page. I find you extremely sexy, but I don't do messy either, and I don't do relationships anymore. So, friends?" He asks this so nonchalantly, like he didn't just say he thinks I'm extremely sexy. Not just sexy, but *extremely sexy*. He also indicated a bit of a backstory, where relationships are concerned, that I'm curious to hear more about. Setting his cup of coffee on the table between us, he shoots his hand out toward me. I set my cup down too and let his palm envelop mine.

"Friends," we say together as we shake, and dammit if electricity doesn't zing up my arm like I just touched a live wire.

Our eyes snap to where our hands meet, and then back to each other, gazes locked. He felt it too, I know he did. We release our grip, pick up our respective coffee cups, and sit in amicable silence, all the while taking in the view and our new friendship status.

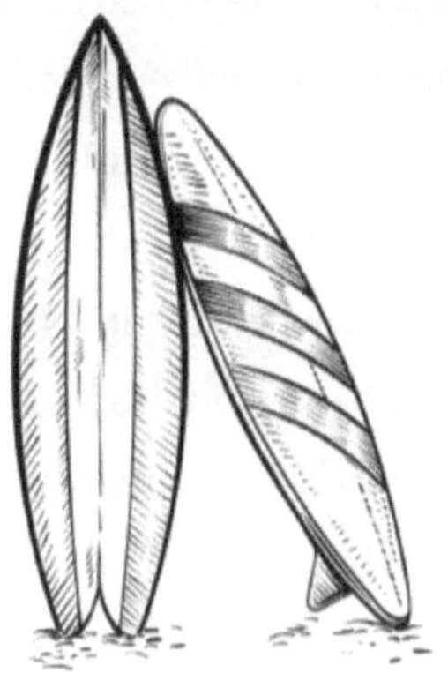

CHAPTER NINE

WES

The light breeze whips my hair around my face as I stand on the curb outside my new building. Breck is on his way to pick me up for lunch, and I can feel the year since we last saw each other stretching between us and pulling taut the closer he gets. When I was flown to the hospital in Hawaii after the crash, he dropped everything, took time off work, and was on the first flight he could get. He stayed with me for a week and he's been a constant source of support since.

We'd been close friends since I studied abroad here in college, but after Hawaii, he became my *best* friend. My friends from back home hardly keep in touch, and I don't know that I would feel comfortable accepting the support from them that I've sought from Breck. That's how you know the fair-weather friends from the true ones—they show up. And here is Breck showing up when I need him most and giving me a much-needed escape.

A sleek grey Toyota Hilux pulls up with a loud honk. A grin splits my face at the sight of him bounding around the front of the truck like a golden retriever, headed straight for me. I brace myself as we collide and he wraps me in a hug unlike anything I've experienced in... well, probably since I saw him last. Breck is the most physically affectionate man I've ever met. When he hugs you, it's a full-body experience, not like those bro-hugs or the handshake/back slap hybrids either. It's just part of who he is.

I'm struggling to remember the last time someone hugged me that wasn't my sister. Even my parents don't hug like this. In the Navy, buttoning down your emotions is expected, and rightfully so when compartmentalizing is key, but it usually trickles down into your friendships and relationships as well. Things have never felt like my bond with Breck does, like they exist deeper than surface-level. *Almost* never, I should say, but that's not a thought I allow in.

I squeeze him back, putting all the feelings I can't find words for into it, hoping he understands.

"Fucking finally, mate! I can't believe you're really here." Breck's warm laugh surrounds me as he nearly picks me up off the ground.

All my stress, the worries, the anxieties... the guilt, seem to drop to the sidewalk like a stone as he releases me. Leaving his hands on my shoulders, he looks me over. My somewhat disheveled appearance is probably a shock to him, and I smirk remembering the way Joss appraised me in a similar fashion earlier. Even in college I had a buzzcut. I may not have been in the military yet, but I knew where I was headed and I made sure to fit the part. I know I look a little shaggy by comparison now, and I'm just waiting for him to comment on it.

Breck, on the flipside, looks exactly the same. Six feet tall and built like a rock. His ability to surf and snowboard with the grace of a dancer has always blown my mind. His sandy-blond curls blow in the wind and his bright blue eyes shine with open excitement.

"Man, it's good to see you." The emotion in my voice threatens to spill over, so I pull him back in for another quick hug.

"You have no idea. It's been way too long!"

I hear the passenger-side door open and look over Breck's shoulder to see Talia standing there. Her olive skin tone and dark hair pair perfectly with her rich hazel eyes. She's sporting a small smile, amused by our bromance unfolding in front of her. I know her too, but not well. She was around a bit in college, but being two years our junior, we didn't overlap much. And it wasn't until a few years after graduation that she and Breck got together.

"It's good to see you, Talia. Thank you for the pizza and beer yesterday, you're a lifesaver." She walks over and I give her a side-hug then drop my arms. I'm not as comfortable with physical touch as Breck is, especially when it comes to his girl. I sneak a glance at Breck and find his eyes have turned mushy—he's a goner for her.

"I'm so glad you found it. I knew you'd be wrecked after that flight." A gust of wind tunnels between us then, and she motions toward the truck. "Lunch, yeah?"

"Oh yeah, I'm starving."

I can feel Breck watching me as we head for the truck, like he's running a mental diagnostic on how I'm really doing. How I'm coping. I put a little more effort into the smile I flash him, but I think he sees right through it.

"Willow has school, huh? Her favorite uncle moving to town didn't warrant a skip day?" I open the front passenger door for Talia but she hops in the back, motioning for me to take it.

Breck's smile goes wide as he climbs in. If he's a goner for his girlfriend, he's even more so for their daughter. "I thought about it, but she already missed a few days last week with a cold. I'm supposed to give you a hug from her."

Willow was a surprise that neither Breck nor Talia was prepared for. They'd only been dating a few months when they found out Talia was pregnant. As soon as Breck told me he was going to be a dad, I deemed myself Uncle Wes—even if I'd hardly get to see the kid because of the distance.

"Yeah, yeah." I roll my eyes. "Look at you being the responsible parent," I say, but we both know he's so much more than that—he's an amazing dad.

"We'll have you over this weekend and you can see her. I doubt she'll let you out of her sight the whole time," Talia chimes in from the back seat as we pull away from the curb.

Riding shotgun next to Breck, we shoot the shit about work and life. Driving down familiar roads feels like a dream after all this time. He slides into a parking spot with ease like he isn't commandeering a beast—the man has always loved his toys, and it's nice to see that hasn't changed.

The café we've pulled up to is quaint, with little tables out front and a sandwich board propped on the sidewalk. I laugh at the words written on it. On one side, it says, "A meal without wine is called breakfast," and on the other it says, "But a breakfast without champagne is not a breakfast." The café is warm and inviting, and my stomach grumbles loudly at the smell of fresh bread. I planned on getting something to eat this morning but was promptly distracted by a beautiful brunette.

The fresh coffee aroma washes over me and I realize that I forgot to buy some at the store. I'll have to make a stop later; otherwise, I'll be pounding on Joss's door in the morning.

"Tell me about this new neighbor." Breck says, fishing for information after my text about her being prettier than him. He's practically salivating at the prospect of a woman in my life. *Not happening, bro.*

"Sorry to disappoint you, but there's not going to be anything happening there," I reply, the words sending an unwelcome pang through my chest.

I can see the disappointment as his face falls, but he recovers and smiles again. "Why's that? She got a boyfriend or something?"

I think back to our conversation. I never actually asked, but I doubt she would have had me in her house and spoken of her attraction to me if she did. No, I think I can confidently say she isn't in a relationship.

"No. She's just not interested in anything casual, and I'm not interested in anything serious. You know I'm not one for messy and complicated, which is exactly what it'd end up being."

"Wait." His head rears back in surprise. "You've actually discussed this with her? Didn't you just meet?"

How can I explain this without sounding nuts... I guess it would seem odd to most people, but I loved that we were able to be up front about it. No mixed signals or wrong ideas here.

"Sort of..." I run a hand through my hair as I trail off, trying to think of how to start.

"What do you mean *sort of*? You've been here less than twenty-four hours... Is she from school?" Talia asks with way too much interest.

"No, not from school. She was a flight attendant on my flight in. We ran into each other again this morning at the coffee shop just down from my building and, turns out, we're neighbors."

"What are the chances?" Breck lets out a low whistle.

"Right?"

"I mean, come on, Wes. This is like the plot to every romance novel—you have to pursue her. It's fate!" Talia is not letting this go. I scrub a hand across my stubbled face trying to think of a way to diffuse this situation before she gets carried away planning my wedding.

"Talia..." Breck chastises her, but he does it with that megawatt smile of his, dimples on full display, so she doesn't seem to mind.

"What? I'm just saying." She shrugs her shoulders like this should be a foregone conclusion.

"Look, I get it," I say. "But we're *neighbors*, Talia. It would be a shit show if things went south. Anyway, we like each other, and it feels easy being around her. As friends." I let out a chuckle at her crestfallen face before directing my next words to Breck. "She cracked a *Silence of the Lambs* joke. An honest-to-god serial killer joke. I almost died."

Breck laughs. I know he's going to like her.

"So, when do we get to meet her? Any friend of yours is a friend of ours, right, Tal?" Her eyes swing to him and soften with a small nod.

"I'm not sure, she works a lot. I think she's off for the next few days though. We're planning on surfing dawn patrol tomorrow."

I can hardly wait to get in the water. I surfed a bit in my first two years of college in San Diego, but it wasn't until I transferred to Sydney that I really threw myself into it. Breck was always dragging me out with him in the mornings before classes and to random surf camps up and down the coast. I know he doesn't get to go nearly as often now between work and family stuff. He's busy, and I get that, but it used to be a huge part of his life.

"She surfs?" His eyes brighten, and he sounds even more excited about meeting her. "I haven't gone to Bondi in ages, I'd love to join you. Tal, you don't mind, do you?"

It bothers me that he has to ask. I know they live together, have a kid together, *and* work together, but still, Breck's a waterman. Talia's eyes drop to the table as she gives a little shrug.

"Yeah, it should be fine. I can take Willow to school, but we have a nine-o'clock meeting that I need you to be at."

"I won't miss it!" He leans and plants a kiss on her lips. She blushes and looks around as though embarrassed. They've been together for over eight years, you'd think she'd be used to his publicly affectionate ways by now.

"Thanks, babe."

He looks back at me with those dimples carved into his cheeks. He's like a big puppy who just got a treat, and I don't know why it doesn't sit right with me.

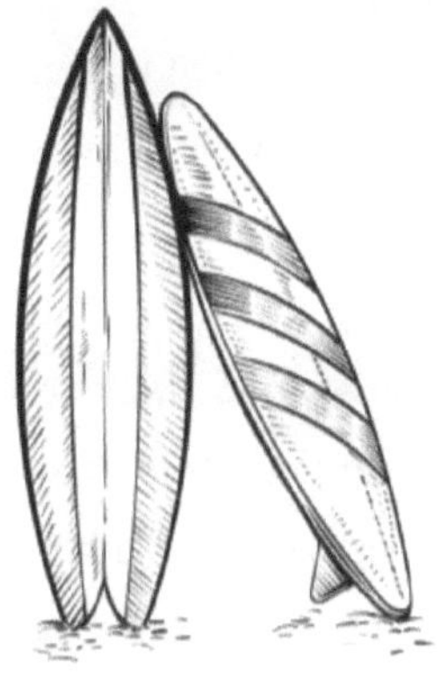

CHAPTER TEN

Joss

My alarm blares from the bedside table and I'm this close to reaching for it and throwing it across the room. Five in the morning is indecent. Part of me wants to roll over and go back to sleep, but the other part remembers why I'm awake in the first place.

I pull on my bikini, blushing at the vivid picture in my mind of Wes's face yesterday when he sized it up. Maybe I should wear a different one? I'm not looking to make this harder on either of us, but I do love this suit.

Oh for goodness' sake, Joss. He'll hardly see it under your wetsuit!

I slip on a pair of ripped jeans and my favorite hoodie. I take a minute to brush my teeth and braid my hair back, letting it fall across my shoulder before I head for the door. Will Wes actually wake up for this? He's got to be completely knackered and dealing with jet lag way worse than I am. I'm pretty much immune to it after so many years of constant travel.

All thoughts are banished when I open my door and find Wes leaning casually against the wall. Why is it so sexy when men lean? It should be illegal.

His board shorts hang low on his hips—something I only know because his University of Sydney hoodie isn't pulled down all the way and I can see the sliver of skin dipping under his waistband. There's a long, jagged scar across the top of his knee and another along the side that disappears under the hem of his shorts. I guess the old adage is true—chicks dig scars. And *those* I want to know the story behind.

His hair is tousled, definitely looking like he just woke up, and his eyes still have that soft quality about them like they might slip closed again at any moment. But he's here, and the smile on his face makes his dimples pop. I can't help but offer him a grin in exchange. It's not until he speaks that I finally snap myself out of my less-than-neighborly perusal.

"Morning, Grey." Even his voice sounds sleepy. A little gravelly. I think I might like his morning voice better than his normal one.

"M-morning," I stutter, looking for something to say that isn't *I'm thinking about your bedroom voice and wondering about your scars.* "Nice board."

There, see? Not so difficult.

His board looks like it used to be white but has yellowed with age and old wax. The only contrast to the color is a single navy-blue stripe down the center.

He shifts a little to glance at where his board is propped beside him before taking in the one I've got gripped under my arm. "You too. I hope you don't mind, but I invited my buddy Breck to come this morning. He offered to pick us up downstairs."

He mentioned his friend yesterday, but I didn't realize he was joining us. I really don't mind, though. I like having people out there with me, and it's been a while since anyone's been willing to get up this early.

"Awesome." I look between our two boards again. "I hope he drives a ute." The board rack on my car only carries two boards; we'll need the extra space with three. A hint of confusion crosses his face followed by a light of recognition.

"Oh yeah," he responds with a laugh, "he does. I forgot you Aussies have bastardized the word *truck*. There should be plenty of space in the bed."

I laugh and it feels like the most natural thing in the world—to laugh with Wes. "We should probably get going then so he doesn't think we overslept."

Wes grabs a grocery bag that contains his wetsuit and a towel off the floor, and I eye it with curiosity.

He shrugs. "My backpack ripped, remember? Until I can replace it, I don't really have anything else to carry my stuff in."

Then he reaches across and grabs my board from me so I can lock up, but he doesn't hand it back as we walk to the elevator. No, like a gentleman, he just continues to carry it, and I can't help but smile at the way that makes me feel. It's been a long time since I let anyone help me. With anything.

A Toyota Hilux idles at the curb with a very attractive man leaning against it. It's obvious this is Breck with the way he pushes off the ute and drags Wes into a rib-cracking hug. I nearly laugh because it's just so blatantly affectionate, which isn't something you often see with men these days.

"Hey, mate, glad you actually woke up for this," Breck says, giving him one more slap on the back.

"I wouldn't have missed it. It's been too long since we've paddled out together," Wes replies.

When Breck pulls back, his eyes land on me and his smile only grows. Damn, between these two, I will not be hurting for eye candy. He has dimples like Wes, but his seem more prominent without any facial hair to hide them. How does he look so genuinely happy to see me? It takes me aback a little, but before I can consider why, he's pulling me into a similar bone-crushing hug.

"It's so nice to meet you, Joss."

"Nice to meet you too." I try to school my features and wipe the surprise off my face at being hugged by this near stranger. I must not do it fast enough though because Wes catches my eye and looks ready to burst out laughing. I roll my eyes at him and relax into the embrace.

"Shall we get going then?" Wes says, and I appreciate his subtle way of getting Breck to release me. He lays our boards out onto the cargo bed, then gestures for me to hop into the back seat. The drive is mostly silent with all of us still waking up, and I give myself a pat on the back for getting out of bed. The early hour means less traffic and no trouble parking.

The beach is quiet—only a few other people dot the lineup. The water isn't particularly warm this time of year, so we all move quickly to shuck our clothes in exchange for wetsuits.

Unlike Breck, who keeps his eyes pointed away, I catch the briefest glance from Wes as I shimmy out of my jeans and hoodie. I'm not going to lie though, the struggle is real to keep my eyes in my head when Wes pulls his hoodie off, revealing tan, muscled skin underneath. There's another scar at his left shoulder that runs about five inches across to his pec, and I once again tamp down the urge to ask for his scar stories. Not that I could speak even if I tried with how tongue-tied the sight of his bare chest makes me. As he wraps himself in a towel, I force myself to turn and face the surf, knowing he'll be sliding his board shorts off under that towel any second.

I appreciate that, as a woman, my bikini easily fits underneath my wetsuit without bunching. So I don't comment on the little surfer's shuffle they're both doing, no matter how much I want to tease them. *Focus on the surf, Joss—not on what you'd see if Wes dropped his towel right now.*

When I hear the sound of two zippers being pulled up, I know it's safe to grab my board off the sand behind me. Being only human, I take note of how well their wetsuits mold to their toned bodies, then shake my head clear of any further thoughts.

We head for the water, soft smiles on our faces, as the sun starts to rise over the horizon. The grit of the sand between my toes is welcome and familiar and I feel more at home than I have in a long time. The sky fills with reds and oranges, making my heart swell in my chest. I'm a sunrise girl, no contest, especially when I'm sitting on my board to catch it.

The paddle out is brisk and invigorating. If I wasn't fully awake already, I am now, and there's a peacefulness that comes with the waves lapping around my ankles. I haven't been prioritizing this enough, and I didn't realize just how much I missed it. As the three of us go wave for wave, I can finally admit to myself why. It stopped being as majestic when it was just me out here—alone.

Jaz might have a point about me not letting anyone into my life beyond surface-level. Even my friends from work don't know me all that well. I don't keep in touch with anyone from my childhood. As far as family goes, well, aren't they the reason I've held myself back all these years? For fear of trusting someone and then having that trust broken. My mind reels as I continue to bob in the water.

Watching the comfortable friendship unfurl between Wes and Breck, I feel slightly envious of how easy it is for them. Neither of them seems to have any issue letting me in, to be a part of their jokes, their conversation. They immediately make friends with the other surfers out here, and I wonder if I could be that easygoing with people if I wasn't so scared all the time.

Oddly enough, it seems easier with Wes than it's ever been with anyone else. I'm even starting to think Breck could be a good friend. As I sit and circle my feet in the cold water, looking toward the shore, observing my city, I decide it might finally be time to set that fear aside and open myself up a little.

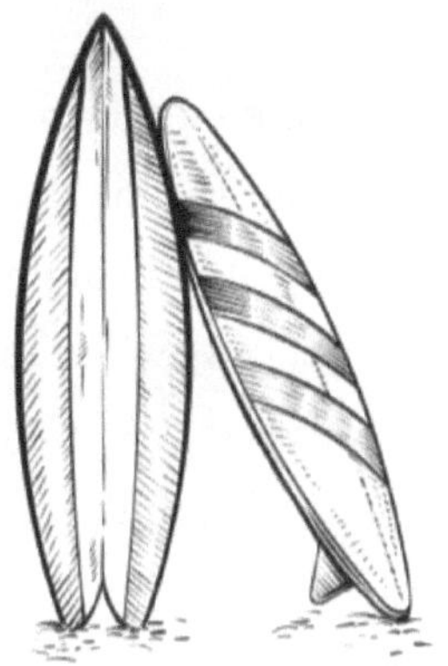

CHAPTER ELEVEN

Wes

You've been gone a whole month… Do you even look the same?

I require photographic evidence.

Okay, fine, I'll accept FaceTime. I need proof of life.

Did we or did we not talk last week? I'll send you an email when I get back to the office… but it may not be the kind of photographic evidence you want. Just try not to freak out, ok?

I laugh as I slip my phone back into my pocket. Rory is going to absolutely lose her shit when she sees the video from this morning's flight—seeing as I wasn't the one flying but the one jumping. Today was my first tandem skydive with Orion, Breck's top jump instructor, and it was exhilarating. I may not be a fighter pilot anymore, but I'm still an adrenaline junkie, and it was such a rush to take that plunge. The initial burst of nerves followed by the feeling of absolute freedom as we flew through the sky was indescribable.

I was anxious about it initially, worried it might cause flashbacks to the crash, but I was surprised to find it almost cathartic. To fall from that plane and land safely, it's like it rewrote whole pathways in my brain, mending some of the unresolved pain from that day. It also helped that Orion was the one landing us, so I was able to keep my legs up and my knee protected.

Today's jump was a celebration of sorts. Now that I've completed the requisite number of flights as a co-pilot, I can finally fly solo next week. I haven't felt this at ease in my career in a long time. Flying for the Navy was thrilling, but there was always a ton of pressure: another qualification to get, another flight to lead, someone to mentor... It was rare that I got to fly for the fun of flying, and clearly I was missing out. The energy emanating off people who want to jump out of airplanes for a thrill is off the charts, contagious even.

I'm still vibrating with adrenaline when I pull up to the office. Jumping out of my company truck, I break into a jog, ready to upload the footage from the camera Orion attached to my helmet.

I feed the SD card into my laptop and attach the files to an email, trying not to imagine what Rory's face will look like when she sees them. We've been struggling to connect since I've been here. The nineteen-hour time difference is really cramping our usual style of constant texting and GIF sending.

We've had to revert back to the way we communicated when I was deployed—using email more than anything—so we don't wake each other up. We have fit in the occasional video call though, and seeing my little sister's face feels both like a blessing and a curse. Having my favorite person behind a screen does the job of reminding me how far away she is.

There's no going back now as I hit send on the email. Maybe I should have waited until this evening when she'd definitely be asleep and less likely to ream me out. *Oh well, it was worth it.*

I send a second email to myself so I'll have the files on my phone. Quickly pulling up the most ridiculous of the pictures, one where my face looks distorted because of the wind and ground rush, I text it to Joss.

Since that first morning, I haven't missed a single dawn patrol, and unless she's away for work, Joss is right there beside me. Breck joins in when he can, but I go by myself if I have to. The routine of that early surf session before heading to work has made the transition to my new life here feel easy, effortless.

Joss has been working for the last few days, and I can't deny how much I've missed the beautiful smile that lights her face when she's paddling back out after getting a wave or sitting next to me waiting for her next one. Head tipped back, those first glimmers of sunlight dancing off the water droplets on her face as she breathes in the cold morning air.

I'm brought back to reality by the vibration of my phone in my pocket. It's become something of a habit for us to exchange texts about our adventures, or just send each other stupid jokes or memes. Anything to try to make the other person laugh. I feel a rush of anticipation when I see the banner and my nickname for her on the screen.

I usually keep my flirting to a minimum with her—boundaries and what have you—but I'll stoop to sprinkling in a little extra charm to convince her to go skydiving. She may not be addicted to adrenaline the same way that I am, but I've learned over the last month that she loves to try new things.

Grey

> Don't hold your breath :-P

Me

> You wound me.

"What has you smiling?" Breck's voice meets my ears as he sticks his head around the cubicle wall.

"Joss." I wave my phone at him.

The knowing smile on his face tells me exactly what he thinks about mine and Joss's friendship, but I don't rise to the bait. We go back and forth about this every couple days as it is.

"How was the jump? Amazing, right?" I can hear the earnestness in his voice, but it's laced with apprehension.

Breck has been great about respecting my boundaries around discussing the crash, and I know he doesn't want the job to set me back for any reason. He had reservations about how comfortable I would be with flying when I got here, so I think he's relieved to see that I've taken to it easily. Had it gone a different way, he would have found something else for me to do—on the ground.

"Absolutely. I'm trying to convince Joss to go with me next time." As soon as I say it, I wince and brace myself for his comments. Breck smirks, eyebrows raised. It's a look that says he's in on some joke that I'm missing the punchline to. "It's not like that. Come on, Breck, you've seen us together. We're just friends."

"I know, I know. You just spend a lot of time together for two people who are *just friends*." He raises his hands, but that damn smirk stays firmly in place.

"We're also neighbors, which makes spending time together that much easier."

"True, I guess. She'll be home tonight, yeah? Back at it tomorrow?" Breck's voice ticks up, enthusiasm over the promise of surfing clear on his face.

"I'm down, but whether she comes with will depend on how tired she is. This was a long trip for her." I hope that she'll want to go. That picture of her pops back up inside my mind and—no. I mentally shake myself, focusing my attention on Breck. "You going to be able to take off early today?"

He looks back toward his office and the papers strewn over his desk. The excitement from a moment ago is immediately replaced with something strained. He's tired. I know he loves this business, that it allows him to pursue his passion, but it can be draining.

"Soon. I'm going home soon, regardless of whether I'm done with all that." He rubs the back of his neck and sighs before walking away.

I feel a twinge of guilt as I slowly pack up my stuff and prepare to head home, knowing he'll be here for a few more hours. In the last month, I think I've seen him leave before five o'clock less times than I can count on one hand. But with all my paperwork done and no flights until next week, there isn't much else I can do around here today.

Joss is on her final flight and will be back early this evening, so we're planning to grab dinner with Jaz. Aside from my coffee runs,

I haven't spent much time with her, and Joss seems excited for me to get to know her best friend. At this point, any friend of Joss's is a friend of mine. Though, Jaz seems to be the only friend Joss ever mentions, and I often wonder why that is. The girl is magnetic.

I walk by Breck's office on my way out and see him hunched over his desk. "See you later, buddy."

"Enjoy your night with your 'friend,'" he says, using finger quotes on *friend*, which earns him an eye roll to go with my wave.

Aside from his jabs, I'm finding that working with my best friend is the most rewarding part of the job. The dynamic in the office between Breck, Talia, and Drew—their business partner—is still something I can't quite get a read on though. The carefree Talia I remember from college is different to the one crunching numbers as the head of the finance department. She seems detached somehow, aloof. More concerning though is Drew. Since he's part of their inner circle, I'd assumed he and I would hit it off. Instead, he feels like a walking red flag. He's overly nice to my face, but I get the vibe he doesn't appreciate Breck bringing in one of his "mates" for a position that would normally be up to him to fill.

Where Breck is the brawn of this operation, creating and organizing each excursion, I guess you could say Drew is the brains. He and Talia run the behind-the-scenes stuff, but they're all equal partners. And from everything I've seen, Drew is as type-A as they come, meaning that my being here has thrown him off-balance.

I pass by Drew's office on my way out and hear his and Talia's voices through his closed door. This is what I mean—why isn't Breck in on whatever meeting they're having? Seeing as everyone else has left for the weekend, I consider stopping and, I don't know...

poking my head in? But that seems ridiculous no matter how much I dislike the guy, so I hike my bag up my shoulder and carry on.

While I wait for Joss to make it home, I grab a beer from the fridge and head out to the balcony. I walk past my bookshelves, giving them an apologetic look as I pick up my Kindle from the ottoman. They look less barren now than when I first moved in, and I've always loved the feel of a physical book in my hands, but the Kindle is just so damn convenient. I settle into the chair and prop my feet on the railing, taking a minute to appreciate the city skyline.

I'm just about to pick up where I left off with my latest thriller when my phone chimes with an incoming call. Nervous energy floods my system when I see that it's a FaceTime from Rory. I always love seeing her, but how mad is she going to be? I drop my head back and take a deep breath before swiping to answer her call.

When her face fills the screen, I'm prepared for the worst. But I'm met by her soft laugh and a small smile playing around her lips. *Huh, that's not what I expected.*

"You look scared, Wessy. Worried your little sister is going to scold you?" She chuckles, and I instantly relax.

"You're not mad?"

"Oh, I'm plenty mad. Unfortunately, you're a grown-ass man and I can't really tell you what to do. Plus, you're in one piece, so..." She shrugs like this answers everything.

"It was incredible, Roars, seriously. I was nervous, but... I don't know. It was good too."

"No panic attack?" Her question is soft, genuine. She'd never make light of the fact that she's seen me in the throes of a flashback.

"No, none. It felt liberating, like some of that baggage fell out of the plane with me and was lost to the wind." I scrub a hand over my face. That probably sounded stupid, but I feel lighter after today's jump.

When I bring my gaze back to hers, there's hope in her eyes, like maybe she's finally realizing this move was what I needed.

"That's really great." She drops her eyes, like she's thinking over what to say next, and then brings them back to mine. "You're doing okay then?"

She and Breck are the two people who fully understand what I'm dealing with. What I left behind. *Why* I left.

"Yeah. Coming here was a good call. It was what I needed. I think... I think this is where I'm meant to be right now."

She nods, but her face is sad. "I miss you."

"I miss you too." I hate knowing I put that look there, that I've put it there too many times. "Maybe you need to come visit. I think you'd love it here. Breck and I can show you around."

Her laugh is light and her eyes say yes, but her words don't match them.

"Maybe. You know I'd love to. Life just feels extra busy right now."

"Yeah. Of course. But, you know, you're allowed to take time off. That's what vacation days are for."

Her eyes flare slightly at the words, almost like I've hit a nerve.

"Have you seen Mom and Dad lately?" I change the subject, and the question earns me an eye roll. I laugh, reminded of a younger Rory, one that had sass for days.

"Oh, they're Mom and Dad. I see them once a week for dinner because *we're family...*" She adds air quotes and lowers her voice to mimic our dad. "Never mind the fact that they've been divorced for twelve years. I'm still required to sit in awkward silence with them both until they ask me once again about my love life, when I'll be bringing Jamie around, how Jamie is doing." She shrugs dramatically. "Or they ask about work, but only to insinuate that I could do so much more if I just put my journalism degree to work. My love life or work, those are our two topics of conversation. They're exhausting."

"I'm sorry, Rory." There's not much else I can say. I haven't lived under their thumb for sixteen years, and I was glad to escape it when I did. Rory has always been there, close enough for them to try to control or manipulate. I've often wondered why she didn't leave like I did. "At the risk of sounding like Mom and Dad, how is Jamie?"

Jamie is Rory's best friend. They've been inseparable for years. Much like our parents, I keep waiting for the day she tells me they're together, but she swears it's only friendship between them, that she's never wanted him like that. I think back to Breck commenting on my friendship with Joss. *Oh the irony.*

"He's great. He's on his way over here to watch a movie actually, so I should probably go. I just wanted to call and yell at you for jumping out of a plane."

"You didn't yell at me."

"Yeah, your scared puppy face when you answered took the edge off. Plus, I'd rather just tell you that I think you're brave and that I love you. I'm here if you need me, okay?"

"Thanks, Roars. Have a good night. Tell Jamie hello from me."

She waves a hand at the screen. "Night, Wessy."

I want to roll my eyes at her nickname for me, but it's what she's called me since she was little, and I'd let her call me just about anything. I wish I could've brought her here with me; she could use an adventure. As far as I know, Tahoe is what she wants. Her whole life is there, but if she ever wanted something different, I would move heaven and earth to help her, just like she's done for me.

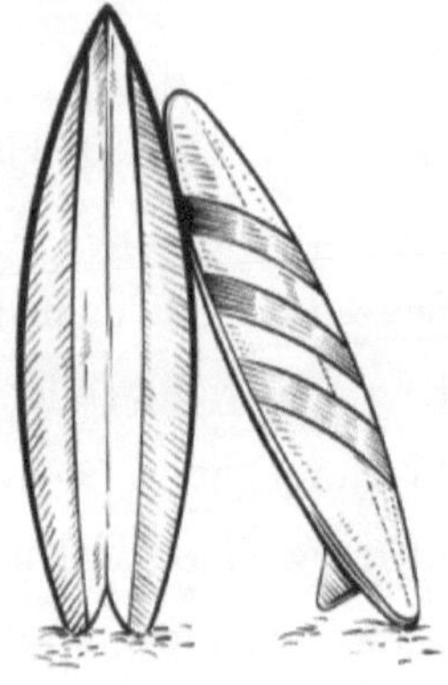

CHAPTER TWELVE

Joss

I'm shaken awake by some aggressive turbulence. Feeling like I only just fell asleep, my heart is racing a million miles a minute. I'm in the crew space where we take turns getting some shuteye on these transcontinental flights. The curtain hangs closed, but it sways with the movement of the plane. There was nothing but clear skies ahead when I climbed in here, so the fact it's bumpy as hell is startling.

My watch tells me I've been asleep for about an hour. Time flies when you're having fun, right?

Rubbing the sleep from my eyes, I don't get up just yet, taking deep breaths to calm my body out of fight or flight mode. It's feeling gentler than it did a minute ago. Maybe I could fall back to sleep?

Or not.

A swish of fabric is the only warning before Sydney appears at my feet. And yes, she's from Sydney. Her parents must've thought they were real funny. "Hey, we've got about two hours until we land. We need all hands on deck to get the food served."

I suck in a deep inhale, wishing she'd take her lovely perky smile and go away. Somehow she still looks as fresh as she did when we took off from London this morning. I, however, feel like a wadded-up tissue. I groan again and sit up, giving her a thumbs-up as she closes the drape and leaves me in peace.

I've felt off this whole trip. What if I'm getting sick?

Nope, nope, nope. Don't even let those thoughts into your head, Joss.

I cannot get sick. I do not have time to get sick. Ever. It's something I simply don't do. I know the other flight attendants are waiting on me, but I need five more minutes to feel human. That way I can put my best foot forward when I step out there to take care of the 200-plus people under our care.

I close my eyes and think about surfing, grounding myself in all five of my senses as I imagine my happy place. The sound of the waves hitting the shore. The feel of the water against my legs as I circle them under my board. The taste of the saltwater on my lips as it drips from my wet hair. The air, salty and clean. In my mind's eye, it's Wes I see sitting next to me, a soft grin on his face, dimples peeking through the stubble on his cheeks.

My heart rate slows, my thoughts resting on the last several weeks. On the mornings Wes and I (and sometimes Breck) have surfed. We've fallen into a steady rhythm—well, as steady as it can be with my constantly being out of the country. Since deciding to be more open to letting people in, I'm amazed at how much more fulfilling my mornings are. It's kind of like when you don't know you need glasses. When you finally bite the bullet and can see the world in its entirety, you realize how much you were missing.

I was content with my life a month ago. I loved my job and Jaz, but there was something missing. A hole I've never been able to fill that feels a little less empty these days. Somehow, in just a few short weeks, the companionship I'm slipping into with Wes feels as easy as breathing. He's my glasses, showing me how much more there is in the world. Getting back to that feeling has been what's kept me going on this trip.

Jaz, Wes, and I have plans for dinner tonight so that they can get to know each other beyond Harbour Grounds. Though, I'm wondering if we should have opted to do it tomorrow—I'm already knackered. Taking one more deep breath, I climb out to go help my coworkers.

The next couple of hours are a total crush, as is often the case with these long flights—everything happening at the beginning and the end, with a lot of downtime in the middle. It's a blur of food service, drink service, clean up, and deplaning. But now that the passengers are gone and we've moved on to general turnover, I can feel the adrenaline wearing off and new sensations replacing it.

Why does the AC feel like it's blasting? But also, why am I sweating? I want to crawl out of my skin. The synthetic fibers of my uniform scraping against it feel almost painful, there's a pounding rhythm in my brain, and the lights are too bright.

"You okay, Joss?" Sydney asks from the back of the plane.

"Yeah, just tired I think," I mumble, trying to steady myself.

She looks unconvinced as she watches me but gives a little shrug, moving on to finish her checklist. I'm just tired.

I'll keep telling myself that until I believe it.

I'm so focused on getting home that I can't remember my walk from the plane to the curb, and the drive is the same. One minute I'm sliding into the yellow cab, cracked leather seats catching on my nylons, and the next I'm outside my building. I must have fallen asleep. Grabbing my bags, I head for the door as the cab drives away, off into the bustle of the city.

Frank looks up, his greeting dying on his lips as he takes me in. "Ms. Morgan, are you alright?"

He's always been more like a protective uncle than a security guard, and I love him for it. I smile, but it must come off as more of a grimace with the way his face contorts in worry. He jumps up from his chair and rushes over to take my bags from me.

"I'm fine, Frank. Just a little under the weather."

I can't imagine what I must look like if Frank is this concerned. I don't think I've seen him be anything but cool, calm, and collected.

"Ms. Morgan, I'm going to escort you to your apartment, make sure you get in okay," he says as he ushers me toward the elevator. I can't even find the energy to argue with him about calling me *Ms. Morgan* instead of Joss.

The metal wall is cool on my skin. When did I lean against it? I close my eyes, taking stock of all the sensations in my body right now. Everything hurts. I'm so cold, like I took a dive in a plunge pool then decided to flounce about without drying off.

The ding of the elevator brings me back to my senses and to Frank, who's staring down at me, eyebrows knitted together. He rolls my bag down the hall while I attempt to remove my keys from my purse, but my hands aren't working properly. They end up on the floor, the jangling sound echoing inside my skull, and all I can do is stare at them.

"Dammit," I mutter, or at least I think I do.

My ears never fully equalized from our descent, and it's hard to judge the volume of my voice right now. I lean against the wall, not having the energy to pick my keys up. Frank moves toward them, but from of the corner of my eye, I see a hand shoot out and get there first. Appearing in front of me like I conjured him is the most handsome man I've ever seen.

Wes.

His long legs, in a pair of jeans that fit just right, are bent to kneel before me. His grey Henley, with the top buttons undone, stretches across broad shoulders and hugs his chest and arms. That face, the scruffy jawline, the deep blue eyes. There's no smile or dimpled cheek like I'm used to. Instead, his brow is furrowed, worry lines bracketing his mouth. I think he's talking to me, but I can't hear it as I slide down the wall and everything goes black.

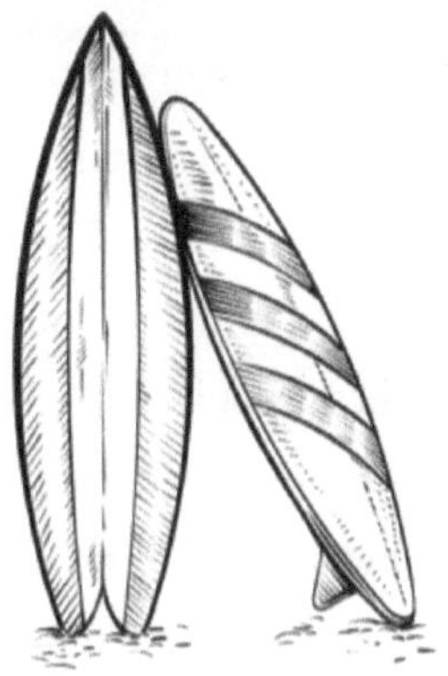

CHAPTER THIRTEEN

WES

I was stepping out of my shower when I heard the sounds in the hallway and figured Joss must be home. The only other apartment on this floor is still vacant, so I knew if someone was there, it had to be her. I'd barely run a towel over my hair and thrown on a shirt when I heard a thump and rushed to open the door. That was when I knew something was wrong. Frank was standing there with Joss's bags while she rested her body against the wall for support. My legs moved on instinct, and by the time my brain caught up, I was kneeling in front of her.

Now, she's looking through me with glassy, red-rimmed eyes, and her rosy cheeks are a stark contrast against her too-pale skin.

"Joss? What's wrong?" My voice is laced with concern as I turn to look up at Frank.

"She told me she was under the weather, but…" He trails off, my same worry mirrored in his eyes.

I look back to where her eyes still rove over me, unseeing. "Joss, let me help you get inside." I move to stand just as she sinks toward the floor, her delicate eyelids fluttering closed. "Shit!"

I catch her in my arms, stopping her slide before she can hit her head. Panic rises in my chest. Her body is an inferno, and yet I can feel her shivering. Hell, she must be down with a fever. The thought of her coworkers letting her push through it on that flight makes me more furious than I probably have any right to be. I slide my other arm under her knees, dropping her keys. Her body curls against me as I lift her in my arms, and it's both a dream and a nightmare.

My hands tremble against her. What do I do? Do I take her to the hospital? How serious is this?

Her eyes flutter open for the briefest of moments. I finally glance away from her face and realize Frank must have let us inside, because I'm standing in her apartment. My eyes land on him and he's looking at me expectantly.

"Sorry, Frank, what was that?"

"I have to get back to the desk." He eyes me warily, like he's not sure he should leave Joss alone in my arms, but it's gone with a blink. Something in my face must've eased his concerns. "If she needs anything, just call down. I have a pharmacy's worth of meds in my office—never know what you might need."

"Thanks. I'll make sure she's okay."

I hear the door click shut as I'm already moving, striding straight to Joss's bedroom. I've never been in here before, and under any other circumstance, my curiosity would get the better of me. Right now, though, all I see is her. I lay her gently on the bed, her eyes finally opening long enough to lock onto mine. Falling to my knees next to the bed, I ignore the protest of my right one. My eyes never leave her face as I trail my knuckles across her warm cheek. Too warm—she's burning up.

"Hey there, you scared me." My voice is rough, almost breaking on the words. I want to be quiet and gentle, but I'm struggling to push the fear of what could have happened down. What if she hadn't made it home when she did? What if Frank or I weren't here?

She gives me a weak smile, leaning into my touch. Her delicate hand covers mine where it rests on her cheek, and I can feel how clammy she is.

"I'm okay, Wes, just tired." Her voice is barely a whisper as she tries to downplay how sick she is, but it's not going to work on me.

"Grey, you're more than just tired. How long have you been feeling like this?"

My eyes move over every inch of her, looking for any sign that she might pass out again. I'd bet my Jeep that's sitting in storage back home that she's dehydrated too. She starts to sit up but seems to think better of it.

"A couple days, I think. I've felt off this whole trip, but it didn't really hit until today's flight. I was too busy to really take note of how bad I felt." She squints and shields her eyes, like the light in her room is too bright. I extricate my hand so I can go pull the shades closed, wanting to dampen the late afternoon light streaming in.

"I'm going to get you some water. Where do you keep your medicine?"

When she doesn't answer right away, I whip around to make sure she's still lucid. The fist in my chest relaxes slightly when our eyes lock.

"I don't get sick. I don't have anything here." The helplessness in her voice cracks my heart.

"Okay, sweetheart. I have some. If I leave for a few minutes, will you be alright?"

She rolls her eyes at me.

"Yes, I'll be fine." She pushes herself up to sit and when I move to help her, she holds out a hand. "No, really, I'm okay. I just need to get out of my uniform."

My worry about her passing out again wars with the realization that she needs privacy. It's not like I can help her change—that's definitely not my job—but I don't want to leave her alone either.

"Let me help you. I mean, not to change, but I can help you move around," I say, injecting more bravado into my voice than I feel at the moment.

"I'm not an invalid, Wes," she snarks back at me. Snark is good, right? You can't be snarky if you're in bad shape. She must see something on my face or sense how on edge this has me, which makes her take pity on me. "But as I see your masculine, caveman side is coming out, I'll humor you."

Now she's making jokes. The vise around my heart releases a little more. She's okay. She's going to be okay.

"Can you grab a pair of joggers and a T-shirt from that second drawer for me?" She inclines her head toward the dresser on the opposite wall from her.

"You're going to let me rifle through your drawers?" I raise an eyebrow at her as I follow her instructions. Pulling the drawer in question open, I see neatly stacked clothes—all leisurewear or pajamas in various shades.

"Just that one," she says with a laugh, but it's weak and turns into a cough that racks her body. I grab the first things I can get my hands on and rush back to the bed. Laying them next to her, I put my hand on her forehead.

"Okay, let me help you to the bathroom, and then I'll run next door to grab what you need, yeah?" I say as I reach my hands out. She takes both in hers, and I barely notice the jolt of energy when we touch because I'm solely focused on how warm she is. She drops one hand to grab her clothes, and I take the opportunity to wrap my arm around her waist and pull her closer. I haven't been this close to her since that first day on the plane, pressed to her body, feeling her breath tangle with mine.

We've made a distinct effort to draw some boundaries since then. It's obvious that in order for us to maintain what has so far been an easy friendship, we need to keep our distance. Now as she melts into my side, the things I'm feeling are as far from friendly as it gets.

This is not the time for that.

The tile is cold on my feet when we reach the bathroom, and I can only imagine how much colder it must be for Joss.

"Do you have slippers or something?"

She looks up at me and peels away from my side. The loss of her touch is like a punch to the gut. She leans back against the counter, her small hands resting on the lip behind her.

"In the closet. You can..."

I'm already moving to grab them before the sentence is out of her mouth. I'm back in a flash, a pair of teal fuzzy slippers in my hands. They make me want to laugh, they're so ridiculous. She smiles when she sees them.

"Thanks," she says, then lets her eyes flutter closed as I make quick work of helping her into them. When I fit the first slipper around her foot, she chuckles, and I draw my gaze up from where I'm positioned, wanting to absorb that sound. "You're like prince charming, except my slippers are made of fur instead of glass."

She's right, the only glassy thing here is her eyes. They're glazed with exhaustion, even under her attempts at levity.

"You okay? You're not going to pass out on me again, are you?"

My stomach clenches at the memory of her sliding down the wall. I stand and swipe the back of my hand across her forehead, then graze it down her cheek where she catches it with her own.

"I'm okay. I promise."

"Alright, I'll only be gone for a minute. Don't push it. Sit down if you're feeling dizzy." I know I'm being overbearing, but as she said, my inner caveman is coming out and I just want to keep her safe. She nods and then shoos me out of the bathroom. I back out with my hands raised. "Okay, okay, I'm going."

I waste no time rushing from her apartment back to mine. I expect to find the door wide open, but it's shut tight. Frank must have closed it on his way back downstairs. I slide through the door, grabbing a sweatshirt from a bar stool and slipping my Vans on while heading toward my bathroom.

I'm really grateful for the Wes of last week who decided to stock up on all the necessities, like cold medicine and pain relievers. It took me a while to figure out the Australian equivalents to the ones I buy in the States, but I think what I have will do.

I shove a few things in a grocery bag then swing through the kitchen, grabbing a couple bottles of cold water from the fridge, along with a box of crackers and some Tim Tams. Joss and I have bonded over our love of the cookies, and it's a show of my friendship that I'll share mine with her.

Next door again, everything but the medicine gets dropped unceremoniously on Joss's counter. I breathe a little easier at the sound of running water coming from behind the closed bathroom door, and I take the opportunity to drop my haul on her bedside table.

"Proof of life, please. You okay in there?" I call out, knuckles rapping gently on the door.

There's an exasperated sigh followed by a small laugh. I can almost hear her rolling her eyes at me. "I'm fine, Wes. I'll be right out."

I press my forehead against the door in relief, my hands braced on the wall on either side. In the darker recesses of my brain, I was terrified she'd be passed out on the floor by the time I got back. I don't let myself think about why I'm so panicked—those thoughts won't do me any good here.

She's okay. She's okay. She's okay. If I keep repeating it over and over, maybe I'll eventually believe it.

The door opens and I'm face-to-face with her. God, even when she's sick she still takes my breath away.

She stumbles back a step, obviously surprised to discover me hovering in the doorframe, and I instantly reach forward to grasp her arms. I want to crush her to me, replace this worry with the feel of her beating heart against my chest, but I need to keep this about her. Her eyes haven't left mine, and they seem more alert than they did before.

"Let's get you in bed, Grey."

I don't let her go, tucking her into my side and wrapping an arm around her waist. I don't miss the way she snuggles into me, allowing me to take care of her. The thought hits me, not for the first time, that I know very little about her family. She doesn't talk about them, and besides Jaz, I don't think she has anyone that takes care of her.

I pull the covers back on her bed so she can sit. There are so many pillows in different shapes and sizes that I'm not sure what she does with them all while she sleeps. She must catch the look that I'm casting their way because she ducks her head.

"I know it's a lot. I love the way they look when the bed is made, but they're kind of a pain in the ass the rest of the time."

"Tell me which ones you need and I'll move the rest."

She settles two normal-looking pillows behind her and pushes the rest over the edge of her mattress. Ah, so that's what she does with them. She slides her legs under the covers and snuggles down. I move to the other side and neatly stack the pillows against the wall.

Her bed did look rather inviting with all of them propped there, like a cloud or one of those foam pits. *You really need to stop thinking about her bed.*

She's watching me intently, and I have to glance away. Thank god she can't read my mind.

"There's cold medicine and pain meds next to the water, you need to take both."

"Okay, bossy."

It's my turn to roll my eyes at her, but my attitude doesn't last long. She's struggling to open the medicine, moving on to the water bottle and having no better luck.

"Here, I've got it." I'm back to kneeling by her side. Popping the caps off both bottles and unscrewing the water with ease. I press it into her hand. "Drink." She raises an eyebrow at my tone. "Please."

Now she smiles; it's weak, but it's there. She takes the water bottle and drinks half of it down. Flying is dehydrating enough—I shiver at the thought of how much worse being sick makes it.

"Thanks," she says, playing with the cap of the bottle, eyes on her lap. The breath she takes is ragged, like she's barely holding it together. "Seriously, thank you. I'm not sure what would have happened if you weren't here."

She finally looks up, and there are tears in her eyes. My heart squeezes. This soft, vulnerable side of her is something she hasn't shared with me. If I were a betting man, I'd put money on the fact she isn't quick to let her guard down. It's not like I can blame her, I'm not exactly the most forthright person about all my shit either.

I lift a hand to her cheek, unable to stop myself from touching her, and swipe away a tear as it falls. "Hey. It's alright. I'm here. I'll be right here for as long as you need. Okay?"

She sniffles and nods, going back to avoiding my eyes. Reaching for the tissue box, she proceeds to use it to hide from me while she blows her nose and dabs at her eyes. Wanting to give her space, I focus instead on reading the label on the bottle in my hand.

"Thank you, Wes."

Her eyes finally meet mine as she takes the offered pills and swallows them back with another swig of water. Burrowing deeper into the blankets, her eyes turn heavy. I tuck her in, swiping a tendril of hair away from her face. She grabs my hand before I can pull it away. I know she'll be asleep in no time, but there's something in her grey eyes that makes my breath hitch.

"Are you leaving?" Her question is shy, confirming my earlier assumptions that she wants me to stay but doesn't know how to ask. What she doesn't know is that I couldn't leave her here like this even if I wanted to, and I do not want to.

"No, sweetheart, I was just going to grab something from the kitchen. Can I sit in here with you?" I want her to say yes. No, I *need* her to say yes.

Her little nod is everything. I give her hand a squeeze before ducking into the kitchen.

Her eyes are closed and her breathing even when I tiptoe back into her room a minute later, headed for the chair in the corner. Where my room has a sleek black leather chair, which I've discovered is more comfortable than it looks, hers has an overstuffed armchair and ottoman in teal green. Rustling sheets and the sound of my name stops me before I can settle in.

She's lying on her side and facing me, arms wrapped around one of her pillows. Her eyes are halfway open, fluttering and heavy-looking. She extends her top arm and pats the bed next to her.

"You don't have to sit all the way over there."

Her eyes drift closed but her arm stays extended. I know what the smart thing to do is—both because she's sick and because of our boundaries—but I'm not feeling particularly smart at the moment.

I grab two pillows from the stack so I can sit upright next to her. The bed is soft as I stretch my legs out in front of me.

As her breathing eases again, I take stock of the pain in my knee. It's a reminder of all I've lost in the last year, and the heightened emotions only bring it to the surface. She's fine. This isn't the same. She won't be another person I lose. The thought has me reaching for that extended hand, trying to ground myself. She doesn't open her eyes, but her fingers curl around mine, and I realize this is the most connected to another person I've been in a long time.

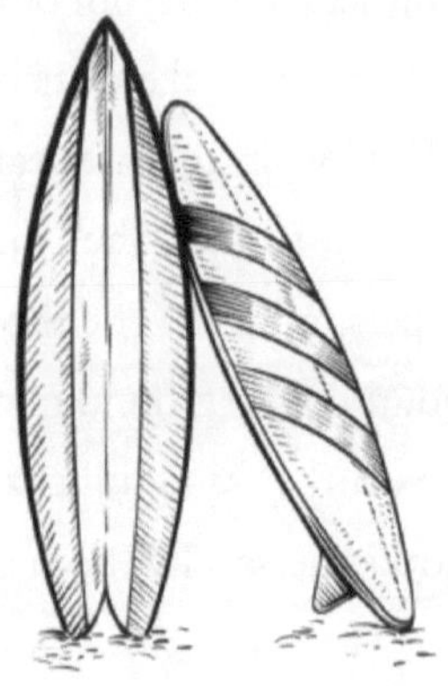

CHAPTER FOURTEEN

Joss

I'm dazed when I wake up. Everything feels heavy and warm around the edges. It's dark aside from the light filtering in from the kitchen. I slowly get my bearings and one thing comes through in vivid clarity. There's a man in my bed, and we are holding hands. His breathing is quiet and steady, his palm dwarfing mine.

He stayed. Wes stayed. He didn't have to, but he did. I feel a constriction in my chest at the thought. My eyes adjust to the low light so I can take in more of his features. Is it creepy to watch him sleep? His Kindle lies across his chest and his arm is thrown over his face, the upper half hidden in the crook of his elbow.

His lips part slightly as he breathes. What would they feel like if I ran my thumb across them? His jaw is relaxed and the beard that was stubble when we met is more pronounced now. I've never been particularly attracted to men with facial hair, but it's different with Wes. The ruggedness only adds to his appeal.

His chest rises and falls as I continue my perusal of his body. *Dangerous, Joss.* He's not under the blankets, so I can take everything in. His shirt has ridden up a couple inches, hinting at the muscles underneath. Seeing a man's stomach is nothing new. I see shirtless men all the time in the surf. It's not even the first time I'm seeing Wes's abs. Despite rushing to get in and out of our wetsuits, it's inevitable. And it is a sight to behold. But here and now, the proximity of it... My mind is reeling with things it probably shouldn't be.

Time to move on, Joss, or you'll stare at that little strip of skin all night.

He should have gone home to change out of his jeans, but I know why he didn't. He was worried, like *really* worried. I could see it written all over his face, feel it in his every touch. My body likely took this particular illness so hard because I never get sick. I can't believe I passed out in the hallway. No wonder he panicked.

His feet are bare, crossed at the ankles. It's such an inconsequential thing, but there's something so *domestic* about it.

The softest squeeze on my hand brings my eyes to where they're joined. Another squeeze. He's awake. The arm that was over his face is now behind his head, and it's his turn to take me in. Not that there's much of me to see, hidden under the blankets like I am. He's searching my face, eyes bouncing between my own. What is he looking for? What does he see? The scrutiny has me breaking eye contact. It's too much, too intense.

He moves his Kindle to the bedside table, and then, without pulling his hand away, rolls to his side to face me. His touch is featherlight as he skims his fingers across my forehead and down my cheek.

"How are you feeling?" he asks in a raspy voice. Concern is etched into the lines of his face, replacing the peace from moments before.

"Better. A little groggy, but better."

We're so close right now, only about a foot separating us, our hands clasped firmly in the middle.

"I think your fever broke. You're not hot anymore."

"Ouch. Way to kick a woman while she's down." The little chuckle I give him is the most I can muster at this point, but I like needling him.

"You know that's not what I meant, Grey." He sighs, pushing a piece of hair behind my ear with gentle fingers. He lingers there, brushing ever so slightly, sending a shiver that has nothing to do with fever down my spine. "You could be throwing up and I'd hold your hair and tell you you're beautiful. There's not a version of you that wouldn't be hot to me."

Well, damn. I blush all the way to my toes. Sleep must've addled his brain to make him say these things. We haven't said anything remotely flirtatious to each other since the day we agreed to be just friends.

I drop my eyes and tuck my chin toward my chest, feeling embarrassed... or maybe I'm pleased. Hearing those words felt way too good. I focus on our entwined fingers and give them a little squeeze before trying to release my hand, but he holds firm.

"You stayed?" I ask the question even though I know the answer. But I can't understand why he did. Stay. No one ever does.

"Of course I stayed. You asked me to, and I wanted to be here to take care of you." His eyes are earnest, boring into mine. The last part of his statement makes me want to cry. He wants to take care of me? I've been taking care of myself for so long I forgot how good it feels to have someone to lean on.

The tears well in my eyes, and I can't stop the first one that falls. Too tired and sick to control my emotions the way I've taught myself to over the years. Instead of pulling back, the way I always expect people to when I show any feelings, he reaches for me and pulls me into a crushing hug.

It's the first time he's hugged me, and the warmth of his body, mixed with the heady scent of him, makes me melt. There's no stopping it now as I absolutely lose it. I haven't cried—*really* cried—in years, and definitely not with someone around to witness it. He's making quiet shushing sounds as he rubs my back, not saying anything, not feeling the need to fill the silence or try to fix me.

"You're okay, I'm here." Wes's voice is lined with an emotion I can't quite place.

The way he runs his hand gently up and down my back soothes something deep inside of me. My brain knows he's just my friend, that this can't be more than that. My body, though? It hasn't gotten that memo, and it's purring like a kitten at his every touch, wanting more. I push my body's pesky feelings down, letting my brain take over and hide them away in a box like I do with all my other emotions. He's being a good friend; this doesn't mean anything.

You're sick, Joss, just take the comfort where you can get it.

I want to say something, explain away the mess that I am so that he doesn't bolt and never come back, but the heaviness of sleep is pulling at me. The last thing I'm aware of before sinking into the haze of cold medicine and exhaustion is a pair of soft lips against my temple. There are no words, at least not that I can hear, but I feel them there as I'm swept away.

Light streaming through the cracks of the curtains pulls me into consciousness sometime later. My head is pillowed on a strong chest that is softly rising and falling. My arm is slung around Wes's waist, and one of my legs is entwined with his. His arm is wrapped around my back, his hand resting in the dip of my waist. Tangled up in him doesn't even begin to cover the way I'm feeling right now.

I thought waking up last night holding hands was intimate, but waking up in his arms is something entirely different. I don't want to move, but I also know I can't stay here. Not like this, not if we have any hope of maintaining our boundaries. Boundaries that we've been pushing since the moment I got home yesterday.

Each movement I make to extricate myself from his limbs is measured until I finally get free and roll to my side of the bed. Not that Wes has a side. No, this whole bed is mine. I slide my feet into my slippers and stand up too fast, watching as the room spins, forcing me to sit back on the bed. Okay, slower this time. I move toward the bathroom at a snail's pace, bringing my water bottle with me.

I'm a sight to behold when I look in the mirror. What used to be a messy bun looks more like a bird's nest on top of my head. There is a distinct line across my cheek from where it was pressed into the seam of Wes's Henley, and there are smudges of mascara and lord knows what else on my face. Wes's words from last night come back to me. *There's not a version of you that wouldn't be hot to me.*

Sighing, I walk to the tub and turn on the water. I need to wash away the grunge of my flight, the clamminess coating my body, and *all* the feelings. Feelings that poured out as a result of Wes's unexpected kindness, and a host of others I can't seem to keep locked up.

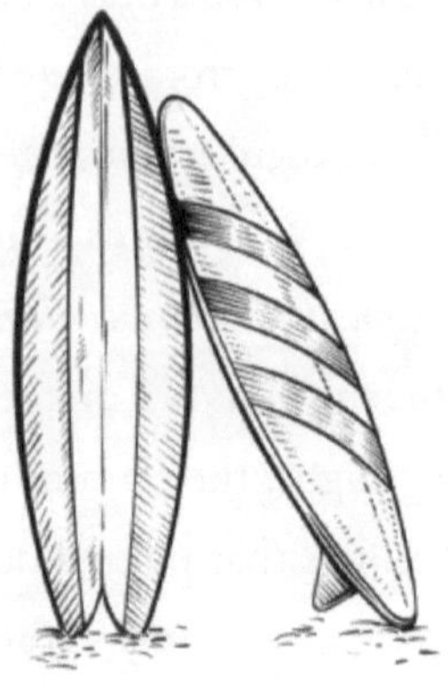

CHAPTER FIFTEEN

WES

The sound of running water wakes me up. My eyes blink away the sleep, and it all comes back. Joss passing out in the hallway. Helping her to bed and taking care of her. Sleeping with her hand in mine. Holding her while she cried. I fell asleep with her in my arms, and it was the best sleep I've had in a very long time. Probably since the crash. I didn't dream, and there were no nightmares.

She's not in my arms now though, and I can hear her humming softly in the bathroom. It's a stark reminder that I also have needs. I wouldn't hesitate to stay in this exact spot all day if I didn't, but I make my way to the half bath in the hallway.

Will Joss feel up to eating? What about coffee? I desperately need both. Finding a pad of paper on the kitchen counter, I leave a note for her.

> Went for coffee
> and breakfast, be
> back in a few, text
> me if you need me.
> W

Grabbing my wallet and phone, I head out the door and down the elevator. There's a text from Breck in response to the one I sent him late last night telling him to count us out for dawn patrol.

Breck

> No worries, mate. You missed an epic sunrise. How is she feeling this morning?

There's a picture of the sun coming up over the horizon that I'll have to show Joss later. I'm glad he went without us; he needs that time as much as I do, and he doesn't get to do it nearly as often.

Me

> Better, I think. Headed out for coffee and breakfast.

I pass Frank, who takes in my appearance with an appraising look. I'm suddenly aware that I'm wearing yesterday's clothes, and that they look significantly more rumpled now.

"How's our girl this morning?" Frank asks.

Besides yesterday, when his focus was on Joss and words were necessary, this is the most he's said to me since I moved in. I smile at the way he calls her "our girl," as if I have some claim over her. Hope rises in my chest at the notion.

"Better. I'm headed for breakfast. Want anything, Frank?" Maybe a pastry is the way to this man's heart, or maybe it was just taking care of *our girl*, because he gives me what looks almost like a smile and asks for black coffee.

The brisk temperature as I walk to Harbour Grounds invigorates my brain. Which is good, because it's lagging this morning. Maybe the coffee on the other side of this glass door will bring me the answer to the question rolling around up there.

How on earth am I supposed to separate last night from the friendship Joss and I are building?

It's only been a month, but I've grown closer to her than almost anyone else in my life. I don't let myself think about the disaster that was my last romantic relationship, and the easiest friendship I've ever had is also something I can't think about right now. Not without spiraling about the crash. Being around Joss though, talking to her... It's as effortless as breathing. There's a familiarity as if we've been friends for years, not weeks.

I pull open the door to Harbour Grounds, and the warm smell of coffee and sugar hits me. I relax a little further. That is, until I hear my name screeched from behind the counter and realize my mistake.

"Wes! Have you heard from Joss? She never texted me after her trip. Did her flight get canceled?" The panic in Jaz's voice is evident as she bolts from around the counter, ignoring the customers waiting to order.

I completely forgot about our dinner plans last night, and Joss must've too. I rake a hand through my messy hair, blow out a breath, and start explaining.

"She's fine. Breathe, Jaz." I keep my voice calm in an attempt to soothe her worry. She stops just short of me. "She's home and she's safe, I promise. She's really sick though—"

"How sick?" Jaz cuts me off. "She never gets sick. You're sure she's okay, have you checked on her this morning? Why didn't she call me? I would have gone over to her apartment." Jaz shoots off rapid-fire questions like nobody's business.

"She's okay," I say when her eyes fill with tears. I reach out, placing a hand on each of Jaz's shoulders. I need her to calm down before I end up with another unconscious woman in my care. "I was there when she came home. She's caught a nasty cold. This last trip really wrung her out and she was dehydrated." I clear my throat, unsure of how much to tell her. I don't want to freak her out, but she deserves to know.

"She was barely conscious, Jaz." I have to turn my face away to hide the emotion behind the words. Her intake of breath tells me that is not what she wanted to hear, but the words just keep flowing. "It was really scary, if I'm being honest. I'm sorry I didn't think to call you, it all just happened so fast. She was getting in the bath when I left to come get breakfast, so she has to be doing better. She slept hard, probably needed it after four days of travel." I'm rambling, and I know I'm trying to convince the both of us that Joss really is okay.

"Wait. Were you with her? All night?" She's eyeing me now, a little warily and a lot shocked. I don't blame her; she doesn't know me very well. Last night was supposed to change that.

"Yeah." I give her a shrug and run my hand through my hair again. I'm uncomfortable with her scrutiny, but I'm also glad Joss has someone so protective in her corner. "I didn't want to leave her alone. She asked me to stay. I was watching out for her—that's all."

Her lips are pursed as she takes me in from head to toe, likely readjusting her understanding of why I look like a rumpled sheet. The next thing I know, she launches herself into my arms and is hugging me, hard. Damn, this chick is strong.

"Thank you for taking care of her. Thank you. Thank you. Thank you."

"She's okay, really. I should probably get that coffee and some food so I can get back, yeah?" I pull back, still gripping her shoulders. "I'll have her text you, okay?"

She nods and presses the backs of her hands against her flushed cheeks.

"Okay. I'll get your order together while Gunther mans the register. I know what Joss will want, what else?"

"Two black coffees, a bagel with cream cheese, and a croissant."

Jaz hurries back behind the counter and whispers something to the other barista. He looks a little put out but doesn't say anything. Joss told me that Jaz is part-owner, so it's not like he's going to tell the boss no.

She's back in front of me with a drink carrier and a bag of pastries in no time at all. I reach for my wallet, but she stops me with a hand on my forearm.

"Don't worry about it, it's on me. As a thank-you for taking care of Joss last night."

I dip my head in thanks and smile warmly.

Back at my building, I stop by Frank's desk and offer him the black coffee and the croissant; he refuses the latter but is almost effusive with gratitude for the former. I mean, he even gave me a full smile, or at least what I assume is the biggest smile he has, and tipped his hat at me. Progress.

The elevator ride feels extra slow. I'm bouncing on the balls of my feet, nervous energy radiating off me in waves. I just need to see her, know she's alright. I rush out of the elevator and straight to her apartment, not giving mine a second glance.

I don't even bother to knock, striding into the kitchen to set down the coffee and food.

"Joss, I'm back. You doing okay?" I call out.

It's quiet and my heartrate picks up, what if she passed out in the bath?

"Joss?!"

I walk straight back to her room and hear quiet music coming through the door.

Take a breath, Wes.

My knock is gentle but my voice is firm when I say her name again. It's loud enough she should be able to hear it over the music. There's a little slosh of water before she responds.

"Wes?"

My head falls forward on the wood with a thump.

She's okay. She's okay. She's okay.

"I've got coffee and breakfast out here if you feel up to it," I say, doing my best to refrain from thinking of Joss, naked, on the other side of the door.

"Mmm. Coffee sounds amazing. I'll be out in a minute."

Hell. That little moaning sound is definitely not helping me keep my thoughts platonic. My hands tighten on the door frame until my knuckles turn white. The effect she has on me is electric. I push myself back from the door before I do something stupid.

Coffee. I need coffee.

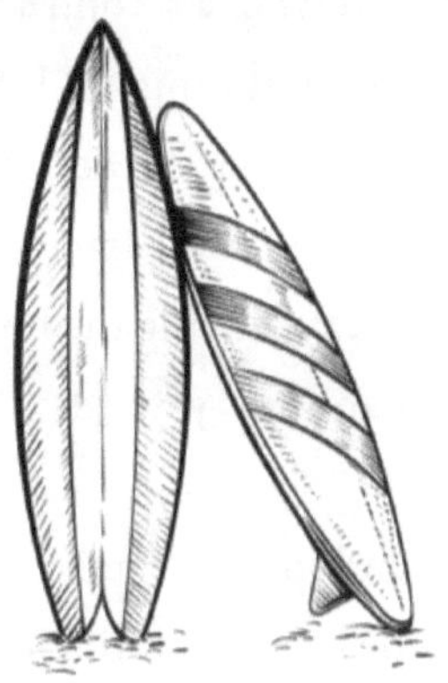

CHAPTER SIXTEEN

Joss

I'm having an internal battle of epic proportions. Luxuriate in this bath forever, or get out and drink the coffee that I can hear calling my name from the other room. Decision made, I lean my head back against the cushion and allow myself one final minute. I thought I could untangle the chaos of my feelings while I was in here...

What happened last night?

You lost control of your emotions, Joss. That's what.

And then there's Wes, who's waiting in my living room with coffee and breakfast. Wes, who stayed with me all night, cared for me. Wes, who has become one of my closest friends in only a few weeks. And something tells me if I don't get out there soon, that very friend might barge in here to make sure I'm alive.

I slip out from the tub and grab my fluffy towel, snuggling into its warmth, and then wrap a second around my damp hair. Giving myself a once-over in the mirror, I give into the reality of just how sick I am. Despite sleeping well, the dark circles under my eyes rival my favorite vampire characters from my youth. My body aches, and I'm already missing the hot water of the bath. I may be feeling better than I was yesterday, but the medicine has definitely worn off.

I peek my head out and spot Wes standing in the kitchen with his back to me, forearms leaning on the bar. His head tips back as he takes a drink of coffee, and I recognize the cup. This man. He walked down to Harbour Grounds for me this morning. He lets out a little groan of satisfaction, and it vibrates through my body like someone struck a tuning fork deep down inside me. Turning my back, I shake my head to clear the thoughts that pop up about what else might make him groan like that.

I flip the light switch, illuminating my closet as I walk in. It's split into two distinct sections. My uniforms hanging neatly, everything ordered and tidy, pressed to perfection. Then there's my everyday clothes—all leggings and jeans, knit tops and T-shirts. I rarely dress up, so the few pieces of nicer clothes hang abandoned with my work wardrobe.

I pick a pair of buttery soft leggings and a cozy hoodie. Wes has already seen me at my worst—I doubt he will judge this look too harshly. *There's not a version of you that wouldn't be hot to me.* His words glide through my head once more. My chest tightens at the earnestness of them, the truth in them, even if I can't seem to believe it.

Feet in slippers and damp hair in a messy bun, I walk out in search of Wes. A pang of disappointment resonates in my chest when I don't immediately see him at the counter. Did he leave? I turn on the spot until I find him, standing alone on my balcony, in the same clothes he wore yesterday, feet bare, dark hair blowing softly in the breeze.

He's so at ease with himself, so comfortable here in my space, and so damn sexy. A tiny voice in my head whispers *mine*, but I shove that into the box. He's not mine. He never will be, and the sooner I accept that the better off I'll be.

Like he can sense me, he turns around and joins me in a few long strides. I'm stunned silent by the way his beautiful blue eyes roam over me. I blush, even though I know he isn't doing it to be flirty. He sets his coffee on the bar, and I see the conflict on his face, like he isn't sure what to do next. *Me neither, Wes, me neither.* We stand and look at each other for a beat, neither of us moving, just sharing the same air, the same space.

His fingers twitch by his side. Will he finally move to touch me, save us both from this tense moment? Those fingers curl into a tight fist, his eyes moving to the floor. Okay, then. Should I say something? Thank him for being here, tell him he doesn't have to stay...? If he's this uncomfortable after last night, I don't know what that means for us.

He looks up and his eyes pin mine. I catch the glassy, misty look in them. There is so much feeling written on his face right now. Even after all his concern last night, this is different.

"Can I hug you?" His throat bobs with a swallow. "Please." The words are hushed, almost pleading. I'm so taken aback that all I can do is nod.

He wastes no time reaching for me and crushing me to him in a hug that tops all hugs. His hold is soft. Careful. My body melts into his as I wrap my arms around his torso. His breath tickles the shell of my ear where he's bent low. I feel his next inhale like it's my own. It's labored, shaky, and when he lets it out, a "Thank you" comes with it.

"For what?" I ask, moving my hands to his arms. If I could push back, look in his face, maybe I could understand what he's feeling right now. But he doesn't let up, holding me to him.

"For the hug." His voice is tight. "You really scared me last night, Grey." The underlying loss and pain in his words wrecks my heart. I know, somehow, this has less to do with me than it does with him.

"Wes?"

I finally manage to put a few inches of space between us. His eyes are red-rimmed and he looks a little frantic.

"I'm okay, I promise." I reach down to grab his hand and place it firmly over my heart so he can feel it beating. "I'm right here. I'm just sick. I'll get better. I'm okay."

I can feel it in my bones that he needs the reassurance. He leaves his hand over my heart but brings his forehead to rest against mine as his eyes slip closed. I'm unsure how long we stand this way. A few minutes? Hours? Time seems to stop when we touch, and I can't bring myself to pull away. In the end, it's Wes who does, but only to bring his hand up to my forehead instead.

"You're warm again, how are you feeling?"

"Better than last night, but still not great. Can you grab me more medicine? And where's that coffee you promised?" I joke, trying to bring some levity to the conversation.

His lips quirk and he finally lets me go. "Coffee is right there. I'll be right back."

He points to the second cup on the counter before heading back to the bedroom. I grab it, turning it in my hands to warm them up, which is when I see Jaz's untidy scrawl.

"Oh my god, I forgot about Jaz."

I slap a hand to my forehead and instantly regret it because it jostles my pounding head. I scan the room, looking for my phone. My eyes land on the luggage stacked by the door where Frank must have left it last night. Oh man, Frank. I owe him a big thank-you as well. I dig through my purse and retrieve my phone. It's dead of course. I'm antsy knowing that I bailed on Jaz last night without a word—she's probably worried sick.

"Wes? Did you see Jaz this morning?" I holler back to the bedroom as I grab my phone charger, but a movement at my side causes me to jump.

"No need to shout." He gives me a little smile and sets some medicine on the counter in front of me. "And, yes, I saw her. I explained what happened, but she's still worried about you. I told her you'd text her."

"Okay, thank you. I can't believe I forgot. I feel so bad."

I'm watching my phone like a hawk, waiting for it to power back up. The little apple appears on the screen, and I let out a sigh of short-lived relief as it begins pinging with notifications from the last fifteen hours or so. Most of them are from Jaz, getting progressively more frantic the longer I wasn't responding. I decide to reply to the last one, which is from this morning.

Jaz

> Bloody hell Joss. Would you text me back already?

My hands fly across the screen. I love her for how worried she was; it's nice to know someone cares.

Me

> I'm so sorry, Jaz. Wes just told me he saw you and filled you in.

Jaz

> Don't apologize, I'm just glad you're ok. You're ok, right?

Me

> Yeah, still not feeling great, but better than last night.

Jaz

> Is Wes still there? Do you need me to come over?

Me

> He's still here. I think I'm good. Call you later?

Jaz

> Yes please. Will you thank Wes for me again? I'm glad someone was there for you.

The last two words tumble in my brain for a minute. Not there *with* you—there *for* you. It's a subtle difference, but in the context of my life, it's kind of eye opening. How many people have been *with* me but have never truly been there *for* me? Jaz has been my best friend for as long as I've been in Sydney, and she's the only one who could possibly understand how much it means to me that Wes stayed last night. I'm not even sure I fully understand how badly I needed that.

That stinging feeling in my nose and behind my eyes returns. Man, what is happening to me? I haven't been this emotional in... well, about seven years. Goose bumps prickle on my arms at the reminder of that time. I guess the floodgates were bound to open eventually.

My gaze lifts to find Wes watching me intently, like he's just waiting for me to pass out again. Or waiting for me to explain why I look like I might start to cry—*again*.

"What are you hiding over there in that pastry bag?" I wiggle my eyebrows, trying to break the tension before it pulls so tight we break instead.

"This bag?" He opens it just a little and makes a show of sticking his nose in and inhaling deeply. "Mmmm, I don't know if I want to share." His tone is teasing, and there's a little flutter in my stomach that I have to ignore.

"But I'm sick." I give him my best puppy-dog eyes and force a couple of fake coughs into my hand. Unfortunately, the action leads me into an actual coughing fit, and I have to brace my hands on the counter to ride it out.

"You're lucky you're cute," he says with a cheeky grin. "And that I know just how sick you are, or I really might keep these all to myself."

He moves on and starts pulling pastries out of the bag. There's an apple fritter and a cranberry orange muffin. My mouth waters at the sight. *My favorites.* I make a note to thank Jaz later.

My stomach chooses then to let out a loud grumble, and it's enough to remind me that I haven't eaten in far too long.

"I guess you're hungry, that's a good sign," Wes says as he hunts through the cabinets, looking for plates. Instead of telling him where they are, I enjoy the feeling of watching him make himself at home in my space. "Table or patio?" he asks once he's located them.

"How about couch?" I ask. My energy is waning again, and I'm not sure the sunlight would agree with the pounding in my head. He nods in a *lead the way* motion, so I settle into one corner of the couch and get comfortable.

Wes puts the food on the coffee table and has my feet in his lap across the couch before I even have a second to think. My eyes catch on the corded muscles of his forearm as he grabs the blanket off the back and covers my legs. Then he casually reaches for his coffee as if he didn't just make my heart melt. How did I get so lucky to have found such a good friend?

I'm still not used to having someone who sees me, who sees what I need and actually acts on it. His big hand gives my foot a little squeeze through the blanket. There's a naturalness to the way we sit and eat in silence. I never feel the need to fill the quiet spaces with Wes. We sit like this a lot when we're surfing, just listening to the waves and taking in the beauty of the world.

He finishes eating before I do and starts rubbing my feet through the blanket. I let out a low moan at how good it feels. Last night was hell, but right here, I think I might be in heaven. My head falls back and I get lost in the feel of his hands on me.

"Oh my god, that feels incredible."

His hands still, just for a second, before resuming their ministrations, but my eyes snap open to find his gaze locked on me. That look is pure fire, and a part of me wants to burn with him. Damn the consequences.

I have to shift my eyes away as a heat that has nothing to do with the fever spreads through my body. I'm sick after all—this is not the time to let those thoughts take hold.

"Um, would you mind grabbing me those meds from the counter?" I say in an attempt to shift the vibe.

I continue to stare resolutely at my muffin, breaking off a piece and popping it into my mouth. I hold back the moan this time, not wanting to reignite the spark I just thoroughly doused. He sets my feet down on the couch and is back a minute later, meds in one hand and a fresh bottle of water in the other.

"Thank you."

"Welcome." There's gravel in that one word, and I avoid looking at him for fear of what I might see in his eyes.

He moves back to sit at the other end of the couch, but he doesn't immediately pull my feet into his lap. Is he trying to reestablish our boundaries the same way I am? The ones we blasted through with the hand holding and cuddling last night?

I feel sleep pulling at me again, so I curl onto my side, feet just barely brushing his thigh. He gently brings them back to his lap, readjusting the blanket as he kicks his own feet onto the coffee table. It's like he can't stand not touching me, kind of like when he asked if he could hug me earlier. Normally, I would scold him about feet on the table, but he looks comfortable enough to make me bite my tongue.

I close my eyes and let the world fall away, wondering if he'll still be here when I wake up.

CHAPTER SEVENTEEN

Joss

I blink my eyes open to find a fresh bottle of water, more meds, and a package of Tim Tams on the coffee table. There's also a note.

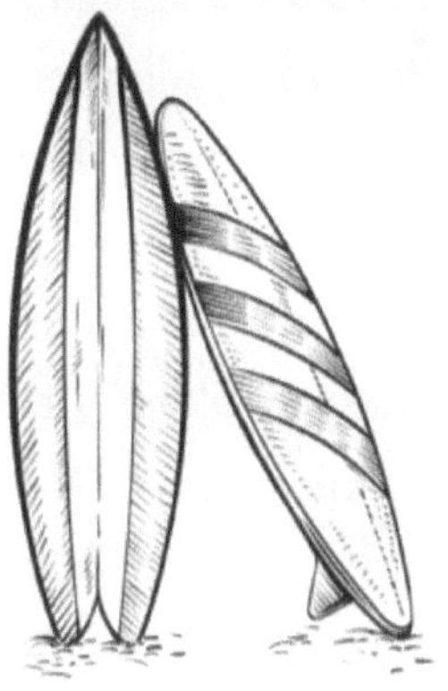

I can't stop the stupid smirk that tugs at my lips. "Bossy," I mumble under my breath while I run my fingers over the tidy handwriting. It's not messy and chaotic like mine, and I like knowing that his hand ran across this page just for me. He's still taking care of me from afar, and it makes my heart constrict in my chest. I do what he told me though and grab the bottle of water, popping the pills into my mouth.

My eyes snag on the Tim Tams. I mean, why not? I tear into the package, grabbing two. The first bite is heavenly as the chocolate coating melts on my tongue followed by the crunchy biscuit and creamy chocolate filling. I close my eyes and do a little wiggle because it tastes so good. Note to self, if I'm going to settle down, do it with a man who buys me Tim Tams.

I push the package away, otherwise they'll be gone before Wes even gets back. There's a bizarre galloping sensation in my belly at the thought. Why do I feel giddy about that? And anyway, he should want to avoid me like the plague I'm clearly carrying.

I pull myself up to sitting, waiting for the pounding in my head to start again, but it never comes. I should take a shower myself. The bath this morning was great, but there's just something about a scalding hot shower when you're sick to make you feel human. Two more Tim Tams just so happen to disappear from the package before I make my way back to the bedroom, humming a little as I go.

Walking into the living room thirty minutes later, freshly showered and in clean leggings and a tank top, the first thing I see is a bouquet of flowers on the table. They're stunning. But they don't hold a candle to the man standing in my kitchen, heating soup on the stove. Wearing an apron. He hears my chuckle and turns to face me, giving me an eyeful of him in my *Kiss the Cook* apron, hair still a little damp.

"I saw it hanging on the pantry door. Thought it was worth a shot." He gives me his megawatt smile, dimples on full display even under his beard.

I can't help the laugh that trips out of me. "Nice try. I don't think you want my germs though."

"Hmmm. Good point, I might have to take a rain check." He turns back to the soup and continues stirring. The flirty way he's talking to me has my head spinning, wondering if any of our boundaries have stayed intact.

"The flowers are from Frank, by the way," he throws out over his shoulder.

I'm glad he's facing away from me so he can't see the twinge of disappointment that mars my brow. I guess some of those boundaries are still up.

Platonic friends don't buy you flowers. BUT they also don't hold you in bed all night.

I sigh and walk over to my flowers, wishing I could smell them. Stupid stuffy nose. I can see there's a note tucked inside.

> Ms. Joss, I hope you're
> feeling better.
> x Frank

The note is so Frank—short and not at all flowery despite the fact that it came with flowers. But he actually called me Joss. Now I just need to get him to drop the "Ms." and we'll be home free. I giggle to myself, and Wes looks my way.

"What?" He's got a lopsided grin on his face. It's cute.

"Nothing, just Frank being Frank. I can't believe he bought me flowers."

"I think you really freaked him out last night. He seems pretty protective of you and was nervous to leave you alone with me." He chuckles, then puffs up his chest. "He's finally warming up to me now though." The look of pride on his face has me stifling another laugh.

"You think so, huh?"

"Yeah, I bought him coffee, and he even smiled," he says, waving the ladle around to look back at me. "That's got to mean something."

"Maybe, Wes. Maybe." The words escape as a sigh as I walk into the kitchen to retrieve dishes and silverware. Wes fills me in on both Jaz's and Frank's visits, which I missed entirely in my cold-medicine-induced coma on the couch. Before I know it, he's ladling chicken noodle soup into the bowls and cutting thick slices of crunchy bread for us.

The image gives me pause—the domesticity of this moment is something I haven't experienced in a long time. There's an intimacy in it that conjures long-forgotten memories of family dinners around a table similar to this one. My throat feels a little thick at the thought, and I have to clear it before I can speak. Needing to get my mind off my family, I ask Wes about his instead.

"Well, you know they all live in Tahoe," he starts, putting his spoon down and folding his hands. "My parents own investment properties around the lake, and their world has always revolved around that." He stops to rip off a chunk of bread, then continues.

"They weren't bad parents by any means, just kind of self-absorbed and absent. They made sure we had everything we needed, so I guess it could've been worse."

I don't tell him how much I can relate to the "absent" part. I asked him this question to take my mind off my own parents, not make me think of them more.

He gives me a shrug, and I gesture for him to keep going. "I think I got lucky because I left for college before the fighting started. I always felt bad that I couldn't protect Rory from that." He grimaces, a look of remorse crossing his features. "They split when she started high school, which was pretty rough for her. Though, their business relationship has never been better," he adds with another shrug and a small shake of his head. "They were always better business partners than they were marital partners anyway.

"My sister though... She is the best of us all." There's a wistfulness to his voice now as he talks about Rory. "I hope I can convince her to visit so you can meet her. She's eight years younger than me, but she's always been the mature one, you know?"

I wish I could say yes, that I do know, but I don't. I wonder how different my life would have been if I'd had a sibling. And not the one I've never met—nor ever intend to—but one I could've shared memories with.

I continue asking Wes questions about her, and I'm quick to learn that despite their age difference, they were thick as thieves. And how, even though they don't get to see each other that often, their bond is as tight as ever.

We move to the couch, our bowls empty and stomachs full. Groaning, I sink down into it, pulling the blanket I'd been asleep under back over my lap. Wes pulls out his phone to show me pictures of him and Rory snowboarding a few years ago, scrolling back through his Instagram feed. Each picture prompts another funny story to go along with it.

When he scrolls past a picture of him laid up in a hospital, I grip his arm. His right leg is propped up in a cast, a bandage wrapped across his forehead and his left arm held in a sling. He looks terrible, broken, and it makes my heart beat fast.

"What happened?" I murmur. I didn't even know him then, but I'm devastated to see him in such a state. His eyes are wary, looking back at me nervously, like he isn't sure he's ready to share this with me yet. But then he takes a deep breath and starts talking.

"That was a little over a year ago." His voice is hoarse, and he has to clear his throat a couple times. "I was in a plane crash." His eyes shut tight and his face crumples with silent pain.

"Oh my god," I whisper, hand tightening on his forearm as the other covers my mouth.

"My best friend—" He breaks off, his throat working. "Bobby was in the other plane." The way his voice cracks on his friend's name is enough to tell me that he didn't survive. I can't stop the tears that spill over or the little gasp I let out, but I hold back a sob, not wanting to make this harder for him.

"We'd been on that damn aircraft carrier for ten months and we were *one day* from pulling into the base in Hawaii. Fuck. We were home free." Each word is a hiss through clenched teeth, his head falling back, the tendons in his neck taut. I don't know how to react... Do I touch him? God, I'm so out of my depth here.

"But Bobby and I wanted one more flight together. He had orders to move cross-country as soon as we got home from deployment, and it would be the first time in our careers where we wouldn't be stationed together." His gaze locks straight ahead now, and I don't know if it's that he won't look at me, or if he can't. "It was supposed to be a good deal. Just a joy ride. No mission, just an hour to fly over the ocean with my best friend."

I wince at the picture he's painting. His guilt is so palpable I feel like I could choke on it. I offer the lightest squeeze to his arm, just a subtle reminder that he's not in this alone right now.

"A storm popped up out of nowhere between us and the ship. I've flown in a hundred storms, but never like this. When caution alerts started popping up on my HUD, I knew something was wrong. Every emergency procedure that had been drilled into my head came to me like second nature, but with one already failed engine and another throwing damage and fire warnings at me, I knew." It's like he's still sitting in that plane as he speaks—as if talking it out could change the outcome somehow. I'd guess he hasn't shared this with anyone in a long time, or maybe ever.

"I wasn't going to make it back to the ship, and I couldn't communicate with Bobby. The electrical damage I sustained in the storm knocked out my radio. I needed more altitude so I could eject. I pulled up, praying my second engine would get me there." His voice is flat, almost detached now, all his emotion leashed somewhere deep inside. "I expected Bobby to head back to the ship, land, tell them what happened... but he followed me and..." His swallow and the way he rakes his hands through his hair, pulling at the strands at the nape of his neck as his head hangs, tells me enough, but he continues anyway. "I ejected. He didn't."

I can feel the weight of his guilt from where I sit. It's oppressive, completely debilitating.

"I'll never know exactly what happened. It was all too fast..." He rubs absently at his knee, like talking about this has brought on a new surge of pain. "I lost consciousness before I even hit the surface of the water."

He stares straight ahead again. "Ejecting is always a risk, but my leg..." He clenches his jaw, hand tightening around the offending limb. "They told me it got tangled in the parachute. It shouldn't have happened. But it cracked my knee and tore several of the ligaments around it."

I can only imagine that the physical pain was nothing compared to the agony of learning why Bobby wasn't there when he woke up.

"Nothing about that flight went as planned. I just wanted one more chance to fly off my best friend's wing, to watch the water ripple below us, and remember what a privilege it was to fly together." He presses himself back, letting his head hit the back of the couch, speaking to the ceiling. "Instead, it ended with me in the hospital and him in a flag-laden casket."

Jesus. His pain radiates off him in waves, building and cresting. He pitches forward, elbows coming to rest on his knees, hands pulling at his hair again. Rage and sorrow spiral around him in a vortex.

"It was my fucking fault." He spits out the words, full of self-loathing.

He hasn't cried, but I can tell he's so strung out it wouldn't take much to push him over the edge. I shake my head, though he can't see it. I don't think he can even feel where my hand now rests on his back or the way my body is pressed to his. I don't even remember moving this close.

"No." My voice breaks on the word, barely able to get that one syllable past my lips. I swallow, steeling myself to say more. "No. It wasn't." I don't know how I know it, but I do. "God, Wes, I'm so sorry. I'm just so sorry."

I manage to keep my voice mostly even as I say the words. I just want to hold him, take it all away. But I'm not sure that's what he needs right now. I reach my other hand out, gently pulling on his wrist, trying to get him to look at me. When he finally lifts his head, his eyes are almost pleading.

I repeat his words from earlier. "Can I hug you? Please."

He nods and I wrap my arms around him, and I feel his shoulders slump. He's so tall that I'm awkwardly kneeling on the couch to embrace him, but I couldn't care less. His shoulders shake as he hugs me back, squeezing me with everything he has, like I'm the breath he hasn't taken in years. He lifts me, bringing me closer until I'm flush against him, my thighs bracketing his hips to straddle him.

He buries his face in my neck as I rest my head on his shoulder, whispering all the comforting words I can think of. Knowing they'll mean nothing, but hoping they'll ease the ache in his heart a fraction. I let him take what he needs, the comfort of my body against his, the freedom to let himself go.

Everything starts to fall into place as I think about this story in the grand scheme of his life and why he's here. This must be the catalyst for why he got out of the military. The scars on his leg and shoulder that I've noticed when surfing finally make sense. This is what he's running from—everything he lost at home.

I don't know how long we sit like that, wrapped in each other. At some point, we quietly shift to lie on our sides, continuing to hold each other close as we drift off to sleep.

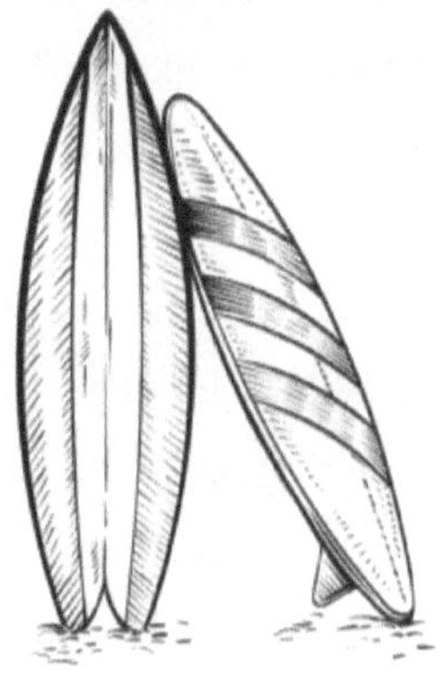

CHAPTER EIGHTEEN

WES

I stand under the hot spray of the shower, letting my mind wander over the two months I've spent in Sydney. Some days it seems as if that time has flown by, but when I think about how far I've come, I'm surprised it hasn't been longer.

I reflect on the night I told Joss about Bobby. I hadn't planned to pour my heart out to her, laying bare all my grief and guilt over what happened, but somehow, I've felt lighter in the weeks since. Prior to that night, I barely ever talked about it. Most people don't know how to handle holding someone else's grief, and it was just easier to deal with it in my own way.

My own way being me waking up sweating from flashbacks and nightmares every night, and then brushing it back under the rug every morning. I mean, at least I've finally accepted them for what they are and I'm not pretending they're just "dreams" anymore. Progress is progress. Yet, in the month since I spilled it all to Joss, I haven't had a single nightmare. It's like my body and my brain were just waiting for me to let it out some other way so they could stop badgering me while I slept.

I feel a difference in myself. Life seems a little easier to manage. I can see now that I'd been faking a lot of my confidence and swagger since the crash. A year of putting on a show for everyone around me. But now it feels more like the old Wes is back, the one who embodied that confidence, that self-assurance, the one who loved life. Joss has been a huge part of that. Anytime she sees me getting into my head, she reminds me that I'm not to blame for what happened.

A small smile crosses my face as the water beats down my back. Joss has me actually talking about Bobby again. I've started to share all the good things I remember, all the memories that I locked away because they were just too painful. I wish he could have met her; he would call me an idiot for not making her mine. Maybe I am an idiot, but I still haven't let go of my hang-ups surrounding relationships. One step at a time. Besides, our friendship means too much. *She* means too much.

We were out on our boards at dawn this morning, so it's only been ten hours since I saw her, but I've spent all day looking forward to tonight. I love our daily routine when she's home: surfing down at Bondi, grabbing coffee before I go to work, eating dinner at either one of our places. Sometimes we read on one of our balconies or watch something stupid on TV. When we watched *Silence of the Lambs* last week, we both went into hysterics remembering the day we met (for the second time).

We text constantly while she's working. I usually wake her up with a picture of the beach or the sunrise, or she wakes me up with a selfie of her making a silly face on an airplane. Whenever my phone pings and I see it's her, I can't help my face splitting into a huge smile. Like it's doing now.

Our rhythm with each other has become easy, our expectations low. I know she has work and a life just like I have my own, but slowly they're intermingling more and more, and I can't complain. Even our friend groups are starting to overlap. Breck joins us for dawn patrol when he can, and Talia has even met us for coffee a couple of times after she drops Willow off at school. And after my weekend of taking care of Joss, Jaz accepted me with open arms.

I shudder at the memory of how sick she was that weekend. We *still* can't believe I never got what she had. I know I'm a total man-child when I'm sick, and I wouldn't have wanted Joss or anyone else to have to put up with that. Last Christmas when I visited Rory, I was laid up with the flu for days on end and she still makes fun of me for how absolutely horrific I was as a patient. I was completely useless.

Come to think of it, I probably need to call her this weekend to check in—see how everything is back home. The idea of home feels so strange these days. Sydney feels more like home than any of the duty stations I was assigned to over the last twelve years in the Navy.

Shit, that's a scary thought.

One I don't dwell on as I flip off the water and immediately hear a knock at the front door, followed by Joss letting herself in. We've gotten so used to sharing these spaces. Dinner here, a movie there, coffee on the balcony. But we never sleep over—not since she was sick.

Do I think about that weekend? The way it felt to hold her in my arms? The way it felt for her to straddle me on the couch? I mean, what man wouldn't let his mind wander there occasionally. Still, it's not something we plan on repeating, actively putting in the effort to resurrect the boundaries we blurred.

"Are you ready?" Joss calls just as I'm stepping out of the shower.

Remembering we need to get going so we're not late to Breck and Talia's, I hustle to slip on a pair of black boxer briefs. I turn to leave the bathroom, but stop dead in my tracks when I come face-to-face with Joss.

"Hi!" She squeaks out the word before turning on her heel to face the other side of the room.

"Hi yourself," I purr, amused at her reaction. I'm not one to get embarrassed, especially about my body.

I check her out from behind, a favorite pastime for a masochist like myself. She's in a pair of jeans that make her ass look amazing and those legs... Damn. She's wearing a chunky knit sweater and suede boots. The way her hair hangs in waves down her back makes me want to wrap my hand around it and—*nope, nope, nope, stop those thoughts right there, Wes.*

"Are you going to put some clothes on?" She sounds flustered.

Good. She's the one who walked in on me, let her be flustered.

"Why?" I ask as I pull myself away from the perusal of her body, my desire to tease her taking over. "Don't like what you see?"

"Wes!" she admonishes, but her tone is breathy and not nearly as chiding as I'm sure she meant it to be.

My smile just grows wider. "That's not an answer, Grey." I make a low humming sound in my throat as I step closer to her.

"Wes." It's more of a plea this time. Does she think saying my name like that will make me stop teasing her?

I take another step. "Joss?" I draw her name out like a caress. I'm within touching distance now. *Fuck, what am I doing?* This is a terrible idea. "Did you see something you liked, sweetheart?"

She goes entirely still as her breath catches. Did I push too far? I may have pushed myself too far, my body reacting to her being so close. It's not like these boxer briefs are leaving much to the imagination, and if she turns around it'll be game over.

I don't think she's going to answer, but in the quietest voice, she finally does.

"Yes."

One word. One little word, and my restraint snaps. My ability to keep this flirtatious and light goes out the window. I take the last step and press my body against her back, my heated skin brushing against the fabric of her clothes. I slide one arm around her waist and use the other hand to pull her hair to the side so I can bring my face to the crook of her neck.

"What did you see that you liked, Joss?" I whisper, letting my lips dust the shell of her ear, my breath hot against her skin. The little self-control I still have keeps my lips off her, knowing I won't be able to stop if they make contact. She gives an involuntary shiver at the same time her head rests back against my chest, leaning into my touch.

"You." She clears her throat, and from this angle, I watch it bob with the effort to swallow. "All of you."

Her breathing comes fast, and I can feel her every movement against my bare chest. She's being coy, but I know what she's saying, and to prove it, I press all of me against her back. I drag my nose down her neck, taking in the amazing way she smells. She moans, her back arching slightly, exposing more of her throat and pushing her hips further into where I'm pressed against her.

We're on the precipice, a point of no return. I could spin her around and crush my lips to hers, making sure we never make it to our friends' place. Or I could back away, put my clothes on, and we can pretend this never happened.

I don't get the chance to choose though, because Joss's hand comes over mine at her waist. It's not a needy I-want-more kind of touch. It's a soft one, the kind you use when you're about to step away. Which she does. It's not a rejection, just her coming to her senses, and I can tell it's a struggle for her as much as it is for me.

She clears her throat again, her shoulders lifting and settling back, her spine straight as she walks to the door.

"I'll meet you out here, yeah?" She doesn't turn around. She doesn't take another look. She just walks away, closing the door behind her as she goes.

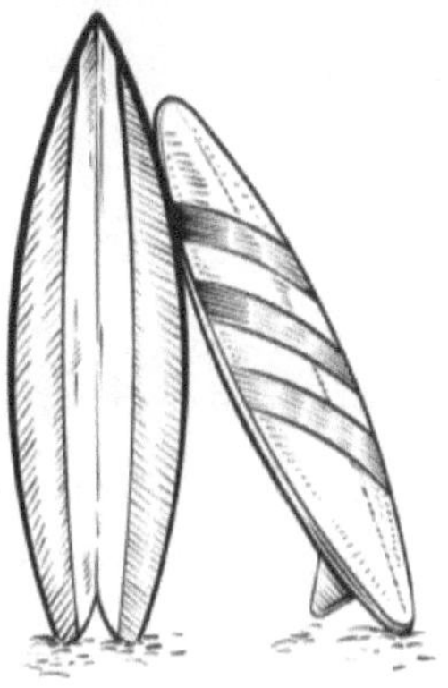

CHAPTER NINETEEN

Joss

I swing the door to the balcony open and take in a lungful of the chilled winter air. The railing feels cold under my arms, even through my jumper, and I drop my head to my clasped hands. What in the hell just happened? I know the tension has always lingered there, but we've done such a good job of holding it at bay that I almost forgot the power it has over me when I let my guard down.

How many times have I stalked into this apartment over the past few weeks without even thinking about the fact that Wes could be naked? It didn't even cross my mind as I walked into his room tonight. Yet there he was, in all his toned glory. Wet and glistening from his shower, not a lick of clothes on him before he pulled on those boxer briefs. I'll never look at a pair of plain black boxer briefs the same way again.

And if I thought his ass was perfect under a pair of well-fitting board shorts, it was even better in the flesh. My cheeks heat at the memory of the way his muscles flexed and stretched, his body angling as he slid the fabric up his sculpted legs.

I should have walked straight back out as soon as I first saw him, but I was stunned stupid and couldn't seem to make myself move. That all would have been bad enough but, oh my god, what happened after... I'm so embarrassed—no, not exactly embarrassed. Flustered, maybe? Turned on, definitely. *Crap.* How am I supposed to look him in the eye now?

I drag in a deep breath as I relive the last few moments in my mind. We were so close to crossing a line I don't think we could come back from. I was so desperate for his lips on my skin, but I could tell he was holding back, restraining himself.

"Shit."

I run my hands into my hair, letting my head hang as my mind races. I can't lose this friendship, can't afford to mess it up. He doesn't do relationships, and I don't do casual. I don't really do anything these days, honestly. After Eric, I decided I needed a break from putting myself out there. Why bother when the outcome is always the same?

If it's casual, they leave. If it's serious, they leave.

But in the back of my mind, I know I want someone to share my life with. It's what I've always wanted, craving what I never had with my own family. But I also know it can't be with Wes. He's only supposed to be here a year. I can't fall for someone who isn't able to offer me stability. I won't.

When he comes out, I'm going to pretend nothing happened. Rebuild those boundaries brick by brick if I have to. I push off the railing and take a few deep inhales, sending the apprehension in my chest out with them.

"Hey. Ready to go?" Wes says from over my shoulder. His voice is quiet but sure, steady, and I'm almost afraid to turn around and see what he's thinking. I prepare myself to find regret in his eyes, silently hoping there will be some residual heat there too. I don't know what I want him to feel, probably because I'm drowning in my own uncertainty.

I suck in one more breath before spinning to face him, but end up refusing to meet his eyes.

Chicken.

"Yup," I say, popping the P a little more than necessary. *Goodness, I'm awkward.*

My eyes fall on his torso—the safest place I can think to look—and I take in the way his arms are braced on the sides of the doorframe. I wonder if he plans to move. Before I reach him, he steps sideways just enough so I can slide past him with only a hair's breadth of space between our bodies. I ignore his sharp intake of air and walk straight to the door, Wes following me without a word.

The elevator ride is silent. Even in the early days, we couldn't help but banter with each other, and now I can barely bring my eyes to his, though I can feel him watching me. When the doors open, his hand instantly comes to my back, and it burns through the fabric of my top like a wildfire. There's not a hint of tentativeness in the touch as his fingers flex against me, and I finally gather the courage to look up at him from under my lashes.

He smiles his regular old Wes smile. Cool and confident.

I let myself smile back. *This will be fine.*

There's a car waiting at the curb, as neither of us wanted to worry about driving home later. He opens the door for me and I slide in, letting him take the lead and chat with the driver as we head out of the city toward Bellevue Hill where Breck and Talia live. I stare out my window, distracting myself by watching the buildings and lights fade into trees and houses. At some point, Wes covers my hand with his.

"Hey."

I sigh and sink into my seat slightly. Wes's salty ocean scent surrounds me, reminding me how it clung to my pillows for days after he slept in my bed.

"I'm sorry," I say at the same time Wes says, "You okay?"

We both laugh and I let my eyes roam his face. There's no discomfort or awkwardness there. He motions with his hand, indicating that I can talk first.

"I-I shouldn't have barged into your room like that. I'm sorry."

He huffs another laugh. "No worries. I probably should have closed my door since I knew you were coming over."

He sounds so unaffected, nonchalant. Am I just blowing this out of proportion? So I've seen him naked—it's not like I've never seen a naked man before. I'm about to open my mouth, to talk this out just like we did that first day on my patio when we were honest and earnest in acknowledging our attraction, but the car comes to a stop and my words die in my throat.

"We okay?" he asks, his thumb skimming over the top of my hand.

"Yeah, we're okay," I reassure him as a shiver coasts down my spine.

He climbs out of the car and lopes around to my side, opening my door for me. He takes my hand to help me step out, then settles his on the center of my back again to lead us up the path. He doesn't bother with the doorbell, just turns the knob and walks right in. I'm reminded of my excitement for seeing him in his element with his friends.

I've surfed with Breck a lot, and I've enjoyed getting to know Talia the few times she's met us for coffee, but this is more intimate. I also finally get to meet Willow tonight, which feels big somehow. With the way Wes talks about her, you'd think they actually share blood.

We follow the voices through the quaint and cozy house. It's simply decorated and follows a neutral pallet from the look of each room we pass. That must be Talia's doing. I would expect something much more vibrant and eclectic from Breck, or at the very least beachy. I'm also surprised there aren't toys and kid stuff everywhere. Talia is clearly tidier than I would be if I had a seven-year-old.

We reach the back door and I can see the leaping colors of the bonfire in the backyard as Wes pulls it open.

"I can't believe you got started without me," he calls in mock-outrage.

"Uncle Wes!" A sing-song voice carries across the yard followed by a tiny body running to collide with his legs.

He catches her, lifting until her feet kick above the ground and ruffles her hair, an affectionate smile on his face. "Hey, kiddo."

"We all know the party doesn't start until you get here, don't worry." Breck walks over, planting a kiss on my cheek then pulling Wes into a hug, effectively sandwiching Willow between them.

"Daddy! You're squishing me!" Willow squirms between them and Wes lets loose a full-body laugh.

Breck releases them both and Willow slides back to the ground only to have her eyes land on me.

"Willow, I want to introduce you to my friend." Wes looks between us. "This is Joss. She lives next door to me."

What will Willow think of her Uncle Wes bringing a friend to her house? I couldn't blame her if she'd wanted him all to herself. I offer her a smile and extend my hand—do you shake hands with a seven-year-old? No, apparently you do not. She launches herself at me this time and wraps her arms around my legs.

"Hi!" she squeaks out. I chirp a laugh at how adorable she is. She is so like her dad—over-the-top affectionate in the best way.

"Hi there. I've been looking forward to meeting you. Your dad and uncle have told me a lot about you." I run my hand down the sheet of smooth dark hair that is just like Talia's. She pulls back and I'm met with a striking combination of both her parents. Talia's olive skin tone, Breck's bright blue eyes, and a smile accented with dimples to match his on her cheeks.

"Mom and Dad said I needed to get ready for bed." She juts out her bottom lip. "But I made them promise I could stay up to see Uncle Wes." She turns to her dad with big puppy-dog eyes to go with her pout. "Can't I stay up a little longer, Daddy? Please." She elongates the word, clasping her hands in front of her like a prayer.

Talia appears over Breck's shoulder and addresses her daughter with her no-nonsense mom voice. "Willow, love, you can come back out to say good night after you brush your teeth and get your pjs on."

Her little shoulders sag and she offers us a dejected wave as she trudges into the house.

Breck watches her go looking almost as sad as she did. "We could have let her stay up a little later." His eyes come back to Talia.

"You're too soft on her." She presses her hand to Breck's cheek. "We already let her stay up to say hi to Wes and meet Joss." She turns to us. "Can I get you two something to drink?"

I glance down at my empty hands and then up to Wes as realization dawns. "I forgot the bottle of wine on the counter." I turn back to Talia, feeling a niggling of frustration with myself. I hate showing up to something like this empty-handed. "I had a bottle to bring and completely forgot it."

"You were a little distracted." Wes winks at me and his smile pulls wide. I blush crimson at the insinuation, then swat at him with my hand.

"No worries. We have plenty. Can I get you a glass?" There's a smirk playing around Talia's lips, one that tells me she's picking up on whatever energy Wes and I are throwing out tonight.

"Sure, that would be great," I say, willing my face to cool.

"Talia made her famous laksa and we have Tim Tams for dessert—your favorite," Breck says, and though it's directed at Wes, I smile because they're my favorite too. We've eaten our way through more packages in the last two months than I care to think about.

He jumps in to show us where the food is, and points to the cooler for Wes to grab a cold one. A few people are already sitting with drinks and bowls of laksa, chatting and enjoying the warmth from the fire. Wes told me there would be a mix of work and college friends here, and some are both. He doesn't move his hand from my back as we walk to the circle of chairs. It's not possessive, just friendly, like he wants to make sure I know he's here, that we're okay.

The group around the fire stands as we approach, and so begin the introductions. There's Drew, who I've heard a good bit about from Wes. He's not Wes's favorite person, but I'm not about to write him off without getting to know him first. Nancy is another colleague from Adventure Chasers, but she was also in Breck's business program at U of Sydney. So was her husband, Steve, who grips me in a strong handshake and offers a kind smile. The last couple lives next door to Breck and Talia, and it appears Wes hasn't met them yet either, making me feel a little less like an outsider.

"I'm Jimmy," the tall, bespectacled man offers, then gestures to his wife. "This is Jane… and that over there is Joey." He points to the pram sitting next to their chairs. "He's out for the count and can sleep through anything, so don't worry about waking him up."

Talia brings me a glass of red wine and offers me a woolen blanket for my legs as I take a seat by the fire. August nights are still brisk, but being out here and seeing the stars in the sky is well worth it. I love watching the city lights from my balcony, the way they dance on the harbour waters, but you don't get the stars.

"Want some laksa?" Wes asks.

With my head tipped back to look at the night sky, his voice slides down my neck as he bends to meet me. Shivers prickle along my arms at this closeness, and our eyes lock for just a moment. It's a pointless question though because he knows I'm not one to turn down food and I've been hearing about this noodle soup for weeks.

"You know I do. Thanks."

I watch him walk over to the table where Talia nearly pounces on him. I only catch the way he motions with his hands and glances back at me, grinning cheekily. He's back a minute later, handing me a bowl that smells delectable as he drops into the chair beside me.

With a startling "Boo!" Willow appears at Wes's side. He almost drops his bowl, leading to riotous laughter around the fire. Willow's girlish giggle stands out above the rest. He sets his bowl aside so she can wrap him in a big hug. She releases him and pulls me into a matching embrace. What must it be like to give affection and love so freely? I think I could learn a thing or two from this tiny human.

"Good night, kiddo," Wes says, a soft look in his eyes.

"Good night, Uncle Wes. Good night, Joss," she says over her shoulder as Talia ushers her off to bed and she pouts all the way up to the house. It's the most adorably sad thing I've ever seen.

The group falls into comfortable conversation, everyone eating and complimenting Talia on dinner. College stories are shared between Breck, Wes, Nancy, and Steve. Talia was there for some of them, but she didn't seem to be a staple member of their friend group at the time.

I get to hear about some of the tours they've set up recently, how the skydiving venture is going, and get the inside scoop on a surf trip they hope to do in the summer. I take note of how excited Wes sounds about going, my brain already whirring with the decision to take a week off work to go with him. I rarely take time off—haven't had much reason to outside of my big trips with Jaz.

It doesn't take long for me to pick up on the weird vibe that Wes must get from Drew at work. There's something there under the surface, but it's hard to pinpoint. At first, I think it's because he's the only one in the group who isn't part of a couple. Not that Wes and I are that, but we came together, we're sitting together. Drew is kind of the odd man out.

Yet he seems overly aware of Talia, and it gets my hackles up. I eye the way he watches the group, but particularly her, especially when she's with Breck. Breck's affection is on another level with her. Not that I can blame him, he's at his own home for goodness' sake, but Drew seems to bristle at the public displays. Like when Breck pulls her in close, nuzzling into her neck, or when he grabs her hand to tug her into his lap by the fire, covering them in a cozy blanket.

It's not until I catch Drew's eye that I shut down my people-watching (read: spying) and accept that I'm probably picking up on something that's not there. Or that I'm already biased from what Wes has told me and not giving the guy a fair chance.

I yawn and roll my head along the back of my chair to look at Wes. Legs out long in front of him, hands behind his head, elbows wide—he's the picture of ease. He's at home here, I realize.

I wonder if he could see himself putting roots down, or if he's just biding his time until he goes back to his true home in the States. It makes my heart hurt to think of him leaving, which is exactly why we can't be more than friends. He must sense my gaze because he turns his head my way, giving me a smile that brings both dimples into sharp relief in the firelight. He's so beautiful like this.

"You getting tired? We can go."

I don't want to drag him away from his friends, but it's been a long day and I'm fading fast.

"I think I'll help Talia tidy up a bit." I move to stand, and he starts to follow. I reach out and stop him, letting my fingers graze over the hairs of his forearm. He's pushed the sleeves of his shirt up, warm from sitting this close to the fire. "No, I got it, you stay. Enjoy your friends."

He glances down at my hand and smiles just a little wider. Does he know what his forearms do to me? He gives me a small nod and leans back in his chair, rejoining the conversation with the rest of the group.

I head over to where Talia is gathering everything from dinner and offer to help, grabbing as much as I can fit in my arms before following her into the house. We set everything on the counter, and she starts moving around the kitchen.

"How can I help?" I ask.

"Just keep me company, this shouldn't take me long." She glances over her shoulder, scanning the room to make sure we're alone. "So, what's going on with you and Wes?"

I probably should have seen that question coming, but nope. I am completely blindsided by it. My mouth hangs open like a fish, and I'm unable to form a coherent thought.

"Oh, um, nothing. We're just friends." I fumble out the response, and she throws me a *I don't believe you for a minute* look.

If she had asked me yesterday, I probably would have been a bit more convincing. As it is, with the memory of a naked Wes and the way he pressed himself into me earlier, I don't think I can convince myself there's nothing going on here. Even if there shouldn't be.

"Oh, come on now." She gives me another one of those looks. "Even Breck has told me he's never known Wes to be like this with a girl."

I prepare my protest, ready with all the reasons we're just friends—can only *be* friends—but she continues.

"Even with Brenna. Of course, Breck never saw them together in person, but still."

"Brenna?" I say the name with too much emphasis to get away with it being casual. *Who is Brenna?*

Talia's head whips around like she heard the words I didn't say. Her dark ponytail nearly hits her in the face, surprise evident in her features. She must've assumed I know who Brenna is.

"Brenna..." She trails off. "She's Wes's ex. He hasn't told you about her?"

"He told me he wasn't a relationship guy." I give a noncommittal shrug, trying to pretend it doesn't sting.

"You've never wondered why?" she questions, and I want to roll my eyes. Of course I've wondered.

"I mean, I know his parents didn't have a great relationship. He's also moved around a lot. I guess I just figured he didn't want to settle down."

"You're probably right there. He's not really the 'settling down' type, but the closest he's been was with Brenna. You know about the crash, right?" The condescending tone in her voice grates on me. As if she knows oh-so-much about him and I'm clearly out of the loop. As if her being with Breck somehow makes her the resident expert on all things Wes. This is the first time I've seen this side of her, and I don't care for it.

"Yes, I know about that, but what does—"

"It has everything to do with it," she cuts in. "Wes was with Brenna when he went on that last deployment, and my understanding from Breck is that she fancied being a fighter pilot's girlfriend. Hoped she'd eventually be a fighter pilot's wife."

She pauses for emphasis, eyebrows raised, lips pursed, and I nearly lose my dinner at the thought of Wes married to someone else. Someone *else*? God, what does that even mean? I'm almost thankful when Talia continues talking.

"Between his injuries and the PTSD from the crash, Wes decided he couldn't be a fighter pilot anymore. She left." Talia's arms are crossed against her chest and though she's not exactly smiling, there's this vibe under the surface, like she knows she just dropped a bomb and she's content to watch the world explode around it.

"*What*? Even after everything with Bobby, she just left?"

My face is hot with the anger I feel on Wes's behalf. Seriously, how do I find this Brenna person and kick her ass?

"Yup. I don't think Wes has dated since. I think he pretty much swore off relationships and women after that." She smiles, and it seems genuine, but this whole interaction has given me whiplash. I continue to stand there in stunned silence as she looks me dead in the eye and says, "Until you."

My heart falters a beat and I can't find words to respond.

"So I guess I should ask you again... What's going on with you and Wes?"

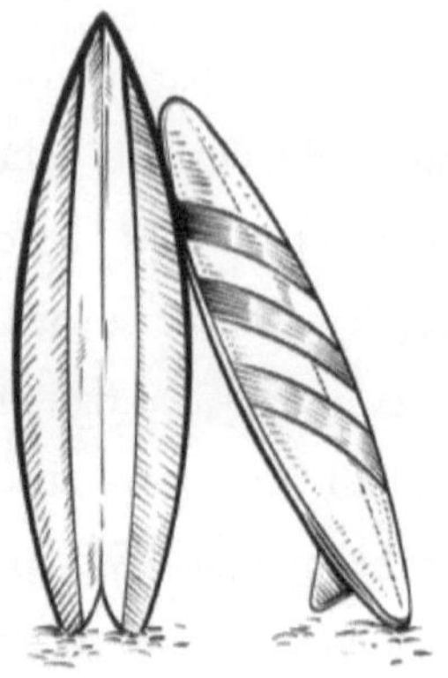

CHAPTER TWENTY

WES

The ride back is quiet, and I don't know what to make of it. Everything felt pretty normal between us once we settled in around the fire. Sitting with Joss's feet draped over the arm of her chair so they rested in my lap. Laughing with my friends. Eating delicious food and talking about all the surfing we've been doing. She never once flinched away from my casual touches.

Yet there's been a distance between us since she left me sitting by the fire. Maybe Talia pushed her Hallmark-movie meant-to-be bullshit like she did with me while I got our food. She doesn't seem to understand that that just isn't our reality, no matter the feelings I'm having to squash down more and more often. The ones screaming that maybe it could be.

By the time we make it up the elevator and the doors slide open on our floor, I can't take the silence between us anymore. I thought I played off the incident after the shower well, I thought we were okay, but maybe we aren't. Maybe she's more upset about it than she's letting on.

"Joss?" There's a tentativeness to my voice that I'm unfamiliar with. I'm not used to feeling unsure of myself.

"Hmm?" She glances briefly over her shoulder before continuing down the hall. The tired look in her eyes almost conceals that there's something more brewing beneath the surface. Almost.

"Can we talk? Please." I stop her with my hand on her elbow and turn her toward me. Her shoulders are hunched and she won't look at me. Her posture looks almost defeated, and my heart wrenches in my chest.

"Wes, I'm really tired. Can we do this tomorrow?"

A pit in my stomach yawns open at the thought of leaving things this way, of going to bed tonight not knowing where we stand. My brain knows that if it doesn't happen tonight, it might not happen at all.

"Joss. Please." She looks up at me, our eyes finally meeting. That look I couldn't place before... I think it's sadness. Whatever she sees in my face makes her soften a little and she nods, stopping at my door when we reach it.

I let us into my apartment, eyes catching on the wine right where she left it on the counter. Just before she walked in on me naked. Fuck. I run my hand through my hair at the thought.

She walks straight to my couch and collapses onto it. Pulling a pillow into her lap and facing the center, she leans back against the arm rest. I feel a little relieved that, whatever's going on, she's still comfortable here in my space. I join her, sitting on the opposite side of the couch. Everything in my body tells me to grab on to her and never let go, but I give her space.

"Is this about earlier?"

Joss speaks at the same time, saying, "Why didn't you tell me about Brenna?" in a similarly rushed breath.

My laugh at us talking over each other chokes off in my throat as her words register. *Why didn't you tell me about Brenna?*

Why in the world would she want to know about Brenna? How does she even know about Brenna? *This* is why she's been quiet? It's not about earlier. It's about *her*.

I glance around, looking for a fire, or maybe a volcano—some explanation for the burning pit I just fell into. I want to crawl out of my skin. It suddenly feels too tight, uncomfortable, squeezing the breath out of my lungs. My heart unable to beat like it should.

Dammit, Talia.

"It's not her fault," Joss says. "She assumed I knew."

I guess I said that last thought out loud.

"No, Joss, I don't think she did." Even to my ears, my voice sounds foreign and curt. I've never been angry around Joss, but I can't keep my emotions in check right now. I scrub at my face, as if that will somehow dissipate the overwhelming anxiety taking over my body at hearing her name.

I physically can't sit still as my mind reels. Shoving off the couch, I only just notice Joss's flinch. I can't breathe the way I could a minute ago. It's like Brenna's name being spoken in this space, where it's never been before, has suddenly changed the air.

Shit. I'm on the verge of a full-blown panic attack. It's been a while since I've had one, and the realization only fuels the inferno. I stride to the patio door and swing it open, gulping down the cold air as it whips around my face. Thinking of her brings that time in my life back in a way that nothing else can. Not even talking about the crash with Joss hit me like this.

I think I hear Joss's voice, but it sounds quiet, like she's talking to me from underwater.

Just breathe, Wes.

There's a trickle of awareness that punctures the fog.

Hands.

On my back.

My breaths are still too fast, but I register the feeling of a soft caress up and down my spine. I think she's counting, but her voice still sounds too far away. I try to match my breaths to the rhythm of her hands. Inhale as they run up my spine, exhale as they run down. Four counts in each direction. The first few breaths feel stuttered and shallow, but I eventually slow them down, focusing on nothing but the feel of her. Joss.

"You're okay, Wes. You're safe here."

Am I safe here? I've felt like I was this whole time, but damn... If simply hearing Brenna's name can send me into a panic attack, am I really safe anywhere? I take a measured step back, my eyes still closed tight, all my focus going into keeping my breaths even. Arms wrap around my middle, Joss's small body pressing into the back of mine.

The image of a koala wrapped around a tree flashes in my mind. Maybe my brain isn't broken if that's what it's conjuring up at this moment.

She stands there, holding me close. I have no words for the gratitude I have for her at this moment. The only other person who's witnessed me in this state is Rory, and though she was as helpful as she could be, I think I prefer Joss's methods better.

"Well—" I break off as my throat catches around the raw emotion running through my body. My mouth feels sticky and my throat is dry. I swallow and try again. "When I said we should talk, this was not how I saw the conversation going."

There you go, Wes, deflect with humor. I can feel her smile against my back, but she doesn't laugh. I turn in her arms, needing to see her—even if it's pity I'll see written on her face.

But when I open my eyes and look down at her, it's only concern and care staring back.

"I'm sorry, Wes, I shouldn't have—"

I cut her off with a finger to her lips. God, they're soft. I appreciate their ability to distract me, if only for a second.

"No, it's not your fault, you had no idea I'd react that way. Fuck, *I* had no idea I'd react that way." The air I attempt to blow out of my lungs is stilted and weak. "Can we sit? I need to sit."

Her arms loosen, but instead of letting her go, I just collapse into the patio chair, taking her with me so that she's sitting across my lap. It creaks and groans under our weight, and I send up a prayer that it holds strong. This is not the *friendliest* position, but I'm not ready to let go of her comfort yet.

"Hearing her name caught me off guard," I say, trying to play it off.

I look at Joss's furrowed brow and feel the moment tilt and expand. I *want* her to understand. Resting against the back of the chair, I find myself wishing for the starry sky in Tahoe.

"Brenna..." I barely get her name out, my voice shaking over the two syllables. It's the first time I've said it in so long, and it feels like acid on my tongue. I clear my throat and start again. "Brenna was my girlfriend, which I'm guessing Talia told you. Did she tell you what happened?"

"She told me she left... after the crash. After Bobby."

I snort out a sardonic laugh.

"Yeah, I guess that's true. But that's not the whole story." I can't look at her while I talk about this, so I just keep staring out at the skyline. "I haven't let myself think about her much less talk about her since she left. Fuck, why is this so hard?"

I squeeze my eyes closed and focus on the soft feel of her fingers trailing across my chest. Back and forth, back and forth. Soft and supportive, just like when I opened up about Bobby. Remembering how safe she made me feel then keeps me going.

"I never wanted a girlfriend. Being in a relationship had never appealed to me. I moved around too much, and my parents were far from a glowing example. But being the only single pilot in our squadron was lonely, and I was staring down the barrel of another deployment. Everyone would be getting packages and letters and calendar squares from their significant others, and I just... I didn't want to do it alone. Again."

I wish I could skip all of this, but it needs to be said. I want Joss to understand.

"Brenna just kind of happened. I'm not proud of it, but I started dating her because it was convenient, and she loved the idea of being there for me in those ways. I didn't see the cracks at first. Like how we functioned better as a couple when we were oceans apart. Then Bobby..." I have to clear my throat again as it catches on his name. Joss hears it and gives me a nod, encouraging me to go on.

"When Bobby died and I was flown to the hospital in Hawaii, she didn't come. That should have been the breaking point. I went through three surgeries and was there long enough to start PT. Breck came. Rory came. Even my egotistical, self-centered parents came. She always had an excuse."

The tension in Joss's face does little to mask the fury behind her eyes. If she's mad now, it will only get worse.

"Something that started as a convenience had turned into me relying on her support. She was different when I finally made it home though. I couldn't fly for the first six months because of my injuries, but she was always pushing me to get back in the jet. Like it was a bike that I needed to get back on. It was always veiled as encouragement, support, but I see it now for what it was." My lip curls in disgust, the words tasting sour in my mouth.

Sitting here with a quiet Joss in my lap, her hand on my chest and empathy on her face, highlights the difference between true support and the warped version I got from Brenna.

"I only made it back up in a jet once. Due to my struggles with PTSD and a few of the lingering issues with my knee, flying didn't feel the same. I couldn't do it anymore. When I told her that I was done flying, at least in the capacity she knew, she told me I was a coward." I have to hold back a flinch at the word. "She said she couldn't be with a man who would give up on his dreams so easily."

Fuck, it hurts to remember how quickly it became apparent that she was with me for all the wrong reasons. She wanted the prestige that came with my career, but she didn't really want *me*.

"That last tether of support suddenly snapped. It was good that I was already done flying because I spiraled even worse after that. I'd trusted her, needed her at the worst time in my life, and she abandoned me. Her leaving solidified for me that people will tell you that they love you whether they mean it or not. That trusting someone to take care of your heart is foolish."

My brain is a wreck, struggling against these ideas even as I say them aloud for the first time. Is this really how I feel? Do I believe this still? That solid wall I built feels on the verge of collapse, and I'm not sure what to do with that.

"I'd just lost my best friend, the career I loved. Losing my girlfriend and the support that went with it right after was the universe solidifying those beliefs. It fucked with my head, and I developed some trust issues. Obviously." I stop and laugh sardonically, but Joss remains silent, still rubbing my chest in that soothing motion. "I haven't gone on a single date since. I swore off relationships and decided it was best to learn to take care of myself rather than be vulnerable with someone like that again."

Joss pauses her movements. God, I just word-vomited all over her. I tilt my head slightly only to find silent tears tracking down her face.

"Hey." I brush my thumb across her cheek, catching one as it slides down toward her mouth. "I'm okay. I know it might not seem like it after that, but I am. And if she hadn't done what she did, I wouldn't be here now."

"I'm sorry, Wes. I'm just so sorry." Joss buries her face in my chest, sniffles rocking her whole body. I know she doesn't like for me to see her cry—for anyone to see her cry—so this is oddly the most comforting thing she could do. Like she's giving me a small piece of herself. I wrap my arms tighter around her, a silent thank-you.

"What do you have to be sorry for, sweetheart? You didn't do anything wrong."

"I brought her up. I was jealous and mad that you hadn't told me about her, even though I had no right to be."

I *know* there shouldn't be a swooping feeling in my stomach at hearing her admit she's jealous.

"Joss, you have no reason to be. She couldn't hold a candle to you if she tried. And I wasn't exactly keeping it from you. Like I said, I just don't talk about her, period."

She sits back, eyes clearer, and I can only hope I haven't said too much. I never know when I'll end up on the wrong side of the flirtatious friendship and outright attraction line these days.

"Can I ask you a question?" She hesitates, biting her lip. "You don't have to answer. I don't want to make it worse."

My body tenses, and she must see the nerves cross my face. Her delicate hand reaches up to brush across my cheek and then her thumb presses between my furrowed brows.

"What caused the panic just now? Was it just Brenna or... something more?" She drops her hand, her fingers fiddling in her lap, pulling nervously at the hem of her sweater.

I cover them with mine, lacing our fingers together. "I think she was the trigger. I wasn't expecting her name to come up, so that was a shock, but under other circumstances, it might have been different."

"Other circumstances?"

Now it's her brow that furrows, confusion marring her beautiful features. Here goes nothing.

"Things have been a bit tense between us tonight. After... earlier." Heat rises in my body as it remembers the way she felt pressed against me. "I could feel you pulling away from me in the car. There was a distance between us that hasn't been there since we became friends. I've been playing off what happened, but the worry that my stupidity earlier was going to take you from me had me on edge. And then to hear her name on your lips, to know that she was part of what created that chasm between us, that I could lose *you* because of *her*... Yeah. It rattled me."

My heart rate ratchets up again, that same panic rising like it did earlier. I can't lose Joss.

"You panicked because of me?" Her voice is quiet. Her eyes are locked where our hands are twined in her lap.

I reach my free hand to lift her chin, forcing us eye to eye. Grey to blue.

"No, Joss. I panicked because I don't want to lose you." The lines are becoming blurrier the more I talk, the tighter I hold her in my arms.

I don't know what I want anymore. I don't even know who I am anymore. I'm not a fighter pilot. I'm not in the Navy. How can I be something more for someone when I don't even know myself? That's why I'm here, right? I can't be what Joss needs. I'm not enough for her. She deserves so much more than the broken shell of a man that I've become.

I'm sure I've said too much, sure she can see all my thoughts written on my face. That she'll run from the wreck that I am. She surprises me with a smile. A *smile*. It's such a small gesture, but everything in me loosens. I'm hanging on tenterhooks for what she'll say, if she'll let me in on whatever has put that look on her face. I never know with this girl.

"I'll never be able to understand how she could leave you." Her smile morphs into something mischievous and playful.

That's definitely not what I was expecting.

"Especially now that I've seen you naked." She draws out the last word and wiggles her eyebrows. She's teasing, and I am so grateful for her in this moment.

My head falls back as I laugh.

If you'd asked me when I walked out here, mid–panic attack, if I'd be laughing just a short while later, I would have said you were crazy. Joss is laughing now too, and the sound does something to my heart. It's like a balm to all the shattered and bruised places I've been trying to mend for the last year.

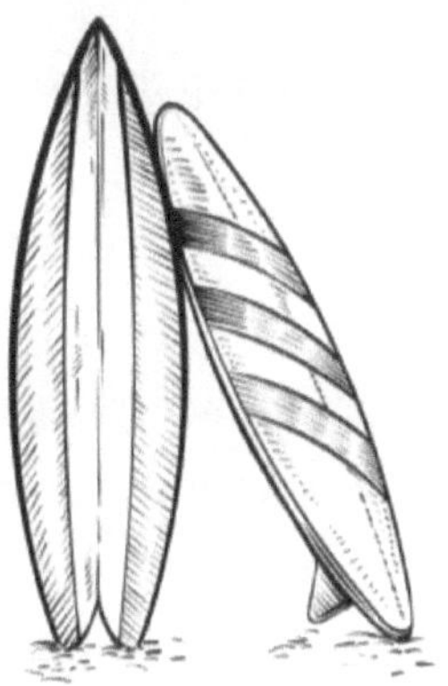

CHAPTER TWENTY-ONE

WES

"Remind me what exactly it is we're doing again?" I call out to Joss through her closed bedroom door.

"Jaz has a date," she calls back, and I sigh. I know this part. The part I'm fuzzy on is where Joss and I come in.

"Yes, that I get. What are *we* doing?"

"Well, Jaz really likes this guy, and he suggested a double date with a couple of his friends, but they had to pull out last-minute. So Jaz, in a moment of sheer stupidity, suggested that *we* go instead."

"Correct me if I'm wrong, but isn't the second couple on a double date usually, you know, a couple?"

She finally walks out of her room in a pair of tan suede leggings and a cream sweater that drapes off her shoulder. There's something in the way it hangs, like if I gave it a little tug I could see more of her—*all* of her.

"You're gorgeous." I can't stop the words, though they come out a bit breathless.

My eyes rake over her in a way that is decidedly *not* friendly. When I finally drag my eyes to her face, her cheeks are flushed in that way I love, and the grey of her eyes looks darker.

"Thank you." Her eyelashes flutter as she glances away. "And to answer your question, yes, *usually* that is how it works, but she panicked and we were the first people she thought of."

Her gaze comes back to me in a slow perusal. I see myself through her eyes—my dark jeans and button-down shirt that ironically matches the color of her sweater. I don't have a lot of dressy clothes. I anticipated a lot of surfing and flying and not much else on my schedule this year. When Joss told me we were going out tonight and that I needed to dress up, I scrambled for over an hour. Based on the look in Joss's eyes though, I didn't do too bad. I follow her throat as it bobs with a swallow before she speaks again.

"Are you okay with this? I didn't know how to tell her no."

She's chewing her lip nervously. Is she really worried that I wouldn't want to spend the evening with her, especially when she's looking like that? I step toward her and pull her lip free with my thumb, then let it linger on her chin.

"Grey, seriously, it's fine. What's the plan?"

She's flustered by my touch, and as much as I love it, I know I need to tread carefully. I take a step back, putting some distance between us before I do something stupid like kiss her.

We're always a little flirtatious these days, but the last thing I want to do is anything that might drive Joss away or scare her off. We've been honest with each other since the beginning about our different stances on relationships. That hasn't changed... as far as she knows.

For me, there's been a shift these last few weeks, in more ways than one. Since the night at Breck and Talia's, I've felt lighter. I've caught myself a dozen times daydreaming about waking up next to someone, sharing about my day, fingers entwined with another's. Laughing with someone over the little things.

And not just someone. Joss.

It's only Joss I see when I consider this possibility. But how can I pursue something with her when my time here is destined to run out? It would only end up hurting us both.

Joss's voice pulls me out of my head. "Jaz's date, Paul, got tickets to whatever show they have at the Opera House tonight—I think she said it was *An American in Paris*." There's a glimmer of excitement in her eyes. "And a reservation for dinner at Aria beforehand."

"Wow, fancy. No wonder you asked me to dress up. So are we..." I trail off, wondering how to put this in a way that won't freak her out. "Are we, like, a couple for the night?"

Her eyes dart away. "We don't have to act any differently. No need to make it weird."

"Make it weird?" My head tilts to the side, eyebrows raised.

"We don't have to kiss or anything. We just act like us, and I'm sure we'll be fine."

"Okay. No kissing, got it. Time to go?"

It's good to know, but damn, I wish that wasn't her hard and fast line. I wouldn't mind having an excuse to get my mouth on hers. One where there aren't expectations. The mouth in question is worrying that bottom lip again, and I don't think she realizes what the action does to me.

"Yeah. Yeah, let's go." She looks me over one more time, eyes burning a trail down my body, before she grabs her coat. "You look nice too. I meant to say that before."

She doesn't quite meet my eye and the color in her cheeks deepens again. Tonight is going to be fun.

The restaurant is situated to have a gorgeous view of both the Harbour Bridge and the Opera House. I swallow and smooth down my shirt. This is the fanciest restaurant I've been to in a long time. My usually confident demeanor wavers, wondering if they're going to let me inside in my jeans. What if I ruin this night for everyone? Not to mention this is my one chance at a date, no matter how real, with Joss.

The hostess doesn't bat an eye at my attire, and I breathe a little easier. We've beat Jaz and her date here, so I lead Joss to the bar, my hand coasting down her back to rest at her hip before pulling out a stool for her.

"Drink of choice when you're out at a bar?" I ask. This feels like something I should know, but seeing as most of our nights include pizza and beer or takeout and wine, this is all new terrain.

"Gin usually. G&Ts are my go-to, unless there's something more fun on the menu." She picks up the cocktail menu, smokey eyes scanning the options. A smile breaks across her face as her finger stops on a blueberry gin martini. "That's the one for tonight."

"It's on me." I wave the bartender over and order her drink, along with a scotch—neat—for myself. At some point during my naval career, I became a scotch man, though I don't usually buy it to drink at home. When he returns with our drinks, we clink our glasses together, eyes holding over the rims.

A little hum slips from Joss's mouth, her eyes fluttering closed, clearly enjoying the taste. She does a little shimmy with her shoulders, which I take to mean she approves. I've seen her do this with food too, and it never fails to make me smile. She catches me staring and, in true Joss fashion, crimson floods her cheeks. I love how reactive she is to my attention.

"Joss!" The voice that calls out is distinctively Jaz as it carries across the bar.

She has her hand linked with a tall man in a navy-blue suit. His skin is a richer, darker shade of brown compared to hers. The smile stretched across her face indicates how into this guy she is.

She pulls Joss into a hug, releasing her date's hand in the process. They hug and squeal their hellos, as if we didn't see her for coffee after our surf this morning.

"Hi. I'm Wes." I introduce myself to her date, chuckling over the spectacle the girls are making.

He extends a well-manicured hand. "Paul. I'm glad you two could join us. I'd have hated to see these tickets go to waste."

Joss extricates herself from Jaz and the rest of the hellos go by in a blur of hugs and handshakes. I settle my bar tab right before our name is called, and we follow a waitress to a table in front of floor-to-ceiling windows. The view is stunning. Lights dance on the surface of the harbour, and the reflection of its iconic bridge against the water is mesmerizing. The water is so smooth you can almost imagine there being an entire city sprawled underneath.

My hand settles low on Joss's back again while I pull out her chair. There's the smallest shiver that spreads across her skin at my touch before she takes her seat. I claim the chair next to her, our thighs rubbing beneath the table and shoulders bumping as we get settled. I relax in my seat, throwing an arm around the back of her chair. That ever-present electricity hums to life at our proximity.

I take in the couple cozied up across from us as we chat and look at the menu. Paul rotates between holding Jaz's hand under the table and running a hand along the nape of her neck, brushing her russet curls over one shoulder tenderly. It warms me to know Jaz has someone so attentive at her side.

The pair orders a round of drinks a few minutes after we're seated, then we get straight into the *getting to know yous*.

"Do you like sports, Wes?" Paul asks, glancing sidelong at Jaz—who rolls her eyes.

"Don't let him get started, Wes, or he will talk your ear off about cricket all night."

I laugh but humor Paul. "I was really into hockey in high school and still keep up with how the Sharks are doing when I can. Unfortunately, I doubt they'll get much coverage here."

We only bore the girls with sports talk for a few minutes before Jaz pivots the conversation to travel, something we all seem to have in common.

"Joss spent most of our time in the Maldives in the water—on one board or another—while I spent most of my time in a hammock or on the beach with my book and a drink."

"It's not my fault you're athletically inept," Joss jokes.

"Harsh. I went snorkeling, remember?" Jaz says in her own defense.

"Yeah, because you refused to scuba with me." Joss's eye roll sends the two of them into a fit of giggles, leaving Paul and I to exchange a look of bewilderment.

A scuba story of my own pops into my head. "I went scuba diving in Thailand and my buddy Bobby saw a leopard shark. I swear he nearly crapped himself." I chuckle, along with the others, surprised at the ease I feel talking about Bobby. "I missed it, too interested in following a little blue fish through some coral. But when he finally got my attention, he was holding his hand up in front of his face like a fin, eyes bugging out of his head."

I feel a light squeeze above my knee. Joss's way to signal her support, to show me she's proud I'm taking the steps to move forward—to talk about him again.

"How did you two meet?" Paul questions, looking between us.

"You want to take this one, Grey?" My laugh starts low in my belly, my shoulders shaking a bit as the vivid memories chase me down.

Joss's eyes dance with laughter too, and I remember her attempted retelling of this story with Jaz that first day at Harbour Grounds. She elbows me in the ribs, and I catch her arm, sliding my fingers down until they lace with hers. The look in her eye turns warmer, heated.

"Fine, but you know I'll be sure to portray you in the worst possible light, right?"

"Oh, I would expect nothing less." I wink at her, and her perfect smile spreads wide across her face.

She tells the story from the airplane, ensuring that my falling on her and groping her are front and center in the narrative. She remembers more details than I would have expected, like how I stumbled through trying to talk to her. She gets some good laughs from the table at my expense, but I don't mind.

When she gets to the part where she chased me down in the airport, she pauses, a question in her eyes. "What were you thinking when you saw me coming after you?"

Huh, not the question I was expecting. How have we never talked about this?

"I guess I couldn't quite believe my eyes. I'd watched for a sign from you as I made my way off the plane, hoping you'd give me one more look, but you didn't. I assumed I'd never see you again. Then, there you were, calling my name, face painted with that beautiful flush"—I run my thumb across her cheek, eliciting a small gasp—"and I thought I must be hallucinating."

This next part, if I share it, will lay more of me bare than I've ever given her, more than she's likely ready for. But this could be the perfect chance to say these things, without the pressure of it all being "real."

"Looking at you standing there, my name having just slipped from your lips..." At the word, I swipe my thumb across hers. "My only real thought was *mine*."

Mine. Mine. *Mine mine mine.*

I remember the way my heart beat faster seeing her there, how it jolted when that single word flitted through my mind. It was possessive, and I couldn't understand why on earth I had thought it—about a complete stranger, no less. But there's always been something about Joss, and something in me knew it wanted her from the start.

I don't look away, just letting the word hang heavily between us. I wish I could read her mind because I sure as hell can't read her expression. I don't think she was expecting the earnestness—neither was Jaz if the look on her face tells me anything. It's softer, almost knowing, like she's in on some secret. I'd love it if she'd explain it to me, because I feel like I'm adrift after that confession, and I need something to pull me back to shore.

Joss glances away finally to look at Jaz, jutting her thumb my way.

"Knew it. He was a possessive caveman from day one."

Paul laughs and runs a hand down Jaz's arm, drawing her attention away from whatever look she was exchanging with Joss. I feel Joss trail her gaze from where our hands are intertwined between us, up the length of my body, until she reaches my face. My breath hitches at the way her lips part and her tongue runs across them.

Jaz and Paul are talking now, giving us a moment. The heat of Joss's body infiltrates my space as she leans close. Is she...?

She brings her mouth close to my ear. A small shiver of disappointment runs through me when I realize she's not going to kiss me. But then she whispers words that are just for me. "I don't think I would have chased you down if you were anybody else. I think part of me felt like you were mine too."

I can't find enough air in the space between us, and I don't know how to respond. I pull back just enough for our eyes to catch and hold, more being said in the silence than we're ready to say out loud. Trying to silently scream across the inches between us that this doesn't feel fake.

Jaz shatters the moment when she asks Paul what he first thought when he saw her at Harbour Grounds, and we launch into more easy banter as we make our way through our meals.

By the time dessert rolls around, I'm stuffed. Paul must be feeling the same way as he stretches and groans across from me. "We have about half an hour before we need to be at the Opera House. What do you say we walk off that dessert and stroll through the Botanic Gardens for a bit?"

It sounds perfect to me, but I look to Joss for confirmation. She's the one in heels. She gives a lazy nod, and I can't help but lift my hand to swipe a tendril of hair behind her ear.

We aren't acting any differently than we usually do, but in the context of this double date and the restaurant's romantic atmosphere, every touch feels like more. Every look feels like more. There's so much *more* to be had with Joss, and I can't decide whether that exhilarates or terrifies me.

The walk to the gardens doesn't take long, and though I've been in the city for a few months now, I haven't made my way down here yet. I'm disappointed to see that the bats that used to cling to the trees in droves are gone now.

When I was here in college, you'd walk through these trees during the day and they'd be completely black from all the bats that covered the branches. At night you'd hear them swooping around and see them as they flew through the skies. It was majestic. When I ask about them, Paul tells me they were relocated shortly after I graduated.

I reach for Joss's hand as we continue our walk, bringing her closer, unable to keep from touching her in some way. She looks up at me, grey eyes shining bright under dark lashes. Her beauty stops me in my tracks. Stops my heart too. The lights in the garden are soft, meaning that most of what I see of her face is thanks to the glow from the moon above us.

There's a moment when I almost just say "fuck it" and kiss her, and a similar one in which I see that same desire mirrored on her face. But then she turns to keep walking, dragging me behind her, and it's gone.

What she doesn't know is that the more she pulls me along, the more I realize I might just follow her anywhere.

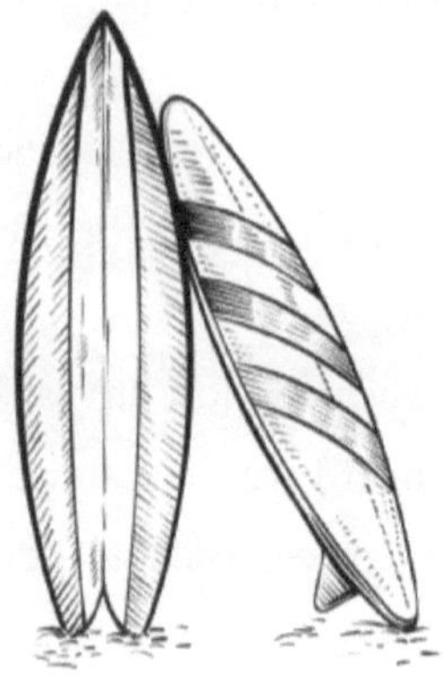

CHAPTER TWENTY-TWO

Joss

After our non-date last week, Wes and I have moved forward, business as usual. We haven't talked about Brenna since the night on the balcony, the shower debacle is well behind us, and we did not kiss under the moonlight, so I'd say we're doing just fine. Totally fine.

But each flight of this trip, each subsequent night in a hotel, each new airport I've walked through has been filled with thoughts of it all.

The irony isn't lost on me that we both have abandonment issues when it comes to relationships. Or that we manifest our desires for a future in completely different ways. His way of coping is to reject any form of long-term relationship, preferring not to open himself up to get hurt. My way of coping is to reject any form of casual relationship, only wanting something if I know I can trust the other person to never leave me.

How well has that worked out for you, Joss? I practically roll my eyes at the thought. Not well, obviously. Eric being case and point.

I don't want to see Wes, this amazing man, go without love because some vapid woman couldn't love him for the right reasons. Especially after experiencing what *dating* Wes would be like. And that wasn't even the real thing—yet, his words continue to pop up in my head any chance they get.

My only real thought was "mine."

The possessiveness of those words should probably bother me, but instead there's a flutter in my stomach every time I remember his confession. This man. A man who doesn't want a girlfriend, doesn't want a relationship. His first thought at seeing me, even when he thought he never would again, was *mine*. Bloody hell. I really didn't expect to like that so damn much.

I have spent way too much time thinking about this. Thinking about me and him. Us. Could there be an us if we weren't both so screwed up from our pasts? I keep pushing those thoughts away, unwilling to entertain the possibility of being rejected by Wes. Worse though are the thoughts of him leaving and never coming back when his time here comes to an end. It's already been three months and they've gone so quickly—nine more doesn't seem like enough.

As I stare out a hotel window in New Zealand, taking in the flow of late-night flights at the airport in the distance, I'm jolted by the thought that I'd rather be home. Wes and I have been texting back and forth nonstop about plans for this weekend, and each ping of my phone has me grinning like a schoolgirl at the small lit-up screen.

Me

> I was thinking we should hit up a surf camp or something? Get out of the city. Do something different.

Wes

> That sounds amazing. Breck and Talia are having people over again, but we could blow that off.

As much fun as I had that night by the bonfire, I can't shake the feeling that Talia had ulterior motives for bringing up Wes's ex. And with the weird vibes I picked up with Drew and her, I don't know if I want to be around her all that much at the moment.

Wes

> Let's go somewhere.

Did he know I was hesitating? Probably, and I love that entirely too much.

Me

> Ok, I'll look for some options and send them your way.

Wes

> Cool cool cool.

> My apartment is lonely without you next door. And I have to order dinner for one which just seems sad.

Tell me about it. Eating pizza alone in this hotel room is not nearly as fun as eating it at your place with a movie.

When are you back again?

Thursday evening. You think you could take Friday off?

I'll check the schedule and make sure I don't have a flight, but I think I can swing it.

The next two days are a blur of airplanes and hotel rooms, and by the time we set up for landing, I'm ready to be home. A kaleidoscope of pinks and purples melt into the Pacific, greeting us on our descent, and the puffy white clouds we drift through shift from yellow to deeper orange. There is no better view in the world.

I've called this city home for nearly twelve years, and there's not another place I'd rather be.

The second the plane touches down, I reach for my phone. This morning I sent Wes my plan for the surf trip and I've been giddy to hear what he thinks. I can already see it in my mind's eye. Packing up the car before the sun rises, then driving north and spending a few carefree days relaxing, surfing, and enjoying the company of my new favorite person.

Instead of Wes's name being the first thing I see, it's a message from an unknown number, and my heart sinks to the pit of my stomach. My pulse spikes as I stare at the words on the screen. My stomach roils like it's full of snakes and my nausea has nothing to do with the gusty landing we just made.

I'd love nothing more than to turn my phone back off and not deal with this. Stick my head in the sand and pretend I never got this message, but from experience, I know that won't lead to me getting what I want.

How does she even have my number? I've changed it since the last time we saw each other, needing as much distance as I could put between us. I hear her voice in my head: *I'm your mother, Joss, you can't hide from me.* Words that were once a joke when I was a kid playing hide and seek. She was always good at finding me, even in my best hiding places.

Unknown number

> Darling! I'll be in Sydney this weekend, need to see you! Please make time for your mother, it's been too long.

No shit, Mom. It's been seven years.

And still that somehow doesn't feel like long enough. My gulping breaths attempt to fill my lungs. Seven years since we've seen each other, seven years since we've spoken, and yet now she wants to see me? What am I supposed to do with this? For all she knows I could be working this weekend. Not that she'd care; she'd expect me to make time for her regardless.

Oh *hell* no! That is definitely not happening, not after last time. And who is "we"? God, if she thinks she can bring *him* back into my house, she has another thing coming. My breath kicks up and no matter how hard I try to settle the pounding in my chest, I'm left gasping and sweating. Is this a panic attack? Is this how Wes felt?

Shit, Wes. We're supposed to leave town tomorrow. My thoughts are a wild jumble. Impossible to follow as they jump from my mother to Wes. I make myself lean forward, head toward my knees.

"Joss? You okay?"

It's Katy, the second flight attendant, and all I can do in my current state is lift my right arm and give her a thumbs-up.

Yup, totally fine. Obviously.

I need to get it together. I have a job to do—I can figure this out when I get home. I take a couple more deep breaths, going to my happy place and grounding myself in it.

I'm at least a tiny bit calmer when I sit up and see Katy eyeing me speculatively.

"I'm okay, really. Just got a bit dizzy. All good now."

Deplaning and cleaning takes a lifetime. By the time it's finally done, I just want my sweats and some wine and to pretend that I never got those messages.

One foot in front of the other, I walk off the plane. My emotional state resembles a dumpster fire. I've stewed and stressed over how to get out of this. I've run through every scenario I can think of. I know she won't give up; she'll just keep spinning it until I finally give in and agree to make time for her. There's no way she can stay with me, especially if *he* is with her. Just thinking of it makes bile rise in my throat.

I'm so far into my own thoughts that I barely acknowledge Frank as I pass through the doors to my building. I'm even less alert as I walk out of the elevator toward my apartment, completely missing Wes opening his door when I pass.

It's not until he's by my side, pulling on my arm and saying my name, that I register he's there.

"Joss? You okay? Are you sick again?" His brow is furrowed as I watch his lips move.

I'm so out of my head that I reach up and use my thumb to soothe away the lines carved between his brows. This gets me an eyebrow raise, which does fix the lines at least, but the smirk and confusion on his face finally break through my stupor.

"Oh, yeah. Yeah. I'm okay." Am I? I turn back to my door and try to get it unlocked, but my hand shakes. My frustration is rising, threatening to crest like a rogue wave, when warmth covers my hand, steadying it. Steadying me. It's this touch, the electricity of it, that brings me fully back to my senses. I look up into his eyes as the door swings open and let out a little sigh, shoulders slumping. "I guess it's time I tell you about my mother."

A look of surprise takes over his handsome face. I've never said a word about my parents to Wes. He asked once and I deflected. He hasn't brought it up again. Lately, there's been a nagging tug in the back of my mind telling me that trust goes both ways. Wes has trusted me with his darkest moments, maybe it's time I trust him with mine. I don't know that I have much choice now anyway.

"Oh-kay." He swoops his hand out to the side. "Uh, let me grab something from my place and I'll be right back, yeah?"

"Yeah, I need a minute anyway. Gotta change out of this stupid uniform."

"Nothing stupid about that uniform, Grey." He gives me an exaggerated wink and smiles, all dimples, as he walks backward toward his door. He's trying to lighten the mood, and amazingly, it does just that.

"Get out of here, you." I swat the space between us. He keeps smiling until he's at his own door and slips inside.

Two minutes. I was in his presence for two minutes and he somehow took me from a spiraling mental mess to a smiling fool. He makes me feel more at ease than I have with any man I've ever met.

I close my door, head for the bedroom, and slip into my well-loved purple sweats before dropping my entire uniform into the laundry basket. Good riddance for another five days. I slide on a white tank and throw Wes's old college hoodie over my shoulder. He left it here one night about a month into our friendship, and I've since claimed it as my own. I'm not sure he realizes I have it, and I'm not about to tell him how often I end up sleeping in it. Tonight, I plan on pulling from it the strength I don't feel.

I hear a light knock before Wes lets himself in, followed by an obnoxious "I'm walking into your apartment, please make yourself presentable."

The small smile I had on my face two minutes ago pales in comparison to the full-on laugh that escapes me now.

"Staahhhppp," I plead as I join him in the living room, and he laughs in earnest. "You just had to bring that up. It was *one time*."

I bump him with my hip and trudge over to the fridge.

"The best time of your life, am I right?"

"Oh geez, there he is. There's that cocky man I met on the plane, I wondered where he went." I roll my eyes and reach for the bottle of rosé I stocked earlier in the week.

"Is this a big glass or small glass kind of talk we're about to have?" Wes's voice is casual, but I can hear the undercurrent of concern there.

When I look over the fridge door, he's standing with one of each in his hands, weighing them up and down.

"Definitely the big one," I say with a smirk.

"I knew you liked big ones." The way he deadpans this statement nearly makes me drop the bottle of wine.

I recover quickly and volley my comeback. "True, not sure why I hang around you then. All you've got going on is that big ego."

I shoot him a devilish smile, proud of myself for that sick burn.

"Ouch, Joss. Taking size jokes to a whole new level." He shakes his head at me like he's disappointed. "You get the small one for that—and I'm taking my hoodie back too."

He moves to put the large wineglass back in the cupboard.

"No! I'm sorry." I put my hand on his arm to stop him and give him my biggest doe eyes, rapidly blinking my lashes.

"Okay, you can keep it, but only because you're my favorite," he says before giving me a little peck on the cheek. Placing the small glass back in the cupboard, he grabs a second large one and turns to walk into the living room, leaving me stunned.

I recover quickly, grabbing the bottle of rosé with a grin, my cheek pleasantly raw from his stubble. Steeling myself, I walk into the living room to have a conversation with *my* favorite person... about my least favorite person.

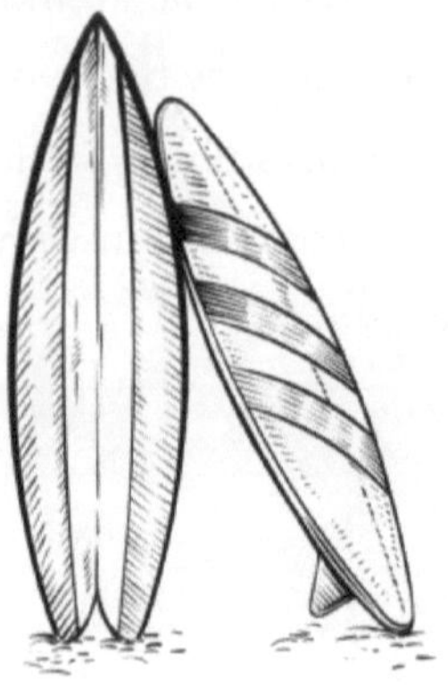

CHAPTER TWENTY-THREE

Joss

We're sitting on opposite sides of the couch while I fiddle with the hem of Wes's hoodie. He's quietly watching me, giving me the space to talk when I'm ready. I don't think I'll ever be ready for this. The way he never talked about Brenna... That's how I am with my mom. The difference being that his silence lasted less than a year, and mine has been going for seven.

I pick up my glass off the coffee table, taking a fortifying sip of liquid courage, and lock all my emotions up tight so I can get through this. Then I start at the beginning.

"My dad left when I was fourteen. He had an affair, and another daughter as a result. He started another family and I... I haven't heard from him since. He chose them over us."

"Shit, Joss, I had no idea. I'm so sorry."

I shake my head. I don't want his pity, especially on this. That's just a small part of the story, and if he's feeling sorry for me already, things will only become more difficult as I keep going.

"It's okay. Well, no. It's not." I huff out a breath, my shoulders sagging. "But it's not your fault, and honestly, that betrayal was just the first of many."

He reaches across the couch to grab my hand and gives it a light squeeze. When I finally look at him, that pity I thought I heard has been replaced with concern. He's giving me support so I can keep going, and it feels like everything.

"After he left, my mom... She didn't cope well. She moved us around a lot, trying to find me a *new dad*." I add air quotes, rolling my eyes at the idea. Wes stays silent, and it gives me the strength to continue. "I went to five schools in four years. We moved from one man's house to the next—Melbourne to Adelaide, and just about everywhere in between. My mom was always so sure that each would be *the one*. They never were."

It always made me so mad how she pretended it was all for me. In reality, *she* wanted someone who would provide for her. Whether that extended to me was just a bonus.

"The first few guys weren't too bad, but they got progressively worse. The last one before I turned eighteen took the cake. I don't know what exactly he did to keep himself and my mom living the lifestyle they had, but I suspect it wasn't above board."

The memories of that house weave through my mind. "I can't tell you how often I stayed with friends or slept in my car just to avoid being there. The number of times I slept in the back of the surf shop I worked at—something I never told the owners. It's a wonder I was never arrested." I shake my head. Those weren't details I'd planned to tell Wes. The fact that I'm about to share the next part makes my heart rate spike and blood pound in my ears.

"Just before I graduated high school, there were some things I needed from the house, so I went home after school. That day, my mom was out but Tom was there." I gulp down air and slide my wineglass onto the table as my hand starts to shake. Wes sees it and envelopes it in his, anchoring me. I lock eyes with him, seeing the fear etched there, of what I'll say if I keep going.

"When he realized we were alone, he made a pass at me. He... he grabbed for me." I shudder, tensing up, but Wes's hand holds mine steady. "He must've thought he'd be able to overpower me, but he was drunk and I was fast. I was out the door and in my car before anything could happen. I never went back. I stayed with a friend for the last few days of school, and then right after graduation, I got in my car and put Adelaide in my rearview for good."

The rage rippling off Wes is palpable, and I have to look away. I've refused to give the memories the power of making me cry, and I plan to keep it that way.

"I'd already set up an interview in Sydney for a job with Qantas, so I drove the fifteen hours straight through to get here. I wanted to leave all that darkness behind me, and when the opportunity to train as a flight attendant came up, I gave it all I had.

"My mom eventually tracked me down. The car was registered to their insurance, and I still had my phone that they paid for. I'd left everything else behind in that house though, so I had to start over from scratch, make my own way."

I rush to get the next part out. "When I told my mom what happened, I expected her to leave him, to finally stand up for me, to rage and rush to defend her daughter. She didn't. Instead, she blamed me. It was my fault that he'd kicked her out. It was my fault she lost everything."

I sigh, wanting to just be done with this story. "I guess Tom didn't like being made a fool of, and that was how he felt when I got away. I'd wondered why my mom hadn't shown up to my graduation. It turned out she was angry I'd cost her her meal ticket."

When I put all the pieces together, the despair and loneliness I felt was deep enough to cut, and it had nothing to do with being new in a big city.

"God, Joss. No wonder you never talk about her." Wes's words break through my stream of consciousness, and I'm thankful for it. I catch the way his nostrils flare and feel his grip on my hand tighten—he looks about ready to burst with anger on my behalf while he tries to process. He's almost vibrating with it, and if this whole situation weren't so fucked up, I'd probably laugh at the irony.

This man, who I've known for just three months, is reacting the way I thought my mom would when I told her I was nearly assaulted by her boyfriend. I give his hand a little squeeze, running my thumb back and forth, silently thanking him for being the man he is. He looks on the verge of losing it, and this isn't even the end of the story. I hope he can hear it without breaking anything.

"Yeah, well, it gets better." I try to infuse my tone with as much nonchalance as possible, taking the power away from the events

I'm about to relive, but I know it'll be a feeble attempt. There's no disguising the pain of what broke us for good.

"I told her to leave me alone. She went back to him and begged him to take her back—because of course she did." My head shakes as I say the words—they still seem unbelievable even to me. "I took over my phone bill and the insurance, cutting myself off from their finances and influence entirely. I thought that would be enough. They were together for a while, but I knew they'd broken up when she called me a few years later and told me she'd moved again but that this time, she'd found *the one*. Again." I scoff, and it comes out maniacal. "She claimed she was so happy. He was so wonderful. Blah blah blah."

I should have known better. I should have never taken that call. I should've changed my number when she didn't believe me and took the word of a predator over her own daughter. There were so many things I should have done, but thinking about them isn't going to change anything.

"She sounded genuinely happy, and we slowly started reconnecting. Emailing, calling, just checking in. She seemed different, better. She was happy for me that I had a job I enjoyed and that I was finding success for myself. She asked if she and her new boyfriend could come visit me in Sydney. At that point, it'd been several years since I last saw her. She said she missed me, that she really wanted me to meet him because she thought they might get married, and she wanted me to be there when they did."

I can still remember that whole conversation like it was yesterday. The little girl inside me was desperate for us to be okay, for her to want to have a relationship with me. I close my eyes and can hear all her words in my head. When I open them again, Wes is watching me intently, still holding my hand. My rock in this storm.

He's closer now too. Sitting in the middle of the couch, one leg bent in and the other hanging off the side, my feet just against his shin. He's got one arm propped on the back of the couch, holding my hand, and the other looks ready to grab on to me at any moment.

"I said yes." My words come out hollow, sad. "I wanted to reconcile. I hoped it would fill the void my dad left, that *she* left. They came and stayed with me for a couple days. I was living in a tiny one-bedroom apartment at the time. There was barely enough room for us all to be there, but they brought an air mattress, and for the first two days, it was nice. Almost normal. They took me out to dinners, we walked around the city, and we even splurged to walk overtop the Harbour Bridge together. I introduced them to Jaz and we drank too much coffee at Harbour Grounds. I was just so happy to feel like I had family again. I let my guard down."

God, I can't even look at him now. The fingers of my free hand pull at the hem of the hoodie until I'm afraid I'll shred it if I don't stop. I swallow the lump in my throat, wanting this to be over, for it all to be out there.

"It was a Wednesday. I'll never forget. I had to get up early for a trip in the morning, and my mom and Bill—" I break off. I haven't uttered his name in seven years. "They weren't moving very fast that morning. I was going to be late, so I kissed my mom goodbye and told them to lock the door on their way out. I was gone for three days, and when I got back, anything that was easy to move, easy to sell, everything of value that I owned was gone. My laptop, gone.

The few pieces of jewelry I had, gone. I didn't have a lot, but they took anything they could fit in their car."

I feel the first tear slip down my cheek, and Wes's thumb brushes it away. The second follows a few seconds later, and then it's all over. Fuck.

"God, this is so embarrassing." I close my eyes, wiping at my face and looking up to the ceiling. I still carry so much shame and anger over what happened because it was my fault. I should have never trusted her.

"Joss?" My name is a gentle question. He waits for me to look at him, and when I do, there's no pity, even the burning rage has dissipated. Instead, all I see is sadness—because he cares. "That was not your fault, you know that, right?"

"Yeah, but I chose to trust her, to trust him. I allowed them into my house and I left them alone there. I should have known better."

"But Joss, you were young. You were, what, twenty-two? Twenty-three? You're supposed to be able to trust your own mother. This is not on you—this is on them."

My shoulders shake with the sob I can't contain. Aside from the few times I've allowed myself to cry with Wes, I hadn't cried a single time since that day. Not once since I walked into my ransacked fourth-floor apartment in Marrickville and realized what she'd done. I locked my emotions up tight. I thickened my skin. I never opened myself up to be hurt by someone again. It's why I react instinctively now with anger over sadness. Anger feels empowering, controlled. Sadness, tears... Those emotions feel weak and unrestrained.

His words wash over me again and again. I've told myself those things so many times, and Jaz has insisted them even more. She's the only other person who knows my past because she was there to pick up the pieces. Yet hearing it from Wes is different. The words sink below that thick skin and begin to take root.

I take a steadying breath, needing to finish this story so we can move on. "After I got home and realized what happened, I changed my number. I even moved in with Jaz for a while until I could find a new place. I couldn't stay there any longer. It had been so utterly violated by them that it made my skin crawl. I cut all ties with her and haven't heard anything from her in seven years. Until today."

I'm about to lose it and start crying again. My lip quivers and my vision blurs with unshed tears. Then Wes's strong arms engulf me, and I sag against him in relief and exhaustion while he holds me tight.

I want so badly to stay here in this moment with him, to never let go, to forget the rest of the world, my mom, all of it. But I have bigger problems, and I need Wes to help me figure them out. I push away from him and reach for my phone. I've felt it buzzing in my pocket for the last hour. I can only assume what the messages will say.

I unlock the screen and there they are.

Unknown Number

> Joss, I know we left on bad terms last time, but please let me explain.

> I need to talk to you, we need to make this right.

> Please, Joss. This is important. I'm your mother, you can't just ignore me.

> We will be there Saturday morning. I promise it won't be like last time.

> I love you.

I want to scream and throw my phone across the room, but what would that solve? I hand it to Wes. His eyes widen as they slide down, and I swear his whole body tenses when he reaches the end. The anger and sadness mixed in his expression make my heart ache.

"You're not letting her come here, right?"

"I don't want to. I haven't responded, obviously, but it sounds like she's coming whether I want her to or not." I shrug, feeling almost resigned to that reality.

"But she doesn't know where you live. You've moved."

"She also shouldn't have my number," I say, feeling so frustrated with this invasion of my privacy. "I honestly wouldn't put it past her to know my address."

"Who's coming with her? Is it this Bill guy? They should be in jail, Joss. They robbed you." He's indignant, tossing the phone on the table like it's burned him. It feels good to have someone in my corner.

"I have no idea, Wes. I know exactly as much as you do based on those texts. What do I do?" I need him to tell me what I'm supposed to do here. How am I supposed to deal with this? His grip on my hand grounds me while he takes a steadying breath of his own.

"You should ignore her. She can't get in the building. We tell Frank to keep an eye out for them, and to refuse them entry if they come here. We can still go on our trip; we won't even be here for her to bother you."

Shit, the trip.

"Wes. I don't know if ignoring her is the best idea. I don't know why she's decided now is the time to reconnect, but I'm sure she'll just keep trying. Maybe if I see her, just this once, I can finally leave it in the past."

God, that sounds terrifying. Is that really what I want? If you'd asked me yesterday, I would have said hell no. But today, in light of finally sharing this burden with someone, I think it actually might be.

I can tell by the pinch of his lips and the furrow in his brow that he hates that idea. I use my thumb to press into the lines between his brows again, smoothing the skin.

"If you keep making that face, it's going to get stuck like that."

My lips lift and I'm met by a warm smile in return. His fingers tighten around mine and he brings them to his mouth. It's the smallest touch, just the lightest kiss against my thumb, but I feel it everywhere.

"I don't like the idea of her being anywhere near you, especially not knowing who she's bringing with her. Tell me I can be with you when you see her, please?" The way he says *please* melts my heart.

I lean forward, pressing my face into his chest, and force down the ever-present feelings for this man. It's going to tear me apart when he leaves.

"I wouldn't have it any other way." I breathe into his chest before turning my head and resting it there, listening to his beating heart. "Thank you."

His shoulders relax in relief and he pulls me just a little bit closer.

"Wes, what do I say to her? I can't have her just showing up here. We need to set something up away from my apartment—there's no way she can stay here. I'll struggle to stand my ground... You don't know her. She won't take no for an answer."

"Then you tell her your boyfriend says no."

I pull back so fast that I crick my neck.

"My... boyfriend?" No way did I hear him right.

"Your boyfriend. You tell them that I live here with you, that I'm your boyfriend, and that I'm not comfortable with it. You blame it on me, and then they can't force the issue."

Ah, so this is a show for my mom, got it. My stomach sinks a little, but I push that thought aside. This could work.

"You'd be my fake boyfriend? While they're here?"

I watch him intently, hoping I can pick up on more of what he's thinking, but his face is calm, almost unreadable except for the fire in his eyes. It's hard to tell if it's directed toward me or if it's because he's fired up over the situation.

"Yes." He's so resolute and sure of himself. God, I wish I had half as much confidence.

"Okay. But how would this work exactly? I've never had a fake boyfriend before."

"And you'll be my first fake girlfriend, so I guess we'll have to figure it out together."

The way my heart soars when he says girlfriend is stupid and irritating.

"Why are you doing this?"

"You know why." He fingers a tendril of my hair and slides it behind my ear, giving me goose bumps down my neck. His fingertips trail my jaw to my chin. Holding me there, forcing me to look at him. If I didn't know better, I'd think he was about to kiss me. "I'm not going to let anyone take advantage of you, Joss. You mean too much to me. You've become my closest friend. I need to know you're okay."

That instantly cools the heat that was pooling in my body at his touch. Friend. Right, of course. He isn't interested in a real relationship with me, and I'm not interested in being with someone who can't offer me the stability that I need.

I pull back, needing space, needing to breathe. I stand up, grabbing our glasses that are now very much empty, and head for the kitchen.

Breathe, Joss.

"Hey. You okay?" I hear the concern in his voice, but I can't look at him.

"Yeah, today's just been a lot. I'm getting tired and should go to bed. We can figure out a plan in the morning, yeah?"

I glance over and see him eyeing me. Can he feel me pulling back, just as he's pressing forward?

"Yeah. You sure you're okay? Do you want me to stay awhile?" The sad puppy-dog eyes he's sporting almost break me, but him staying won't help anything. I'll only be digging myself deeper into this hole of feelings that I'm quickly falling into.

"Nah, I'm alright. Just need sleep. Coffee and pastries in the morning?"

Instead of dawn patrol the morning after I get home from a trip, this has become our tradition, so that I can sleep in and decompress.

He nods and closes the distance between us, picking me up in a bone-crushing hug. I melt into it, enjoying the way he's so comfortable holding me, like his arms were made for me.

"Thank you," I whisper into his ear. I let his scent wrap around me like a blanket. "For being you and for being here."

"There's nowhere I'd rather be, Grey."

I sink further into the embrace and let myself believe him.

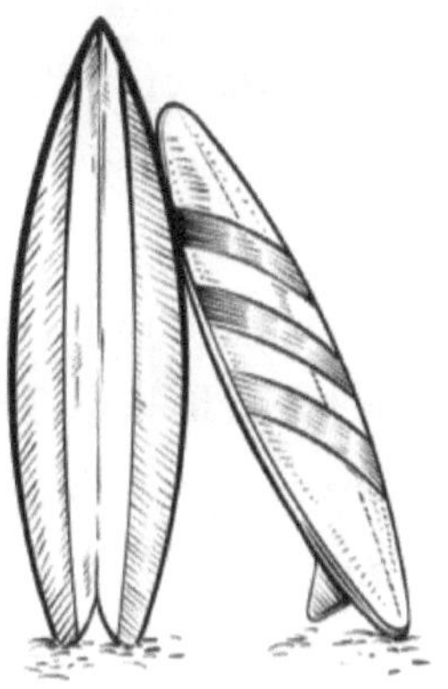

CHAPTER TWENTY-FOUR

WES

Sleep evaded me last night, the conversation with Joss about her mom running a loop around and around in my head. It explains why her circle of friends is so tight, and why she's reluctant to open up and be vulnerable. It's not like my parents were all warm and fuzzy, but to steal from their own kid? Never. They love me and Rory, even if they aren't the best at showing it. But this, what Joss has been through—she deserves so much more than people who abandon her and take advantage of her.

I relax into my couch and prop my feet up on the grey ottoman before taking my first sip of coffee. What is it about that first sip that makes it better than all the rest? I hum as it slides across my tongue and down my throat, easing the tension and tiredness. Since I was up early, I was able to get our coffees and my pick of the freshest pastries this morning.

Jaz hooked us up with an array of Joss's favorites, and she even gave me the locals' discount. For such a small gesture, it made me feel like this could be home for me.

My front door swings open and Joss appears. Did this woman learn nothing? I could be naked in here. The reminder sends my brain down the gutter. *Snap out of it, Wes. This is not helping when you've just agreed to fake date her.*

Fake, not real.

It shouldn't come as a surprise to me that with how tangled up my feelings are becoming, offering such a thing was a terrible idea, but I'm committed now. Her mom is arriving tomorrow, giving us very little time to work out the details.

"Hey, gorgeous," I say, jumping up from the couch and pulling her into a hug. The purple bruising under her eyes tells me she didn't sleep well either, but I'm a smart enough man not to mention that to her.

"Hey, handsome." Her greeting is less enthusiastic, but it's also the first time she's given me a pet name. I've been using them for her since the day we met because I can't help myself, but it's a bright spot hearing one fall from her lips.

"Look at us being all cutesy. We're totally going to kill this pretend relationship thing." I manage to sound like I mean it, even though it's not how I feel. Pretending with her feels just plain wrong. Everything between us has always been honest and true. Joss's face falls a little, and I hope she's not reconsidering. It's the best option we have to get her through the weekend.

"Right, yeah. About that..." she says, her bottom lip finding its way between her teeth while her fingers pull at the hem of her hoodie. *My* hoodie, but I like it on her. "I think we need some ground rules."

Rules, right. I like rules. In fact, they used to make up ninety percent of my day-to-day.

"Okay, but first, coffee. Jaz went all out this morning." I grab her hand and lead her over to where I've laid out a tray with all the pastries and her coffee, which she reaches for first. Then she folds herself comfortably into the corner of my couch.

"Why is the first sip always the best?" she says as she brings her cup to her full pink lips and inhales, a little hum coming from somewhere deep in her throat.

I laugh at where her head's at—the same place mine was just moments ago. I can't seem to drag my eyes away from her when she's relaxed like this, content. That look on her face is not there enough.

I clear my throat and reply with a lame "Yeah, it's the best."

That's all I can think to say, even though my body urges me to say more. To tell her how I wish I could taste *her* instead, that I know she would taste better than any cup of coffee. To say that *she's* the best. But I don't say any of that, I tamp all of those things down because we have enough going on without me throwing around feelings that even I don't understand.

We eat our pastries, avoiding the elephant in the room. Catching up on our lives from the last week feels normal, so we lean into that instead. She tells me about her flights—Sydney to Auckland, Auckland to Honolulu, and then back again in reverse order. I fill her in on my flights and how many amazing jumps I got to see happen. I love the adrenaline even when I'm only flying. It's contagious with so many people preparing to jump out of the plane. Most of them for the first time.

I wish I could tell her that Drew and I are finally getting along, but it would be a lie.

"I don't know what it is with that guy, but he gets under my skin in a way no one else has, which is saying something considering some of the cocky bastards I've worked with over the years." I take a sip of my coffee, emptying the cup, before returning it to the tray. "I tried to skirt the issue with Breck this week, but he insists Drew is just hard to get to know. It feels off though, the way he always gravitates toward Talia."

"Yeah, I didn't get any kind of good vibes from that guy. And you're right, he is weird with Talia, Breck too, but more so with her." She chews on her lip, and I can practically see the wheels turning.

"Exactly, and I get that working in close quarters is part of the job description since they're business partners, but the door to Drew's office is closed more than it's open. Just him and Talia ensconced in there, alone." My brow furrows. Saying all of this aloud only leaves me more confused. "And with Breck constantly out of the office, it just doesn't feel right."

I think of all the work Breck does, all the hats he wears. The last thing he needs is to be worrying about what's going on back at the office. Not when he's responsible for operations and setting up the logistics of all our tours: everything from surf trips to group tours of Sydney's Olympic Park to private winery tastings.

"You don't think there's something going on between them—Drew and Talia I mean?" Joss's voice breaks me out of my thoughts.

"God, I hope not. That would destroy Breck." I shake my head. The idea of Talia cheating on Breck makes my skin crawl. "Maybe there's something going on with the business."

"Maybe... It's odd that they'd exclude Breck for those meetings if so though."

"Hm. Yeah." I blow out a big breath, rolling my shoulders back and throwing an arm across the back of the sofa. My fingers lightly brush against her shoulder, eliciting a small shiver of awareness.

"Let's talk about something else." I say, veering away from Drew-related conversation. "So, ground rules, yeah?" Joss hums and a soft blush heats her cheeks as her glance moves to her lap. Bashful is a new look for her, and I like it.

"I texted my mom back last night after you left. Here, I'll show you." She reaches into her pocket and hands me her unlocked phone with the thread pulled up.

Joss

I'm not sure how you got my number, but if you insist on meeting Saturday, we can. You will need to find somewhere else to stay. My boyfriend isn't comfortable having someone he doesn't know stay in our home, and I agree. If Bill is with you, don't bother coming.

Mom

Bill?

Oh, Bill! Yeah, no, he's long gone. Please reconsider letting us stay with you. It's so hard to find somewhere to stay in the city. I didn't know you were living with someone, do tell.

I hate that she saved her mom's number. I don't think she deserves that courtesy after how she's treated her daughter.

Joss

We won't be reconsidering. We can meet for brunch at Opera Square.

Mom

Fine. You don't have to talk to me like that. I am your mother. Regardless of how you feel about our past, I will always be your mother. Can't we meet at your apartment? It will be more private that way. We just want to be with you.

"Well, shit, she sounds like a real treat, Joss. I can't wait to meet her." I let the sarcasm and disdain drip from every word. How did this person somehow produce the kind, beautiful, and adventurous woman sitting next to me?

"You're sure you want to do this, Wes? I understand if you'd rather not be a part of this mess."

Her eyes shift away from me while she fiddles with the hem of her shirt again. I've noticed she does this when she's nervous or anxious.

I don't ever want her to be those things with me, so I reach across and fold my hand over hers.

"I wouldn't have it any other way." I repeat her words from last night, wanting to reassure her that nothing about her mother is going to scare me off.

"Okay. Well then, first things first. What do I do about where we meet? I don't want them in my apartment; I'd rather not have to move again." Her voice shakes. "She's so stubborn though, and she's going to keep pushing about meeting in private. God knows why."

"We can do it here." It's out before I even think it all the way through, but it makes sense.

"What?" Shock is written all over her face.

"Yeah, even if she knows your address somehow, it's only one off from mine. We can play it off like she got it wrong. We have them come here, that way your space remains safe but they feel like they're winning with the private get-together."

"Okay." She drags out the word. "You're sure? That's a lot to ask of you."

"Joss, I offered. You didn't ask."

She shifts, looking around the room, taking it in with different eyes, and nods.

"We'll have to grab some of my stuff though, make it look more lived-in. You haven't made any changes to the stock furniture and decor since you moved in, have you?"

The observation makes her look a little sad. Why would my not decorating make her sad?

"I haven't had time, I guess," I say with a shrug, my shoulder brushing hers with how closely we're sitting now. "I've never been good at the whole decorating thing, and I've moved so much that I rarely put much effort into it. I just go to your place for that homey feeling anyway."

Her smile comes back at this, and her eyes brighten. She must know that she's what makes this place feel like home to me.

"Oh, okay then. I'll still bring over some stuff to make it feel more *homey*." She winks. "What's our backstory going to be? You've only been here a few months; I don't know how believable it will be to my mom that I moved in with someone so soon."

"Maybe I'm just that good in bed." It's out before I can stop it, and since the damage is probably done, I wink and waggle my eyebrows at her for good measure. She bursts out laughing. "What? You don't believe me? That hurts me, Joss." I jut out my bottom lip, pouting.

"You stop that." Her swat to my shoulder makes my smile reappear. "This is serious, Wes. She'll know. She's like a bloodhound, she'll sniff out the lie if we don't sell it properly, and I don't want her knowing how much effort I'm putting into keeping her at arm's length here. If she senses that weakness, she'll exploit it."

"You're not weak, Grey. You're protecting yourself. I promise I'm taking this seriously. I'll be the best fake boyfriend you've ever had."

"Easy title to achieve since you're the only fake boyfriend I've ever had."

"And I better be the last." At my words, her eyebrows rise a little and I rush to cover for what just slipped out. "That was me showing you how possessive your fake boyfriend can be." I send her another wink, and her eyebrows relax.

I wasn't saying I want to be the last boyfriend she'll ever have—I don't think. Her home is in freaking Australia. My home is... where?

Nope, not going there. Those thoughts need to go somewhere else to be dealt with—well, probably never, but definitely not right now.

"She doesn't need to know I've only been here a few months. We can fudge the timeline a little. We can keep how we met the same. It's such a great story after all." I bump her shoulder with mine. "One for the grandkids, am I right? But we just make out that it happened, what? Six months ago? A year? What do you think she'll believe?"

"Split the difference, nine months? We've been living together for three. We can skip the part about us being neighbors first, yeah?" Her body relaxes with each detail as they fall into place.

"Sounds good." I nod, watching her intently, enjoying the warmth of her body where it presses against the side of mine.

"Ground rules. I want us to still be able to look at each other after this, so we'll need to make sure we don't cross any lines that might affect our friendship. Maybe something similar to our date night with Jaz?" She swallows, and I watch her throat bob. It's like she really had to work to get those words out. Her cheeks are pink and she looks uncomfortable. She turns so her back is pressed into the arm of the couch and her knees are pulled in tight to her chest, her toes skimming my thigh.

"Well"—I up the flirtation in my tone—"if we're living together, she'll assume we're sleeping together." The pink flames to a bright red, but she doesn't look away as I continue. "That obviously won't be happening while she's here, but we need to be comfortable touching each other. If you haven't noticed, I'm a pretty physical guy. Maybe not as much as Breck, but um, yeah. I'm going to need you to spell out what those boundaries are for you. Because I'm not going to lie, if you were mine, I'd probably be all over you all the time."

There's that word again. *Mine*. Fuck.

The blush moves down her neck and I reach over to feel it as it warms her skin. Her eyes are focused on mine and that electric pull between us has my heart pounding in my chest. She's barely breathing as I touch her, like she's unsure of what I might do next.

Instead of letting go and allowing her to lead this conversation, I shift on the couch so I'm facing her. My shin presses over her feet and I leave my left hand resting on her neck, my thumb on her cheek.

"Is touching you like this okay?" I ask, and it comes out more ragged and gravelly than I intended, but I'm not in control of much right now.

She nods, like she can't quite form words. *Me too, Joss, me too.* But I find a way to get them out as I continue. "Holding hands, yeah?" I slide my arm from the back of the couch, trailing it down hers to interlace our fingers.

"Mm-hmm, yeah." Her thumb coasts over the back of my hand, and it's like a live wire brushed my skin.

I bring her hand up, turning it in mine as I press my lips to the underside of her wrist. "What about kissing, Joss?" I bring my eyes back to hers, watching them darken slightly at my words. Good. She is just as affected by our proximity as I am. Whether it's a good thing or not, I'm not actually sure, but I'm sure as hell not going to stop. I can't.

"Um—I-I don't know," she stutters out, but it's barely a whisper.

"What aren't you sure about? Tell me what you're thinking in that pretty head of yours." I let my hand fall farther down her neck so my thumb can coast over her pulse point. It's fast and erratic, just like mine.

"I just... What if kissing is too much? I don't want to jeopardize what we have, our friendship, for a stupid lie. We're too important."

Her eyes are closed now, and I can sense her fear. I'm scared too, but I also haven't felt this alive in a long time.

"Joss, there isn't a single thing that could jeopardize that, I promise you."

She still has her eyes closed, like she's not sure what she might see in mine if she opens them.

"Look at me, Joss. Please." I need those grey eyes boring into mine. "I am *not* going anywhere. Whether you let me kiss you or not, whether your mom is a raging bitch or not, whether this ruse succeeds or not... I will still be here at the end of the day. You're the closest friend I've had in a long time—maybe even more than Breck. I'm not letting anything ruin this, Joss."

She lets out a little laugh, and I think I've finally gotten through to her. Saying the words out loud helps me to believe them too. She rubs her thumb across the back of my hand again. "I didn't figure you and Breck ever got *this* close."

My laugh is unfettered, my shoulders shaking with it. I love that she can somehow crack a joke at a time like this. She always knows just what to say to make me smile.

"No, we've definitely never been this close." I wrap my fingers around her nape and pull her closer to emphasize the point. "You didn't answer my question."

I'm holding her churning grey gaze with my blue one. I wish so badly I could hear her thoughts.

"Can. I. Kiss. You?" I let the words sink into the space between us. Her eyes dart to my mouth then back up to meet mine.

"Yes."

Her tongue darts out, wetting her lips, and it's almost my undoing... But I need to be sure.

I watch her roll her bottom lip between her teeth.

"Right now?" I drag my eyes from her mouth to look her dead in the eyes, knowing it's there that I'll see her answer. I don't want our first kiss to be in front of her mother, and I can't think of a single valid reason to keep from kissing her right now. Another drag of my thumb over that pulse point, and I'm holding on by a thread. Those mercury pools swirl with want as she says the two words I need to hear.

"Yes. Please."

It's all I need to close the inches between us and press my lips to hers.

Finally.

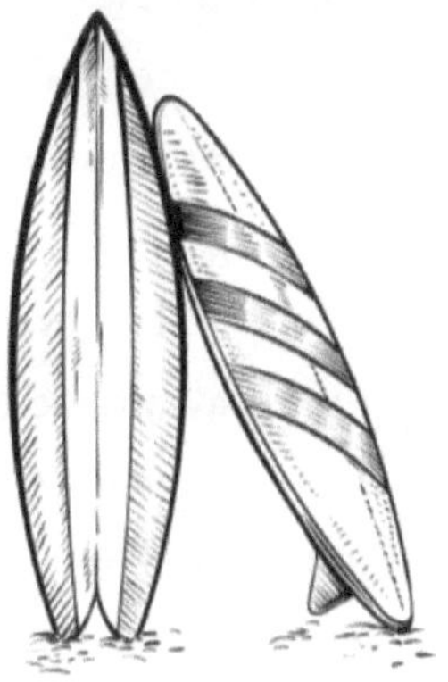

CHAPTER TWENTY-FIVE

Joss

*F*inally.

Wes's lips meet mine in a tentative, cautious kiss. It must be taking every ounce of his self-control—unless he isn't feeling the intense pull between us the same way I am. If I were in control of this kiss, I'd probably have him on his back already. His velvet lips move gently against mine. God, I knew this would be amazing, but it's so much better than I imagined.

He pulls back and leans his forehead against mine. His breaths are quick and shallow, his eyes closed tight. I run my free hand up his arm and grip his bicep. The little squeeze I give it is mirrored in his grip on my neck, holding me close. A tiny whimper escapes me at that possessive touch, and his eyes fly open, searching mine. They're darker now, like the sky at twilight.

This time it's me who presses forward, brushing a soft kiss against his even softer lips. My tongue teases the seam of his mouth, begging for entry. He tastes like coffee and sugar, my two favorite things. I hum, my lips parting, and Wes seizes the opportunity to explore. When his tongue slides against my own, my restraint snaps.

My hand tangles in his hair, and I try to pull him closer, but my bent knees are in the way. I've always wondered what it means in my romance novels when someone "growls in frustration," but I think I get it now. I need more, and I need it now. I let my right leg fall open to the side and tug at his hair.

His low moan vibrates through me as his body shifts. Releasing my hand, he pulls me with him until we're laid out on the couch. My left knee bent, trapped between his body and the back of the sofa, my right hugging along his hip on the other side. He mimics my hold on him by sliding his hand into my hair and pulling gently, exposing more of my throat.

I miss his lips on mine until they find the spot beneath my ear and work their way down my neck. I moan at the feel of him. The heat. The pressure. The way his beard scrapes across my skin. My body lights up. He nips at my collarbone with his teeth, and I could float away on the tide of sensation.

Where I could barely breathe a minute ago, I'm panting now. My breaths are fast and labored, matching his. Oh god, I feel like I could combust. How long has it been since someone touched me like this?

Wes's arm slides from behind my back, his hand pressing into the crease of my hip and thigh as his body rocks forward. I stifle the cry that's so close to escaping, and rock up against him. Holy shit. Are we really dry humping on the couch like a couple of teenagers? Yes, yes we are. Do I want to stop? No, no I do not.

"Fuck." Wes growls out the word, extending that one syllable like a prayer. It's barely more than a breath against my skin as he kisses his way back up my throat, leaving a blazing trail of fire in his wake. When his mouth meets mine again, gone is any and all tentativeness. This kiss is bruising and raw, our tongues a tangle of heat as we try to get more of each other. Like we're starving for each other.

"God. Wes."

"Only one of us is here, Grey." His voice is light, filled with humor, as he chuckles against my lips. It's the brevity I need to clear my head, if only a little. We need to stop.

"Yeah, we kind of forgot to leave room for Jesus, didn't we?" A full laugh bubbles up, and I press my forehead into Wes's chest as I let my shoulders shake. I've effectively stopped our kiss and given myself the chance to breathe, reveling in the scent of him for just another minute. The smell is comforting, fresh and masculine, and entirely Wes.

"The teachers said that here too?" I hear the smile in his voice against my hair. I nod into his sternum, still not ready to break away. "I was never very good at that. The eighth-grade dance chaperones hated me."

I look up to catch that signature smirk of his, dimples on display. I melt at the sight of them and nearly lose all restraint again.

"Of course you weren't," I answer with a smile. "I guess that makes two of us."

I'm so nervous for what comes next. Afraid that no matter what Wes said, we'll never be able to return from this. He's still bracketed solidly between my thighs and damn if it isn't sexy as hell. I want to reach for him and pull him back to me while simultaneously needing to push him away so I can pretend this never happened.

I'm saved from the need to decide by the sound of my phone ringing on the coffee table. I know it's her, and the moment is doused in the cold that washes over me. I let my head fall back and close my eyes. I haven't heard her voice in seven years, and I don't know what it'll do to me when I do.

"I don't want to talk to her," I say, feeling cowardly and embarrassed that I can't handle a single phone call. How am I supposed to deal with seeing her tomorrow?

I feel a slight shift above me and hear Wes's voice. "Hello?"

My eyes fly open, looking at where he's propped himself above me with one hand, holding my phone to his ear with the other. Bloody hell. I can't quite hear what's being said on the other side of the line, but I can tell it's a woman's voice.

"This is Wes, Joss's boyfriend. She's running errands and left her phone at home."

This is a different Wes than I'm used to. This is not the sweet, flirty, charming Wes that I know him to be. This is a more calculating Wes, his protective side on display.

"Yes, she told me you'd be visiting."

More talking on the other end of the line. Damn, now I wish I could hear it.

"Sorry, no, we don't have space for overnight guests, and I wouldn't be comfortable with it even if we did."

Go Wes! This is only making him hotter in my eyes. He is totally unflappable and not giving her an inch. I can't take my eyes off him.

"If you'd like to come here for lunch, we can make that work. I'll have Joss send you the address when she gets back."

More talking from the other end of the line.

"Okay then. We'll see you tomorrow."

He hangs up without another word and I am dumbstruck. Setting the phone back on the table, he sits himself up on the couch and runs a hand through his hair, looking irritated and a little sheepish, before glancing at me.

"I'm sorry," he says, "I should have checked with you."

He looks almost nervous. That... what? I'm going to be mad at him for taking charge? As if. That was the nicest thing I think anyone's ever done for me.

"You're kidding, right? That was amazing! Thank you." I launch myself up and wrap him in my arms before pulling back just enough to look at him.

"Now teach me your ways, because how you just handled my mother was"—I make the little chef's kiss motion—"perfection."

"You're not mad?"

"Hell no. I said I didn't want to talk to her, and I never would have been able to hold the line like you just did."

I release him, pushing all the way back across the couch. A little breather from the physical touching feels necessary.

"Was she mad?" I worry my bottom lip between my teeth. "When you said they couldn't stay?"

"I don't know if she was mad per se, but I think she thought she could convince me otherwise. As you heard, that was not going to happen. I won't jeopardize your peace of mind." His hand comes to my face, his thumb trailing over my bottom lip before lightly pulling to free it from my teeth. "If you're going to see her, you're doing it in a way you can control."

My heart melts at his words. He never fails to make me feel seen and safe. It's like he knows the deepest parts of me, the broken parts, even better than I do.

"Thank you." It's all I can say, and it doesn't feel like nearly enough.

"Sweetheart, you never have to thank me for making sure you're taken care of. I do it because I want to. I do it because you deserve to have someone who will."

He curls a finger around a piece of hair at my temple and slides it behind my ear. I feel that small touch all over and I think that if I would just let myself, I could fall in love with this man. Maybe I already have.

The next few hours are a blur of activity while I work on moving things next door, helping it to look more like a home we could both live in. I keep having to remind myself, especially after that kiss, that this fake relationship is fleeting and that my very real friendship with Wes could be too. He's here on a work visa. He has family at home. There's no telling when he'll decide it's time to leave Australia. I may need to lax my boundaries over the next couple days, but they'll go right back up after we're done with this little charade.

While I wait for Wes to get back from picking up pizza, I settle into the couch and take in the space. My throw pillows and a blanket on the couch add pops of mint and coral. My blown-glass vase filled with peonies sits on the table runner. I brought over a couple of framed pictures of Jaz and I on vacation to put on his bookshelves, along with a bunch of my books. The kitchen has a few of my favorite knickknacks scattered around the counters, and I added some magnets on the fridge. I buy one in each new place I go, and it's become quite the collection. One that brings me joy whenever I look at it, and it seems to bring me even more joy now that it's on Wes's fridge.

No, *our* fridge.

The door swings open and in strides Wes with two large pizza boxes, a six-pack of cold ones, and another small bag, contents unknown. I jump up from where I'm sitting to help him get everything onto the counter.

"How much pizza did you order? We're only two people, you know." I playfully smack his arm and look at all the food. Not like I'll complain about leftover pizza for breakfast before dawn patrol tomorrow, but still.

"Actually, we're going to be four. Breck called to ask how the surf camp was, wondering if it was somewhere he could partner with for tours. I had to tell him we didn't end up going, and then I kind of invited them over. I hope that's okay? Willow's at a sleepover, so it's just Breck and Talia."

His uncertain gaze meets mine, and I'm once again grateful for his thoughtful nature. I'd completely forgotten that we should be surfing right now, without a care in the world. How can twenty-four hours change so much?

"Of course. Wes, this is your house." I laugh lightly and look around it. "Though it looks a little more like mine now. How are we going to explain that to them?"

"They probably won't even notice." He shrugs, like having my stuff all over his apartment won't send a message I'm not sure we can come back from. At least not with his best friend, and definitely not with Talia.

"But it looks like I live here."

"Yeah, that was kind of the point, Grey." We both laugh, his smile reaching his eyes as he bounds over to me. "It'll be fine, okay?"

His arms engulf me in a way that drives every worry from my mind. Well, almost all of them. We still need to talk about this, figure out what to say to his friends when they get here. The words are on the tip of my tongue when the door opens, and Breck and Talia's voices cut short at the sight of us embracing by the couch. Then Talia squeals in delight.

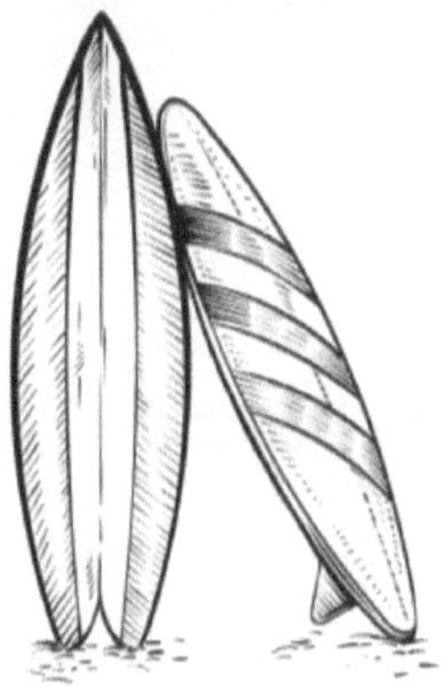

CHAPTER TWENTY-SIX

WES

Well, shit. I'm facing away from Breck and Talia when they walk in, but the excited squeak only confirms that Joss was right, and I'm an idiot. Here I am holding her in the middle of an apartment showcasing Joss's feminine touch. What did I think would happen? We have only a moment to set the record straight, because I'm guessing Talia is already planning our wedding.

I look to Joss and find her eyes filled with panic. Crap, how do I fix this? The first step is probably letting her go, so I slide my arms from around her, missing her warmth immediately.

When I turn around, it's Breck's look of shock that draws my attention first. His mouth is agape, eyes wide, one hand halfway through his hair. God, I wish I could snap a picture of him like this. Talia is the complete opposite. She's bouncing on her toes, hands clasped in front of her heart. She reminds me of Anna from *Frozen* with how excited she is. Yes, I've watched *Frozen*—Willow is very persuasive.

"Hey guys, glad you could make it," I say, mustering as much chill as I can, like this is normal. Everything is totally cool, nothing to see here.

Breck finally snaps out of it, pulling his hand from his hair and scratching his neck while he levels us with a look. Before he can speak though, Talia breaks in.

"I knew it! I freaking knew it! Didn't I tell you Breck? I knew it!"

Wow, she is really emphatic about her so-called predictions.

"When did this happen?" Breck's calm voice fills the air, and I look my best friend in the eye. He looks confused, almost hurt.

"It's not what you think."

Really, Wes? That's the best you can come up with? That's definitely just going to make them believe it's *exactly* what they think.

Joss giggles behind me. Obviously she's moved past her panic and is enjoying the way I'm floundering. Her unsaid words come across loud and clear in the way she looks up at me as she steps from where I'm blocking her with my body.

I told you so is said with a squeeze at my elbow while her eyes say, *Don't worry, I'll take it from here.*

"It's really not what you think," she interjects. "My apartment had a leak while I was gone and I'm staying here for a few days while they fix it. That's why we canceled the surf trip. It's been chaos. Wes was just trying to pull me out of my stress spiral." She looks up at me again, a smug smile on her face. Damn, she's good. I don't think

I could have spun a story that solid if I'd had weeks to come up with it. Forget being a flight attendant, she may have missed her calling as a writer.

Two boxes of pizza, six beers, and half a bottle of wine later, we're all sprawled around the living room, joking and laughing. This has been one of my favorite nights in Sydney so far. I love having my best friend here, and getting to see him and Talia together outside of work and away from Drew makes me think I must be making that whole situation up in my head. Breck is so happy with her—it's almost nauseating. And other than his obvious nerves over Willow being at her first sleepover, they're both at ease, comfortable.

The disappointment of Joss and I not being an "item" was a tough pill to swallow for Talia. Though she keeps asking if we're sure we aren't together. Probably because I can't keep myself from touching Joss at every opportunity, not to mention how my heart lurches whenever she reciprocates with a touch of her own.

Now, she's nestled by my side on the couch. My legs stretched in front of me, propped on the ottoman, while hers extend out across the cushions. She leans against my side, my arm slung on the back of the sofa, her head lightly resting on my chest. She's been quiet the last few minutes. Leaning down to see if she's still awake, I take the opportunity to breathe her in—lilac and something that reminds me of the sun and sand, coconut maybe? I could get lost in that scent.

Bringing my gaze across the room to where Breck sits with Talia in his lap, I mouth, *Is she asleep?* to him. He gives me a little nod and a knowing smile. Talia is bright-eyed and grinning, like she has been all night. I click my tongue and shake my head. Every time the words "just friends" have slipped from my lips tonight, they've felt like a lie. She isn't making this any easier.

We continue to talk for a bit longer while Joss snoozes against me. I bask in the feel of the beautiful woman in my arms. Letting myself imagine, just for a minute, that this could be my life. That we could be this way all the time, that there's not a ticking clock on all of this, that we want the same things.

When Breck gets up to use the restroom, Joss stirs and looks up at me, her grey eyes hazy with sleep and something else I can't quite place. I bring my free hand up to cup her cheek and rub my thumb across it, then down to her lips, unable to stop myself. They're soft and pouty. I want mine there, but that definitely won't help convince Talia that we're just friends.

Ugh, those words again.

"You're tired, Grey. Time for bed?" She nods but holds my gaze a minute longer before trying to push off me. "Oh no you don't."

I hold her to me more tightly, then maneuver around so that I can pick her up. She gasps but then lets out a little giggle before leaning her beautiful head against my chest, her eyes closing again.

"Where you going?" Talia asks from behind me as I walk toward the front door with Joss in my arms.

"What?"

I turn around to face her just as Breck walks out of the bathroom, looking me up and down where I stand holding Joss.

"Isn't your room that way?" Talia points down the hall, toward my bedroom.

Right, Joss is supposed to be staying here for a few days. I can't take her back to her place right now.

"Right, yeah."

I brush it off with a laugh but Breck eyes me curiously again. I stalk past him and head straight into my room. It's the first time I've been in here since I left for the pizzas, so I haven't seen the little *touches* of Joss around the room. I guess she figured her mom might get snoopy tomorrow.

There are twice as many pillows on my bed as there were this morning. The black leather chair in the corner now has a friend in her teal one. The table is tucked between them, looking as though we sit there with our coffee every morning.

Did she drag that thing in here by herself? I picture her doing just that and can't help the small chuckle that reverberates from my chest.

I lay Joss on the bed, moving some of the new pillows out of the way. I'm not sure if she has a side she prefers, so I put her on the opposite of the one I consider to be mine and sweep the hair off her face. She's fast asleep again. I can move her to her place after Breck and Talia leave, so I just cover her in the brightly colored throw blanket I find at the foot of the bed. I kiss her forehead, and the twitch of her lips sends mine tugging up at the corners. My heart soars as I look down at her, asleep in my bed, before I walk back out to the living room to say goodbye to my friends.

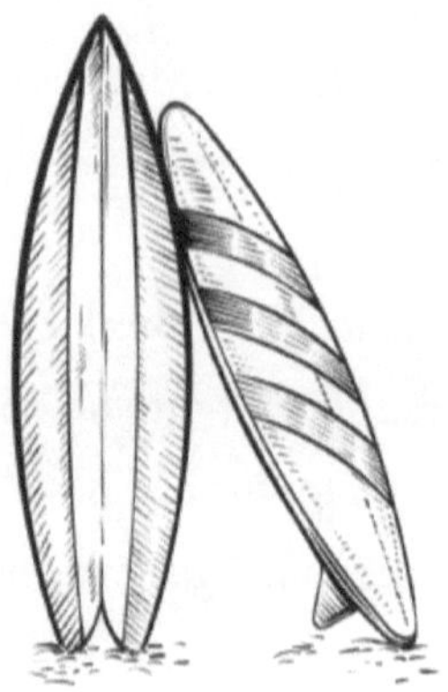

CHAPTER TWENTY-SEVEN

Joss

The hum of voices drifts through my consciousness from the other side of the bedroom door. It's just loud enough to keep me from falling into the deep oblivion of sleep that beckons me. With the click of the front door closing, the quiet engulfs me again.

"Hey, beautiful." The whispered words match the featherlight touch of Wes's hand moving my hair off my face. I want to sink into that touch. "Do you want me to take you back to your place?"

Do I want that? I reject the idea by burrowing farther into the soft, warm mattress, pulling the blanket closer to my chin. Nope, I don't want to go anywhere. I just want sleep. A slight shake of my head and a little pout earn me a chuckle from the man by my side.

"Okay, sweetheart." A brush of lips against my forehead draws a mewling sigh from my lips. Could he stay there, just like that, forever? "I'll be on the couch if you need me."

The couch? Why is he going to the couch? My subconscious perks up just enough to tell me that is not where I want him. Of course, I shouldn't want him at all, but alas, my sleepy mind isn't functioning at that high a level. My arm, heavy as lead, reaches after him, grabbing his hand in mine.

"Stay. Please."

Even without opening my eyes, I know he's debating what he should do.

Please. Stay. They're the only words in my foggy mind, like a skipping record. Please. Stay. Stay. Please.

His hand feels so big in mine, engulfing it in his warmth. A squeeze for reassurance.

"Okay." One word. That's all he mutters, but it's enough. I release his hand and finally give my body over to sleep.

I don't know what time it is when I wake up feeling both too hot and too cold. The throw blanket I'm using is insufficient for all-over warmth, yet my jeans are stifling. My brain feels foggy and I'm confused. Why am I still wearing jeans? Why am I not under my comforter?

I shimmy out of them and fling them to the floor with a thud. The throw is gone too, likely having slithered down to the floor in all my wiggling, but I don't need it now. I scooch the comforter down just enough to slide under it, and the cool fabric against my skin is soft and welcoming. The hazy part of my brain takes note of the different feel of the sheets, the denser pillow under my head, but then the haze thickens to a full fog and I'm lost down the rabbit hole of exhaustion once again.

Sunlight streaming through open windows draws me to the surface like a moth to a flame. My eyes are squeezed shut, but the light feels blinding all the same. Red spots pop behind my eyelids like little fireworks. Why is the sun torturing me? I have blackout curtains for this very reason. I throw an arm over my face to block it out, not yet ready to wake up.

Something else needles at my subconscious despite my attempts to ignore it. No, not something—someone. Someone with warm, bare skin pressed against my own. I register the legs first, tangled with mine. Then the heavy weight across my midsection, holding me in place where I lie on my back. I remove my arm from across my eyes and squint, watching as the form beside me takes shape in perfect clarity.

Wes is asleep on his side, wrapped around me with a contented look on his face. He's relaxed, no lines or worry marring his flawless features. It's unfair how beautiful he is.

My eyes drift lower, noting that he's shirtless. Oh so very shirtless. His torso is a work of art, etched and chiseled from hours spent in the gym or on a surfboard. Someone should sculpt this man. Though, no matter their skill, they'd never get it right. Each defined muscle, the pink puckered skin of his scar, every detail. I want to trace them all, and not just with my fingers.

I squeeze my eyes shut again. *Jesus.*

I chalk my straying thoughts up to the fact that my best friend's half naked body is pressed against my side and I have very little self-control before my morning coffee. That much is clear when I open my eyes and continue my perusal of his body. His arm is slung across my abdomen, possessive in how his fingers dip around the side of my waist. The muscles of his abs flow into an impressive V that disappears below the waistband of his—wait, is he wearing only underwear right now? Must be, because there is no second waistband in sight that would maybe, you know, belong to a pair of pants or shorts.

At this very opportune moment, my brain reminds me that I took off my own pants last night in a fit of exhaustion and discomfort. So, here we are. Both very nearly naked and pressed awfully close together. Wes's hand rests between the wide band of my thong and the white fabric of my cami, which has ridden up to my ribs in my sleep. The soft hair of his forearm, with its sinewy muscles and veins, tickles across my stomach and sends a shiver down my spine.

The subtle movement causes Wes to stir, just enough for his hand to tighten on my waist, pulling me closer to him. Warm, so warm, and the hard lines of his body press solidly against mine—

Oh my god. Is that...? That cannot be what I think it is. But one more slight press of his hips into my side and a quick glance down tells me that *yup*, it absolutely is. *Breathe, Joss.* This is completely normal male behavior. He's sleeping. It's morning. This has nothing to do with me. Or my body being the one he's pressed against. Just a natural reaction. This is fine. Totally fine.

Except, my body is reacting to his body reacting and I. AM. NOT. FINE. The heat in my cheeks is nothing compared to the inferno raging through the rest of me. I'm going to combust at any moment if I don't extricate myself from this man. Like, now.

I can do this.

An image of a magician yanking a tablecloth out from beneath dishes flits through my mind and distracts me from all the other thoughts in my head. Good, that's good. Okay, quick like a magician. I tense, ready to pull away, only to find myself tugged onto my side, facing Wes instead. His arm is banded around my back now, my chest pressed to his. My hand braces against his shoulder as his leg slides between mine, entangling us further.

I have to bite my lip to stifle a groan, or is it a moan? Hell, what's the difference? He's doing this on purpose, right? There's no way he's still asleep. I study his face, looking for evidence that he's messing with me. But no, his breathing is even, unlike mine which is fast and shallow, matching my heart rate.

What do I do now?

I need to move away. Seriously, I need to do *literally* anything other than continue to lie here getting hot and bothered. Because I *am* getting hot and bothered. But I don't and, like it has a mind of its own, my hand moves from his shoulder up to his neck to tangle in the curls there. *Stupid, traitorous appendage.* My nails scratch softly at his scalp and a rumbly growl escapes him that I feel all the way to my toes. I trail my gaze to his face. His eyes are open now, locked on mine, and even though they're heavy with sleep, the heat in them burns me to my core.

His hand flexes on my hip, over the band of my underwear. "You're not wearing any pants, sweetheart." His voice comes out gravelly, either from just waking up or from desire, I can't be sure. He keeps his eyes pinned to mine, not looking down to where our lower bodies lie exposed, the comforter having shifted somewhere along the way.

"Neither are you," I whisper, glancing down to where our bodies are pressed together.

"Eyes up here, Grey." The command snaps my eyes back to his. "We already know you like what you see. Now tell me, do you like what you feel?"

His leg shifts, and with how it's bracketed between my own, I feel that movement everywhere. How does he have the power to electrify my body this way? It's like watching lightning arch and arc through the sky during a thunderstorm. It originates in one spot but branches out, lighting up everything in its path. I'm the one moaning this time, and he chuckles darkly, air puffing against the top of my head where it's level with his mouth.

"Is that a yes?"

I can't find words for everything I'm feeling right now, so a nearly imperceptible nod is the best I can offer. He leans his forehead down to meet mine, eyes squeezing shut, restraint evident in the tension pulling at his neck and shoulders. I feel every small flex and movement under my hand and reflexively squeeze at the back of his neck. He's holding himself back, and part of me understands why—I'm doing it too—but the other part of me wants to beg him to let go, consequences be damned.

"I want to touch you." His words are a growl through clenched teeth, making everything in my body tighten. The tension between us pulls taut like a bowstring, my self-control an arrow against it, the timbre of his voice making it quiver, ready to fly.

"Can I touch you?" Each syllable is pained as his lips move to my neck, just below my ear. Not quite touching, but *so* close. "Please, Joss."

It's not his playful *Grey* or endearing *sweetheart*, but my real name. And the reverence with which it's said breaks the last vestiges of my control and sends that arrow sailing.

"Wes." It's a plea for him as I tighten my grip in his hair. His eyes, blue and churning with desire, meet mine once again, but he doesn't move to touch me.

"I need to hear you say it, Joss. I need the words. Need to know you're here with me."

Where else could I possibly be? I am lost in him, in this moment, in his touch. The words slip from me like a prayer. "Touch me."

His lips slant over mine.

This kiss is soft and languid. Almost like dancing with a new partner when you're still figuring each other out. His hand slides to cup my face, and I melt into him with a sigh. The parting of my lips flips a switch and we both become more insistent, unrelenting, in our attempts to get closer. We roll as one until he's braced above me with a hand on either side of my head, my thighs hugging his hips where they press into mine.

He takes my mouth with kisses that are barely on this side of control. His tongue ravishes my mouth, and I nip at it. He responds by sucking my bottom lip between his teeth. It's push and pull, a different kind of dance now. Our chests heave against each other, sharing the same air, and it's not enough. I pull at his hair with both hands, looking for purchase in a moment when I feel untethered from myself and everything around me.

He releases my mouth and moves down the side of my neck. Oh god, I'm going to combust. Just burst into flames right here and incinerate us both. His lips are thorough as they wander. Side of my neck—nip, kiss, suck. Collarbone—nip, kiss, suck. Shoulder—nip, kiss, suck. Hollow of my throat. Down my sternum. Each touch leaves flushed, sensitive skin in its wake.

He stops where my cami covers my heaving chest.

"Is this okay?" he asks quietly. How he seems so in control, I'll never know.

I wish I could say the same for myself. I am a mess of want, and my whole body shivers as his breath falters against my heated skin. His eyes lift just enough to meet mine, questioning. I give another nod, words still failing me. If I had the brain power to form words, I'd be talking myself out of this whole thing, but unfortunately—or *fortunately*, rather—I don't.

"You are so damn beautiful."

I flush a deeper shade of red, the unexpected compliment taking me by surprise. I close my eyes, feeling suddenly shy, exposed. I have never been more vulnerable with a man than I have been with Wes. The thought scares me as much as it excites me. Because this is Wes. My best friend. Oh god, what are we doing?

My lungs catch, unable to breathe, as his teeth graze the top of my tank, catching the fabric between them. His fingers loop around each strap, peeling them down inch by inch—

Knock, knock, knock.

The neckline of my cami snaps back against my skin while Wes's fingers freeze, straps pulled just to the tips of my shoulders. His head lifts until our gazes lock. The quiet is deafening. Maybe we imagined it?

Knock, knock, knock.

We startle at the sound, as if we weren't expecting it to come a second time. His fingers slip away as he pushes himself up, bracing on both hands and head snapping toward the source of the noise.

The burning heat of the moment turns to ice. Not from the heavy dose of reality at what we were about to do, the line we almost just crossed. No. It's the voice I hear that acts as a frigid plunge pool to my body, my mind. Everything inside me goes numb in an instant as my mother calls my name from beyond the front door.

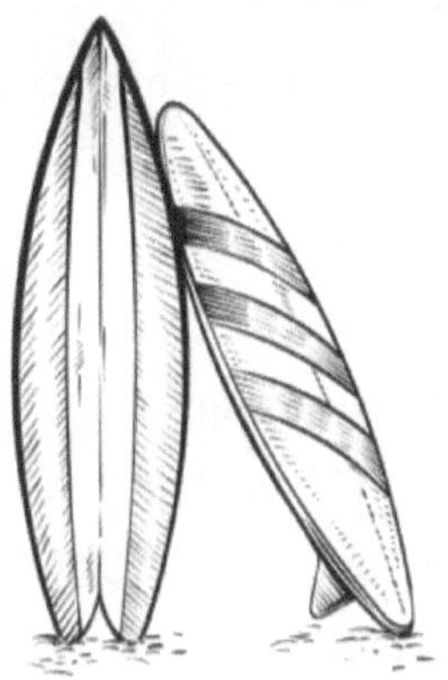

CHAPTER TWENTY-EIGHT

Joss

No. No, no, no, *no*.

She's early and I'm not prepared. We were supposed to have time this morning. I was supposed to formulate a rock-solid plan, and now I'm out of time.

Wes's head hits my chest with a little groan and I want to laugh, I really do. But I can't.

"She's early," I choke out, my voice sounding far away even to my ears. We both look at the clock at the same time. Ten a.m. Two hours, we should have two more hours. We also well and truly missed dawn patrol. Whoops.

"I'll get it," Wes says, and pushes himself off the bed.

His eyes linger over my body, splayed out in nothing but my underwear and cami. A burn re-emerges, my skin heating in direct correlation to the path of his gaze. I can see the desire there and know it's mimicked in my own eyes.

Another knock sounds across the space, and I wince. My brain wakes up to the fact that I can't avoid this any longer. The last thirty-six hours have been an oscillation of worry over this visit and living in wishful ignorance that it would never come. Well, it has. And I can't hide behind Wes for this.

"No, it's fine. I'll get it," I say, sliding out of the bed in his wake.

My feet hit the floor, toes scrunching in the soft carpet. My jeans lie splayed next to the bed. I pull them on in a rush, grabbing a discarded hoodie of Wes's. The smell of him, masculine and heady, fills my nostrils, and I give myself just one second of bliss to breathe him in.

I catch a glimpse of Wes in grey sweatpants, a T-shirt in his hand, walking from the closet as I head out of the bedroom. Another knock penetrates the silence. God, talk about impatience.

"Joss, wait."

But I can't wait. Now that I'm moving, it's like a fire's been lit and it's burning out of control. I just want this part over. The doorknob is cold under my palm, the click of the deadbolt loud in my ears. I have the briefest moment to take in my mother standing at the threshold before she shrieks, "Surprise!"

I'm shocked back a step when she pulls me into a hug, and my back hits a bare chest. Wes's chest. Where is his shirt? I crane my neck enough to get a glimpse of his torso before his shirt slides into place. Ah, he was pulling it on as I opened the door, and now I'm trapped in a Wes-and-Mom sandwich.

"Mom."

I don't know what I expected, but this hug as if nothing happened isn't it. I can't look at her, so my eyes flick back to the door. My entire body goes rigid as a sickening realization crests over me like a wave. She didn't bring Bill. She didn't bring some random guy she's shacked up with. My vocal cords thaw just as my mom pulls back and turns to face the man standing in the hallway.

"Dad," I gasp.

Wes's arms band around my middle in a heartbeat, the word throwing him into action. He pulls me tight against his chest again, away from my mom. She's looking between us with a smile on her face. This is why she was so vague about who she was bringing. She brought *him*.

"Hi, Joss," my dad says, sounding tentative but hopeful.

Just hearing his voice hurts. It's like a finger pressed to a long-healed wound. One where the scar tissue is almost more painful than the original blow. That voice, all these years later, brings with it an onslaught of memories. I'm thankful for Wes's steady presence and the way it's keeping me upright.

I can't speak, my voice has seized yet again. I was prepared for Mom—or at least as prepared as I could be—but this? There is nothing I could have done to prepare for this. Wes's arms lock tighter around my waist for just a second, a silent promise. *I've got you.*

One arm loosens from where he's wound around me, reaching forward to my mom.

"Hi, I'm Wes. I'm afraid you caught us still in bed." He lets a laugh loose, a real laugh, and the entire mood lightens. Awkward chuckles from my parents echo around us. I hear it all through a fog as I force a smile onto my face. It probably looks deranged.

My mom's hand meets his and her smile grows. He's charming her already. "Andrea. It's so nice to meet you, Wes."

When my mom moves aside, my dad takes a step forward and I tense. Our matching grey eyes haven't left each other since the first moment I saw him. His arm moves as if in slow motion, extending toward Wes. Their hands meet, and at the same time, Wes's other hand slips just underneath the hoodie, his thumb rubbing circles over my hip, soothing an ache he can't even see.

"I'm Brian. We're sorry for disrupting your morning."

He's less than a foot from me. This man I haven't seen or spoken to in sixteen years. Not since I was fourteen years old. All at once, it's too much, and I wrench myself free. My stomach pitches. I'm going to be sick. I barely hear Wes's pained voice calling my name as I run for the bathroom.

My knees hit the tile and I relish the sharp pain, the pressure, as I heave and heave over the porcelain bowl. There's nothing but ringing in my ears, blocking everything else out, so I don't hear him coming. His hands reach around my face to pull my hair back, fingers grazing my cheek, my neck. A soothing hand glides up and down my back from where he's crouched around me like a protective animal.

There's nothing left in my stomach, but my body continues to shudder against the onslaught of dry heaves until I finally slump sideways into Wes. The force knocks him off-balance and he falls back against the bathtub with a thud, me in his lap.

"Shit, I'm sorry," I say, attempting to move, but his arms wind around me, twining vines of support, intent to hold me steady. I relax into his grip, my head lolling onto his chest.

"Don't apologize, Grey. I'm good."

A washcloth materializes in front of my face. Grabbing it, I wipe my face, feeling disgusting and still a little queasy.

"So, uh, that's your dad, huh?" The irony in his tone isn't lost on me, and my answering laugh is humorless and rough.

"Yeah. That's him."

"What can I do, Grey? Do you want them to leave? This isn't what you signed up for with this visit."

Is that what I want? I mean, at this point, they're here. Maybe I ought to take this opportunity to... Shit. I don't know. There must be a reason they're here now, right? They wouldn't have traveled all this way for nothing. Oh god, are they here together? Like, *together* together? My stomach clenches again, and if there were anything left to throw up, I would.

Deep breaths, Joss. Inhale. Hold. Exhale. Hold. Again and again.

Wes presses a kiss to the top of my head and I sink into him further. I want to stay cocooned on the bathroom floor and forget that my parents are sitting in the living room waiting for us.

"Are they just sitting out there?" I say into his chest, letting my fingers splay across the muscles there.

"Yeah, I wasn't sure what else to do with them." His hand drifts up and down my arm.

"Okay." I exhale loudly on the word. "I need to take a shower. I can't go out there like this. Can you—"

"I've got it, take your time. We'll be there when you're ready."

I nod against him, not wanting to get up but knowing I need to. It takes me another full minute to will myself to stand. Wes presses himself off the floor, uncurling gracefully like a cat.

"You okay?" His eyes hold the question, and I think back to how many times he's asked me the same thing since this all started.

"Yeah." I clear my throat. "I will be. Thanks, Wes."

"Anytime, sweetheart." This time it's my forehead he kisses, soft and light, but he lingers just a second longer than would be considered "friendly." A deep sigh escapes him when he finally pulls away.

I shut the bathroom door behind him, listening to him move around his room for a minute before the click of the bedroom door makes its way to me. The steam from the shower fills the space, warm and inviting. I strip off my dirty clothes, wishing I could strip away the last fifteen minutes and end up back in bed, snuggled up with Wes.

The hot water against my skin burns and scalds, injecting life back into me and leaving me feeling invigorated. I scrub every inch of my body, enveloped in the scent of Wes's bodywash, my mind set to the task of figuring out what the hell I'm supposed to do now.

I feel raw and exposed. These last few months I've been lowering my walls, letting Wes in little by little, allowing my emotions to take the reins more than I have in years. Yet sharing my family history and being vulnerable with him left me unprotected from the shock of my dad being here in a way that I hate. I showed weakness to the two people I can't trust not to exploit it.

Dammit. This is why I have that box inside myself where I keep all this shit locked up tight. Letting it out does nothing but bring me pain. I guess Eric and Jaz were both right when they said I don't let people in, but how can I when this is the result?

The water beats on my shoulders, every motion on autopilot as I rebuild my walls brick by brick, until I'm back to being the Joss that I'm comfortable as. The Joss that can handle this whole situation. The one who can keep it together in the face of her father who abandoned her. The Joss who doesn't care about the mother that stole from her and broke her trust.

The woman I am when I step out of the shower is not the same woman who stepped in. I look at myself in the mirror. The hard lines of my jaw. Eyes a dull grey, closed off, no emotion to speak of hidden in their depths. Shoulders rolled back, spine straight. I take a deep breath. There's not even a waver or quiver in it. It's strong and controlled.

I gather my clothes off the floor, wishing I had extras to change into. When I enter the bedroom, the tiniest crack forms in my armor. A clean hoodie lies on the bed, beckoning me forward. I slip on my jeans, wishing I had fresh underwear, before pulling the hoodie over my head, relishing the soft fabric against my bare skin.

There's no point in putting this off any longer. I stalk to the door, pulling it open quietly, ready to get this over with. Every step comes with an extra brick, reinforcing those walls that I rely on for protection, cramming putty into the cracks made by Wes's latest bout of thoughtfulness. I don't have space even for him to be inside these walls right now.

It's my dad's voice that carries to me first. "—and you're American right?"

"That I am. Can't seem to pick up the Australian accent, no matter how hard I try."

The laugh that ensues from across the room is a replica of my own. If not for the fortress around my heart, the sound of my mother's laugh might make me sad or nostalgic, but instead, I feel nothing.

"That's okay, babe," I say as I join them, infusing my voice with confidence to match Wes's. "I like your American one better anyway."

He turns, his eyes becoming smoldering sapphires when he sees me, and I walk directly into his arms. His nose is buried in my wet hair, my face pressed to his chest, toes dangling above the floor.

"I'm so proud of you," he whispers across my skin, low enough for only me to hear. "Also, as your boyfriend, I'm really excited to have my hands all over you."

He pulls back and winks, pressing yet another kiss to the top of my hair. I try not to linger on the fact that he didn't say "fake" boyfriend. He lowers me to the floor and I draw strength from him, letting everything else fall away. He takes up the space behind me as I step toward where my parents sit, watching me warily from the couch.

"What is it that you're here for?" There's no feeling in my voice, exactly how I want it to be. My mom looks taken aback by my tone, her gaze darting around anxiously. My dad is still staring at me though, as if it's not his fault he hasn't so much as laid eyes on me in sixteen years.

"Joss, we... your dad and I... we wanted to see you. Isn't that enough?" Mom's voice sends ice down my spine, and I repress a shiver in response.

My dad shifts in his seat, looking uncomfortable.

"I wish it could be, but you haven't given me a lot of reasons to trust your motives, now have you?" She recoils like I slapped her and instantly looks to my dad. What has she told him about our history? Nothing, if I had to guess. "Is that why you're here, Brian? Just wanted to say hello?"

I may still call him *Dad* in my head, and it may have slipped out when I first saw him, but he won't get the honor of that title out loud again.

"Joss, I—" His voice breaks on my name, a hollow, sad noise that, if not for the walls, might actually make me want to go to him. "I did want to see you. I do. I know it's been a long time, too long, but there's things I'd like to say."

He can't look at me now, his gaze flitting from one thing to another as he takes in the room.

"Then say them. Tell me how your family is. You know, the one you left us for."

His countenance sags, and when his eyes do finally meet mine again, the grey is rimmed with silver tears. They don't fall but I can see them, speaking to the emotion coursing through his body. I let no such emotion show. He looks to his lap, hand smoothing the hair that is so like mine in color aside from the streaks of grey that glint in the sunlight streaming through the windows.

"That's a long story, one you deserve to hear." His voice quavers. "But, I—god, I'm so sorry, Joss. I know there's nothing I can say that will make up for what I did, but if you hear nothing else, please hear this: leaving you was a mistake. The biggest I've ever made."

The facade slips just enough that my mouth falls open, complete shock radiating through my body. Those were words I never thought I'd hear, and yet there they are, hanging between us.

Wes must feel me drowning in them because he reaches for my hand. "How about a cup of coffee, yeah? Then we can sit and talk." His eyes bore into mine, asking me questions that I can't even begin to answer.

"Yeah. Yeah, coffee would be good."

With one more look toward my dad, one lone tear sliding down his cheek, I turn and walk to the kitchen. Wes's hand held tight in mine.

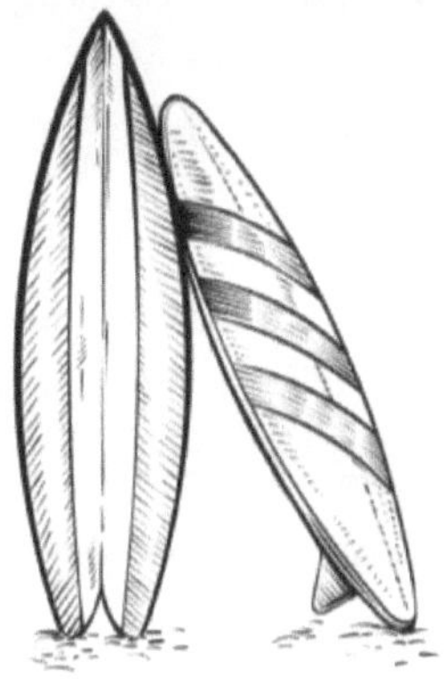

CHAPTER TWENTY-NINE

Joss

Coffee was a good idea. The hot cup in my hands warms me from the outside as each sip of hot creamy liquid works its magic from the inside. I shouldn't have been surprised to see both milk and sugar nestled amongst Wes's things in the kitchen, even though he doesn't use them. I swear his thoughtfulness knows no bounds. He didn't lie either about touching me as often as possible. Even though my parents' view of the kitchen was limited, he still had a hand on me at all times in some way or another.

Now we're sitting in the chair across from my parents, Wes having pulled me down into his lap unapologetically. I don't know if it's just because he wants the excuse to touch me or if it's for moral support, but either way, I'm not complaining.

The awkward silence stretches between us, and I can't take it any longer. I know there's more to this visit, and I'm ready to have it all out in the open.

"Mom, why are you really here? It's been seven years. Why now?"

She glances at her hands, then to my dad.

"Seven years?" Confusion distorts his features, and his eyes bounce between us.

"Andrea, why didn't you tell me?"

Of course she didn't. Well, I think it's high time he understood just what he left me to deal with when he hightailed out of his marriage. Out of our family. Out of my life.

"I'm not surprised." I rub at my temples, resigned to the direction this conversation is going. I ignore my mom, her eyes pleading with me not to continue. I stopped caring about what she wanted a long time ago. I want to see the look on my dad's face when he finally sees the fruit of his actions. "After you left, Mom moved us around a lot. From place to place, man to man. To whoever would take us, since you weren't there to provide for her lifestyle anymore."

The color drains from his face with every word I say, a twisted look of agony wrecking it until he finally moves his eyes to my mother.

"Each guy was worse than the last. I don't know if that trajectory has continued over the last seven years though. We haven't so much as spoken since her last visit to Sydney." I finally look at my mom. Her face is beet red and tinged with anger. This interaction is not going the way she'd intended, but she seems incapable of speaking. "The one where she and the man she brought with her pilfered my home and stole everything they could get their hands on."

Aside from my heart pounding in my ears, there's not a sound in the room. I never understood the phrase "the silence was deafening" until this moment. The quiet is full of swirling emotions: anger, betrayal, hurt, shock. I'm sitting in the eye of a tornado, knowing everything will implode the second the storm shifts.

"Andrea. Tell me this isn't true? Tell me you didn't steal from your own daughter? From our daughter." His voice is calm but his face is ghostly pale, like he might be sick. I can't blame him. When I walked into my apartment that day, I barely made it to the toilet before I lost the contents of my stomach. Oddly reminiscent of today, actually.

"You—you don't understand. He wasn't a good man, Joss," she pleads, and the glistening in her eyes indicates real emotion, but I've seen her crocodile tears more than enough times to remember what a good actress she can be. "I didn't know who he really was until it was too late. I didn't know he was going to do that, but I couldn't stop him either. You have to believe me."

No matter what excuses she comes up with, it will never be enough. Not after all this time.

"You know, Mom, this would have been a good conversation to have seven years ago. A call, an apology, an explanation... It would have gone a long way. But now, it feels like too little too late."

"You don't mean that. I'm your mother. It's never too late." She swipes at her face. A face that looks so much older, yet very much the same. A face I've let myself forget for so long. A face that should have brought me comfort but never did.

"Being my mother doesn't mean that I owe you my peace or my happiness."

I lean into Wes, the only person I've felt those things with in a long time, and he presses a soft kiss to my shoulder. He's been a silent support until now, but I feel him shift behind me and I can sense he's about to become a more active participant. I turn my head, anticipation coursing through me when I catch the expression on his face. His eyes are full of fire as he watches my parents, his lips a hard line.

"Andrea. Brian. Joss asked you a question when you arrived, and I haven't heard an answer. What is it that you're here for?" His grip tightens on me as he continues. "You should be able to understand her wariness after your last visit, Andrea. And Brian, you may be her father, but she doesn't know you anymore, and you don't know her either. She deserves some answers. Otherwise, you can see yourselves out."

Hot damn. This man and his ability to control a situation. It's just like when he talked to my mom on the phone and put her right in her place. I lean in and press a kiss to the underside of his stubbled jaw—a silent thank-you passing between us. Both my parents look completely stunned to be spoken to this way, and I wonder who will crack first under his steely gaze.

Mom's eyes lock on her lap, where she's fiddling with the hem of her jumper, much like I do when I'm anxious. I hate that even my nervous tics come from her.

"Joss, honey, I understand you being angry about what happened with Bill. I am sorry for how everything transpired and that I was never brave enough to try to fix it," she says, addressing her hands. "Your dad and I want to try to make everything right between us. We've all made mistakes, but we're hoping there's a way forward."

I have to hold back a retort questioning what mistakes *I've* made, but I need to let them finish. And if I'm honest, that's more of an apology than I ever expected from her. With the way my dad bristles at her words though, I don't think he likes her talking for him—not now that he knows everything.

"I owe you an apology too, Joss." The halo of silver tears reappears in his eyes as he keeps them locked on mine, and I couldn't look away if I tried. "I should have never left the way I did. I should have kept in touch. I should have explained myself. I should have done a lot of things." He lifts a hand to rub at the back of his neck, anguish and shame on his face. "But I did love you. I *do* love you. I always wanted to do right by you. That's why I'm here."

He clears his throat, looking uncomfortable. "Even after I left, I wanted to make sure you'd be taken care of. I continued to contribute to your trust—"

"My what?" My voice is loud and sharp, shock slipping through all my armor, rocking me to my core. What is he talking about? That shift in the storm I was waiting for... This is it. Wes must feel it too. His hands slide up my back, bringing me a small modicum of calm.

My dad looks uncertain, like this is something I should know. He glances at my mom, who refuses to look at him.

"Your trust," he pushes. "I started it when you were born, and I never stopped adding to it. I always wanted to take care of you, no matter the terrible decisions I made. Your thirtieth birthday is coming up, which means the trust will turn over to you."

"And what, your stipulation is that we have some kind of relationship for me to get it?"

He jerks his head back like I struck him. "No, I..." He trails off, horror in his eyes, body tense. Every emotion that rolls off him rings true to me, but I don't know if I can trust my instincts where he's concerned. "No, I'm not trying to force your hand here. I just wanted to talk to you about it in person. I reached out to your mom to get your contact details. I didn't expect that she'd want to talk to me, but I was hopeful you would be open to it. She was the one who suggested we come to see you together. But the trust is yours on your birthday, regardless of whether you want a relationship with me."

"So... what does that mean exactly?" I furrow my brow, trying to come to terms with what he's saying.

"Well, it's very simple. There are no stipulations for you to access the trust fund; there's just some paperwork we need to fill out and then it's yours."

There must be a catch, strings he isn't telling me about. This man who abandoned me can't possibly be offering me a pile of cash. "And if I don't want it?"

My dad seems surprised and my mom looks absolutely horrified that I'd even consider not taking it. I can understand their reactions. I mean, who wouldn't want a lump of cash? But I don't want to be attached to them by money or anything else if I decide a relationship isn't in the cards.

"It will still be there if you ever change your mind. Legally, it's yours. I can't keep it from you, and I wouldn't want to." He leans forward, eyes locked on me. "Look, Joss, I understand why you're hesitant to trust me, and it sounds like you have things you need to work through with your mom as well." He shoots her a look that says he's not happy about being left out of the loop. "But this isn't about us; this is about you receiving what's rightfully yours.

"I wish I could erase all the hurt I've caused you, and I wish things were different, but I can't make that true." His breathing is a little shaky and there's sorrow and remorse heavy in his features. "I would love the opportunity to fix things, the opportunity to be in your life, but I understand if that's not something that you have any interest in—"

My mom places a hand on his knee. "Brian, I'm sure—"

"No, Andrea." He stands and crosses the room. "I don't want to put any pressure on her. If she's not interested in a relationship with me, then that's her decision."

I take them both in. She watches him with dollar signs in her eyes—it's a look I know well—but he watches me. I wonder how much of her desire for this little trip is to get her hands on either him or a piece of my trust. I wish that wasn't where my mind goes with her, but she's made it that way. I can't trust that she'll ever want me for me.

"I think I need some time to process this. How long are you in town?" I ask, directing the question to my dad.

"Until Tuesday. Maybe we could all go out for dinner? After you've had some time to think."

I watch him, feeling more and more like he might actually have good intentions here. As for my mom, the jury is still out.

"Yeah, okay. I'll let you know."

"Okay. Can I give you my number? That way if you have any other questions, you can reach out." He reaches into his back pocket and pulls a business card from his wallet. "We have rooms downtown—not far from here—if you need anything."

"Yeah, that would be good." I nod my head, still reeling from all of this. When we stand from the chair, Wes reaches forward and takes the card, nodding to my dad. My mom looks uncomfortable, unsure of what to do next. Standing, she fiddles with her hands, looking down at her shoes.

"Joss..." I can tell she wants to say more, convince me to forgive her or maybe to let her stay here—I don't know.

But my dad cuts her off a final time as he walks to the door. "Come on, Andrea, let's leave her be. You'll call or text me and let me know about dinner?"

"Yeah. I will."

My dad reaches out a hand to Wes and says, "I'm glad she has someone like you in her corner. She deserves someone who loves her like you do."

Love. That seems a bit extreme. He's only seen us together for, what? An hour, tops?

Wes clasps his hand, cranking up the fake boyfriend charm and responding with a "Yes, she does."

My dad nods and then turns to my mom, motioning to the door he just swung open. She walks out without another glance, but Dad's sad eyes linger on mine as he walks out after her.

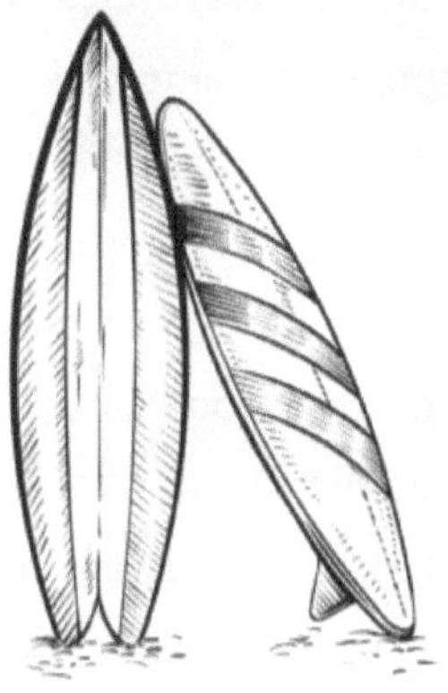

CHAPTER THIRTY

WES

The door clicks shut and I turn to face Joss who is rooted to the spot.

"Hey, sweetheart. Come here."

She doesn't make a move toward me, so I close the distance instead, taking her into my arms. Her body feels stiff, and she's not sinking into me the way I've grown accustomed to. It's almost like we aren't touching at all despite being close enough for me to feel her breaths and the beat of her heart.

"Joss? Are you okay?" I whisper against her hair.

Her hands find my pecs and she resists the pressure of my hand on her back. I release her, sensing she needs space, but it hurts like a physical blow. If only I could read her mind. I want so badly to know what's going on in her head.

"Yeah. I, uh... I need to go change. These jeans are dirty." Her eyes are downcast, looking anywhere but at me as she speaks.

My brain reels, trying to come up with a reason for the chasm growing between us with each second that passes.

"Right, okay, yeah. You didn't really drink your coffee, want to get brunch after? Get out of the house for a bit."

"Sure. I'll, uh, bring your hoodie back over for you. Thanks for..." She stops, clearing her throat like it's hard to speak to me, studiously picking at the hem. "For letting me borrow it."

I reach for her, unable to hold back any longer. Her chin tips up when my fingers slide along it. The usual fire in her eyes isn't there. I haven't seen it since her parents arrived, and I want it back. Because right now, she's looking at me like I'm a stranger, not the man who had her flat on her back in bed this morning.

"You can keep it if you want." I'm not sure I'm talking about just the sweatshirt, but I continue. "I like you in my hoodie, Grey."

What I don't say is *I like you in my everything*. In my house, in my clothes, in my shower, in my bed. I don't know where her head's at right now, but I know it's definitely not a place where she's ready to hear that. Being in that headspace is new and terrifying for me too, and I'm at a loss for what to do.

She nods, the faintest pink stretching up her neck to her cheeks like she could somehow hear my thoughts. But even that blush doesn't loosen the knot tightening in my chest with every passing moment. As it wraps itself taut, it's like I lose my grip on something else. Something I'm not sure I ever really held.

She pulls her chin from my hand, turning for the door, and walks away without a word. The snap of it closing reverberates through my empty apartment, my empty chest, because I'm pretty sure my heart just walked out that door with her.

My feet carry me toward my closet, but I detour to the shower. The wet towel Joss used hangs beside mine and my fingers brush against it like maybe I can absorb the feel of her body from it. Shaking my head, I strip down and turn the water as hot as I can stand it.

By the time I'm done, I feel infinitely more human. I had a good pep talk with myself about how Joss just needs time to sort her feelings out, that she's in shock from seeing her dad after almost two decades. Everything will be back to normal soon. It will all be fine.

I walk out of my closet in jeans and a black Henley and hear Joss moving around my apartment. *She came back.*

"Hey there, beautiful," I say as I walk down the hall.

She takes me in, from my bare feet to my wet tousled hair. There's a small smile playing across her lips, but it doesn't reach her eyes. "Hey yourself."

She's still in my sweatshirt, the dark jeans from yesterday replaced with a pair of light wash ripped ones that I like even more. She has tennis shoes on and her hair is tied atop her head. She looks fresh, and I notice her cheeks have more color.

"Ready for some coffee and food?" I ask.

"Yeah. I was just tidying up while I waited for you to get out of the shower."

"What? Didn't want a repeat of the last time you came over while I was showering?" I wag my eyebrows at her. *Come on, Joss, play with me.*

She tucks her chin, eyes averted, but she can't hide her blush. At least that's something.

"Shall we go?" I extend my hand to her, hoping beyond hope that she'll take it. She finally looks at me and our eyes lock. Blue and grey, like a stormy sky. *Take it, Joss*, I implore her. Please.

She does, and my heart soars.

We're both caffeinated, fed, and less on edge when we walk back into my place a few hours later. We stopped by the store so Joss could stock her fridge, and I was shocked how doing such a mundane chore with her like getting groceries felt so natural. I've never had an easy relationship. Nothing ever felt effortless with Brenna; it was always an uphill battle. Joss and I aren't even a real couple, but our forty-eight-hour fake relationship feels more real than anything I ever had with my ex.

The question I keep coming back to now, in between our bouts of conversation, is whether a real relationship is what I want. I haven't ever been interested in settling down. My parents were never a great example of a loving marriage. My lifestyle in the military didn't feel conducive to a stable relationship. To be fair, my lifestyle *now* doesn't feel all that stable either.

Joss deserves someone who will be her rock, who's there for her. Can I be that person? I don't even know how to be that person for myself, let alone for someone else. If I were ever going to try though, it would be for her. She's so much more to me than my friendly neighbor, but am I enough for her? Am I the kind of man that she needs? That she wants?

It's really not helping that she's been withdrawn since her parents left. I'm gathering she needs to do this on her own. And that would be okay, I could give her the space to do that even though it would kill me, but ever since she told me about them, we've been a team. Now I feel like she's adrift in the middle of the chaos, and even though I want to pull her onto my life raft, she won't take my hand.

"You're awfully quiet over there," I say, watching how she's leaning back against the counter, arms across her chest, staring out across my apartment like she can see to the ends of the earth.

"Sorry, just got lost in my brain there for a minute."

"Yeah, I noticed. Want to share any of those big thoughts with me?" I ask, knowing I'm holding back my own.

Her shoulders lift with a big inhale and then she sags back against the counter as she blows it out, her eyes dropping to her shoes. "I don't know where to start. Honestly, I think I just need to be alone to sort through some things. Is that okay?"

"Of course that's okay. I'm not going anywhere, Joss, you know that."

She nods. "Yeah, thanks. I better go back to my place. I should clean up over there. You probably want your apartment back anyway. I'll come over tomorrow to move my stuff out."

She's still not looking at me, at least not directly. What the hell happened? The space between us yawns open again, growing even wider. Maybe everything I'm feeling is one-sided and I'm alone in wanting our arrangement to change and develop.

"There's no rush, Joss, don't worry about that."

I knew this was fake. I knew it was supposed to just be a show for her parents, but her moving her stuff out feels final. Like the end of something we never really had.

"Yeah, okay." Her hands tighten on the counter before she pushes away. I can't just let her leave like this.

"Joss?"

"Yeah?"

"I know you feel like you need to do this on your own right now, and that's alright. But I need you to know something." I finally have her attention, eyes fully on mine, and there's something stirring underneath. I slowly step closer. "You deserve to have people in your life who will be there for you no matter what, okay?" Her eyes turn misty, a single tear sliding down her cheek that I can't resist swiping away, leaving my hand cupping her face. "Do you believe me, sweetheart? I need to hear that you understand I'm not going anywhere. I'm willing to share the burden if you want me to. Tell me you believe that."

She shakes her head, another tear escaping when her lids close tight. She's breaking and I don't know how to hold her together.

"I don't know how to believe that, Wes. I just don't."

For the second time today, she turns away from me and walks out, shoulders shaking under the weight of everything she's always had to carry alone.

I pace my apartment. The hours between Joss walking out of here and now have stretched on for what feels like an eternity. My stomach chooses this moment to rumble, and the thought of eating alone, not sharing dinner with her like we do almost every night, feels like one more punch to the gut.

Every minute of the last few days runs on a loop in my head. The way she let me in, telling me about her family. Our first kiss on the couch. Waking up this morning tangled in each other. The taste of her skin, the feel of her body. How she let me hold her on the bathroom floor, and the way she handled her parents. The look in her eyes when they finally left. The way she just shut me out. All of it, again and again and again.

If today felt overwhelming for me, it was a hundredfold harder for Joss. I wish she would talk it out with me, let me carry some of it. She trusted me enough to let me in, and it was an honor that she did. I don't understand what happened between then and now, how I somehow lost that trust. I'm desperate to find a way to fix it.

I run my hands through my hair, knowing it must be a mess by now. I take in each and every item that she placed in the apartment. I want to hold them all, these pieces of her that she left behind. The blankets, the pillows, the books, the frames—

A jolt goes through me. Walking with purpose to the kitchen, I grab the paper bag that's been sitting there since last night when I came home with the pizzas. I'd completely forgotten about it when Breck and Talia showed up. Pulling out the contents, my fingers caress the smooth metal, coasting just above the glass.

My heart clenches as I take in every detail. The picture is one Breck sent me. It's a candid of Joss and me at the bonfire. Her legs are draped over the arm of her chair so they lie in my lap and my hand rests on her thigh possessively. Our faces are lit by the firelight, and we aren't looking anywhere near the camera. No—we only have eyes for each other.

I don't remember that exact moment or what we were talking about, but my heart yearns for it. A stolen moment, forever immortalized. I had it printed and framed yesterday. At the time, I told myself it was just a part of the ruse, a way to prove our relationship to Joss's mom. But looking at it now, I understand it better.

I saw this picture and it let me in on a secret I've been keeping from myself: none of this is fake. That the *faking* is what we've been doing all along, well before this weekend. Pretending that our connection is less than it is when really, it's everything.

Holding the picture, I walk to the couch and pick up my phone. I'm ready to call Joss and force her to talk to me, to share this revelation with her. I flip it over in my hand only to see my little sister's face on the screen, her FaceTime call coming through. I try to remember the last time we talked. Too long. I hang my head, feeling guilty. I haven't been the best brother the last couple months. I slide my finger across the screen, setting the frame on the table as I sink down into the couch.

"Hey, Roars," I say, and she grimaces.

"Hey there, stranger," she says. She's always hated that nickname. As she takes me in, her face softens. "I've missed you."

"I know, I miss you too. I'm sorry I haven't been great about calling. I've just been really busy."

"How are things going? How's the flying?" I can feel her worry through the phone.

"It's going great. I love taking these groups up, it's so chill. Nothing like it was in the Navy. And working with Breck, getting to do life so closely with my best friend... it's freaking cool."

"Wes, that's awesome. I'm glad you and Breck are getting this time together after so many years apart."

"How are you, baby sister?" I pry. "How's work been? Gearing up for winter already from what I saw on Instagram this week."

"Work's fine, I guess. Posting snowy pictures just doesn't feel right in September, but I guess that's life when you work for a ski resort." She shrugs sounding resigned. "But..." She stretches the word and her turquoise blue eyes brighten. "Jamie and I did a photoshoot together last week. It was an elopement actually. He was the officiant for some friends of his, and I did the pictures. It was so amazing."

There's an excitement laced in her words now, a stark contrast to the indifference of her tone when she was talking about work. Maybe it's time for a change for her too. "I'll send you a couple of the proofs. We're even talking about doing more of them. Just as a side hustle—for fun." Her face is alight with joy at the prospect. It's always been obvious to me where her passions lay, and it's not in content creation for our hometown ski resort. Seeing her with a camera in her hand was all I ever needed to know she was meant to be a photographer.

"That's incredible, Rory. Really, I can't wait to see the photos." I let all the pride I have for her permeate every word. I know she doesn't get that praise from our parents.

"Hey, I was thinking that maybe I could come for a visit in the spring. Are you still planning to be there for a year?"

Her question hits home, and I'm not sure what to say. After everything that was revealed today, everything going on with Joss, I can't imagine leaving her.

"Earth to Wes? Where'd you go there, brother?" Her voice snaps me back, and I try to smile.

"Yeah, sorry. Yes, I'll be here for at least the year. Maybe longer, I'm not sure yet."

I can't make eye contact with her. Even with the screen and thousands of miles between us, she's too good at reading me, and I don't know if I'm ready to tell her about what I'm feeling for Joss yet.

"Longer? How much longer?" Her voice pitches higher with each question. It's not like her to spool up over stuff, so I know I've hit a nerve.

"Roars, nothing is set in stone here. I just know that at this point, I'm really happy with what I'm doing and I'm not ready to come home."

"*Yet*, right? You're not ready to come home *yet*?"

My eyes shift away. If what I have with Joss is the real deal like I hope it is, I don't know what that will mean for where I'll end up long-term.

"Wes?!" she yells through the phone.

"Look, Rory, I don't know, okay?" I shout back, and then feel an immediate pang of regret. When I finally make eye contact with her, she looks shocked and sad. Shit, are those tears in her eyes?

"Fuck. Rory, I'm sorry. It's just..." My head falls back. I'm going to have to tell her. Maybe it'll do me some good to get someone else's opinion on this anyway. "I've met someone, Roars. I think she might be it for me."

Her eyes are wide when I lift my head.

"I think I'm in love with her," I add, because why not.

More silence, and then she swallows and lets out a low whistle. "It's your neighbor, right? Joss?"

"How did you know that?" I snap forward, getting closer to the phone like it will actually bring me closer to my sister who, I'm realizing, I need right now.

"Wes, I know you. You talk about Joss even more than Breck anytime I ask what you've been up to. She's the main character in most of the stories I read in your emails. I'm not stupid, I'm just surprised. You've always been sort of a date 'em and skate kind of guy. I don't mean that in a bad way, you've just never been interested in anything serious. Even with Brenna..." She stops short and gives me an apologetic look. "Sorry, I didn't mean to bring her up."

"It's okay. She's not someone I worry about anymore."

"That's good to hear at least." She sighs. "Wes, I just want you to be happy. But I wish you could be happy here. I miss you. All the time." Her face falls. I wish I could reach through the phone and give her a hug.

"I miss you too, Rory. You know I do, and you know I love Tahoe. It's just..." I exhale, trying to get my thoughts in order. "I've never felt this way about anyone. I wish I could have both, but I don't think I can."

She takes in a shaky breath, clearly trying to keep it together. God, I hate causing her pain. But then she looks up and smiles.

"Have you told her? How you feel, I mean?"

I rub my hand along the back of my neck, avoiding eye contact as I voice my greatest fear to her. "We've only just *kind of* moved out of the friend zone. I don't want to scare her off by being too much too soon. I don't know if she wants this."

"Wes"—her gentle use of my name draws my gaze—"you're a larger-than-life guy. You *never* hold back. Don't start now. This may be the first time you've truly fallen in love, but I've seen how you love your family and your friends. How could she not want that? How could she not want you?"

Damn. Now I'm the one having to squeeze my eyes shut against the tears threatening to spill over. I had no idea I needed to hear this.

"Jeez, Rory, way to make me all misty-eyed," I say with a weak smile. "I get what you're saying, I do. She hasn't had a lot of people who were there for her throughout her life, you know? She hasn't gotten the love she deserves. Even though that's exactly what I want to give her, she's skittish and has trust issues. I think that's been on her mind from the beginning. That I'm temporary."

I rub at my eyes. Saying these things out loud for the first time makes them real. "For me to prove to her that I'm in this, I think I'd have to move here permanently." I open my eyes and see my words hit home. It breaks my heart a little more to see the initial look of pained shock cross her features.

She sucks in a big breath and closes her eyes, a single tear dripping down her cheek. Part of me wants to take it back, but I know I can't. I don't know how to comfort her, but when she looks at me again, I realize I won't have to. Her face has a determination in it, filled with that fierce loyalty I know and love, and her voice is strong. "Then that's what you'll do."

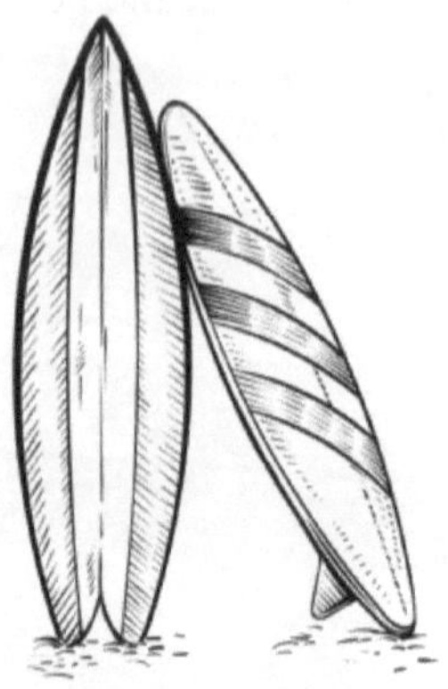

CHAPTER THIRTY-ONE

Joss

The water laps around my legs, my board gently rising and falling. My eyes are locked on the shore as I watch the sand turn from a dull grey to a soft pinkish orange.

It's quiet here, just beyond the waves. Too quiet. I used to come out for sunrise by myself all the time, but it's been months since I've been out here alone. *Without Wes.* My mind supplies his name in an instant, and my heart constricts. Dammit, can't I just have a moment of peace from everything?

My head tips up, the cool spring wind coasting across my face. Maybe it could carry away all the worries that feel too heavy to shoulder. That's why I came here. My apartment was closing in with each passing moment I spent in it. What better place to find peace and quiet than the ocean? Yet it's not bringing the clarity I expected.

After I left Wes in his apartment yesterday afternoon, I'd just barely slipped through my door before the sobs racked my body. I didn't even make it past the foyer, sliding down to the floor, knees pulled tight to my chest. The hour spent with my parents was an assault on every single wall I've built over the years. I didn't have anything left to keep them up by the time Wes hit me with those final words.

You deserve to have people in your life who will be there for you no matter what... I'm not going anywhere... I'm willing to share the burden if you want me to.

Those words continued to tumble around and around in my head, over and over, like a broken record. While I cleaned my apartment. While I attempted to read. While I attempted to sleep. I know he meant them. But what happens when he leaves and my "no matter what" disappears, when there's no one left to share my burdens? What happens then?

Mixed into the tumult are my dad's words. A second record skipping across my brain at a painful rhythm.

Leaving you was a mistake. The biggest I've ever made.

It should bother me that my mother seems to be barely an afterthought considering she was the one who set all of this in motion. She said nothing that made any difference to the way I feel about her. Yes, I'm glad she finally gave me some semblance of an explanation for what happened with Bill, but it doesn't make up for any of it, and the way she manipulated this entire situation only goes to show that she hasn't changed.

A wave lifts my board, and my arms and legs move of their own accord as I paddle. The momentum pushes me forward, and

I press against the board with both hands, jumping to my feet as the water sprays across my face. There's nothing quite like the drop into your first wave of the day, the rush and excitement that builds from within. A smile lifts my lips without any conscious thought.

The rush of the water by my side, my hand gently slicing through it, clear and cold, awakens my senses. Each pump of my legs builds my speed. I carve through the water, my focus solely on the wave beneath my board. This is what I needed. I feel the push start to wane and kick out, coming down to my belly, breathing in short, shallow gasps.

It's when my eyes scan the space around me, the space just beyond the swell, that my heart sinks. I'm looking for him. Seeking out his smile, his arm pumping in the air after watching me catch that perfect wave. Listening for his *whoop* of encouragement and excitement. Instead, I'm met with silence and an empty horizon. Not a single person there to see me. I'm completely and totally alone.

"Joss?" The voice catches my attention as I walk down the street toward Harbour Grounds. My head swivels to the side, to the man standing next to me, a man I didn't even notice in the haze.

"Eric?" I croak. Shock and surprise rush through me. Somehow we've avoided running into each other for months, and here he is, today of all days. Seriously, how many emotional twists and turns am I expected to go through in a twenty-four-hour period?

"Dawn patrol?" He nods toward where my car is parked—board dripping on the roof through the rack.

"Oh, yeah," I respond, letting my hand coast through my saltwater-laden hair, the texture grounding me into my senses. I used to go out most mornings when we were together. He sat on the beach to watch a few times, but it was rare. It was my thing, and I didn't really like to share it with anyone. *Until Wes.* My heart rate picks up at the thought of him.

Very helpful, Joss. I mentally shake myself and ask, "How are you?"

He looks the same as ever, dressed comfortably in jeans and a T-shirt, his jacket unzipped over the top. His short blond hair is styled perfectly, black-framed glasses covering green eyes. His smile is tight, and I wonder if he's as uncomfortable as I am.

"Good. Good. Um, I'm guessing you're headed for Harbour Grounds." He waves a hand in that direction. "Want to grab a cup of coffee? Talk?"

I'm shocked to find myself nodding. *What am I doing?* We fall into step side by side, an awkward tension between us until we round the next corner and the shop comes into view. I breathe a sigh of relief just knowing that caffeine is near.

The bell over the door dings as Eric holds it open for me. When we reach the counter and Jaz's head lifts, her jaw drops, then words tumble out in a flurry. "Uh, hi. Hey. Joss. Eric. What are you guys doing here?" She's nearly incoherent, her surprise reminding me of that first day here with Wes. Another spike in my pulse.

"We bumped into each other outside." Eric's hands are in his pockets, the earlier awkwardness seeming to have dissipated.

"Just finished my surf."

"Right. Right, okay. Well, what can I get you both?" Jaz is still flustered, and I can feel her eyes snagging on me every few seconds.

I order my post-dawn patrol usual—a coconut latte with caramel and chocolate sauce. Jaz even named it the Dawn Patrol and put it on the menu after I started ordering it every morning, and it's become pretty popular with her customers.

The silence descends around us again as we sit in the corner—my sweet delicacy and his plain black coffee steaming on the table between us.

"Are you okay, Joss?" Eric asks, and there's true concern in his voice. "I didn't mean to make you uncomfortable by asking you to grab coffee."

My head snaps up and our eyes catch, holding like two magnets, unable to break apart. I wonder what he sees in mine now.

"No, Eric, you didn't. I'm sorry. My head is somewhere else this morning."

"I kind of noticed." He chuckles uncomfortably. "I said your name two or three times before you finally heard me on the sidewalk. Do you... Do you want to talk about it?"

Do I want to talk about it—my parents, Wes—with Eric? How many times did he ask me a question just like this, only for me to tell him there was nothing to talk about. That I was fine.

"It's been a rough couple of days," I decide to say. "My parents are in town." I can't seem to stop the words from tumbling out.

He looks shocked that I actually offered something up, but he recovers quickly. "Your parents? I didn't think they were in the picture."

I scoff. That's the understatement of the century.

"Yeah, they aren't. Weren't. It's kind of a mess." I chew on my lip. I don't have any intention of sharing the whole story, all the nitty gritty details. If I didn't want to share it with him when he was my boyfriend, there shouldn't be any reason to start now.

And yet, as I take fortifying sips of my coffee, that is exactly what I find myself doing. Not all of it, and not about Wes, but enough for him to be stunned into silence by the time I've finished.

"Wow. That is kind of a mess. I'm sorry you're dealing with that." The words are sincere, not a hint of pity behind them.

"Not your fault. Sorry I just dumped all that on you. I don't know what I was thinking." God, I'm mortified. I move to stand, ready to bolt, when he places a hand over mine on the table.

"Hey, it's fine. I'm glad you did. I just..." He clears his throat before continuing, his eyes searching my face. "I just wish you would have told me while we were together. All those times I asked about your family, you just shut me out."

I open my mouth, ready to defend myself, but he holds up a hand to stop me.

"I'm not blaming you. It was your story to tell, and you weren't ready. I get that. I just hate that you were holding it all while I was clueless to the pain you were in."

I take a deep breath, letting go of the defensiveness as I exhale. "You're right, I wasn't ready. And you were right when you said I never let you in. I'm sorry for that. I didn't see the point of dredging up the past when it could just as easily be left there. Why would I want to dump my own crap onto someone else when I could just deal with it myself?"

"Joss, no. You do it because you *shouldn't* have to deal with it by yourself. You do it because the other person wants to know you. That's all I ever wanted. I just wanted to know the real you."

There's a sting behind my eyes at the honesty in his words. He says them with care, without a hint of harshness, but they cut deep. He's right. Jaz was right. And didn't Wes say the same thing to me just yesterday?

I am willing to share the burden if you want me to.

But I've never wanted to. I've always kept all my pain, all my hurt, to myself. Afraid that if I shared it with someone else, they would choose to leave. Protecting my heart became the reason people didn't stay. How did I never see it? How did I not see that my keeping others at arm's length was the thing hurting my relationships?

A tear slides down my cheek and I swipe it away, embarrassed. Eric has never seen me cry.

"Hey." His tone softens. "I'm sorry, maybe that was too harsh."

"No, no. It wasn't. God, I'm sorry. This is so embarrassing."

"Having feelings is nothing to be embarrassed about, Joss. They're what make us human."

My watery eyes search out his, and I catch how wet they look behind his glasses. It hits me that I never saw him cry either, that he might've kept his emotions in check because I always did. I feel the burn of shame at the realization that I missed out on getting to know this kind man.

"I'm sorry that I hurt you, Eric. I'm sorry that I couldn't be what you needed. I really hope that you find what you're looking for, that you're happy now."

He wipes under his eyes and sniffs, but he doesn't look uncomfortable with this show of emotion. He actually smiles. "Thanks, Joss. I am happy. Really happy actually. I, uh, met someone. We just moved in together."

He looks away, like he's afraid of how I'll take the news. But all I feel is glad that he's found someone to make him happy. It's also not lost on me that the words on the tip of my tongue are to tell him that I found someone too, but I can't do that. I can't claim Wes that way.

I smile for Eric, even though my heart has never felt so bruised and battered. I yearn for Wes, even though I know I don't deserve his kindness. Not after pushing him away.

"I'm so happy for you, Eric. Truly. That's amazing."

"You deserve the same. You know that, Joss? You were dealt a crap hand growing up, but that doesn't mean you have to continue playing it. Maybe it's time for fresh cards, or a new game entirely."

I repeat the words under my breath. Feel them sink into my skin, my heart.

Maybe it's time for fresh cards, or a new game entirely.

He tells me he needs to go meet his new girlfriend and her parents for brunch, and we hug goodbye. I slump back into my chair, not ready to confront the outside world just yet. My cup is empty, and I glare at it. It feels like a metaphor.

Right on cue, Jaz slides in the chair vacated by Eric, two mugs in hand. She passes me one and I take it with a smile.

"Thank you, friend. You're a lifesaver."

Her emerald eyes are laced with concern, and I can almost hear the questions swirling behind them.

"You taking a break then?" I motion to the cup in her hands.

She sinks deeper into the chair, taking a big sip and nodding her head. "Yeah, it was time. You okay? Looked like a pretty intense conversation you were having over here."

I almost wish she'd been eavesdropping so I wouldn't have to repeat it all.

"Yeah. I told him about my parents." I look up to catch her eye and nearly laugh at the look of utter disbelief on her face.

"What? Why?"

I can understand why that seems not only out of character, but also out of the blue. I haven't told her they're in town. She's the only one who knows my history, and I didn't even bother to tell her they were here. Why didn't I lean on her for support too?

Because I like to do it all myself.

"Well... they're here. I saw them yesterday." I try to downplay just how huge a deal this is, but she's too quick.

"Wait, both of them?" Her voice rises an octave and I look around, hoping we aren't drawing the attention of the whole café.

"Yup." I take another sip of coffee and wait for her to flip out.

"Are you okay?"

My head cocks to the side. Isn't that just the question of the day. "Honestly, I don't know. Between my parents, Wes, and now Eric, I have a whole lot of thoughts piling up, and I'm at a loss for how to sort them out."

"Is this why you didn't go on your surf trip this weekend? I wondered when I saw you walk in this morning, but it was kind of driven from my mind when I saw you with Eric."

"I wasn't *with* Eric. We just ran into each other. But it felt good to clear the air. I finally understand what you've been trying to tell me. How I don't let people in, that I push people away before they have the chance to hurt me."

"Yeah?" She raises an eyebrow at me, so many questions hidden behind that tiny gesture.

"Yeah. Now I just need to figure out what I'm going to do about it."

"Well, it sounds like you're on the right path. I'm here if you need to talk, you know?" She reaches for my hand and gives it a little squeeze before standing up. There's a line forming again at the counter. "Right now, I need to get back to work, but I'm here for you. Always. Call me later and fill me in, yeah?"

"Thanks, Jaz. I don't know what I'd do without you."

"For what it's worth, I think Wes might be worth the risk."

I pull my best friend into a hug, and part of me wishes we could sit for hours and unpack how terrified I am to open up and potentially have my heart broken—and not just by Wes. But I know she needs to get back to work, and even though I'm learning I don't have to do everything on my own, the plan I have forming in my mind is something that I do.

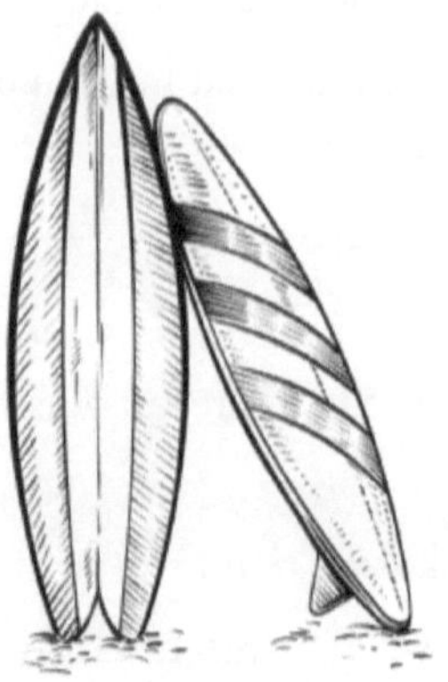

CHAPTER THIRTY-TWO

Joss

My knee bounces beneath the table, hands fiddling with my napkin as I try to center myself and take in my surroundings. I'm tucked away in a booth toward the back of the restaurant. It was the only table that would provide a modicum of privacy for us.

I rarely have the opportunity to dress up, and other than that double date with Jaz, I never go out to fancy dinners. So now, especially with what I'm about to do, I'm feeling more than a little uncomfortable in my skin as I shift in my seat.

What if he doesn't show up? What if he decided I wasn't worth the trouble and went home? I'm on the verge of getting up and walking away when I hear a voice behind me.

"Joss." It's just my name, but the fact that he's really here calms me enough to face him.

"Hi, Brian." My voice feels foreign, wavering over the name. Just like my resolve never to call him Dad again. Because in the light of today, with just the two of us here, I almost want to. I stand and take him in as he approaches the table. I was so focused on keeping my control yesterday that I never took the time to look at him closely. He's still so tall, just like when I was a kid. I haven't grown much since then, and I wish I could have gotten some of his height.

His navy suit is expensive-looking—exquisitely tailored and pressed to perfection. I never was very good at ironing; it's the bane of my existence as a flight attendant. The slate grey tie matches his eyes. Eyes that are just like mine. I'd forgotten how alike we are in the nearly sixteen years it's been since I last saw him.

His hair that became so disheveled yesterday as he ran his hands through it is styled neatly today. The same brown as mine but with grey streaked throughout, yet it only seems to make him look more distinguished. I can see a few women around the restaurant sending him appraising looks. He looks younger than he is. He has a wary smile on his face, like he's nervous about this dinner too. It's enough to make me drop my shoulders from my ears.

"Can I give you a hug?" he asks with tentative softness.

My throat closes up for a second, and I can see the same uncertainty mirrored on his face.

"Yes, I'd like that," I say, realizing the words are true.

Since he left the apartment yesterday, I've had more than enough time to think about everything that unfolded. There are questions I need answers to, and he's the only person who can give them to me.

He opens his arms, hope sparkling in his eyes. I walk into them, allowing his scent to surround me. It's the same as it was when I was a kid, and it's like a hit to my senses. I haven't been in these arms in sixteen years. I haven't smelled his woodsy smell in *sixteen years*.

My eyes fill with tears, and I have to pull away to keep a sob from ripping through me. It's getting harder and harder to keep my walls up. Like they're more permeable, breakable, now that I know what I need. They used to be fortress-like. Nothing and no one could get past them. But I'm determined to start fresh, and what better place to give it some practice than here and now. I step back and swipe under my eyes, careful not to disturb the makeup I spent twenty painstaking minutes on earlier.

We slide into the booth across from each other, and I inhale a few times to calm my system, grabbing the water in front of me and drinking half of it down. He looks just as out of sorts as I do.

"I'm really glad you called. Yesterday didn't go quite like I planned. Seeing you grown…" He swallows hard, the words catching in his throat. "Well, I wasn't prepared for how hard that would hit me. I don't think I adequately expressed just how sorry I am about everything that's happened."

"Well, if I'm being honest…" I sigh and look him in the eye. "You showing up on my doorstep was not something I was prepared for either."

"I am sorry for that too. Your mom was so sure you'd be okay with us showing up early. I should have made her call."

"No." I shake my head, knowing he's misunderstood my meaning. "I mean, yes, that was unexpected, but I'm talking about *you* being there."

He looks confused, his eyebrows pulling together.

"What do you mean? Your mother didn't tell you I was coming?"

A weak laugh escapes me as I shake my head.

"She told me she was coming and that she had someone with her. I assumed it would be yet another one of her horrible boyfriends. Seeing you in the hallway..." I have to stop, blowing out the breath that feels caught in my lungs. "It was like seeing a ghost."

His eyes go wide with horror. "God, Joss, I'm so sorry. I had no idea. No wonder you reacted the way you did." He scrubs at his face, looking genuinely distraught. "Why would she do that?"

"I stopped trying to figure out why she does the things she does a long time ago. There's a reason I asked you to meet me here without her. I needed to get a feeling for this situation without her attempting to pull the strings."

"You said you haven't seen or talked to her in seven years. She stole from you?" The question in his voice is almost pleading, like he's hoping that was a joke and I'll have a new story this time around.

"She did. I don't know what to make of her story about Bill, whether any of that's true. My only interaction with him was during that visit." I didn't plan to go into all the details, but he's here, and I don't know if I'll ever get another chance to explain it to him. So I do, and he listens patiently while I tell him about that horrible time, never once interrupting.

"Jesus, Joss. I'm so sorry. I-I never would have brought her to your door if I'd known." He shakes his head and looks indignant, frustrated. "I was struggling to find you on my own, and she was easier to track down. She seemed so excited to come visit you. She never once mentioned that it had been years since you spoke."

"You're not responsible for her actions."

"Aren't I, though?" I feel the anger, even though I know it's all directed at himself. "I left, and it drove her to become whatever she's become."

"I think she thought if she could just find a new husband, we would be okay. But she was a mess, and she's never been a good judge of character. The men we ended up living with..." I shudder as I think about how terrible some of them were—Tom in particular. I catch the look of concern on Dad's face, but I continue. "I left the day I graduated high school and never looked back. But we kept in touch, at least somewhat. Until Bill."

"I want you to understand something, Joss. Although I know it can't change the past, I need you to know that I never wanted to leave you."

I stiffen at his words. How can he say that to me? If he hadn't wanted to leave, he wouldn't have.

He must see my apprehension because he holds a hand up. "Wait, please, let me finish. Your mom—she was so angry at me, rightfully so, for cheating and wanting to be with someone else. But I never wanted to leave *you*." He emphasizes the word, and my body locks up at the implication.

"I wanted to figure out a way to share custody of you. I even offered to take you full time. She told me she'd ruin me, my reputation, and destroy me in court if I even tried." He hangs his head, bringing a hand up to the back of his neck. "I was too much of a coward to fight for you then, so I left. And as the years went by, my cowardice only got worse. I was too afraid to see you and be met with the hate in your eyes—as would be your right. It was easier to stay away."

"You wanted to take me with you? You wanted me?" I barely whisper the words as I stare at the table in front of me. This changes everything, and also nothing. I feel his warm hand over mine and lift my gaze to see his face.

"I always wanted you. I'm sorry I was too spineless to fight for you."

That sob from earlier comes back, and I don't bother holding it in this time. I have to pull my hand from his so I can cover my face. I could have had a relationship with him all these years...

"How could Mom do this?"

"I won't make excuses for her, but I know she was angry with me, and she probably figured you'd be better off without me as well. She wouldn't even cash the checks I sent for you, not wanting a single thing that would tie us together. I eventually stopped sending them and put it all in your trust instead." He looks heartbroken.

"But she listened to me cry myself to sleep for weeks and weeks after you left. She saw the way your leaving affected me. She let us live in those terrible places. God..." I look around the room, glad that it's not crowded. Less people to witness my breakdown. The server's eyes glance toward our table and quickly away—clearly having no desire to get in the middle of it either. "I've been afraid to trust anyone not to abandon me for sixteen years, all because she was a spiteful bitch."

"Joss. I-I'm sorry."

I shake my head, trying to make sense of all this new information, to make it fit together with the life I lived, with all the things I believed to be true all these years.

"Joss," he starts, the word filled with such sadness but also something that sounds like love. "If you believe nothing else I tell you today, believe this. I have always loved you and wanted you. My leaving never had anything to do with you. You deserved better than what your mom and I ever gave you."

I take a minute to absorb his words. *He loves me.* He always did.

"Why wasn't I enough for you to stay?" I can't make myself look at him, but I hear his broken sob and know that he's just as much of a mess as I am over this.

"Oh, sweet girl. It was never that you weren't enough to keep me, it was that I wasn't strong enough to stay. I'm sorry I made you doubt that. Joss, please..."

I look up, knowing my makeup is surely wrecked now, and wish that I could hide away from him, from the world, for a while.

"*You* are why I'm here. Not your mother, not even because of the trust. Just you. I couldn't go another day of my life without seeing you, without trying, without at least telling you how much I love you and want you in my life."

The click of my heels on the sidewalk is the only sound penetrating my mind as I walk back to my building. I feel emotionally drained. Physically drained too after my five a.m. wake-up to surf. The conversation with my dad left me with so many things to think about. How could Mom cut me off from him without giving me a chance to be a part of that decision? She let me hate him when we could have had a relationship this whole time.

Before I know it, I'm exiting the elevator and approaching Wes's door. I want to walk straight inside, into his arms, but I need a few more minutes to process everything on my own. I let myself into my apartment and slump against the door. Taking a deep breath, I let the smell of home calm me.

My apartment feels strange with so many of my things over at Wes's place. My room feels different too, cold and quiet. We fell so easily into sharing his space, like it was meant to be ours. The way our two homes melded into one was nice, and now I find myself craving the comfort and rightness of that space more than this one.

I slip out of my dress and shoes, groaning in pleasure as I stretch my feet. Those heels were not my best idea in conjunction with my choice to walk to and from dinner. Wes's hoodie is on my bed, where I left it earlier. I've worn it almost nonstop since I walked out of his apartment yesterday, needing some semblance of connection to him even as I was pushing him away.

And I *was* pushing him away. I realize that now. I've known from the very beginning that his being here was temporary, that he would go home eventually. I created special boundaries just for him, yet over these last few months, he's done a good job of dismantling them piece by piece. I never stood a chance, and then this whole fake relationship thing obliterated all that was left.

It opened us up to think of each other differently—at least for me—and now where are we? Attracted to each other, closer than ever, and still with a looming end date. But now I know how he tastes, how his body moves over mine, how it would feel to be his. Really his. It was simple to pretend with each kiss that he wanted what I wanted, with each touch that we could be more to each other. But all I've really done is leave myself vulnerable to have my heart broken. It's become more complicated than I could have possibly imagined.

The words he exchanged with my dad float to the surface of my mind.

I'm glad she has someone like you in her corner. She deserves someone who loves her like you do.

Yes, she does.

Wes was never interested in a relationship. Love has always been out of the question for him, and yet his words contradict that at every turn. The things he says, the way he is with me, I'd love to believe that they mean more than they do. But if I do and he still leaves, then I'm just the stupid girl who fell for the guy who as good as said he'd never love her.

Jaz's words are what I hear now.

I think Wes might be worth the risk.

I know he is, but I'm struggling to rewire over a decade of protective tendencies. The idea of putting myself out there completely, telling Wes how I really feel, terrifies me.

I've been standing in the middle of my room unmoving for at least five minutes now, his hoodie still in my hands. I finally pull it over my head, letting the comfort of his scent engulf me. I lift my phone off the bed and pull up our text thread. There have been two messages since I walked away yesterday—the first came through shortly after I left and the second came through a couple hours ago.

Wes

> Take all the time you need. I'll be here if you need me.

> Grey, I'm really trying here, but I'm worried about you. Please don't shut me out. I miss you. My apartment doesn't feel right without you in it.

My heart seized when those words came through on my walk to dinner. I've repeated them an unhinged number of times in my head. So, when I hear a sound through the wall of his apartment, I can't stop my feet.

He says he misses me, that his apartment doesn't feel right without me. Well, same here.

I'm out my door and standing on the other side of his in the next breath.

Can I just walk in? Do I deserve that privilege after ignoring his attempts to help? I don't know, but I slip my hand around the handle anyway. I just have to hope he'll forgive me for running scared.

I know he's here, but when I get through the door, I don't see him. Everything is exactly as I left it yesterday. It makes me smile to see one of my blankets haphazardly strewn on the couch next to his Kindle, like he was snuggled under it just a minute ago.

His voice draws me toward his bedroom. "Yeah, I was already thinking I'd apply for the airlines. That's the easiest possible transition."

The airlines? Transition to what? Oh my god, is he—is he leaving?

"I didn't want to leave you high and dry, but it sounds like the timing might actually work out well for both of us." His words freeze me in place. Who is he leaving high and dry? "That's an amazing offer you got. I'll really miss working for you though."

No. I let out a shaky breath. I'm only a few steps from him, but it feels like an insurmountable distance. I'm frozen. Unable to move, unable to speak, as my heart cracks in my chest.

"Yeah. Yeah, I'll call you tomorrow and—"

Wes swings the door open only to find me on the other side, eavesdropping. I can't even pretend that I wasn't. Shock flits across his face, but it's instantly replaced with relief.

His thumb hits the end button, effectively hanging up on Breck, before he slips his phone into his pocket. His hands reach for me, but I flinch away, pain searing through me as his words echo through my head. But he doesn't stop, not until his thumbs coast down my cheeks and I realize they're wiping away tears.

"Joss? Sweetheart, what happened?"

I yank out of his grip. How can he ask me that? How can he call me sweetheart when he was just talking about leaving like it was a foregone conclusion?

I do what I do best. Run.

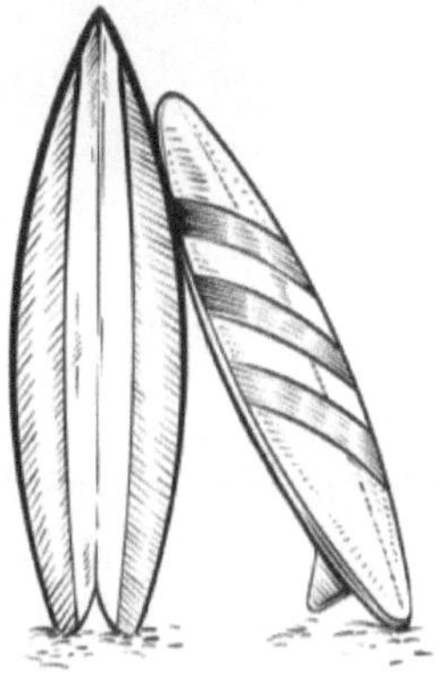

CHAPTER THIRTY-THREE

WES

"Joss, wait!" I charge after her, but she spins on her heel to face me, hurt and anger radiating off of her. We nearly collide as I try to stop my forward momentum. The look on her face could derail a freight train. Fuck, what happened?

"Who are *you* to tell me not to run? Isn't that exactly what you're doing?" she spits, pushing a finger into my chest.

"What? No, what are you talking about?"

"I heard you, Wes! Just now, on the phone with Breck. He's selling Adventure Chasers, right? You're going to leave and get a job at an airline."

Her face crumples, tears falling in earnest, arms wrapping around her middle. Dammit, I can see the conclusions she's drawn from what she overheard, and it physically hurts that she thinks so little of me. Like I could just up and leave her without a second thought, without a conversation.

"Joss, please. Look at me." I'm begging her, my heart breaking with every tear. Her trust is so fragile, and she looks more broken now than she did yesterday. "Joss, the sale will take months, getting a new job will take months. Neither of those things are happening right away. I'm not—"

"You're not what, Wes?" She cuts me off, and I have to rake my hands through my hair to rein in the frustration that she won't let me finish, won't let me explain. "Leaving *yet*? Oh, we've got months, right? Well, I don't want *months* with you. That's what I came over here to tell you. I-I'm such an idiot. The last few days have been purely pretend to you. You were always going to leave, and I was stupid enough to fall in love with you anyway."

Everything stops. It's like the whole world has fallen away. There's no sound. Not even the rasp of Joss's breathing permeates the space. Her eyes are wide and terrified, the words dangling in the space between us. I stagger back a step, like they carried a physical blow when they hit me square in the chest.

"You..." I can't seem to form the words, in my head or out loud.

"Don't, Wes." She holds a hand out in front of her. "You don't have to say anything. I have to go."

"No!" I reach for her, catching her hand before she can bolt. She tries to yank it free, but I hold fast. I'm not letting her go. Not again. Not ever. "I'm not leaving, Joss."

The tension releases just enough, the instinct to flee leaving her body as her eyes search mine.

"I'm not leaving. I'm not," I say, beseeching her to believe me. To trust me. "Yes, Breck is selling, but that will be months from now. Enough time for me to get applications in with the airlines. *Australian* airlines, Joss. I'm not leaving, I'm looking for a new job *here*."

"Here?" Her voice cracks, making it sound high and squeaky, barely contained. She's not letting herself believe it.

"Here, Joss. In Sydney."

I tug her forward, our chests not quite touching but close enough that I can see the way hers rises and falls with unsteady breaths. I place her hand over my heart, because it's hers if she'll take it.

"It was never fake for me, Grey. I didn't pretend for a single second. I think I always wanted it to be real." My hand finds her chin, tilting it up, my thumb caressing her bottom lip. Silver tears shine in her eyes, and I can just see the glimmer of hope there, battling with her doubts. "You know what I figured out last night, Joss? The pretending? It's what we've been doing all along. For months. Pretending we weren't everything to each other when we are. Pretending we didn't belong to each other when we do. You are everything to me, Joss. Everything."

I can't wait any longer, I crush my lips to hers, pulling her body flush against mine. I can't take another second of us not touching, of not being together. She finally relaxes, all the fight in her falling away. Her hands lift to my neck and slide into my hair, making a mess of it as she pulls and tugs it between her fingers.

"Wes, I..."

The words are just a pant between breaths, my lips interrupting her ability to continue. She pulls her head back slightly, so I move on to her neck, her pulse a frantic beat under my lips, matching the one in my chest.

"Say it again, Joss." I punctuate each word with a kiss down her throat. She whimpers when I nip at her collarbone. She looks nervous as I meet her gaze, unsure even after all I've told her. "Trust me, please."

I know I'm asking her to take a leap of faith. To trust I won't break her. She let the words slip in fear earlier, but I want to hear them in hope this time. Her eyes shutter closed, a stilted breath escaping her before they open again. My sapphire blues meet her graphite greys and there's nothing here but me and her.

"I love you, Wes."

Her heart sits between us, almost like I could reach out and touch it, and I have no intention of leaving it there. It will never be anything but mine. *Mine.*

"I love you too, Joss."

She moves first now, pressing up to her tiptoes, chest brushing against me as her lips meet mine. I feel it all in this kiss. Her love, my love. The way we move, like two halves of a whole that have finally found each other.

My hands slide low, from her back, over her ass, and down to her thighs. Gripping tight, I lift her, those firm, sexy legs wrapping around my waist. The way her hands tighten in my hair drives me wild and I growl against her mouth. I have never wanted anything in my life more than I want her. Not just her body, which I very much want, but all of her. Her heart. Her trust. Her smile. Her very soul. I want every part of her. I want everything with her.

She moves against me, a moan slipping past her lips, giving me access to slide my tongue along the seam and into her mouth. Tasting her, needing more.

I pull back just enough for our eyes to meet again. The burning heat there and the soft nod of her head all the answer I need to the silent question between us. Our lips crash against each other again. Muscle memory carries me toward the bedroom, unseeing, lost in this kiss. We break apart only long enough for me to find the door with my foot and kick it closed behind us.

We made love twice before needing to come up for air. Our bodies sated and tired, I wrapped Joss in my comforter and carried her to the balcony where we now sit, cocooned together watching the sparkling lights of our city.

She's quiet, and I let her be, knowing that she'll tell me what's going on in her head when she's ready. I smooth soft kisses over any inch of skin that peeks out from beneath the blanket, watching goose bumps erupt in their wake.

"I had dinner with my dad tonight."

"You did?" I try to keep the tension out of my voice. The protective part of me hates that she went alone, wishing I could have been there. I must not hide it well enough because she laughs under her breath, turning on my lap so she can see me.

"Yes. And I knew you weren't going to be happy about it."

"It's not that I'm unhappy you went, especially if that's what you needed to do. I just wish I'd known so I could have gone with you. It's the caveman in me, I guess. I know how much you love that side of me."

Her laugh breaks free. Good. After all the tears of the last few days, it's a relief to hear that laughter, feel it deep in my bones. If she's genuinely laughing, she must be okay, and that's all that really matters.

"I do love that side." There's that word again. My heart swells every time I hear her say it, no matter the context.

I *really* liked it when it slipped out between her breathy moans as our bodies melded together earlier. I shift under her, and the look on her face, one eyebrow lifted, smirk across her lips, tells me that I'm not doing a good job of hiding just how affected I am by her.

"Sorry, uh, ignore me. You were saying you had dinner with your dad?"

"Yeah." She pulls her lip between her teeth. "And I had coffee with Eric this morning after dawn patrol too."

"Eric, your ex?" I ask, and she nods. "Hold on, did you say you did dawn patrol this morning? Alone?"

If she wanted my attention, she's definitely got it. I stay fully focused on her as she walks me through the last day and a half. I don't know how she's still conscious at this point between the early wake-up and the emotional toll of her conversations with both Eric and her dad. I kind of wish I could hate her ex, but it sounds like that chance meeting was exactly what she needed.

Then there's everything with her dad. I know it's on him for leaving and not fighting for her, but what kind of mother keeps a child from their father out of spite?

"I don't know, Wes. I don't think she's changed at all. I think she sees an opportunity here, with either me or my dad—or maybe both—to have her needs met. I hope I'm wrong, but it doesn't feel that way, does it?" she asks, and I can see the sadness in her eyes at even having to voice such a question about her mother.

"I obviously don't know her like you do, but no, sweetheart. If I were a betting man, I would put money on the fact that she's only here because of your trust fund."

Her head hangs forward.

"Why am I never enough for anyone just on my own? Not enough for my dad to stay, not enough for my mom to want me just for me, just never enough." Her head is in her hands now and I pull her shaking body closer, wrapping my arms around her.

"They failed you. Their mistakes are not on you." I hate to see this beautiful, strong woman so broken. "They're just two people, Joss."

"But they're my *parents*. Of all the people in the world, they're supposed to be my biggest supporters."

Her arms come around me, her face in my neck, and I can feel the wet tracks of her tears against my skin.

"I know, Joss. But that doesn't mean other people won't love you like you deserve. Look at Jaz and how much she loves you. Joss... look at me." Her eyes meet mine as she pulls back. They're red and puffy but full of hope, waiting for the words. "Look at how much *I* love you."

I bring a hand up to wipe a tear that's making its way down her cheek. I let her sit in the moment and soak up my words. She's still learning to believe them, and I'll continue saying them until she does.

When she finally moves, it's to fist her hands in my shirt, her gaze never leaving me as it searches out the truth on my face.

"I told you earlier that we're everything. You might not have been their everything like you should have been, but believe me when I say that you are my *mine*, Joss."

She sucks in a breath and her eyes flutter closed as she rests her forehead against my sternum. My heart is hammering, and I'm sure she can feel it. It's still new for me to put my heart in her hands too, and as much as I'll continue to do it, I have fears laced underneath that I have to fight.

She finally pulls back, her shoulders straightening, her head held high as she brings her eyes to mine. She smiles then. It's small at first and then it grows before she finally speaks.

"You're *mine* too."

My heart explodes and I'm finally able to take a full breath before I pull her into me, holding her tight. Her head tilts up just as mine tilts down, and we fall into the perfect kiss. It's slow and languid, and the fire beneath it burns strong and steady, unlike the blaze of those that came before it. This one is full of unsaid words. It's full of promise as we sink into it, deeper and deeper.

She's reluctant to pull away, and I don't let her go far.

"Wes, I..." She falters, and I give her the space to find her way to what she needs to say. "What happens now? I mean..." She glances away. "Your visa, your plans—I know you said you were staying, but you can—"

I bring my finger to her lips to stop whatever it is she thinks she needs to say. I can see the protest forming on them. She isn't ready to trust that this is true yet, but she will. I'll make sure of it.

"I love you, Joss. I'm staying. We'll figure out the rest as we go."

The lip under my finger starts to tremble and her eyes are now so shiny with tears that another one spills over. I lower my hand so that I can kiss her again. I know that words aren't the way to show her that I'm in this for the long haul. It'll be my actions, showing up for her again and again until she believes it down to her very bones.

When I finally pull back, there's a smile on her lips. It's one of wonder and excitement at what comes next. Her hand lifts to my face and, touching my cheek, she laughs lightly.

"You know I swooned over your dimples that very first day in the airport terminal, but you've made me fall for you in so many ways since. I just couldn't let myself admit it."

"I might have fallen for you the moment I saw you in your sexy flight attendant uniform, but I *know* I fell for you the night I held you in my arms while you were sick. I couldn't imagine being anywhere but where you were."

"So." She blows out a breath. "Now what?"

"Well, sweetheart, we figure out what you want to do about your parents first. We have all the time in the world for the rest, yeah?" I say, and she silently nods, pressing her forehead against my chest again.

"But I don't want to think about them right now. I just want to be here with you, in this moment. Can't we worry about them tomorrow?" She looks up at me with a little pout on her lips, and I melt at the sight. I want to take that lip in my mouth and nibble on it, or maybe do something else with her mouth entirely.

That thought definitely doesn't help my resolve that we should focus on the situation with her parents first. I reach up and run my thumb across her bottom lip, making her mouth drop open in a perfect O. When she pulls my thumb into her mouth, giving it a firm suck, I lose all semblance of self-control. Fuck, I want her again and I want her now.

"Fine. You win."

With that, I stand from the chair and throw her over my shoulder before walking straight to the bedroom. She giggles and attempts to tickle me, which earns her a light swat to her behind. She squeals as I toss her onto the bed, the comforter falling away. We're lost to everything else as we find each other. Again and again and again.

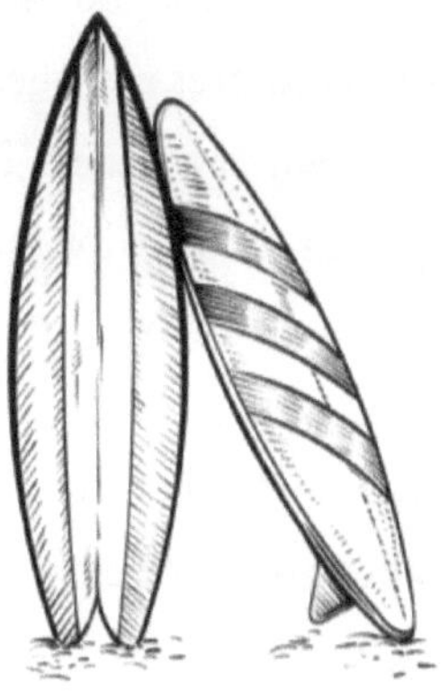

CHAPTER THIRTY-FOUR

Joss

I woke the next morning blissfully tired and sore from the night's activities. Unfortunately, there was no avoiding the subject of my parents in the light of day, so we forced ourselves out of bed and headed for the one place that brings us both peace: the ocean.

We talked as we bobbed in the waves, the sun rising behind us, and unpacked everything my dad revealed last night. We talked about my mom over breakfast and coffee at Harbour Grounds. We talked about how I feel about all of it when we got home. We came to the conclusion that dinner tonight would be the best course of action.

As we got ready to go, Wes was encouraging and supportive. He did his best to keep me present and calm, but my mind was all over the place. I just wanted it *over*. Deciding to walk again tonight, I opted for a pair of black over-the-knee boots with no heel.

The way Wes's eyes coasted over me when I stepped out of my room made my skin prickle with awareness. I paired the boots with my burgundy suede leggings, a black long-sleeve bodysuit, and a black leather jacket. Not my usual style, but I needed a confidence boost to get through tonight.

Now as we walk into The Gidley, I can feel other eyes on me, and self-consciousness about my choice of outfit prickles. But Wes, being Wes, senses my discomfort.

His lips ghost my ear with words that are just for me. "You are the sexiest woman in this room. And you are *mine*."

His possessive claim growled against my neck has me shivering as I melt into his side. I want to kiss him senseless, but I spot my parents waiting for us by a table near the windows. My spine stiffens, and Wes links his hand with mine, giving it a squeeze, letting me know he's with me.

I hug my dad when I approach the table. I hadn't planned on it, but after the one yesterday and talking things out with Wes, I can't help myself. My mom looks shocked to say the least. As far as I know, she isn't aware of our dinner last night.

When she opens her arms to me, expecting the same, I can't make myself do it. I'm not prepared to give her any more of myself. Thankfully Wes steps in, pulling her into his side as if it's the most natural thing in the world, saving me from having to reject her.

I take my seat and Wes moves to sit next to me, but before he can, my dad approaches him, hand outstretched. Wes takes it and then pulls my dad into a hug as well. As someone who knows his hugs well, I can tell *this* one is genuine. Dad looks taken aback but smiles before moving to take his seat on my opposite side.

We exchange pleasantries and small talk for a few minutes while the server brings us water and takes our drink orders. My glass of wine cannot come soon enough as my nerves ramp up. Wes places a hand on my thigh to keep me from bouncing it into the table and shaking the cutlery. After our drinks arrive, I ask our server to give us some time before we order dinner. I look at Wes and I'm met with a smile and a wink, encouraging me to say what I need to say. This man.

"Mom. Dad. I've thought a lot about everything you said. There is a lot of pain and trauma in my past associated with both of you. Things that have caused lasting damage." My mom starts to interrupt, but Dad stops her with a look. "I have some things that I need to say to each of you. I know they probably won't be easy to hear, but I need you to listen."

Wes gives my thigh another squeeze, and I take a deep breath before continuing.

"Dad." I turn to him first, and I can feel the nerves radiating off him. "You broke my heart when you left. I loved you so much." His face falls, and I see the quiet sadness in his eyes with my use of the past tense. "Without you there, I spent years lost in a storm of uncertainty and instability. My fear of abandonment and a feeling of never being enough has wreaked havoc on my relationships and contributed to my trust issues for years."

I turn in my seat, focusing my attention on my mom.

"Mom." She looks at me with such hope in her eyes, and I will never understand how she thinks there is anything for us in the future. "You were heartbroken too when Dad left, I know that, and I won't deny the pain that it caused you. But I've since discovered you held the key to the one thing I desperately wanted—a relationship with him. And you withheld that from me, all because you were angry and hurt."

Her eyes flare before she turns her glare on my father. Her shoulders rise and she looks about ready to yell when I hold up a hand.

"No. I'm not finished." She slumps back in her chair a little, but her eyes still burn with rage for the man next to her. "You never told me that he still wanted me. You allowed me to believe that I was the problem, that I wasn't enough to make him stay. You dragged me from house to house to live with whoever you could find that could fill the void in your life, while never once thinking about the void you were creating in mine. I won't even get into the fact that you didn't believe me, your own daughter, when I told you one of your boyfriends came on to me when you weren't home. That I no longer felt safe there."

My dad's gaze snaps to me and the look of fear and distress on his face has replaced any and all sadness. My mother at least has the decency to look sheepish at my revelation, but she says nothing. Shocker. When my dad turns that look on her, it's morphed into something else entirely. He looks like he might be the one to start yelling, so I grab hold of his arm, bringing his focus back to me.

"It's okay, Dad. I'm fine, nothing happened." I look back to Mom and keep going, on a roll now. "I may have had trust issues initially because of Dad leaving, but those only grew because of what you put me through.

"And then you came to visit with Bill, and you broke every semblance of trust that I had rebuilt. You destroyed any love that I still carried for you when you allowed a man into my home to steal from me."

Mom sniffs, and I think there's genuine fear in her eyes now. I have to hold back the emotion clawing its way up my throat and finish, because no matter how hard this feels, I know that it's the right way forward. The only way forward.

"I may not understand the dynamics that were at play, but nothing will ever justify what happened. Not only was my home—my safe space—violated, but I lost my mom that day. I wish I could say there's a way back from that, but the truth is that I will never be able to trust you enough to be in my life again. I will always wonder if you're only here for what you can get from me. Especially now that I'm about to come into some money."

"Joss, honey." A look of panic has taken over her features.

It's Wes who stops her this time. "Andrea, she's not done."

"I'm in a really good place now, and I won't jeopardize that by allowing you back into my life. I won't apologize for putting myself first. In the end, we all have to make choices. You made yours, and now I've made mine."

I hold her gaze because I want her to see that I'm not going to waver in my decision. I will not break down and change my mind. I'm done living a life where she has the power to come in and flip it upside down.

"Joss." Her voice quivers. "I'm sorry. I know I wasn't a good mother to you, but please, don't write me off. I can be better. I know that I can. Your father and I both can, please don't do this. We can do better for you."

"I appreciate the apology, I really do, but it's too late at this point to fix the damage. Even overlooking all the terrible situations you put me in over the years and the stealing, it's the fact that you made a decision to keep me from my father—encouraging me to hate him as much as you did so that I would never want him back. *That* is what I can't forgive. You stole time I can never get back because you were hurt, and you never once thought about what I needed."

I look at my dad now and reach a hand out to grab his.

"We can't get those sixteen years back, Dad." My eyes fill with tears, and he squeezes my hand, looking just as grief-stricken at that loss as I feel. "But we can try to rebuild now."

I look back to my mom, her eyes ping-ponging between Dad and me like we've each grown an extra head.

"You're choosing him?" Her voice rises, drawing attention from the surrounding tables. "You're choosing a man who abandoned you over the mother who stayed? You're choosing a homewrecker, a man who, no matter what he says to you now, never wanted you? He only wanted to hurt me."

"Andrea," my dad says, attempting to stop her tirade.

She continues as if he didn't speak. "It's because of the money, right? He offers you a big bank account and, like a money-grubbing whore, you let him back into your life."

"Andrea!" Dad's voice rises above hers, but the damage is done. I feel the sting of her insult like she physically slapped me. "That is enough. I will not sit here and allow you to attack Joss this way.

She's made her decision about how she wants to proceed. You are embarrassing yourself."

He's vibrating with rage, and beside me, Wes is nearly out of his seat. He said his sister was fiercely loyal, but it must be a family trait based on the way he looks like he wants to pick my mom up and throw her out of this restaurant. Their outrage on my behalf is helping me to stay calm, and I give them each a squeeze to let them know I'm okay. I'm just ready for this to be over.

"Mom," I say, voice steady. "I'm not forgetting the pain Dad caused me, but much of that could have been avoided. I want the chance to see if there is a relationship to salvage there. But with you, as your outburst only proves... there is no future here. I won't subject myself to your selfishness any longer."

She sits in stunned silence. Her mouth hangs open slightly, her eyes wide as she continues to look between me, my dad, and Wes. It's like she's waiting for one of us to say *just kidding* and pretend the last few minutes never happened.

"Brian, surely you can talk some sense into her," she says with an arrogant indignance. "I am, after all, the one who brought you two back together. You wouldn't even be here if it weren't for me."

It's my dad's turn to look like she's slapped him. "You can't be serious. I would've never needed to track you down if you had enabled contact from the beginning. I've taken responsibility for my actions, and I won't downplay their damage, but Joss's choices are her own. I won't attempt to influence her."

"But you already have!" Her voice rises again. "How does she even know, Brian? Clearly you told her in a ploy to turn her against me. I was *protecting* her so that she wouldn't get hurt by you in the same way I did. I figured it was better to do it all in one fell swoop."

"That wasn't your decision to make," I interrupt. "It should have been mine, and you took it from me. I won't allow anyone to do that to me again."

I take her in, knowing this will be the last time I see her. It doesn't make me as sad as I thought it would. Her reaction was exactly what I expected, and to be honest, it's only going to make it that much easier to move forward.

"Fine. If that's your decision, I guess it's time for me to leave." She stands, grabbing her purse off the back of her chair. "I don't need to stay and be attacked further for trying to reconcile with my own daughter. You don't want me here, I'll leave." She pauses only briefly to look at me, like I might change my mind and beg her to stay. I stay planted in my chair, not needing the firm hand Wes has placed on my thigh but appreciating it all the same.

"Goodbye, Mother," is all I have left to say.

She blanches momentarily before lifting her chin and stalking out of the restaurant. So many eyes follow her before awkwardly looking away.

Once she's out of sight, I let my head fall to my hands, not out of sadness but out of sheer exhaustion. Wes gently rubs my back, his fingers trailing up and down my spine. I raise my head to look at him, finding a small smile tilting his lips. And with that, I release the last of the breath I was holding.

Picking up my glass of wine, I raise it to the two men at the table.

"To new beginnings."

They raise their glasses to clink with mine, then I wave to the server to come take our dinner order. I'm not sure I'll be able to eat, but as I look at the men beside me, the knot in my stomach loosens. They both stood up for me, defended me, and it feels odd to have people who are truly on my side.

"I am so proud of you, Grey. So fucking proud," Wes says, his breath ghosting my ear. "Watching you hold your own, fight your battle, and come out the other side with your head held high... I don't think I've ever been more in love with you."

His lips find mine and I close my eyes, letting him anchor me. His hand tightens around my thigh, making goose bumps shiver across my skin.

My dad clears his throat, and Wes's laugh is right against my lips before he pulls back. "My apologies, Brian, I couldn't help myself." His eyes finally leave mine and he sits back in his chair to look at my dad. My cheeks are ablaze with the heat of his words, his kiss, and the knowledge that my dad witnessed all of it.

"As I said the other day," Dad says, eyes soft as he looks at us, "I'm glad she has you, Wes. She deserves someone who will love her like you so clearly do."

"Thanks, Dad." I tuck my chin, trying to hide my emotion.

"Now." Dad claps his hands together, drawing my attention back to him. "How did you two meet?"

Wes and I look at each other, smiles growing across our faces until we both burst out laughing. Wes tucks a strand of hair behind my ear and says, "Grey, try not to make me look too bad, okay? This is your dad after all."

I shake my head at him, a smile I would not have anticipated wearing this evening wide across my face as I dive into our story.

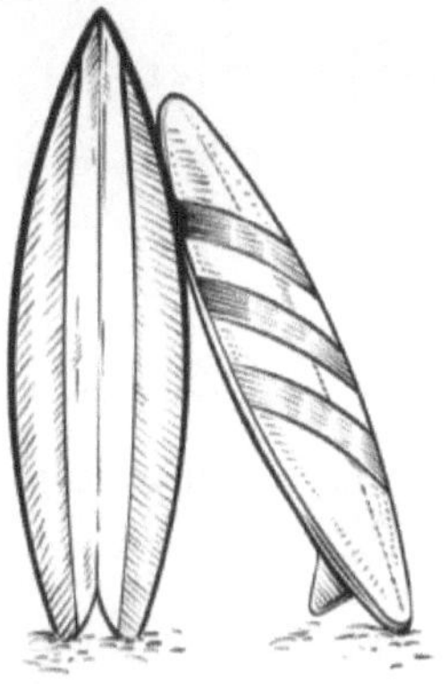

CHAPTER THIRTY-FIVE

WES

I come in for a landing at the airfield and smile as the wheels touch down. It's been a long week filled with multiple flights daily and lots of new people to meet. I'm soaking in every minute, fully knowing that when I eventually change jobs, I'll miss the energy that comes with this. Being busy also keeps me from counting down the days, hours, minutes until Joss gets home. She's been on an extended trip, and damn if I don't miss her constantly.

We're going on two months since her parents were here, since we officially became a couple, and she's been gone at least half of that time. We make do with FaceTime and texting when she's away, but those things don't hold a candle to the reality of having that woman on a surfboard next to me every morning, in my space... in my bed. We aren't officially living together. Yet. It's more like we have a two-bedroom apartment that happens to have two kitchens and living rooms. It doesn't matter where we sleep or where we eat though, if we're home, we're together.

I run through all the final checks on the plane before hopping in the company F-150 I use during the week. I suppose I'll have to look into getting a car of my own when the sale of Adventure Chasers finalizes. Pulling my phone out of my pocket and turning it back on, I'm greeted by texts from my two favorite women.

Grey

> Just landed in New Zealand. Going to grab a drink with a couple of the flight attendants, wish you were here. You'd love NZ!

Rory

> Hey, just had a question for you about Christmas. Give me a call when you can :)

I smile as I read them, feeling lucky they're my people. I respond to Rory first because I want to make sure she'll still be awake when I get home.

Me

> I have some ideas about Christmas, but I might not have a firm plan for a few more days. Will call you in a bit if you're up and we can discuss ;)

Rory

> What's with the wink?

Me

> You'll have to wait up and see

Going back to Joss's message, I send a quick reply, unable to keep the smile off my face.

Before I fling my phone into the passenger seat, I send one more text to let Breck know I'm on my way back to the office. His truck sits between Talia's car and Drew's SUV when I pull up. Good, I was hoping to catch up with him for a few minutes. Every time I've been in the office this week, he's been out. I jump down from the truck, double clicking the key fob to lock it. I rarely take it home on Fridays, but I had several larger packages delivered here to avoid Joss seeing them. I also need it for my weekend plans, so Breck's letting me use it.

I walk in the door and see my packages stacked along the front wall. I grab the first one, figuring I'll load them up now and talk to Breck when I'm done. I don't make it back to the door before I hear raised voices coming from behind his door, and though I can't make out what they're saying, I know it's him and Talia.

Well, that's a new development. I've never heard them fight before.

I have a clear view into Drew's office from where I stand. His eyes are trained on the source of the shouting.

"How long has that been going on?" I ask, walking to lean against his door jamb.

He shrugs. "Today? Or in general?" He turns away, refocusing on his computer.

His response surprises me. Maybe it's less of a new development than I thought. This just seems so out of character for them, especially Breck.

"Meaning what?" I press.

"They've been at it a lot lately. Not my business." He shrugs again, like he couldn't care less that his business partners are fighting in the other room.

"Right." I want to roll my eyes at him, but I hold back. "Since it seems like they're busy, I won't hang around to talk to Breck. Can you ask him to give me a call when they, uh, finish up?"

"I'm not a secretary." Drew's voice is flat and irritated.

I blow out my breath in a huff, an attempt to keep myself from asking what his problem is. "Whatever, I'll just text him." I turn on my heel, grab my packages, and walk back out to the truck.

Once I'm settled behind the wheel, packages stowed in the back, I pull out my phone.

Me

> Taking the truck for the weekend, give me a call when you're done at the office.

I still don't know what to think. Breck has been stressed lately, but I assumed it was all to do with the sale. Maybe it is, and maybe that stress is putting strain on their relationship. I rub the back of my neck, relieving the tension there. I'll have to see if Breck can get out for a night soon, just the two of us.

I park the truck in the lot by our building and pile the packages into my arms, regretting having them sent to the office. I awkwardly make my way up to my apartment, having to drop the packages in the hall to dig my keys from my pocket.

Once I'm inside, I feel the buzz of a text in my jeans.

Grey

> I'd love that. Last night away and then you're all mine for a week! I can't wait. Call you later ;)

A wink from Joss means something completely different than the one I sent to Rory. As it should. I shudder to think of my sister sending a text with the same meaning to anyone. I want to remain blissfully ignorant of my sister's love life for as long as humanly possible. Maybe forever.

Me

> Yes please. You have your own room tonight?

Grey

> Yes sir

I nearly groan out loud.

Me

> Are you trying to kill me, woman?

Clearly her being gone for a week has made a weak man out of me if her flippant use of the word "sir" takes my brain down the gutter.

I get down to business opening the boxes, looking over into the corner where the other things that arrived this week sit, fully assembled and ready to be arranged. I have a lot to accomplish before Joss gets in tomorrow—I think it's going to require a beer or three.

Waking up without Joss in my bed has become the worst kind of torture. She's only been gone for a week and her scent has nearly completely evaporated. I miss hearing her sing in the shower when she gets ready in the morning. Hell, I miss *joining* her in said shower.

I still can't believe that in the span of five months, everything about my life has changed. I came here trying to escape the man I was, the man I'd been forced to leave behind when I left the Navy. Instead, I ended up finding myself in more ways than one. Joss has played a major role in the way I now envision my future, and I'm enjoying showing her how committed I am to making things work with us. Earning that trust has been a special privilege.

Even though I took the day off, I have a lot to do today. When I told Rory my plans last night, I swear she was thrilled enough to jump through the phone. She even had a few ideas on how to make the weekend better.

Nothing helps to dissipate the excited energy rolling off me, making me eager to go for a run. I haven't spent much time pounding the pavement since the move, allowing surfing and swimming in the complex's pool to fill most of my workout time. Plus, running with my knee can be a challenge, but there's still something cathartic about it that I crave.

As I run down the street toward the harbour, I take in the beauty of this city that is now my home. It's still bizarre for me to think of Sydney in that way. I miss Tahoe, but I've lived such a nomadic lifestyle with the military that it hasn't been *home* for me in a long time. The contentment I feel as I look around, knowing that I don't have to leave this place, that no one is going to order me to upheave my entire life and move somewhere new, is incredible.

If you'd asked me a year ago how I'd feel about having complete control over where I lived, I would have told you that the prospect was terrifying. There was comfort in being told where to go and when, of not being rooted to any one place. That terror played a huge part in me running to Sydney, to somewhere I assumed would be a placeholder until I decided what I really wanted to do. But now, knowing that I can choose Joss, choose Sydney, choose to be here without the prospect of another move, another change being right around the corner... It's freeing.

I run past St. Mary's Cathedral before heading into Hyde Park and I can't help but smile. Turning back toward the apartment, a sense of calm envelops me, knowing that it's my future I'm running toward, and I'm so ready to get to it.

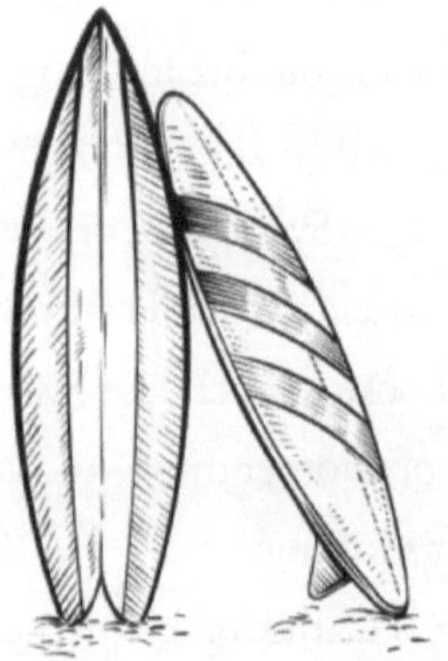

CHAPTER THIRTY-SIX

Joss

My flight into Sydney is as smooth as can be, and I'm so appreciative of the ease with which everyone disembarks so that I can finish up on the plane and get home. Wes mentioned a surprise, so I've been filled with a nervous anticipation all day. Hopefully whatever it is includes us staying home so I can climb him like a tree the moment I walk in the door.

I check my phone as I walk off the plane and see his name there.

I'm always impatient when it comes to you.

I giggle and can't help but squirm at the butterflies in my stomach. I have never experienced anything like how I feel with him. He makes me better, makes me want to *be* better, makes me want things I've never let myself want before. I'm smiling like a fool, not paying attention as I walk out past security in the direction of the taxi rank, when I run into a firm chest.

"Crap, I'm—" I break off when I look up and into the face of the only man who's ever taken my breath away. "Wes!" I throw myself into his arms, my rolling bag clattering to the floor behind me. "When you said you were waiting for me, I assumed you meant at home."

I pull back to look at him, taking in every detail, ensuring he hasn't changed in the week since I last saw him. His beard is trimmed and I can see his dimples peeking through, making the butterflies feel more like the beating wings of a dragon. He's also wearing that freaking baseball cap, the one from his first day in Sydney. It sits backward on his head, giving me an unobstructed view of his sapphire blue eyes.

My feet dangle above the floor, and his arms around my waist may be pulling my skirt indecently high up my thighs, but I don't have a care in the world. I'm in his arms and he's looking at me with so much love that I could melt into a puddle on the floor.

"You know what they say when you assume, Grey?" He chuckles and brings those perfect lips to mine. I sink into him, oblivious to the airport full of people milling around, and grip his hair under his hat to bring him closer. I said I wanted to climb him like a tree, and that's what I'm about to do if we don't stop soon. I break the kiss, my breathing fast and shallow, while Wes slowly lowers me back to the ground. I feel a little wobbly on my legs, like I'm standing on stilts, but he holds firm to my waist, keeping me close.

"Damn. That was…" He clears his throat, his Adam's apple bobbing. "I mean, the whole 'absence makes the heart grow fonder' thing must be true, because… damn." He lets out a low laugh, and I feel it rumble through my whole body. My fingers run along his jaw, then down his neck to his shoulder.

"What are you doing here?" I breathe.

"I couldn't wait a single minute longer to see you, and I told you I have a surprise." He waggles his eyebrows and I pick up on his giddy excitement. I can feel it in the way he moves, the way he smiles so big and wide.

"Okay…" I draw out the word. "So are you going to tell me what this surprise is?"

He reaches around me to grab my bag off the floor. Then, grabbing me around the waist again, he pulls me into his side and leads me toward the doors.

"Now what would be the fun in that?" He leans down and presses one more quick kiss to my temple, leaving me to wonder what on earth he has planned.

When Wes said he had a surprise, I never would have guessed it would entail a long drive up the coast to Blueys Beach. He apparently rebooked the trip we were supposed to take two months ago for this weekend so that we could get away from the city and enjoy our first mini-break as a couple.

When we got into the ute at the airport and I spotted the boards in the back along with our overnight bags, I was speechless. Yet nothing compared to how stunned I was when a private beach bungalow waited for us at the end of our long drive.

I take in every detail of the gorgeous space, the wood floors warm against my bare feet. Inside the expansive room, there's a large king-sized bed with a gauzy white canopy overhang like something out of a fairytale. Opposite the bed is a small sitting room and kitchen space, filled with late afternoon sunlight.

The coastal-inspired décor—all tans, mints, and blues accented with furniture made from driftwood or wicker—makes the room feel light and airy. There's a decadent clawfoot tub in the bathroom, and there's already a picture forming in my mind of me sinking into it. A full week of flights and hotel room beds has me sighing at the idea.

"Beautiful," I say, scanning the room one more time.

"I agree," Wes husks, and when I bring my eyes to his they're not looking at the room. They're glued to me.

When I walk back to him and snake my arms around his middle, I tilt my head back and smile at him. There's no disguising the look of desire in his gaze as he rakes it over my body. I'm still in my uniform and want nothing more than to strip it off, but I'm caught in his orbit and don't think I can move.

His hands slide up along my outer thighs, to my hips, and then my waist. Each inch a slow tease of his warm skin through the fabric.

I shiver when his hands reach my rib cage and his smile turns wicked, both dimples popping under that beard that I've come to love so much.

"What do you say, Grey? Shall we see if the bed is to your liking?" Without warning, he picks me up and within two strides tosses me onto the bed like I'm feather-light and not a whole person. I squeal when the soft mattress catches my fall, my head landing amongst the many pillows.

Wes's laugh is carefree, but his eyes are dark, hooded, and the smoldering look he gives me makes everything inside me tighten in anticipation. He kneels at the end of the bed, first reaching up to remove his hat, tossing it across the room where it lands with a thud, and then to pull off his shirt with one hand. My mouth goes dry at the sight of him. There's so much more than the physical attraction between us now, but damn if I don't love to look at this man. Damn if our unrelenting love for each doesn't make that attraction burn brighter. I want him. I want him forever.

As he climbs over me on the bed, he whispers in my ear, "I want you forever too, Joss."

I guess I said that last thought out loud. It doesn't matter though, because there's no more thinking after that. There's only touch, only breaths, only us as we let our hearts and bodies do the talking.

The next morning, we wake up to the sound of waves on the beach and slide into our bathers without saying a word. The quiet is part of what makes an early morning surf so beautiful. There's no need to fill the silence. You just allow the crisp, cool water to wake up your senses and your mind in whatever way you need on that particular day.

Only once we've paddled out and are bobbing on the waves does Wes finally speak. "I love you, Joss." The words are a caress, filled with so much feeling, and when I look over, I see it all detailed in his features as well. The softness to his eyes, the adoring smile tugging at his lips.

"I love you too, Wes."

The sun continues to rise behind us as we take turns paddling into the waves and riding to our hearts' content. By the time we're spent and boneless, lying in the sand outside our bungalow, the sun has fully risen and my stomach is screaming for sustenance. I flip onto my side, taking in every inch of exposed skin on the man beside me. It's warmer here, in the throes of spring, so Wes is in nothing but a pair of navy boardshorts.

The way they hug his backside makes them my favorite. They've pulled up a few inches on his legs, and I can see the entirety of the scars that surround his knee and extend up his muscular thigh. I feel incredibly honored that he chose to share the story of how he got them. That he trusted me with them, trusted me to hold those broken pieces of him.

I scooch closer to him on the sand, letting my hand trace over the scar at his shoulder where a piece of metal lodged itself in the crash. His body jerks at the contact. "Sorry," I say, but he's already relaxed again into the sand as I move my fingers up and down the raised skin. A low hum emanates from his chest and he catches my hand in his.

"What are you thinking right now?" he asks.

"I was thinking about how badly I wanted to know all your scar stories when we first met. Now I do."

He brings my fingers to his lips, letting his eyes fall closed as he lies relaxed in the sand.

He begins to say something but stops when my stomach grumbles loudly. His laugh puffs out against my hand, and I giggle next to him.

"I was going to say we should go get cleaned up in the outdoor shower where you could more thoroughly examine all of my scars... but maybe I need to feed you first."

He shifts so he's lying on his side facing me, our eyes locked on each other, grey to blue, and I have the briefest thought of what the eyes of our children would be like if we ever have them. It startles me, not because I don't want kids but because I've never been at a place in my life where thinking of them felt like anything but a faraway possibility.

"Breakfast, yeah?" he asks, his hand coasting over my stomach when it grumbles again.

"Yeah," I breathe, but instead of moving to get up, I press my lips to his. He groans, letting his fingers tighten around my waist for just a moment before he pulls back.

"We better stop." He laughs against my lips. "Otherwise I'll have you laid out under me in the sand, and I'm not sure it will be nearly as sexy as the movies make it out to be." He presses a kiss to my forehead before pushing himself to stand, hand outstretched. He wiggles his fingers at me a little, and it pulls a bigger smile across my face.

"You're probably right. I don't want to be washing sand out of places it was never meant to be for the next week." I slip my hand into his and he pulls me up, using all his strength so that my momentum carries me straight into his body.

"This feels familiar," I say, looking up at him with joyful amusement as I think back to that first day on the plane when we ended up in a very similar position.

"Yeah, but this time, I'm not letting you go."

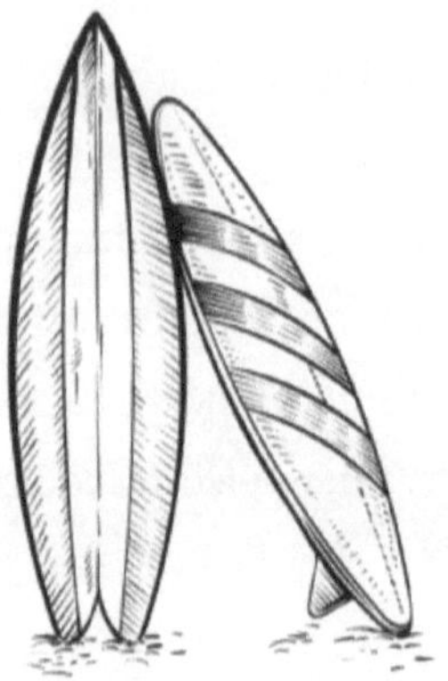

CHAPTER THIRTY-SEVEN

Wes

I did indeed pull Joss into the outdoor shower, our desire for each other outweighing the need for food. Though I did make good on my promise to feed her afterward. Now she's relaxed in the hammock that's stretched across our little porch, reading a book, a small smile playing on her lips. When she opened her bag last night and found four new books laid out on top of her clothes, she burst with excitement.

I knew she took her Kindle with her to work—she never goes anywhere without it—but I know how much she cherishes paperbacks. Jaz recommended a couple, namely romances starring stubbled cowboys, musicians, and hockey players, as well as a thriller that takes place at a beach resort that seemed fitting. Joss is currently curled up with the hockey romance. I didn't know this was a genre, but based on the giddy grin on her face, Jaz picked a winner.

In addition to pulling in help with the books, Rory offered her advice on how to make this weekend extra special for Joss. She sent me a YouTube video of how to set up my phone camera so that we can take some sunset pictures on the beach, which I have planned for later tonight. She also recommended bringing everything for a beach bonfire and for bubble baths.

"Hey," I say quietly, and she places her book down on her lap. "Have you talked to your dad this week?"

Joss and Brian have been slowly figuring out a new dynamic following our explosive dinner at The Gidley. Before he flew home to Brisbane, he told us about how his wife, Alex, died of cancer less than a year ago. From the sounds of it, she'd been encouraging Brian to try to reconcile with Joss for years leading up to her passing. Her death and the realization that life is fleeting played the biggest role in him reaching out.

"Oh, yeah. I actually talked to him yesterday." She purses her lips. "He, uh, well... He really wants me to talk to Isla." Her shoulders sag. "I'm not sure I'm ready for that."

Joss's half-sister has been a bit of a sore subject as she and Brian try to find their footing. Isla isn't to blame, and Joss knows that, but that doesn't change the reality or make it any less complicated. There's still a lot of hurt there for Joss, and I can understand why she's struggling.

Then there's the added layer that Isla starts her final year of high school in the new year and plans to attend the University of Sydney after she graduates. Brian has already flirted with the idea of moving to Sydney as well, his desire to be near both of his daughters being a driving factor. Joss feels the pressure to be a big sister somehow to someone whose very existence is a constant reminder of what she lost. Needless to say, it hasn't been all sunshine and rainbows trying to navigate the nuances of having Brian back in her life.

I stand up from the porch steps and force her to scoot over so that I can slide in beside her in the hammock.

"I know this is a complicated situation, but you can take all the time you need to decide what you want. You know that, right?" I lean in and kiss her temple, banding my arms around her.

"I know. I just..." She exhales and shakes her head. "She's just a kid. Am I being selfish? Her mom died last year, and I'm sure she could use a big sister. I just don't know if I can be that for her." She groans and leans her head back. "Not that you'd understand, what with the amazing relationship you have with Rory."

"Joss." I bring my fingers to her chin and tip it up to meet her gaze. "No one can decide that but you. You know I love having a sister, she's a huge part of my world, but our situations are very different. Do I think Isla would benefit from knowing you? Having *you* as a sister? Absolutely. But it's your call, and no one will judge you for putting your needs first."

She nods, her head falling against my chest. "You're right." Her lips press into my sternum, and that simple touch radiates out until I can feel it everywhere. "I won't be making any life-changing decisions while we're here though, so let's talk about something else."

"What shall we talk about, Grey?" I let my hands roam down her back, sliding my top one down her thigh until I can hitch it up over my hip. Her head tips back so we're eye to eye.

She lets out a throaty hum and her voice is like smoke when she says, "This doesn't feel like talking."

"Talking is vastly overrated," I say, my lips coasting along her neck and back up until I capture her mouth in a kiss that sets my blood on fire. Who needs a bonfire when I have Joss to keep me warm.

Her hands tangle in my hair, pulling me closer, and she shifts her weight to bracket my hips. Unfortunately, we both forgot we're in a hammock and the whole thing rolls. One minute we're mid-makeout, the next we're sent sprawling onto the wooden planks of the porch.

We're a tangled heap of limbs, and I can't breathe because I'm laughing so hard. Joss is right there with me, her loud, uninhibited laughter like music to my ears. This is the kind of life I want. One that's filled with fun and silliness and love. One that's filled with Joss.

"The hammock clearly didn't approve of your attempt to seduce me, Grey."

"Oh, so this is all my fault?" She smacks her hand against my chest but quickly chases away the sting with a kiss.

"Pretty much." I lift my head to kiss her nose. "I was thinking we could get in another surf this afternoon if you're up for it, and then maybe have a bonfire tonight?"

"If that means I get to ogle you in your boardshorts for a second time today *and* I get to snuggle with you by the fire, then count me in." She presses herself up to stand and extends her hand for me with a smirk on her lips. When I take it, she does her best to pull me from the ground, but I barely budge from my place on the porch. She pouts, and my shoulders shake with laughter.

"Sorry, Grey, that's my move. Now, let's go surfing."

Joss sits between my legs with her back to my chest while we watch the fire dance and spark in front of us. The blanket we're sitting on keeps the cold from seeping up from the sand and the fire staves off the chill of the freshly set sun. The only sounds are those of the waves crashing on the beach and the crackling logs in the fire.

Our second surf was long and we're both exhausted, content to sit in each other's arms and just be. I've been mulling over my words for the last half hour while sitting here quietly, waiting for the perfect moment. For someone who never gets nervous, I don't know why I am now.

I've finally worked up the nerve to spit it out when Joss speaks first, still looking at the fire. "Will you move in with me?"

My body jolts in surprise, not because of what she asked, but because she beat me to it. It takes only a split second to recover, and I let out a bark of a laugh, tightening my arms around her waist.

"Way to steal my thunder, Grey. I was about to ask *you* to move in with *me*."

She spins to look at me. "You were not!" Her eyes are crinkled around the edges with the wide grin that splits her face.

I lean forward and kiss her lips softly. "I absolutely was. I was just trying to work up the nerve, and you had to go and do it so casually and confidently. Damn—you put me to shame, woman." I shake my head.

"You didn't answer my question," she says with a smirk, and I let my hands cradle her head as I marvel at how beautiful she is. I can't imagine spending even a minute of my life with anyone but her.

"I'd have thought my answer was rather obvious. But yes, Joss, I'll move in with you. There's nowhere else I'd rather be." I lean in to kiss her again, but she pulls back slightly, a small crease between her brows.

"Why were you nervous?"

"I mean, I was pretty sure you'd say yes since we basically live together already, but still, it's a big deal." I scratch the back of my neck. "I've never lived with someone before, never wanted to, but I want everything with you. It still scares me sometimes." I clear my throat and look into her eyes. The way the flames dance in their depths makes them look like molten silver.

"I love you, and sometimes that scares *me* too. But you know what, every day it gets easier to accept that you aren't going anywhere, that we're everything to each other, and our love is a gift. *You* are a gift."

We move at the same time, meeting in the middle until our lips brush together, soft at first but quickly growing more insistent. We kiss like that for minutes, or it could be hours, before everything slows. I roll to my side, facing Joss, and watch the dying flames cover her in dancing shadows. Her eyes are closed and she looks so content, peaceful.

I hum and grin at her. "I have one more question for you," I say. "Yes?"

"Will you go to Tahoe with me for Christmas?" I'm running my fingers up and down her arm, making goose bumps erupt in their wake. "I want you to meet Rory. I want to show you where I grew up. I'd like to introduce you to my parents, even if they're kind of an acquired taste—"

"They can't be worse than my mom." Her laugh draws my gaze to her lips.

"Nah, they aren't that bad, and they'll absolutely love you. Do you think you can get the time off?"

"Yeah, I think so. I'll try, anyway. I'd love to go home with you and meet your family, Wes."

"It's not my home anymore, Joss." I've known that to be true for a while now. "That's here, with you."

She sucks in a short breath, and the firelight catches the tears in her eyes for just a moment before she closes them, leans in, and kisses me again. I'm not sure how I manage to get to my feet, Joss in my arms wrapped in the blanket with our lips still fused together, but I do. The final embers of the fire die out as I carry her to the bungalow, footsteps creaking on the boarded steps, until I get her laid beneath me on the bed, exactly where I want her, and I find my way home.

Joss and I had to drag ourselves away from our little home away from home this morning. It was the perfect escape from the rest of the

world, a place where we could just be. We fit in a final surf, riding every wave as if it were our last, before packing up to get on the road. Then we spent the hours-long drive talking about the upcoming move, deciding it would be best for me to move into her place, since she owns all her furniture. I assumed that would be the case, so my final surprise of the weekend should work out to be the grand gesture I was going for.

I'm not *completely* oblivious to all those romance novels Joss leaves lying around. Although they're not my usual style, I've picked up some tips from them over the last few months, occasionally borrowing one while she's away. Call it research.

When we pull up to our building, it's with a sense of relief, a readiness. I run around the front of the truck, reaching Joss's door before she gets the chance to open it herself. Her answering smile and small blush at the gesture don't go unnoticed.

"Thank you." She hops out of the truck and presses up on her toes to lightly brush her lips across mine, sending desire skittering down my spine. Will I ever get enough of her?

She grabs our bags as I hoist the surfboards out of the back and we trudge through the doors, headed to the elevator.

Frank looks up from his newspaper and smiles. "G'day, Ms. Joss. Mr. Anderson." I'm still working on getting him to call me Wes, but I'm not holding my breath. He talks to me now, and that's progress.

"Hi, Frank," Joss and I say in unison, and she continues. "Enjoy what's left of your weekend."

We step onto the elevator and Joss lets the bags drop to the floor with a thud and a sigh.

"Maybe those four books were a bad idea?" I needle her, knowing that she'll happily carry a heavier bag if it means she can have her books.

"Definitely not. I'm just exhausted. That last paddle out was a lot of work and my arms are limp noodles."

She picks everything back up with a groan and we exit at our floor. My heart rate kicks up in anticipation as I lead her toward her apartment instead of stopping at mine.

"What are you doing?"

"Let's drop your stuff off first," I prompt, and she looks at me with suspicion but pulls out her keys to unlock the door.

When we walk into the living room, she stops dead, eyes scanning the entirety of the space.

"Wes..."

There's a vase of fresh-cut yellow roses sitting on the dining table and another vase of them on a side table by the couch. She turns on the spot, noticing more changes to the room, where my things are placed amongst hers. My books are nestled with hers on the shelves. Even my shoes are placed by the door.

The picture of Joss and me, from the bonfire at Breck's, is hung on the entryway wall, and surrounding it are more pictures of us. The three canvas prints I ordered to the office hang behind the dining table. A picture of Tahoe that Rory took sits in the middle—a piece of my old home to keep in my new one—flanked by ones of Joss and I surfing. Breck took those on a morning when he showed up a little later than we did for dawn patrol.

Joss turns to face me, eyes soft.

"What... how did you do this?" Her mouth hangs open slightly. Before I can answer, she walks into the bedroom where she finds a second dresser sitting beside hers, and a second chair in the corner so that we can read in the mornings. Mine is a rich navy-blue to complement her teal one. In the closet she finds my clothes hung next to hers. I continue to follow her, smiling and waiting for her to take it all in.

"Seriously, Wes, how did you do this? *When* did you do this?" she says as she walks back out of the closet, eyeing me. There's a smile ghosting her lips, so I know she's not mad.

"Is it okay? Do you like it?"

"Of course it's okay, I love it. I just can't believe you pulled this off. What would you have done if I'd said no to moving in together?"

"I was pretty sure it was happening, and I assumed we would move in here. If you'd said no, I guess I would have felt like a real jackass," I say with a laugh, and she joins in. The look of absolute joy on her face tells me just how happy she is with this surprise.

"Where did that dresser come from? And the chair?" She keeps turning in circles like a top.

"I ordered them a couple weeks ago, again assuming you'd want to live together. I knew I'd need both. I moved them over here the night before you got home. That's when I hung up all the pictures too. And moved my books. There's still some of my things next door, but for all intents and purposes, I'm moved in." I say the last part with a wink, and when she squeals, I can't hold back from grabbing her in my arms and spinning her around.

"Are you ready for what's next?" I ask, lowering her to the ground and pulling back so I can look down at her. I place my hands on either side of her face and press a light kiss to her lips.

"Next? There's more than you moving yourself into my apartment?" She looks curious and excited, her brows pulling together just a little.

"*Our* apartment, Grey, and this is just the beginning. But let's start with me taking my girlfriend, and new roommate, out to dinner, because I think we should celebrate."

She presses herself up, letting her body drag along mine as she pushes up to her tiptoes for a kiss. The intensity of it nearly knocks me backward but I hold us firm, keeping us rooted to the spot as her hands pull the hair at the nape of my neck.

"Keep kissing me like that and we won't make it to dinner."

"I don't much feel like leaving this apartment—this room—tonight. Let's celebrate tomorrow." Her lips ghost my ear as she whispers, "Tonight, you're all mine."

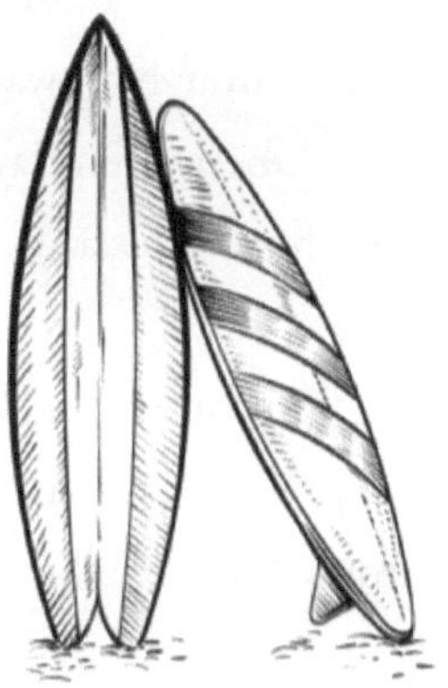

CHAPTER THIRTY-EIGHT

WES

It's been a while since Breck and I got to go out just the two of us, and I'm amped. Ever since I heard him and Talia arguing a few weeks ago at the office, he's been off. Working constantly, not his usual happy self. I'm hoping that tonight will help him relax and blow off some steam.

Breck, Talia, and Drew's cars are all still parked side by side outside Adventure Chasers when I pull up. I give a quick double honk of my horn to signal to Breck that I'm here. I leave it running but step out so I can stretch my legs while I wait. My knee was acting up this morning, and sitting in the plane all day didn't help. It's only a minute or two before Breck walks out of the building with his hands pushed deep into his jeans pockets, his stare fixed on his shoes as he walks.

When he finally looks up and sees me leaning against the front of the truck, there's something there that I can't quite read. He seems sad, dejected. He runs a hand through his wavy blond hair, and the stubble on his face tells me it's been a few days since he last shaved. The only time I've ever seen him with scruff was when we went on surf trips in college.

"Hey," I say, clapping him on the back as he comes closer. I expect a rib-cracking hug, but he just rounds the truck to the passenger side. My eyebrows draw together as my wariness ramps up. "You okay?"

"Yeah, just tired. Haven't been sleeping well lately." We climb into the cab and he immediately flips on the radio, suggesting he's done talking. Nothing about this feels right. He always has something to say, a story to tell, a joke to make, yet there he sits, silent and far away.

"You sure that's all it is?" I'm trying to keep my tone light, but he looks over and must see the genuine concern on my face because he shakes his head, his face falling further.

"Talia and I have been fighting. A lot." He focuses back on the road as I pull onto the street, clearly not wanting to put too much weight on this conversation.

"Yeah..." I grip the steering wheel, not looking at him. "I heard you guys a couple weeks ago." I chance a small glance over at him and watch his jaw clench as he stares out the window. "I've never known you to fight with anyone. I know I'm not around all the time, but I've always seen you as that couple that coos over each other and makes everyone around you sick." I laugh a little, hoping it lightens the mood.

"Oh, you mean like you and Joss are these days?" He smiles, but it doesn't reach his eyes and there's a slight edge to the words. I know he's right—Joss and I are in that disgustingly in love phase. I'm sure it affects some of the people around us, but I never would have expected Breck to feel that way. I thought, of all people, he'd relate.

"Yeah, I guess I deserve that. But seriously, man, what's going on?"

"I don't know. That's the worst part." He hits his hand against the dash and lets out a frustrated sigh. "Ever since we decided to sell the business, she's barely home, and even when she is... she isn't. We always prioritized family time when we could. Now, when I plan something for us, she either bitches about it or bails.

"Don't get me wrong, I'll take all the one-on-one time I can get with my girl"—his face softens a fraction at the mention of Willow—"but I want Talia to be part of these memories. I want her to want to be there, you know?"

"Have you asked her about it?"

"She says she's tired, busy... And I get that, I really do. The contracts, the logistics for the sale—all three of us are up to our eyeballs in it—but still..."

He trails off and I wonder, once again, how much Drew might have to do with all of this, but I'm certainly not bringing that up right now.

"She's always got an excuse, and every time I push back, we end up yelling at each other. I love her, but this doesn't feel like the Talia I fell in love with, you know? It hasn't felt like *her* for a while if I'm being honest. And I know Willow is starting to pick up on it, and I don't want that for her. She deserves better than parents that fight all the time."

"I'm really sorry, Breck. I wish there was something I could do."

He shakes his head. "I'm sure it's just a phase. We've been together a long time; it was bound to happen eventually. Relationships are supposed to be work, but I didn't anticipate our bumps to feel quite so much like mountains."

I'm at a loss for words, and I hate feeling helpless. When we pull up outside Market City Tavern in downtown Sydney, I get a text from Joss that draws my attention away, giving Breck a minute to gather himself.

Grey

Have fun tonight. Tell Breck hi for me.

She got home from a trip yesterday and is spending the evening out with Jaz. Or maybe it was evening in. I'm not sure, they didn't seem to have a plan when we last spoke. Knowing she'll be home when I get home, that we have a few days before she leaves for work again, has me smiling like a fool.

Me

I will. You and Jaz have fun too.

"See? You and Joss are the *worst* these days." He shoots me a smirk.

I bark out a laugh before sliding my phone into my pocket, determined to give Breck my undivided attention.

We head inside and grab a table near the dart board. Maybe a couple rounds of throwing sharp objects will take the edge off for Breck.

"So, where's Willow tonight?"

"Sleeping over at a friend's house." He places his phone on the table face up, glancing at the screen like he may need to put on his dad cape and rescue her at any moment. "I keep wondering when it will get easier."

"You really are such a softie for her." I laugh, and he does too. With the sound, his shoulders relax and he leans back into the chair.

A server stops at our table and we order a couple of local beers and a basket of wings to get us started. It's not long before two pints are sitting in front of us and we settle into comfortable conversation.

"How are the airline applications going?" he asks for what feels like the millionth time since I decided to move here permanently.

"Great. I have an interview with Qantas next month, and if that doesn't pan out, I still have a couple others I'm waiting to hear from."

He nods, lifting his beer to his lips. "You're sure you don't want to stay on with the new owners?"

"Nah. I don't think I could work there without you. And anyway, Joss and I have our trip to Tahoe planned for Christmas next month, and this way I don't have to ask for leave." I take a large gulp of my own beer, steeling myself for my question. It's one he's been avoiding, but the sale will be final—his turnover to the new owners complete—in two weeks.

"Have you..." I pause when I see him stiffen slightly. "Have you thought more about what you're going to do after everything's done?"

He squeezes the back of his neck with his free hand, spinning a coaster on the table with the other. "Not really. I feel like that's part of the issue with Talia. I keep asking her what she wants to do now—what we should do next—but she's not giving me much to go on."

He drums his fingers on the table, watching them with rapt attention instead of making eye contact with me. "I'm honestly at a complete loss as to what to do. You know I didn't want the sale, but I was in the minority, so now it's done and I have no idea where I go from here. That business is all I've ever known, all I've ever really wanted. What do I do now?"

He finally looks at me and I can see the uncertainty in his eyes. Adventure Chasers was his baby. He may have co-owned it with Talia and Drew, but he put his all into it. I can understand, based on my own experience losing a career I loved, how adrift he must feel with all of this.

A lightbulb goes off in my brain and I'm surprised that I didn't think of it before. "Why don't you, Talia, and Willow come to Tahoe with Joss and me? It would be a great way to let off some steam and get away after everything wraps up here. Maybe it would give you the space to figure out what that next step might be."

Breck's eyes brighten and I can see the wheels turning behind them at the idea. "Yeah. Yeah, okay. This could work. You're sure you guys wouldn't mind us tagging along? Maybe the three of us could even stay into January for a bit, while Willow is on her break from school..."

I haven't seen him this excited, this animated, over anything in a while. "We'd love to have you go with us. Can you imagine Willow on a snowboard? She'll be too freaking cute."

His signature wide smile splits his lips at the thought. "Wes, you have no idea, she's going to be so excited. I can't wait to tell her tomorrow when I pick her up. I'll run it by Talia tonight. Maybe this is exactly what we all need. Just some separation from reality for a bit."

The next couple of hours pass in a blur. We ended up shooting pool because Breck had less need to throw stuff after the idea of going to Tahoe took root. He's got a whole plan in his head now, and by the time we climb back into the truck, he's the Breck I've always known. He's lighter, happier... all the negativity and frustration from earlier in the night now firmly in the rearview mirror.

Breck's truck sits alone in the lot when I pull in. A singular light shines through the windows from his office. He hesitates, scanning the lot and the otherwise dark building. "I thought Talia would still be here. She said she had a lot to do this evening and was going to take advantage of the alone time to get caught up." His brow furrows, but with a shake of his head and a shrug, he opens his door and hops out.

"She must have finished up early," I offer. It's almost midnight and I'm ready to get home to my bed after a long day. I'm sure she was too.

"Yeah. Hopefully I can catch her before she goes to sleep and we can talk about Tahoe." His face lights up again. "Thanks for tonight, Wes. I really needed this."

He closes the door and jogs up the steps, turning to give me a parting smile as he lets himself into the building. I reverse out of my spot and turn toward home.

A knock on the front door interrupts me mid-sentence. Both Joss and I turn from where we sit on the balcony to look at it in surprise. We aren't expecting anyone this morning, and the only person on the list to be allowed up without a call first is Breck. My brow furrows and a second knock echoes through the house.

"Coming," I shout, setting my coffee on the table and heading for the door. Joss quickly follows, looking uncertain.

On the other side of the door is a disheveled Breck and a confused-looking Willow—still decked out in pajamas.

"Hey. Wasn't expecting you guys this morning." I ruffle Willow's hair and finally bring my eyes to Breck's. They're red-rimmed and swollen. "What..." I start but Breck gives me an imperceptible shake of his head, so I change tack. "Come on in, we've got pastries. Who's hungry?"

Willow's eyes brighten and she heads straight for the table, Joss following her with a glance over her shoulder that is just as concerned as the one I feel reflected back on my own face.

"What happened?" I whisper to Breck. Looking him over, he's still in the same clothes as last night. The stubble is more pronounced and his hair is sticking out in every direction.

"Can Willow..." The words get stuck, and he clears his throat to try again. "Can Willow hang in your room while we talk?"

"Yeah. Yeah, of course." The tension radiating off him is making me nervous.

"Willow, honey, why don't you take your muffin to Wes and Joss's room to watch your tablet for a bit. We're just going to talk about boring grown-up stuff out here."

"Yes!" she shouts, grabbing the backpack she dropped by the door and heading straight for our room. As soon as the door is closed and I can hear squeaky voices filtering from behind it, I turn to face my best friend.

He doesn't say anything as he stalks straight to the open back door and onto the balcony. A beat passes and I hear him bellow into the wind outside. There are no words, just agony in the sound, his hands braced on the railing, muscles bunched across his shoulders.

"What the hell happened?" Joss whispers, moving closer, her eyes locked on Breck.

"I have no idea." I wrap my arm around her shoulders and we walk as one toward the picture of raw pain and rage leaning against the railing.

"Breck?" I ask from the door, not wanting to crowd him. When he turns, there's nothing but anguish on his face as he sinks to the ground. I lurch forward as if to catch him, but his body shakes with a sob and I'm frozen, unsure of what to do. I've never seen him like this.

He looks up, his hands still in his hair, elbows resting on his knees. "She's gone."

A shock runs through my body. "Talia?" I ask, disbelief wrapped around the name.

He just nods and pulls harder at the strands of his hair. I feel Joss move closer to my side and place her hand at my back, but I can't take my eyes off what's happening in front of me.

"What do you mean she's gone?"

He shifts so he can pull something from his back pocket. It's crumpled and fraying at the edges. "I found this on my desk last night after you dropped me off. She's gone. She left with Drew. They're gone."

I falter back a step. How? Why? What about Willow?

My thoughts are echoed in Joss's voice from beside me. "What about Willow?" Her glance moves toward the wall that separates us from her.

Breck doesn't move to stand, he just holds out a second piece of paper. Joss gingerly takes it from his hand and together we take in the notarized document. My breath chokes off in my lungs and Joss covers her mouth to silence a sob. It's a legal release of Talia's parental rights to Willow. Fuck.

"Oh god... Breck, I..." There are no words for the horror filling my body.

"How could she do this? Not just to me, but to Willow?" His voice cracks on her name. "What do I tell my baby girl? What do I do?" His words are almost unintelligible through his grief. He closes his eyes, pressing the heels of his hands into the sockets and taking a deep breath.

I see the emotions flickering through Joss's eyes—shock, disbelief, anger, sadness. A swirling mess of feelings all vying for the top spot. I understand how she feels. I don't know what to say. Are there *right* words for this situation? If there are, I have no idea what they might be. I take a deep breath, trying to keep my cool for Breck's sake, because I doubt that my losing it would help in the slightest.

His head hangs heavy like the weight of the world rests on his shoulders. I can't bear to see him like this. I cross the balcony and fall to my knees, engulfing him in the most Breck-like hug I can manage. I pour everything I have into it, knowing it's my turn to hold him up now.

"You aren't alone in this. I don't know what we can do, but whatever you need, we'll do it, okay?" I crush him to me, and I feel him break. The anger makes way for the desperate pain of heartbreak as his shoulders start to shake. Joss moves to his other side and I pull her into the hug too.

"I'm so sorry, Breck," Joss says. I look at her and fall a little more in love. For how genuinely she has come to love not just me but my best friend as well. Together, we'll get him and Willow through this.

We finally break apart and Breck's eyes track to the closed bedroom door and he sighs.

"I don't want to be here—not right now." The *in Sydney* is implied.

His face is forlorn. He loves this city, the life and home he built here, so to have it all destroyed in a blink must be devastating.

The plan from last night comes back to me and I offer him the best smile I can. "We already know exactly where you're going to go."

"Yeah?"

"Yeah. You gave me a place to land when I needed it, and now it's my turn." I offer him my hand to help him up. "You and Willow are going to Tahoe. As soon as you finish the transfer to the new owners. I'll take care of getting you a place to stay for Willow's school break.

After that, if you still need time, we'll figure it out. Is that far enough away from all of this?"

"You would do that?" Breck's voice almost breaks on the words.

"I think escaping on the slopes of Tahoe is exactly what you and Willow need."

"Hey, big brother!" Rory's excited voice carries to me across the line from half a world away.

"Hey, baby sister. I need your help."

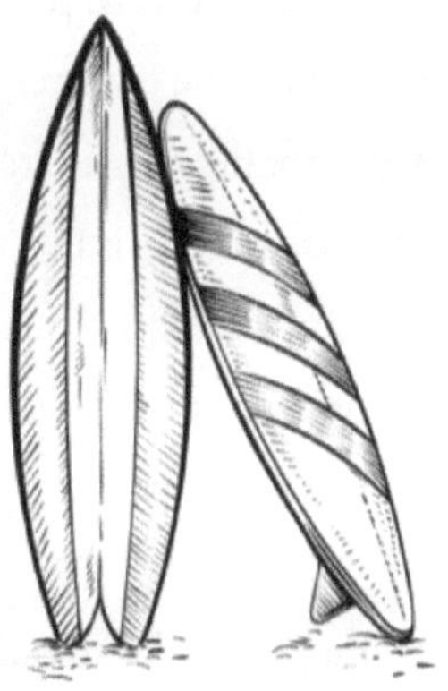

CHAPTER THIRTY-NINE

Joss

I got home late last night to a sleeping Wes, and I passed out almost instantly by his side. I didn't hear him get up, but as I run my hand over his side of the bed and find the sheets to be cold, I assume he's been up for a while. Slowly rolling over, I grab my phone off the table to check the time. It's almost ten in the morning—I don't remember the last time I slept that long or that hard.

I stand and stretch my arms overhead, twisting side to side to work out all the kinks, hearing my spine snap-crackle-pop as I move. The sound of the front door opening greets me, and I bolt for it.

I don't get to jump on him because his hands are full with a drink carrier and a bag from Harbour Grounds. I swoon a little at the sight. Not only is the man an absolute smoke show in his grey running shorts and a fitted athletic shirt, but he's carrying my specialty coffee.

There's no resisting him. Especially when his lips tip up at the sight of me and his damn dimples come out to play.

I help him put everything on the counter before reaching up to grab the bill of his baseball cap, flipping it around so that I can kiss him without taking a hat to the face. His lips are warm and there's a hint of salt there. With the way his shirt clings to him, I deduce that he went for a run before getting our breakfast. I should probably be grossed out, but after a few days away, I couldn't care less that he's sweaty.

"Have breakfast with me?" he asks sweetly against my lips. He pulls back and hands me a cup of coffee. It's a Sleepy Sydney, my favorite, and I take a long drink, letting out a happy little moan at the taste.

"Yeah, okay, because you asked so nicely." We grab the bag of pastries and move to the balcony. Summer weather is just beginning, and the sun is already high in the sky. I know it's an adjustment for Wes, a man born and raised in a snowy climate, to think of December as the beginning of summer.

I smile, knowing we'll be in that snowy climate come this weekend when we fly to Tahoe to spend Christmas with his family. And Breck and Willow. They got on a plane the day Breck finalized the transition to the new owners. They've been in Tahoe for a couple weeks now, and I know Wes is anxious to see how they're really doing—if Breck is coping with everything or just putting up a good front.

"Are you excited to see everybody this weekend?" I ask him over the top of my coffee.

"Yeah, I am. What about you? Ready to meet the family?"

I'm a little nervous about it, but I put on a brave face after much reassurance that they're all going to love me. "Of course. Are you going to teach me how to snowboard?"

"No." He says it so seriously I have to look over at him. All he's talked about has been how much he wants to go snowboarding.

"What? Why not?"

"I'm going to get you a lesson, Grey. Otherwise you'll be mad at me by the end of the day for torturing you on the slopes. I want you to actually enjoy it by the time we go together."

"A lesson? Like I'm a little kid?"

"Yeah, with Willow." He barks out a laugh and slides his fingers into mine, pulling them to his lips. "Kidding. A *private* lesson with an instructor who is used to working with adults. I promise you'll enjoy it much more if I'm not the one telling you what to do."

"But I like it when you tell me what to do." I smirk at him, begging him to contradict me.

"Touché, Grey, touché. But I'm still making you take a lesson."

I drop my shoulders and purse my lips. He just laughs again, like I'm a petulant child throwing a fit.

"Now," he says, drawing my gaze, "do you want to sit here and pout, which won't work by the way, or do you want to get ready for our date?"

I sit up straighter in my chair, spilling a little coffee down my shirt. "What date?" I say excitedly, clapping my hands together.

"I guess that's my answer. Up." He stands and offers me his calloused palm.

"See," I say, "I do like it when you tell me what to do." My sass earns me a swat to the ass when I walk in front of him toward our room.

I notice there are two outfits laid out on our chairs that I didn't see when I first got up. The first is my tiny teal bikini, a pair of shorts, and a T-shirt. The second is a mint-green sundress I've never seen before.

"What are these for?" I ask, running my fingers along the silky fabric of the dress.

"Parts one and two of our date. Right now I need you to get that bikini on so we can commence with part one. It may be too late for dawn patrol, but the surf report looks good all day."

We've been a bit lax about waking up early over the last month. Since surfing was integral in the beginning of our friendship, it makes me smile that he chose to include it in our date.

It takes us longer than planned to get to the beach because getting into bathers required getting naked, and one thing led to another and... Well, I won't be complaining about a couple of missed waves.

We spend a solid hour and a half surfing before we land on the beach winded, wet, and hungry. I can't stop smiling as I look at Wes laid out on the sand with a matching smile. It reminds me of our trip up the coast. Was that really six weeks ago? After a few minutes, when our breathing has returned to normal, he looks at me with a boyish excitement in his eyes that makes me feel giddy.

"Time for part two." With that, he bends to pick up the towel bag and his board. He turns to find me ogling his fine ass and just raises an eyebrow and smirks.

"What? I'm just enjoying the view." I laugh, and it's so carefree and easy with him that I can't quite believe he's real.

We hardly make it in the door, boards and bags discarded around us, before Wes presses me against the wall, using one hand to pin both of mine above my head. The way he looks down my body, stretched long before him, makes me burn. He leans in just enough for our lips to brush before he pulls back, teasing me.

He runs his nose along my jaw and neck, nipping at the shell of my ear and making me gasp. "It's a good thing, Grey, that part two isn't for a couple hours."

He lifts me so my legs wrap around his waist, crashing his mouth on mine until we're nothing but a tangle of limbs and lips and tongues and teeth. He walks us with purpose to the bathroom, where he sets me on the counter and continues to take his time with me. We're in the shower so long that the water runs cold and we have to jump out to save our skin from the icy burn.

We laugh and talk while we finally get dressed for whatever Wes has planned for this second part of our date. When he walks out of the closet in a pair of grey shorts that hug his hips just right, I want to say forget part two and pull him into bed with me. I watch as he does up each and every button on his navy-blue shirt and revel in the way it transforms the color of his eyes to an unfair shade of blue.

As we walk to the waterfront, I can't help but stare at him. His hair is lightly styled in a way that makes it look like he didn't even try, and with the breeze ruffling through it, it gives him that tousled look I love. I could stare at him all night, and I totally intend to. When I slipped into the mint-green dress, I was amazed to find it fit like a glove. The open back is strappy and dips to my tailbone, allowing that same cool spring breeze to caress it and send tingles up my spine. I paired it with white strappy wedges, my damp hair pulled half up with little tendrils curling around my face. I don't think I've ever felt so pretty.

When we reach the restaurant, the host directs us to a table on the deck, and there's a bottle of champagne waiting in an ice bucket. This feels like too much, but I know Wes put a lot of thought into it. I allow myself to just sit back and enjoy every moment. When he pulls my chair out for me, I feel his hand slide up my bare back, and I shiver at his touch.

We order drinks and appetizers, in no hurry to order dinner, and catch up on all the things we missed while I was away. I tell him about the night I spent in Honolulu, grabbing dinner at Duke's with my fellow flight attendants and then surfing at Waikiki. He tells me every detail of his interview with Qantas. He gave me highlights over FaceTime, but hearing about it in person makes it so much more real. It sounds like it went well, and he's cautiously optimistic he'll get a conditional job offer before we leave for Tahoe. A perfect Christmas present.

The sun is setting beautifully across the water, and I feel so content that it takes me a beat to notice the hush that's come over the restaurant. And the fact that Wes is no longer sitting in his seat. Instead, when I look away from the sunset, it's to find Wes on one knee next to the table with a velvet box in one hand.

"Oh my god." They're the only words I can muster as I meet his blue gaze, watching as it turns a little glassy and the smile on his face grows to show those beautiful dimples.

"Joss." He clears his throat, the emotion in it evident, threatening to take over. "I literally fell for you the day we met, and I never stopped. Since then, I've known you're it for me. That you're meant to be mine. I've never wanted anything more than I want you. I've never felt more at home than I do with you. I have never loved another person the way that I love you."

The tears in my eyes spill over now, but I can't stop smiling. I can't believe this is happening. His hand is in mine—I don't even remember taking it—and he gives me a gentle squeeze before continuing.

"I know to some it may seem fast..." He gives me a little wink, and it makes me laugh. "But I have never been more certain of anything in my entire life, and I don't want to wait to start my life with you. Will you marry me?"

His expectant gaze searches mine, and I'm at a total loss for words. My mind is a complete blank, and I'm pretty sure there's something stuck in my throat because I can barely breathe. He lifts a hand to swipe away a tear as it falls down my cheek and I lean into it, drawing strength from this man who has become my everything.

I slowly nod as I whisper a quiet "Yes." It's all it takes for him to pull me into his arms, standing to twirl me around. The exhilaration coursing through my body masks everything else. He sets me back on my feet, pulling my face into a light kiss before bringing the ring box between us.

When he pops the lid open, I gasp. The ring inside is magnificent. In the center sits a brilliant sapphire, outshone only by the eyes of the man holding it. It's surrounded by a hexagon halo of small-cut diamonds glinting in the fading light, with an accent diamond on either side. It's the most unique ring I have ever seen, and it's exactly what I never knew I wanted.

"Do you like it?" Wes looks from the ring to me, and I can see the pulse point on his neck fluttering.

"It's..." I reach my hand out toward the box, almost afraid to touch it, like it might disappear. "It's absolutely perfect."

The smile on his face could light this entire restaurant for years. He pulls the ring from the box and slides it on my finger. A perfect fit. I'm spellbound by the effort he's put into all the details. We've never once talked about rings, never looked at them, yet he was able to find the only ring I want to wear for the rest of my life.

When it's fully seated on my finger and he's done drinking in the sight of it there, he runs his hands up my arms and pulls me in to kiss him again. The restaurant around us explodes with applause, and I remember we aren't alone. I laugh and he laughs with me, our lips still brushing, our foreheads resting against each other. When we finally turn away from one another and find everyone staring, Wes gives a little bow and I flush at all the attention.

I'm breathless when I sit back down, looking between Wes and the ring on my finger. His smile is so wide that I think it must hurt his cheeks, but he doesn't mind and it doesn't waver, not once, as he takes my hand in his.

"I've got one more proposal for you," he says, and it's the first time tonight I find him looking a little nervous.

"One wasn't enough, huh?" I say with a laugh. He certainly has my full attention.

"We leave on Friday for Tahoe." Our eyes hold across the table while his thumb gently swipes back and forth over my hand. "I was thinking, what if we get married while we're there?"

"Like, elope?" I ask, my voice filled with the surprise I feel. That definitely wasn't what I expected him to ask.

"Yeah." He laughs, but I can still see the nerves under the surface because I haven't answered him yet. He continues rambling. "I know you might want to do a wedding here but—"

I finally cut him off. "You don't have to convince me, Wes." I lean across the table to brush my lips against his, somehow avoiding spilling the champagne in the process. "I want to marry you, and I don't want to wait, so this is perfect."

I watch his shoulders relax and his smile reach his eyes again.

"Oh my god," I exclaim as it all really sinks in. "That means we're getting married *this* month, *this* year. How crazy is that?" I shake my head, closing my eyes in complete awe. There's less than three weeks left in December, and I'll be a married woman before it's over.

"Yes, Grey, it does. I can't imagine a better way to ring in the new year than with you by my side, and a second ring on your finger."

He hands me another glass of champagne and we toast to a future that I couldn't be more excited to experience, with a man I met by chance on a flight to Sydney.

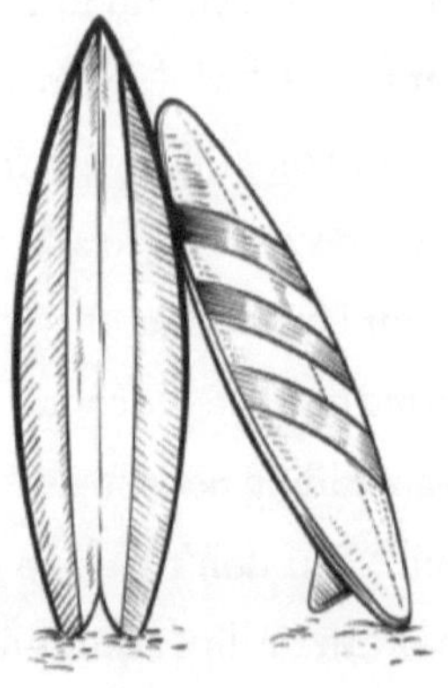

EPILOGUE

Joss

New Year's Eve - Lake Tahoe

I stand at the window, satin pooling around my feet, watching the swirls of snow blur the view of the mountains. Wes booked the honeymoon suite for our last few nights in Tahoe. It's opulent and over the top, but there was no convincing him otherwise. I see myself reflected back in the large windows that line the room and smile at the woman standing there in her wedding dress.

With less than a week in Sydney before we boarded our flight to Tahoe, I didn't have a lot of time to dress shop, but I lucked into finding the perfect dress in the very first store. Or maybe it wasn't luck, maybe it was just meant to be. Like me and Wes.

I turn when I hear the door open behind me and lose my breath at the sight of Wes in a tuxedo. The deep navy-blue jacket fits his broad shoulders in a way that should be illegal, tapering down to his waist where it hits exquisitely over tailored pants to match. I want to ask him to turn around so that I can take in what I know they're doing for his ass. The bow tie at his neck is tied immaculately. I want to ruin it—pull it free and haul him to me by the ends.

Later, Joss, you can do that later.

The smirk on his face says he knows exactly what I was thinking, but it slips into something softer as he takes me in. This is the first he's seen of my dress. His eyes trail over the wide neckline and my exposed collarbones, down the fitted long-sleeve bodice that hugs every curve before flaring out at my knees into a small, delicate train. He takes the same amount of time raking his eyes over me on the way back up my body, and I can't help but blush.

When our eyes finally meet again, I let my lips tip into a wicked smile. Then I turn around to face the windows, giving Wes an unobstructed view of my favorite part of the dress. The fabric cuts low to the small of my back, leaving little to the imagination.

His shaky exhalation is barely a breath. "Damn."

I look over my shoulder with a coy smile, like I had no idea this would be his favorite part too. I laugh when I see his throat bob on a swallow, but it's the heated gaze he pins me with that makes my throat clench. My hair is styled and pinned in such a way that the cascade of curls falls over my left shoulder, and the look in Wes's eyes says he wants to sink his hands into them.

He finally breaks the tension by clearing his throat. "You look incredible." There's a reverence to the words that makes me both catch fire and melt for him.

"You look pretty damn good yourself, Mr. Anderson." My voice is breathy with the heat expanding between us. He finally moves from where he stopped dead in the doorway, walking toward me with a purpose.

I turn and throw my hands up in front of me to stop him, because there's a determined look in his eyes that can only mean one thing. "Don't you dare!" I laugh-scream the words as he pushes past my outstretched hands, grabbing me around the waist and pulling me flush against him. His smile is dangerous, both dimples popping.

He doesn't kiss me though. He just holds me, clearly knowing I'll kill him if he messes up the makeup I worked so hard to apply. His forehead meets mine as he breathes his next words against my skin. "Seriously, if everyone wasn't waiting downstairs, I'd have you out of this dress right now."

I shiver at his words, feeling my heart rate spike. The butterflies that have been happily flapping their wings in my belly all day begin anew, but in a much more frantic fashion.

"But," he says, moving his face so his lips coast just outside my ear, "they are, *and* I don't want to wait another minute to call you my wife."

My wife. Those words are like an electric shock, a live wire, lighting up my entire body, and I feel myself flush even more for him.

"Then I guess it's a good thing I don't want to wait another minute for you to be my husband either." I bring my hands up from where they landed on his hips, my fingers skimming up his lapels. They curl at the top to pull him to me for the briefest kiss—thank goodness for smudge-proof lipstick—before I pull back.

"Are you ready?" His voice is confident and sure now as he steps back, holding a hand out to me.

I slip my hand into his. "I've never been more ready for anything in my whole life."

Acknowledgments

I wrote approximately 100,000 words for this book, but these ones feel the most important. I have loved every moment of writing On a Flight to Sydney (even the ones where I felt stuck or overwhelmed because they still represent a part of this amazing process) and although writing is a solitary thing, there are so many people who I could not have done it without.

First, I have to give glory to God, because everything in my life I owe to him.

Second, to my little family—Traver, Amabelle, and August. Traver, thank you for being an ever-present support, offering your thoughts and encouragement at every turn. I could not have done this without you and I appreciate every time you let me ignore you to write, or took the kids so I could catch up on edits... I love you, thanks for being even better than the best book boyfriend.

The list of those who impacted this journey is long and I know I'll miss someone and lay awake kicking myself over it later, but here we go...

This book is dedicated to my Grandma Dee because she gave me the means to make this book what it is, without her I don't know if it would have happened. Mom and Dad, you have been the best cheerleaders and jumped in at any time to help with the kids so I could pursue this dream. I love you both so much and appreciate it more than you know. Jessica, thanks for being my person and for being my OG book buddy!

Hannah, how do I thank you for inspiring me to write? It seems like something too big for words. If you had never asked me to beta read for you, I might have never realized that I also had a story in me that needed telling. Thank you for always being a light, an encouragement, and a friend whenever I needed it. Walking through this journey with you by my side has been a privilege. Thank you for beta reading for me, working as a critique partner, and all around just being there when I text you or need to be talked off the ledge.

To Stefanie, you have become the best friend I'd never met (you know, until we did. Bozeman will forever be ours!) I don't even have words to describe what your friendship and support has meant to me. The constant texting and voice messaging to answer all of my inane questions about publishing, and also to talk about all our buddy reads... and don't forget all the memes and reels we've sent back and forth. Thank you from the bottom of my heart for just being there, every step of the way, and for championing Wes & Joss the way you have. They may be my characters, but they are yours too. Your unhinged beta comments gave me life and made me smile constantly and I look forward to the nonsense we will get up to as critique partners going forward.

To my beta readers—Ashlyn, Brittany, and Megan (and Hannah and Stef too). This book has grown and developed so much since it was in your hands and you all played a huge part in making it the story it is today. You were kind and constructive, but gave me the feedback I needed to make my writing better. This book is a product of your time and effort and I love you all for it.

To Sam for creating the most amazing cover that I could have ever asked for. I swear you were inside my head and created it exactly how I envisioned, maybe even better!

To Britt and Brooke, thank you for tirelessly editing this book to make it the best it could be for my readers. I learned so much in the process of going through revisions with you and know that I am a better author for it. Plus, I know what an em-dash is now and how to properly use it! Thanks!

To Haley, Kate, and Marissa (and Hannah and Stef... y'all are part of it all) for helping me write the blurb for the back of this book. I had no idea that a 200 word blurb would be harder than writing a whole book, but let me tell you it is, and all these ladies helped me to make it the best it could be!

To bookstagram, all the bookstagrammers, and all the amazing authors I met in this space. If I hadn't decided to join booksta two years ago and met so many amazing readers and authors I wouldn't have realized just how badly I wanted to write a book. I would have had no idea how to publish it. I would have had no idea how to market it. My book would not be what it is without the support of so many amazing readers who have taken a chance on me, supported me, and loved these characters as much as I do. If I listed you all, I'd have a whole second book, but you know who you are... I love you all!

Last, but not least, YOU! The readers. Whether you read an ARC, bought a paperback or ebook, or grabbed it on KU, you make this all worth it. You taking the time to read this book and share in this world with me. I wish I could hug every single one of you because it means that much to me that you took a chance on my book baby! Thank you!

About the Author

J.A. Forde is a romance writer, Navy wife, and full-time mom to two crazy kids (and a furry pup). She currently resides in Nevada with her family where you'll most likely find her with her nose stuck in a book... or more realistically chasing her two kids with an audiobook in her earbuds.

She loves to travel and go on adventures which is why she decided to set her first book in Sydney, Australia. She hopes to write more books set in fun locales both as an escape for herself in writing, and for you as the reader!